# Murdoch's Tale

## Book 1 of Corwin's Chronicle

## by T F Gray

The characters and events in this book are fictitious. Any similarity to real persons, living or dead, is coincidental and not intended by the author.

© 2018 by T. F. Gray

ISBN 978-0980176728

CIP information available upon request.

Pallas Press

PO Box 412

Kenilworth, NJ 07033

Printed in the United States of America

# Acknowledgments

I give thanks to the many friends and teachers who have read my work and commented, and sometimes read again, who have encouraged me to keep going and given me the occasional and much-needed kick in the pants when called for:

Chris Rewa, Tom Soukup, the late and sorely missed Faith Queman, Leslie Beckett, master teacher Eric Witchey, Nina Kiriki Hoffman, Steven Stanley and the other incredible members of The Wordos critique group; David Speiselman and the Act 4 critique group; Jason Dye, Jay Requard, John G Hartness and the other fine writers in the Charlotte Writers critique group; the extraordinary writer/painter/British tour guide Tracey Landmann; dear friend and grandmother to my children Jenna Gibson; the digital (and otherwise) wizard Ivo Dominguez, Jr.; and Dagny Randall of Pallas Press.

I also thank authors Orion Foxwood and John Matthews for sharing their learning with this *quetan*, and the Reverend Patrick McCollum for administering the final kick in the pants that led to publication.

# Chapter 1

*I have found it!* I, Tovan of the *faer*, watched from the shelter of the forest. At the foot of the hill, beyond the cluster of huts where they lived, the *quetan* bent to their harvest, shining blades swinging in the bright sunlight. One corner of the field they would not cut, they could not. There the barley lay shattered on the ground, flattened by a summer squall, and that would be ours. *I give thanks, Lady, for your gift.* I gathered the threads of the *vaira,* sensing the connection, like the tiniest of roots sinking into my being, and sent my joy radiating through it, seeking my kin. I felt their response, the warm, sweet taste of gratitude filling my heart, and the thought, *Brave, Tovan. We will eat well this Winter. We give thanks!*

Then I heard a *quetan* child's shrill voice from the village below. "Corwin! Get back here! You're to be footman and hold my skirts." Hands on her hips, she stamped her foot. "Mum said you must do everything I say!" she screeched, like an angry crow, in the noisy way of the *quetan.* I watched from the wood as a *quetan* boy, smaller than her, climbed toward me, up the hill above the village, his short legs pumping, following a butterfly.

"No," he said, not bothering to turn his head or raise his voice.

The butterfly, blue as a piece of fallen sky, had tattered wings. It must have survived a great storm that blew it from some far land. The boy Corwin reached out his hand to touch it, and it fluttered off. He followed as it meandered, stopping at whiles to sip nectar from the few remaining asters. I felt into the *vaira,* and found the thread that connected us. To my surprise, I felt kindness in this child's heart, so unlike what we *faer* have encountered from the *quetan.* The butterfly was a hurt thing, and he wanted to heal it.

The butterfly flew on, and Corwin doggedly stumped after it, coming close, but still not seeing me, blinded by the *ksh*, like the rest of his kind. Near the top of the hill, the slope grew steeper. Chubby hands grasping at the dying grass, he climbed the steep slope. Where the wood began, the butterfly took off skyward. The boy's breath came ragged. He frowned and sat in the shade at the edge of the wood. The butterfly returned and settled near him, on a dandelion.

Then I felt it, the bitter, metallic taste creeping through the *vaira* into my skin from beyond the next ridge. In the field below the village, his people continued their harvest, the *ksh* blinding them like the rest of their kind. A flock of crows rose from the trees beyond the field, cawing. "Da says that means danger," the boy explained to the butterfly. "Fox, maybe, or badger." But I could feel them. More *quetan*, intent on destruction.

A spark flew through the air, then another, then a shower of them, arcing from the wood at the further side of the field. Black dots appeared in the field and grew into circles that ate both the *quetan*'s harvest and our own. I felt the sourness of my sorrow and disappointment go through the *vaira* to my kin. Unless I could find another shattered field, the Dreaming would be long this year, long enough that we might not live to see the return of food in the Spring.

Smoke rose. The women screamed as they turned and ran back toward the village. The men stopped mowing and grasped their scythes, only to fall, pierced by arrows. Mounted *quetan* came galloping into the village from the ridge. They slaughtered the children and broke in the doors of the houses. Horror seized me, the burning acid itch of their desires etching my skin, and I pulled myself from the *vaira*, as much as is possible to do such a thing. I covered my ears to block the screams, and cast my eyes down.

But one thread would not sever. The boy stood, frozen in fear, in front of me. He was *quetan*, but had shown kindness. I remembered my brother, how the *quetan* had taken him, never to return. Perhaps my taking him would right the balance. I hesitated, fighting the fear that bid me run to the safety of the forest.

I sent the feeling of safety through the thread that connected us. *Run into the forest. Run!* I could feel the pounding of his heart. *Now! Before they see you!* He turned and clambered up the slope and stood before me, still not seeing me, breathing in sobs. He covered his ears with his hands.

*Why do you* quetan *do this?*

The boy looked startled. *Quetan? What is* quetan?

*Come with me. It is safe in the forest, away from the* ksh.

The boy gasped. He still did not see me. Below him, the screams of the villagers ebbed and stopped. The chickens gabbled and the pigs squealed as they, too, were slaughtered. The *quetan* threw torches onto the thatch, and flames roared, sending dense smoke to foul the sky. It took all my will to stand there, feeling the sharp, burning, stench of their cruelty pierce my flesh like jagged blades, infecting the *vaira*.

*We cannot stay here, little one.*

"I want my mum and da." His lip trembled.

2

I hesitated. Could we care for this child? Would there be enough food? I thought of Boronil, and what joy she would take in having a child among us, of Dworning and Bartrym, with a young one to teach. *I will find you a new mum and da.*

He looked for me then, really looked, and at last his eyes met mine. I had never been so close to a *quetan*. Although paler, he did not look so different from us in form, and this one had shown kindness. That gave me hope. I reached out my hand. *I am Tovan, little* quetan, *and I will find you a new mum and da. Come.*

The boy turned and ran. Below, I could see an archer, eye drawn by the movement, take aim at the boy. Corwin saw him and froze. I could stay where I was, my leggings of rabbit fur the color of the bark, my cloak the mottled green of the forest, the ivy twined in my hair like the leaves of a sapling, and he would never see me. I could do nothing, and let the *quetan* way triumph yet again.

Fighting my fear, I raised my head and stepped out of the forest.

The archer's eyes met mine. His mouth fell agape and he lowered his bow. To him, as I had hoped, it was as though a piece of the forest had taken *quetan* form. I seized the child and stepped back into the forest shadow, pulling the *vaira* close around us, hoping it would be enough. I peered between the leaves and saw that he shook his head in disbelief and ran off to join the others despoiling the village.

*I am Tovan. We must leave this place, little* quetan. *There is only death down there. No child, not even a* quetan *child, should ever see such a sight.*

Below us, through the smoke, the brigands heaved the last pig carcass into the cart. One climbed onto the seat and whipped the horse into motion.

*No,* thought the boy. *Molly's a good horse. You only have to say, "Get up," and she'll pull.* After all he had seen, it was this sight that pulled the tears from his eyes: gentle Molly in the hands of such cruel men.

One of those on horseback turned and looked over his handiwork: the flames, the stench, the corpses lying where they had fallen. His gaze raked the land. I sank back into the shade and his eyes passed over us. Smiling grimly, the horseman turned and cantered to the head of the retreating column.

The boy lay his head on my shoulder. No fight was in him, nor will to break away from me, a stranger. His world lay below, all blood and ashes, the Lady's gift destroyed along with it. *I must find another field.* I sniffed the wind and looked at the clouds. Three days, at most, to find and gather grain before the rains spoiled it, and now I had a little *quetan* to care for.

\* \* \*

We followed the ridge, away from the direction the men had gone.

"Where will we go, Tovan?" Corwin asked. "I'm hungry."

3

I put him down and plucked a mushroom. *Here, eat.*

I glanced around, took a step to my right, and plucked a handful of sorrel. The Lady's bounty was good here, not stripped bare like some other places. By the time Corwin finished what I'd given him, I had full hands: nuts, berries, leaves, and had not taken more than five steps in any direction. I looked at him, his pale hair and eyes so different from ours, his form the same. *Can I keep him?* I reached into the *vaira* for Dunwadi's counsel.

* * *

My heart sank as I realized that I could not keep him. I could not care for him and still search for the grain that would feed my people through the Winter. But I had said I would find him a new mum and da. How to find a *quetan* that would care for him without getting myself killed?

I spent the rest of the day in a delicate dance: close enough to the realm of the *quetan* to search for the field that would feed us through the winter and to find a family for the boy, while dodging the fighters who seemed to be everywhere, seeking their kind for the purpose of killing each other. Their madness infected the *vaira* like a stinging itch that nothing could soothe.

As evening came upon us, the forest grew thin between the trampled fields and we came to one of the *quetan*'s roads, a muddy scar across the land. *Lady, we need food.*

I reached into the *vaira* and felt the sweet taste of apples. I turned southward, walking along the road, fearing at every moment that *quetan* would see us. The forest ended and the road climbed a hill. I saw a waist-high stone wall at the top and smelled the stench of burnt flesh. Corwin began to whine with hunger. I grasped his hand and went ahead to the wall, and within it found an orchard, branches heavy with fruit, slashed from the trees and lying on the ground. The trees wept, their pain jagged against my flesh. Still, the apples looked ripe enough to eat. *Thank you, Lady, for bringing us here.* I let the trees feel my sadness, not that it would help them. Only the Lady could do that. Then I lifted Corwin over the stone wall, careful to keep him turned toward me. The smoking ruin of a house stood at the further side, reeking of burnt wood and flesh, and I feared to let him see what, or who, might have burned within it.

I set Corwin down inside the wall and climbed over. He ran to the nearest branch and pulled an apple from it, laughing with delight. I picked, bundling my cloak for a sack, until we had enough to feed us. He wanted to keep picking—he was *quetan*, after all—but did not complain when I lifted him over the wall and handed him an apple. I led him back into the wood and away from the road to eat.

4

As the moon rose, I sat, leaning against a tree. The child slept, curled in my lap. *Would that it were always Summer, and that* quetan *and* faer *could live in friendship.*

* * *

The silence ended as the moon stood high overhead. Corwin screamed, a high-pitched sound like a hare being torn apart by a hawk. He thrashed, his legs running, as he lay in my arms. He was *quetan*, after all, blind to what is present, and alive to things that are not. I patted his chest to calm him. C*orwin, Corwin, you are safe.*

He sobbed, his small body shaking. I reached into the *vaira* to find something to distract him and bring him back to the real. The leaves on the forest floor in front of us rustled and a mouse poked its nose out into the moonlight. *Look, Corwin. A mouse. I think you woke him up.* Corwin sat up and sniffled. I wiped his nose with a corner of my cloak. *Look how close he has come to us. He must be a very brave mouse.* Corwin nodded.

*You must be brave like him.* He nodded again and leaned against me, his fingers worrying at the hem of my cloak until he fell asleep.

*Tomorrow I must find the food that will sustain us for the Winter, and yet I must make good my promise to this child.*

I reached into the *vaira*, seeking.

* * *

At dawn I heard the sound of a cart: the squeak of wheels and the slow clop of hoofs. Would the *quetan* in it be of goodwill toward this child? I reached into the *vaira* seeking the thread to their hearts. I had little time to decide. They came closer. *Lady, help me choose wisely.*

* * *

I crouched in the bushes, watching the cart approach. When the horse reached the place where I'd lain the sleeping boy, it stopped and sniffed at him. Sleepily, he pushed it away with his hand. The horse snorted, a hay-scented gust.

The *quetan* climbed down from the seat. He was huge, even for a *quetan*, with a bushy black beard and lively brown eyes. "Well, what have we here, asleep in the middle of the road?" he boomed in a deep voice.

The boy sat up and rubbed his eyes. Dry leaves and twigs stuck in his hair and left red marks on his cheeks.

"Look, Acha," the *quetan* called over his shoulder to the woman on the high seat of the open cart. "A child!" He bent over the boy, his voice gentle. "Here, lad, now what's your name?"

The boy's eyes widened, but he did not speak. He looked around, but I dared not show myself.

"Now, it's all right, lad. There's naught to fear from us."

"Oswy, there's been fighting here. Look at his rags! The lad's been through Hell."

"No doubt, Acha. Where are your mum and da, lad?" There was no answer except for the child's blank look of despair.

"The poor bairn," Acha muttered under her breath.

Oswy glanced at her and she nodded. "Son, would you like to come with us?" The child's nod was almost invisible. Oswy extended his hand and the boy took it. They walked the few steps to the cart and Oswy's strong hands lifted him to Acha's waiting arms. He did not speak, nor did he weep, but let out a long, shuddering sigh as the woman embraced him as softly as a cloud.

*Thank you, Lady.*

"My name is Oswy," he told the boy, "and I am a blacksmith. Acha and I are going south, to Alnwick, where Lord Eustace has his castle. We'll be safe there." The boy gave no sign of hearing his words. He sank into Acha's arms like a drop of rain into loam.

"What's your name, dear?" she asked.

"Corwin," he whispered. She stiffened.

"The same as your father, Oswy," she whispered. She crossed herself. "A good name, and only fair. This war took him from us and gave us this bairn."

This memory stays with me, and I cherish it: the sight of his little hands twined in Acha's blond hair.

*Fare well, little* quetan. He looked up, expecting to see me, but could see only the tracks of a deer surrounding the place where he had been lying.

# Chapter 2

Corwin saw the butterfly, and was gripped with terror. It always began this way. The insect fluttered, strangely big and gleaming blue, just past the reach of his hand. *Could it be a faery?* The wings were torn, as though a storm had ripped it from some foreign shore and hurled it to Northumberland. He followed as it fluttered weakly from blossom to blossom, climbing higher up the hill, away from his village to the very eave of the wood.

The butterfly flew off, rising beyond his reach. He turned. Below him, his oldest sister Aisley had named herself queen of the May and led the village toddlers in a grand procession down the narrow space between the houses that served as a street. Beyond the village, the men bent to the work of the barley harvest, scythes swinging. The women followed behind, scooping the stalks by the armful, shaping them into sheaves. The older children gathered the sheaves together, and old Aldan drove the cart, stopping at each stack for the boys to load it.

Crows took flight, cawing a warning. On the horizon, behind the ridge on the far side of the barley field, sparks arced through the sky, landing on the golden field. Black circles grew, and his mother and the other women screamed. Then dark shapes crested the ridge, warriors on horseback, the flames from their torches drowned in the powerful light of the sun, the sky above them wavering from the heat.

The women ran toward the village. The men stood their ground, sharp scythes glinting in the morning light.

Archers stepped forth and death fell upon the village. Far below, his parents and the others ran in from the barley field, falling as the arrows found their marks, screaming in pain and terror. His sister shrieked and herded the toddlers into a house.

*Why do you* quetan *do this?*

Dark-clad riders thundered across the field, trampling the crop and the fallen villagers. Flames leapt as torches landed on barley and thatch. Corwin watched, frozen, as an archer caught sight of him and took aim.

Terror froze Corwin's scream.

Suddenly, the archer looked somewhere just beyond Corwin. The man lowered his bow, jaw slack with amazement.

Corwin's sight went dark. He felt a hand cover his eyes and strong arms pull him into the wood.

*I am Tovan. We must leave this place, little* quetan. *It is safe in the forest, away from the* ksh.

Corwin awoke to the sound of his own screams. He lay shivering in the darkness of the loft, breath frantic, eyes searching the dark corners for the *ksh*, not knowing what it looked like. His heart pounded until the faint moonlight reminded him of his surroundings. The dusty roof beams were low enough to touch as he lay on his straw pallet. His shirt hung on its peg, ghostly in the dark. He heard voices below, then heavy steps and the creak of the ladder. *I've done it again.* His heart sank.

Acha's fair head appeared, framed by the ladder's rungs. "The dream, lad?"

"Aye, mother," said Corwin. "I'm sorry." *I mustn't cause them trouble.* He shrunk down under his blanket. *I've nowhere else to go.*

"Did you say the prayer Father Anselm taught you?"

"Aye," he said. The memory would come as it willed, prayer or no prayer.

"Sleep, then, and no more noise. Oswy has work to do in the morning and needs his rest. And you, as well. You're to start work for the merchant at sunrise." The ladder creaked as she climbed back down to the bed where the family slept.

"Ten years," he heard Oswy mutter, as Acha climbed back into bed. "You'd think he'd be over it by now."

But Corwin could not sleep. He huddled closer to the rough stone chimney, still warm from the evening's fire. *Why do men attack each other? My village harmed no one. Why had I, alone of all the village, been saved, only to be abandoned where Oswy and Acha found me?* He had no answer, and still trembled from the force of the dream. He looked at his cramped surroundings and sighed. *What would my life be if Tovan had kept me? Why did he call me "quetan?"*

*And* ksh. The sound haunted him, harsh like the lash of a whip. *What does that mean?*

The questions tormented him, would not let him sleep, and he needed his rest. He would begin to work for Sommer the merchant at dawn that day, in payment of his foster father's debts.

They'd labored for months at Oswy's forge, making pikes and shields for Lord Eustace and his men for King Richard's crusade. Then Eustace left, and his lady wife refused to pay without her lord's permission.

Sommer demanded payment for the iron, or else—the "or else" being that he'd take Oswy and Acha's home. Corwin sighed. He'd hated making weapons, things that men would use to kill one another, even though his role was limited to feeding the fire and working the bellows. *Now I have to work to pay for the iron.* He thought again of Tovan and tears of anger came to his eyes. *Why couldn't I have stayed with Tovan? Why was my village attacked? This should not happen! But how can I make it stop?*

There was no help for it. He had to silence the thoughts. Corwin forced his mind to happier things. He'd make a new story to tell his foster brothers and sisters.

*The Mouse King rode out on his fine swift swallow,* Corwin thought, *and, and . . . Sir Whiskers the Bold rode by his side.* Would the cat tribe try to trick them or would the faery folk come to ask them strange riddles? He turned the story over in his mind, shifting and changing it until sleep took him.

# Chapter 3

*Corwin sat alone in a cave, watching snow swirl outside in the light of the setting moon. He felt the chill air, the softness of a rabbit fur cloak, and the roughness of the cold cave wall at his back.*

"Get up, Corwin!" Acha shouted from below.

*What's Acha doing out here?* Corwin blinked, amazed to find himself warm on his straw pallet, so real the dream had been. He set his feet on the cold wooden floor of the loft and groped for his clothes in the murky dark. He climbed down the ladder, passed by the sleeping family in their bed, and stumbled into the kitchen, where Acha, hair uncombed, had put a bowl of porridge on the table for him. The porridge was cold, saved from the previous day, but what could he expect, since cooking grain would take over an hour? Corwin carved a chunk out of it with his wooden spoon and chewed. "I'm glad I can finally be of some use," he said.

Acha looked at him, eyebrows raised. She took a ladle full of water from the pot on the hob and poured it into the bowl.

"You were such a tiny thing," she said. "We couldn't leave you there to starve." She took the spoon from his hand, chopped up the congealed gruel, and stirred. "And now you've grown to a fine young man, about to go out into the world and seek his fortune."

"Aye," he said. "Well. . ." He didn't know what to say. "Thank you" seemed so feeble. Tears welled in his eyes.

"Remember to take your lunch," Acha said, putting the small basket on the table in front of him. He peeked under the cloth that covered it: half a day-old loaf, a thick slice of cheese, and an apple. "Now remember," Acha said, her voice stern. "Keep your mind on your work. Sommer will have no use for the Mouse King." Corwin nodded. "And no mooning about staring at the woods. We're depending upon you to keep a roof over our heads."

She kissed his cheek and patted his head, smoothing his mouse-brown hair, before dumping a bowl of grain into the pot over the fire and shuffling back to the bed.

The hinge creaked as Corwin left. He crossed the yard, the forge silent and dark, let himself out the gate into the narrow street, and turned toward the center of Alnwick. The night was clear and gilded by frost, the setting moon touching the horizon, giving just enough light for him to find his way. At the corner, where the tavern stood, its diamond-paned windows dark, he turned right and headed toward the more respectable side of town. The eastern sky began to lighten as he passed the tailor's tiny house, the shoemaker's with its giant boot hung over the door, and the church. As he walked, he wondered what Sommer would have him do. *Perhaps if I please him, he will teach me the merchant's trade.* The thought of travel cheered Corwin. *Perhaps, in my journeys, I will find Tovan.* He reached Sommer's door as a faraway cock crowed.

He knocked.

The door flew back. The portly Sommer, still in his nightgown, grabbed Corwin's arm and cuffed his ear. "You're late!"

Stunned, Corwin cowered back and raised his arm to block the next blow.

Instead, Sommer shoved a broom into Corwin's hands, dragged him through his shop to the warehouse door, and shoved him through. "Start sweeping! I expect this place spotless by Matins!" He slammed the door, and Corwin heard the creak of the stairs under Sommer's weight as he climbed back up to his bedchamber.

Corwin rubbed his stinging ear. Blood smudged his hand, oozing from where one of Sommer's rings had cut him. He stood, gulping air to calm his racing heart. *Is this, too, the* ksh *that Tovan spoke of? Will I never escape it?*

He labored among the tottering stacks of chests and barrels, amazed by the hoard that Sommer had accumulated: fifteen cookpots, each filled with iron scrap; barrels of wine and whiskey; boxes, crates, and trunks whose contents only God could guess, all stacked in a jumble, with no organization that Corwin could see. A line of tall shelves cluttered with boxes stood along the edge of the warehouse. Corwin could see thick, dusty cobwebs beneath. He shoved the broom under the nearest shelf. The handle hit the tower of boxes opposite and it tottered.

Corwin dropped the broom and braced his back against the boxes, hoping to hold them in place. They leaned against him; he pushed back. They swayed, then settled, but a chest at the top tumbled off. It skimmed past his head and smashed into the floor with a bang that echoed through the room. The rusted hinge gave way and a torrent of parchment scraps fell out. He scurried to pick them up. If he'd been cuffed for knocking a heartbeat after cock's crow, what punishment would this draw? Frantic, he stuffed the scraps back into the chest. The stairs creaked beneath heavy footsteps. Corwin found a crevice in the mountain of possessions and shoved the chest into it. The warehouse door opened and Sommer's voice echoed from the walls.

"What's all this? Are you damaging my goods? I'll add it to your father's debt!"

Corwin turned and spotted a piece of parchment on the floor. He picked up the broom and swept it under the shelf.

Sommer rounded the corner, still in his nightdress, fuming.

"A rat!" said Corwin. He didn't need to feign panic. "I tried to hit it with the broom, but it ran away!"

"Hmph," snorted Sommer. "That damned Spivins. He should have set the traps." He stomped back to his bed, muttering about the laziness of servants.

Corwin sagged against the shelf. He reached underneath and pulled out the scrap, then stopped to look at the writing on it. He tucked it into his shirt and went back to sweeping.

When the church bell rang at noon, Corwin took his basket to the kitchen. He stood inside the door, unsure of what to do next. The most marvelous smell of stewed beef filled the room and his stomach growled. The table was laid with two places, a silver cup at what he thought must be the merchant's seat and a clay mug at the other. He sat there. Spivins came in from the yard.

"Get off the bench, you little get," he snarled. "That's my seat!"

Corwin retreated to the doorway, clutching his lunch basket. Spivins stood a head taller and looked down at him, smiling his sharp-toothed smile. He snatched the basket from Corwin's hands. "Let's see what you've got."

"My lunch!" Corwin grabbed it and hung on.

"Mine now."

"*Your* seat. *My* lunch."

Spivins twisted the basket and the bread and cheese fell onto the floor. The apple rolled across Spivins's muddy bootprints and through the open door to pantry.

"Spivins . . ." The young woman's voice echoed from the pantry, angry and threatening.

"Oh. Jane." Spivins let go of the basket and turned toward her as she emerged, holding the apple as though she might throw it at him. Corwin caught a glimpse of cornflower blue eyes in a pretty, furious face before Spivins's back blocked his view.

"I just cleaned that floor. Now you've thrown food on it. And tracked mud in!" She bustled about, picking up Corwin's lunch. "Get those muddy boots outside. Take them off!"

"Anything for you, my sweet," Spivins said. He slunk out the door.

Corwin stood clutching his basket, not knowing what to say. "Well, what are you doing here?" Hocca demanded.

"I'm Corwin, here to work off my father's debt. Oswy, the smith." He smiled. "Thank you. That's my lunch." He reached out and took a step toward her.

"Really," she said. "The smith's foundling. You'll not treat my kitchen in this manner." She opened the window and threw the food out. Corwin heard the chickens cackle as they fought over it.

"It was Spivins!"

The merchant came in and took his seat. "What was Spivins?"

Spivins came in from the yard. "He's lying."

"You pulled the basket from my hand and dumped my food on the floor. Then Hocca threw it out for the hens."

"Hmmph," said Sommer, as Hocca filled his bowl with savory stew. She filled another for Spivins. He sat, smiling at Corwin. Hocca placed a loaf on the table and cut thick slices for both men.

"What am I to eat?" Corwin asked. Hunger gnawed at him.

"Not my problem," the merchant replied.

* * *

Corwin stormed home that evening, slamming the door as he left Sommer's shop and again when he got home. The family, seated for supper, looked up in shock and the baby began to cry.

Acha picked up the screaming infant and bounced it in her arms. "Corwin!"

"Sommer backhanded me the moment I arrived." He pointed to his ear. "See where his ring cut me? Then Spivins dumped my lunch onto the floor and Hocca threw it out for the chickens. I've had naught to eat all day!"

"That's no reason to set off the baby," Oswy lectured.

Corwin sat in his place. Tears welled in his eyes. "Please don't make me go back there."

"No choice," said Oswy, "unless we're all to live under a hedgerow."

"Well, what am I to do?"

Acha filled his wooden bowl with porridge "Eat up. We've plenty here."

"Hide your lunch better next time," said Oswy, "and give him no cause to hit you."

* * *

13

When Corwin undressed that night, the scrap of parchment fell to the floor. He picked it up and stared at it, wondering at the meaning of the marks. He hid it under his pallet that night, and on the Sabbath, he took it with him to church.

After Mass was finished, Corwin knocked timidly on the sacristy door. "Enter," the priest called. Corwin slipped in and stood, twisting his woolen cap into a corkscrew as the white-haired priest removed his vestments and folded them carefully.

"What is it, my son?"

Corwin gulped. "Father Anselm, could you teach me to read?"

"To read?"

Corwin nodded.

"My son, I know you for a kind heart and would gladly teach you, but the only book I have here is in Latin. Do you feel a vocation for the Holy Church?"

"No, Father, but could you teach me to read this?" He held out the parchment.

Father Anselm took it and squinted as he searched for a range at which his eyes would focus. "Agreed this day, in the year of Our Lord 1183 that Adam the Cooper will pay. . . . Where did you get this?"

"In a chest in my master's warehouse. It's full of parchment scraps like this one."

"Thieving is the Devil's work, young Corwin."

The young man crossed himself in terror. "Oh, Father Anselm, I've no intention to steal. After I learn to read this one, I'll put it back. I was hoping that next Sabbath I could bring you another and you could teach me it."

The old priest sighed. "You've little enough profit for your labor. So be it, my lad, but remember, those papers are to be returned as you found them." He thought a moment. "And you must say three Paternosters for each one that you borrow."

* * *

Sommer had a finger stuck in every pie likely to turn a profit in the neighborhood of Alnwick. Few liked him, but he had an unerring knack for locating whatever item might be in short supply or likely to become so. As soon as rumor came from London of King Richard's crusade, Sommer had seen to it that every scrap of iron not attached to a horse's hoof within fifty miles found its way to his warehouse. When the demand rose for the iron he had hoarded, he sold it at great profit and turned to acquiring wheat and barley, reasoning that with so many of the menfolk away, the next year's planting was sure to be disrupted.

Corwin loaded and unloaded carts. When that was done, he swept or rearranged the goods in the warehouse. After that first day, Corwin hid his lunch in the loft of Sommer's warehouse, behind the box containing the parchment scraps. At noon, when the others gathered in the kitchen to feast on Jane's bountiful cooking, he would sit in the loft, the delicious scents masked somewhat by the musty warehouse air, and munch his dry bread and cheese while reading. When Spivins returned to the warehouse, slamming the door behind him, Corwin would put the scraps away, scurry down the ladder, and feign industry.

The first week, he had to find the letters A and B wherever they might occur. The second week, the letters C through F. He progressed rapidly, and by Christmas read his first word.

Each Sabbath after Mass, Father Anselm sat listening as Corwin read the accounts and correspondence that filled the merchant's chest. The word *ksh* never appeared in them, not that he expected to find it. They were all old receipts, and the debts they represented were long paid or forfeit. The merchant, in his rat's way, kept the scraps until someone would come to him seeking parchment so that they could be turned to a jingle in his purse. Many were blank on one side, and if not, the writing could always be scraped off and the parchment reused.

Corwin's desire to learn kept him at it, reading the dull, dry records of Sommer's business dealings. Often, he wished for pictures, a tree with the word *tree* written beside it, or a barrel, or a horse or anything to break the dismal, boring contents. This skill, he knew deep inside, was his way out. Someday, by some miracle, he would be free of Sommer and chart his own path.

He sat near the fire through the long winter evenings, telling his Mouse King stories to Oswy and Acha's children. After they fell asleep and had been carried to bed, he would take the burnt ends of twigs and painstakingly write his stories across the hearthstones. He knew Acha would scrub them clean in the morning, but he could not resist the excitement of seeing the words flow from his fingers.

\* \* \*

But one day in early spring, the warehouse door did not slam. Corwin, intent upon ferreting out the meaning of the letters, did not hear the footsteps until they stopped at the foot of the ladder.

"Corwin!" Sommer barked.

Corwin shoved the scraps into the box. He heard the ladder creak. He shut the lid and sat in front of it, clutching the last of his bread.

The ladder creaked twice more and Sommer's head popped up. "I'll not have you lounging about, you little swine."

Corwin looked at the man—his three chins nestling in the fur of his collar; the vast bulk submerged below the loft floor; his turned-up nose, which completed his resemblance to a pig—and bit his tongue. As much

15

satisfaction as exchanging insults would bring, it would gain him nothing. Then the thought occurred to him: *Perhaps something could be obtained.* "What difference does it make how hard I work? At a penny a week, it will take my whole life to pay my father's debt. For ten pence a week, I'll give you fair value."

Sommer scowled. "You dare to bargain with me? You're not the only way your father can pay off his debt."

Corwin sat up straight. "How else?"

Sommer smiled, and the nature of that smile chilled Corwin's heart. "Your sister Daisy is a pretty little thing, and I've no wife."

"You're old enough to be her father!" Corwin sputtered. "Her grandfather!"

Sommer took another step up the ladder and leaned forward, nearly touching Corwin's face, the smell of his breath making Corwin gag. "You will please me, boy, or your sister will."

"Oswy would as soon kill you as let you touch her."

"Aye, and face the gallows. Then how would your family survive?"

Easter passed without word from the castle regarding Lord Eustace's debt to Oswy, and still Corwin labored, dutifully, obediently, Sommer's threat burdening his heart. Now the worst of the bargain became plain. Each day the sunlight began earlier and lingered later. Each day Corwin had less time to write his stories as the daylight lengthened. By Midsummer's Eve, dawn to dusk would leave him few hours of rest, and the merchant insisted upon his due.

Corwin plodded out the door one morning in early June. "He'll be the death of the boy," he heard Acha tell Oswy. "And then what will become of us?" Oswy lay thinking for a moment, grunted, rose, and dressed. He went to Sommer's house, stopping only to take Charles, his hammer, from its place by the forge. By the time he reached Sommer's door, the merchant had let Corwin in and returned to his bed.

"Come back after Matins," roared the merchant, from the second-floor window, in answer to Oswy's thunderous knock. "Keep sweeping, boy."

"I'm here to look at our contract," Oswy shouted.

"Come back at a decent hour."

"If it's a decent hour for my son to begin work, then it's a decent hour for you to get out of bed." The shutters snapped shut. "Sommer! Charles and I are coming in." The hammer smashed into the thick oak door.

The shutters burst open like a ripe seed pod. "Enough! Stop! I'm coming down."

The neck of Sommer's nightgown hung askew beneath his robe and what little there was of his hair stood in six directions from his shining skull. "Here," he grumbled, as he thrust the scroll into Oswy's waiting hand.

Corwin peeked through the warehouse door, broom in hand. "Come here, lad," said Oswy. He handed the scroll to Corwin, who unrolled the piece of parchment and read it aloud.

"'Agreed this day that Oswy, blacksmith, will pay to Sommer, merchant, one copper each week in the form of the services of his son Corwin from dawn to dusk, Sabbaths excepted, until his debt be paid in full.' That's all, father."

Sommer gawked at him. "You can read?"

Corwin handed the parchment back to Sommer. "Yes," he said proudly.

Sommer squinted at Corwin. "How did you learn to read, boy?"

"Father Anselm taught me on Sundays," said Corwin, head held high.

"Humph," the merchant snorted. "I'll have to keep my eye on you." He raised his voice. "And I'll not have you prying into my ledgers!"

Oswy hefted his hammer and took a step toward the merchant. "Charles and I think the contract needs rewriting."

"Her ladyship said she'd not hear of it again. The terms stand."

Oswy grabbed Sommer by the throat and lifted the hammer. "You blasted swine."

"Father!"

"Spivins!" They heard Spivins's feet hit the floor above their heads. "Would you kill me in front of a witness?"

"Father, no. He's right. Where would we be with you hanging from the gallows?"

Sommer smirked. "Smart lad, that boy. Obviously not yours."

Spivins thundered down the stairs and Oswy released his grip on Sommer. The merchant grinned. "Get back to sweeping, boy; the sun's already up."

Oswy left, slamming the door behind him. Corwin picked up his broom. *If only I could find Tovan and live with him. But what would become of Oswy and Acha and the children?* Tears of exhaustion ran down his face. *I cannot run off. It will take a miracle to free me of this Devil's bargain.* With a dejected sigh, he went back to work.

17

# Chapter 4

Three days before the next Sabbath, a small ship full of casks of Calvados brandy intended for the royal court was swept northward by a summer squall in the treacherous waters of the Channel. Its sole passenger, dizzy and nauseated, had insisted on being let off at the first landfall, Alnmouth in Northumberland, despite it being as far from the Cornish soil he sought as could be while remaining in England.

This man of middle years strode into Alnwick and settled himself in a corner of a tavern whose sign bore the crudely painted images of a rooster and a bull's head. The landlord's dog, part wolfhound, part everything else, lumbered to its feet and sniffed at the hand the man extended to it. Satisfied, it sat and rested its massive head on the bench next to the man's knee and sighed noisily.

"He likes you," the landlord said, approaching his customer. "What's your pleasure?"

"Have you wine?" the man said in a heavy French accent. He looked different from his Saxon host. His nose was long and aquiline. His graying hair had once all been dark. His eyes, intelligent and set close together in his long, narrow face, were large and brown.

The landlord scowled. "Ale. The best in three shires."

"Then I will have some. It is warm, this day. Have you food?"

"Beef!" His tone indicated that the man should be impressed.

"But of course. Have you fish? Some vegetables, perhaps? A bit of cheese? Boiled eggs?"

His host looked puzzled. "Well, I suppose so. Let me ask my wife."

"*Sacre bleu*," the Frenchman muttered under his breath to the man's retreating back. "Beef. Don't these Saxons ever eat anything else?"

The ale came quickly. He took a deep draught and sighed. "*Mon Dieu*, this is superb. Surely this must be the mead of Valhalla." He eyed his host and the landlord's eyes met his. "Or perhaps the nectar of the gods of Olympus."

"You are a man of learning."

*"Mais non,* I am simply a teller of tales of the heroes of old."

"A storyteller!" The landlord's eyes lit with more than delight. French or not, this man's presence would be good for business. "No charge," he told the Frenchman. "And what might be your name, so I can tell a few friends of mine you are here?"

"Philippe," the man replied, "from Albi, a city far to the south, in the Midi."

\* \* \*

Corwin dragged himself homeward, stumbling with exhaustion. Pale twilight glimmered and the moon rode high and full. He passed the Cock and Bull and then, as tired as he was, he turned back. Instead of the usual babble of voices and snatches of song, only one voice rang out. It was deep and smooth, the trained voice of a troubadour. Although the accent was strange, the music of it held him entranced. Corwin peered over the shoulders of those who filled the doorway.

His neighbors sat clustered on the benches, and stood shoulder to shoulder along the walls overflowing to the floor. Some sat dreamy-eyed, others openmouthed like codfish. In the center of the room, the light from the candles on the mantel playing on the silver streaks in his black hair, the storyteller plied his craft.

His rolling voice filled every corner of the room and, more than that, it changed to suit each character as he enacted the drama in the small space left him by the crowd: Ermentrude, the dainty princess; Hans, the clever farm boy; the dull-witted giant Stump; and, best of all, Blodderschmuts, the ravening dragon.

"'ROARARAGHARAGHARROOR!' bellowed Blodderschmuts the Dragon. It took a step toward where the princess lay chained to the rock.

'Did you hear that? Of all the nerve!' Clever Hans whispered to Stump the Giant.

"'Well, yeah, I heard it but, uh, he didn't really say it loud enough for a giant to hear.'

"'RAGHARAGHARAGHAROAR!' said the dragon, moving closer to Ermentrude, who had fainted.

"'I marvel at your self-control,' Hans said, 'after what he just said about your mother.'

"'Mummie? What'd he say?'

"'Absolutely unrepeatable, but if I were you, I'd, well, I'd . . . . I'd punch him in the nose.'

"'ROORARAGHARAGHAROOROORAROOOOOOOOOO!' Blodderschmuts howled.

"'If this giant were any slower, he'd be moving backwards,' thought Hans. 'I've got to act quickly, or the princess will be lunch.'

"'Enough!' Hans shouted. 'I can't let my friend's mother be called an olifaunt.' He leapt from the branch of the tree and marched off toward the dragon, waving his fists and shouting, 'How dare you! I'll make you take it back!'

"'RAGHARAGHAROORAHUNH?' Blodderschmuts snorted, looking in his direction. This one would make a nice entrée. He could save the sweet little princess for dessert.

"Hans shook his fist. 'Maybe my friend won't stand up for his mother's good name, but you'll have to answer to me, worm!' The dragon began to slither in his direction, jaws wide open. 'Saint George preserve me,' the boy whispered. The dragon came closer."

Philippe paused, and the crowd held its breath. "The dragon came closer, and closer, slithering along on its fat, scaly, belly." He approached one of his listeners, choosing a slack-jawed youth sitting on the floor in the first row. "It came right up to Hans and opened its jaws so wide he could see all the way down to the inside of its tail." He raised one arm high over his head and held the other outstretched below.

The young man's eyes opened as wide as his gaping mouth and he sat frozen, utterly convinced that it was a dragon, not a Frenchman, towering above him. Philippe paused again, and held the crowd suspended. Suddenly he leapt backwards and stood bolt upright. "'Not stand up for my mother's good name!' the giant bellowed, leaping out from behind the trees. 'I'll show you!' Stump ripped a tree out by its roots and came at the dragon, swinging it like a club."

The crowd burst into laughter. Philippe waited until they quieted.

"Clever Hans had barely enough time to get out of the way. He ran to Princess Ermentrude. 'Wake up!' he shouted. 'I'm here to rescue you.'"

Philippe fluttered his eyelashes and said in a maidenly falsetto, "'You!' she said. 'You're not a handsome prince!'

"'I'm better looking than the giant. Or the dragon.' Clever Hans shrugged and turned to go. 'Oh well, may the best man win. Or beast.'

'Wait! Wait! I'm sorry,' she said, eying the ferocious combat in the valley below them. 'You can rescue me.'

"'And you'll marry me?'

"She nodded.

"'And we'll live happily ever after?'

"'I'll do my best.'

"And that, my friends, is just what they did. . . . Oh, the giant and the dragon? They're still fighting. Sometimes in a rainstorm you can hear them, and see flashes of the dragon's fire among the clouds."

There was a heartbeat of silence when he finished and then hands clapped, feet stomped, and laughter crowned it all. Philippe wound through the crowd, the hat in his hand filling with coppers, nodding and smiling.

Corwin felt as though he had walked into a dream. All thought of his family and Sommer left his fatigued brain. To live such a life! He waited in the shadows of the street as the crowd dispersed, still laughing and telling one another bits of the stories they had heard that evening. When the last had gone, Corwin slipped through the door.

Philippe sat, his feet propped on a bench as he soothed his throat with a tankard of ale. There was a hole in the bottom of his left shoe and the right was not much better. Corwin doffed his cap and stood, not knowing how to begin. After a time, the storyteller looked at Corwin and raised one eyebrow. "You have a name?"

Corwin started. "Oh, yes, sir. They call me Corwin."

"Be seated, young Corwin. What do you wish of me?"

"Sir, I . . . I want . . ." He stopped and swallowed hard. "I want to . . . to do what you do."

"Well, *mon enfant*, it is not all the cheering crowds and the jingling purses, you know." He pointed to the sole of his shoe. "For one thing, you must enjoy walking. You will be a wanderer and may never see your home again, nor your family. And then there is the training. Not everyone has the gift."

The landlord appeared with a half pint for Corwin. "It's on me, son. Tell him one of those Mouse King stories you've told the children." Corwin looked up in surprise. The landlord grinned. "This is a small village, son. Word travels. Although you won't share your gift with us elders, our children tell us your stories, best they can. Everyone knows you can read and write, too. And we know the price that pig of a merchant is taking out of you and your family."

"You can write? *Sacre bleu!* I have been seeking such a man. Tell me of this noble mouse."

Corwin sat there, palms suddenly damp. The stories that filled his mind suddenly abandoned him. He had a brief vision of all of them: mice, faeries, cats racing away in a terrified mob.

"Go on, lad," said the innkeeper. "How about that one about the mouse's tail?"

"Stand, please," ordered Philippe. "Your audience must see you."

Corwin stood. Taking a deep breath, collecting his wits, he began.

"The Tail of the Mouse King

"Now all of you have seen mice, and you think of them as poor, cowardly creatures, who run from your approach."

"Louder," said Philippe. "Your audience must hear you or they will wander away."

Corwin took a deep breath and continued. "But think: Who among you would not run from a giant, such as we are to them? No, as there are degrees of bravery and cowardice among us all, so it is with mice. And the bravest of all was the Mouse King.

"He was a good king, the protector of the poor, generous with his warriors, and ever vigilant against his sworn enemies, the Cat Tribe.

Now in those days, long before your grandfather or mine were born, mice had tails like those of rabbits, little balls of fluff stuck on their backsides. In those days, life was especially hard for the mice. The winters were long and there was no cheese anywhere on the earth. It was all in the moon. The Mouse King worried greatly to see the suffering of his people. He asked his councilors what he should do.

"'Declare war on the cats!' shouted Sir Whiskers the Bold.

"'And how would that feed our people?' argued Sir Pettyfoote.

"'Glory, sir! We may not survive such an undertaking, but the name of the Mouse Kingdom would live forever in glory.'

"'Are there any other suggestions?' the king asked. 'We don't want to overlook any possibilities.' Sir Whiskers grumbled in his seat, but no one said a thing until Milkwhite, the cook's helper, who was pouring their mead for them, said, 'You must ask for the help of the Faerie Folk.'

"'The Faerie Folk!' they all shouted at once. 'But whoever we send might never return!'

"'Hmmm,' said the king. 'We'll need someone very brave. . . .'

"They all sat silent, even Sir Whiskers.

"'Well, I suppose I'll go and ask them myself. After all, I am the king.' Much to his surprise, no one said that he was too important to risk losing, so he saddled his charger, a fine swift swallow, and rode out the castle gate.

"He had no idea where to find the Faerie Folk, so he let the bird fly as the wind took it until night fell. He dismounted near a hole in the ground at the roots of a tree and bade the bird to roost in its branches. He took his sword in his hand and investigated the hole. It was empty. He sat down inside and opened his bag to take his bread and meat. Before he could take a bite, he heard a woman's voice,

"'Mouse King, Mouse King,
I am bereft, my bairns are starving.'
"'What do you want?' he called.
"'Mouse King, Mouse King,
I am bereft, my bairns are starving.'

"The king sighed. 'I suppose she wants some food. Here,' he said, holding the bag out of the hole. 'Take what you need.' When he brought it back in again, it was empty. 'Drat,' he said and he opened his flask of wine.

"'Mouse King, Mouse King,
I am bereft, my bairns are thirsting.'

"'Oh, no,' he groaned and handed out the flask. It was returned without so much as a drop left. He wrapped himself in his cloak and lay down to sleep.

"'Mouse King, Mouse King. . . .'

"'Freezing, no doubt,' he grumbled, taking off his cloak and handing it out. 'What next?' He sat shivering with his back against a tree root and drifted off to sleep.

"He woke in the middle of a grand feast. Faerie Folk, as small as butterflies, sat on every side of him and he sat in the seat of honor, on the right hand of their Queen. The table was heaped with delicacies of every sort, the wine sweet and fragrant, and the hall warm.

"The Queen turned to him. 'Thank you for providing this fine feast. For that we will aid you. But you did not give with an open heart, so you must make further sacrifice to gain your quest.' She took a golden ring from her finger, set with a great blue stone.

"'Take this ring to the waters of the Western Sea.
Throw it in and help shall come to thee.'

"With that, he woke in the hole at dawn, his pouch filled with food and his flask with drink, wrapped in his warm cloak. His steed was fed and brushed. He mounted and rode without stopping until they came to the shore of the Western Sea.

"He stood on the shore and cast in the ring as he was bid and a great fish with a golden crown came to the surface and spoke, 'You have returned to us the Ring of Air, the greatest heirloom of our house. What do you wish for payment?'

"'My people are hungry and beset by powerful enemies.'

"'You must seek the aid of the Crone of the Waning Moon,' the Fish King told him.

"But when the Mouse King turned to mount his steed, it lay exhausted from its long flight. 'How am I to get there?' said the king.

"'I will take you,' said the Fish King, and he slipped the ring onto his fin. Instantly, his fins became wings.

"The Mouse King mounted and off they flew.

"They reached the moon and found the crone weeping. 'Woe betide me, I have no floss to spin! And how shall the stars be hung in the sky and the sun kept to its course if I cannot spin my thread?'

"The Fish King stood silent, but the Mouse King spoke up bravely, 'Gentle Lady, if it will help, you can use the fluff of my tail.'

"She looked at him amazed and dried her eyes. 'Thank you,' she said. He hopped up on the spindle and she tugged and pulled and spun and spun until she had enough thread to tie every star in its place and bind the sun to its proper path. But his poor backside stung like a hive of bees had been upon it and his tail, well, it never regained its true shape.

"'This is for your people,' she said, breaking a piece of moon-cheese off and giving it to him. "It will feed them forever. And as for the cats . . .'

A rooster crowed. "Oh, my God!" Corwin shouted. The sun peeked over the horizon. "I'm late. He'll thrash me!" and he ran out the door.

Philippe shouted after him. "*Mon Dieu!* What about the cats? Is he enchanted?"

"Close enough," snorted the landlord.

* * *

The next day, as Corwin labored, he could think of little else but Philippe. Had he impressed the man? Would the troubadour pay Oswy's debt and take him away? At last, the slow sun sank and he was free to go. He ran to the tavern and waited outside the door until the innkeeper came to lock it.

"Corwin! I'd wondered if you'd show. He's here, waiting for you."
Corwin entered and doffed his cap, worrying at it with his hands as he approached the troubadour. Philippe sat on a bench, tankard in hand. "Well?" Corwin asked, brow knitted.

Philippe sighed and put down the tankard. "I regret that I cannot."

Corwin's heart sank. "But why?"

"First, although you show some talent to create tales, I do not think that you have the gift to perform them, to command the attention of an audience, to bring them into your tale and become a part of it. Second—"

"But I can learn! And I can write! You said you need a scribe."

"This is true, but your friend, my host, has told me of your father's debt. If I were to take you with me, I would need to buy your freedom. This I cannot do."

Corwin thought of the coppers in Philippe's hat, each one equaling a week of his life. "But I could perform and pay you back."

"As I said, I do not think you have the gift to do that."

Corwin sagged onto the bench and buried his face in his hands. *There must be a way.* He thought of his life of toil from cock's crow to dusk, of Sommer's threats, of Spivins's bullying, of the day Hocca threw his lunch to the chickens. *The chickens!* Suddenly a door opened in his mind and a way out presented itself. He began to laugh.

24

Philippe stared at him, eyebrows raised, and exchanged a look with the innkeep.

Corwin looked over his shoulder, at the landlord behind the bar, washing tankards. "Tomorrow is the Sabbath," Corwin whispered. "Come to the merchant's house when the church bell rings for Mass. *Then* you will see me perform. And if my performance pleases you, will you help me?"

"*Oui*," said Philippe. "I will do what I can."

"Here is my plan," Corwin whispered to Philippe.

# Chapter 5

The village had not yet begun to stir on Sunday morning, although the long, slow, midsummer dawn had begun hours before. Corwin stood in the alley in back of Sommer's warehouse. He peeked around the corner and saw the sexton enter the church. It would take him a few moments to climb the stair to the tower and begin to pull the bell-rope. Corwin swallowed hard and stepped into the street. Oswy knew his role and was looking forward to it: to get the family out to church early, and to be angry at Sommer. Acha, as honest as a saint, couldn't be told of the plan, and of course the children couldn't be trusted to keep their mouths shut. It was up to Corwin to convince them. He crossed himself and strutted to Sommer's doorstep, his thumbs hooked into his armpits. Once there, he scratched at the ground with his foot a few times and capered about oddly. The village continued to sleep.

Corwin took a deep breath, stretched his neck, and crowed.

"Cock-a-doodle-doo!"

The street seemed even more silent.

He tried again. "Cock-a-doodle-doo!" The church bell began to chime.

And again, louder. "Cock-a-doodle-doo!!" Corwin glanced over his shoulder. He saw no one. He picked up a rock and flung it at Sommer's bedchamber shutters. In return he heard a mumbled curse. He threw another. "Cock-a-doodle-doo!!" The shutters burst open. Corwin leapt backwards with a fluttering gabble at the sound. Then he began to strut through the street at Sommer's door, looking for worms.

"You!" bellowed the merchant. "It's the Sabbath, you half-wit. Go home."

"Cock-a-doodle-doo!" Corwin replied, flapping his arms. All along the street shutters creaked open. "Buk?" said Corwin, eyeing a pebble beside his right shoe. "Buk buk!" he cried, as he darted down to peck at it.

"Sommer!" bellowed the barber, whose house stood opposite the merchant's. "It's your boy, Corwin, disturbing the Sabbath. Get him off the street."

26

The merchant grumbled and slammed his shutters with a bang that made Corwin flap and roost unsteadily on the hitching rail. A few moments later, unshaven, the tail of his nightdress dragging askew beneath his garments, Sommer crept into the street with Spivins, still rubbing the sleep from his eyes.

Corwin eyed them suspiciously. "Bawk?" he asked.

They approached him with sleep-addled slowness. "Come along, boy," the merchant ordered, while Spivins sneaked around his bulk toward the farther side of the rail.

"Bwk buk?" Corwin replied, cocking his head.

"Enough of your foolishness!" the merchant thundered as Spivins grabbed for Corwin. The young man leapt from the rail onto the edge of the water trough and from there to Sommer's shoulders with enough force to knock him flat on the muddy earth.

At this moment Philippe strolled around the corner from the direction of the Cock and Bull. "*Mon Dieu*," he said. "The Sabbath is a noisy one in this land." He helped the merchant to his feet and brushed him off. Meanwhile, Corwin, flapping and crowing, led Spivins a merry chase along the street until the older man stood panting. Corwin withdrew to a safe distance and resumed his search for beetles.

"The damndest thing—I've never seen anything like it," Sommer sputtered.

"Truly unusual," the troubadour agreed. "But not unheard of. I saw something very like it when I journeyed in Saxony, but it was a goose."

"A goose?"

"*Mais oui*. He thought himself a goose. Poor man, he suffered so."

"From thinking he was a goose?"

"No . . . no, *mon ami*, that lad lived a happy life, wandering the lanes, eating slugs. It was his master who suffered."

"The master?" More shutters had opened and the faces that peered from them were split with smiles to see Corwin's antics as Spivins, who had now regained his breath, chased the boy up and down the street.

Philippe put his arm around the sweating merchant's shoulders and said, loudly enough for everyone to hear, "A greedy villain if there ever was one. He nearly worked the lad to death. It was just at this time of year, when the days are longest. The boy's mind snapped . . ." He snapped his fingers beneath the merchant's snub nose. "Like a dry twig." His voice dropped to a whisper. "You are fortunate that this one is, how do you say it, such a runt. Surely his father cannot be a very large fellow." Sommer eyes widened and he turned pale. Philippe glanced over his shoulder. Oswy and his family, dressed for church, entered the street. "It was painful to see that merchant when the boy's father was finished with him. He hardly had the strength to limp out of town," Philippe said.

"Leave town?" Sommer chins trembled.

Philippe's voice rose. "The whole village held him to blame. Sermons were preached against him. The townsfolk were so enraged they left not one stone upon another of his home. His stores went up in flames."

Beads of sweat popped out on Sommer's forehead.

Philippe nodded. "I could take the boy with me, so his parents would not have daily reminder of this sad thing that has befallen him. I can use him in my trade. He would draw a good crowd. I suggest you find the boy's father and make restitution to him before things become unmanageable, *non*?"

"Corwin, my boy," cried Acha. "There you are! You're not dressed for Mass."

Corwin froze. *This moment will determine the rest of my life.* He made his expression blank and looked past her, at the shoemaker's giant boot, far down the street. "Buk?" he replied, and roosted again, teetering on the hitching rail. "Cock-a-doodle-doo!!" He flapped his arms madly, praying that his family would be convinced. They stood aghast until John, the youngest, took his thumb out of his rosy mouth and pointed at his eldest brother.

"Chicken," he said.

"No, stupid, Corwin's a rooster," said Daisy. "Chickens don't say cock-a-doodle-doo."

"Sommer," growled the blacksmith, "what have you done to my son?"

"I . . . I . . ."

"Corwin, come here this instant," Acha ordered. Instead, he hopped off the rail and resumed his search for bugs.

"He doesn't know us," Acha cried, burying her face in her hands.

The smiles and laughter of the neighbors stopped.

"Sommer, you villain, I'll kill you," Oswy said, taking a firm hold of Sommer's chins.

The neighbors gasped. Corwin heard the murmurs, "Driven him mad" and "That evil man," and redoubled his flapping. "Cock-a-doodle-doo!"

"*Mes amis*, I am sure we need not resort to murder. Surely there is some way . . ." Philippe said.

At that moment Hocca opened Sommer's door. Corwin fixed her with his beady eye. "Buk?" he said. "Buk bwawk buk a bwawk buck?" he crooned. She looked alarmed and shrank back inside. Spivins, taking advantage of Corwin's distraction, crept up to the rail and leapt for him.

*"Bwawk!"* Corwin shouted and darted through the doorway, taking the maidservant with him. He slammed the door in Spivins face. The thud, and Spivins's scream of pain echoed down the street.

"Now he's got inside," moaned Spivins, holding his hands to his bleeding nose. From behind the stout door, they could hear the crash of furniture, Jane's high-pitched screams, and Corwin's crowing.

"My house," Sommer whimpered.

"My son," Oswy growled, tightening his grip.

*"Mes amis,* surely there is some way this can be resolved, some payment, some restitution that could be made for the loss of this young man's usefulness to his family?" said Philippe. Sommer's face was purple, Oswy's red with anger, and the smith's arm showed no sign of tiring.

"First you try to take my house, and now you've driven my son to madness," raged Oswy, bouncing Sommer across the ground as he dragged him toward the wall of his house and slammed his back against it. A cacophony of crashes came from above them in the bedchamber.

"Your house! Your house! Your debt is forgiven. Just get him out of there!" Sommer cried.

At this, the smith relaxed his grip. "I have your word?"

Sommer nodded weakly. "How do we get him out?"

"Is there another way in?" asked Philippe. Sommer shook his head.

The shutters burst open above them and Hocca called out, "Help, he's gone mad!"

Corwin crowed.

Philippe turned to Oswy. "Can you bear the weight of two men?"

"If they're quick about it."

"You," Philippe commanded, pointing to Spivins. "Climb on his shoulders." He extended his hand dramatically. "Someone bring me a handful of grain. I'm going in."

Minutes later, with a fistful of oats, Philippe tottered atop a tower made of Oswy and Spivins. He climbed through the window to find Hocca pinned to Sommer's bed by Corwin, who was kissing her in a most unrooster-like fashion.

*"Avant, bête!"* Philippe cried. Corwin leapt to his feet and Hocca ran screaming down the stairway. "You have talent," the troubadour whispered to Corwin. "Now remember, you cannot expect applause for this performance and it is not yet over. Quiet!" They heard heavy footsteps on the stairs. Oswy, followed by Sommer and Spivins, peeked through the doorway to find Corwin sitting tamely on the bed beside Philippe, pecking at the handful of grain as the troubadour stroked his head.

29

# Chapter 6

They walked southward in the first blush of summer, through heather blooming in its simple grandeur. The narrow path they followed wound through forest and across heath, with hardly a hut along the way. Corwin counted himself lucky to be free of Sommer, yet he walked with his head down, burdened by many thoughts. Each step took him further south, and he'd last seen Tovan to the north. *I am free of Sommer, yet not free. And I have lost my family twice—first to war, and now again.*

"Something vexes you?" Philippe asked.

"I mean no disrespect, and I am grateful to you, but Oswy and Acha cared for me all my life. I couldn't even say good-bye."

"*Mais non*, Corwin. You had to play that part to the end. Imagine what would happen if Sommer were to find out that you tricked him."

"But they took me in when I was tiny and alone. I was useless to them. Never could work iron."

"You have given them a great gift, and saved their home. When they are paid by the duchess, your father will be a wealthy man."

"I suppose."

Philippe stopped and faced his apprentice. He placed his hands on Corwin's shoulders and looked deep into the boy's eyes. "Think well of yourself, young Corwin. Everything good in life comes from that." Corwin nodded, although it was clear it would be some time before he could do what Philippe suggested. "Now," said Philippe. "What would you like to learn today?"

"How is it that you became a troubadour?" Corwin asked, as they resumed their climb.

"It was my father's trade," Philippe replied. He seemed in no hurry to elaborate.

"What was your father's name? Did he write many poems?"

"His name was Henri de Troyes, and my half-brother Chretien was held by many to be the greatest of all troubadours. I have never, in all my travels, met his like for poetry. He could pull couplets from the air like a

30

magician pulls coins from his sleeve. I have already told you his tale of Tristan. Perhaps you know of his master work. It is called *Parcifal*."

Corwin shook his head. They had reached the top of the hill.

"And your mother," Corwin asked, "was she a noble lady?"

Philippe seemed not to have heard the question. "Let us rest and take our bread," he said, sitting beside the boy and reaching into his bag for the loaf and cheese Acha had packed for them. "In all things—in war, in commerce, in art—it is upon the tales they tell themselves, I believe, that the greatness of a people is established."

Corwin shrugged and bit off a mouthful of bread.

"You do not believe me?"

Corwin grinned. "You are a maker of tales. Wouldn't a merchant say that the greatness of a realm lies in the wealth of its trade, or a knight say that its greatness relies on the might of its armies?"

"Well argued, *mon ami*, and no doubt true, but I cannot agree. Do not the artists rely upon the stories they have heard for the images they draw? Does not every knight imagine himself a Roland, defending his lord and his land unto the death? Do not all good Christians carry the image of Our Lord in their hearts, graven there by the stories told in the gospels, as a measure of what we must aspire to?"

"And the merchants?"

"King Midas, or Croesus, *certainment. Mon ami*, it is we, the tellers of tales, who inspire our fellow men."

"I hadn't thought of it that way," Corwin admitted. "I just thought of it as a much better way to make a living than hauling firewood or loading carts." But a chill ran through him. *Could this be the way? Could I tell a story that would make men rethink their desire to fight, persuade them not to resolve their differences through bloodshed?*

Corwin thought for a moment. "Do you think, my master, that a story can change the world?"

"But of course," Philippe said. "Indeed, it is the only thing that ever has. What change would you make?"

"When I was a child, men came to my village." He stopped. The memory washed over him, robbing him of speech. Philippe waited. Corwin sighed and said, "They killed all but me. If I could have my way, if I could work my truth into a story, that would never happen again, to any child, ever."

"That is a *très grande* quest, *mon enfant*, and a worthy one."

"Is it possible? Could I do this?"

Philippe looked into the distance, where the rolling downs merged with low-hanging clouds. "In ancient times, men even had a god of war. They called him Mars in Rome, the Greeks called him Ares before that, and in the lands to the east, he was known as Marduk. This is something, I think, that is deeply ingrained in men, but it is a task that must be done by someone, Corwin, and perhaps that is why you were spared." The troubadour ate the last bite of his bread and chewed thoughtfully. "It will not be easy, though. In many tales the best-loved part is the one where the hero picks up his sword."

"That's true," said Corwin, and his shoulders sagged.

"But it does not mean one must not try," said Philippe, clapping the boy on the shoulder.

Corwin looked up eagerly. "How do you do that?"

"For your stories to inspire your listeners, you—the teller—must first become inspired."

"Oh," said Corwin, taking a bite of cheese. "And how do you do that?"

"First, you must discover your truth. The story that speaks from the core of your soul. *Mon fils*, it is the task of the storyteller to make the world right. One must speak one's truth, above all else, and that is why we tell stories."

"Why not just speak the truth outright?"

"Sometimes the powerful do not agree with one's truth. One must always speak truth, but sometimes one must—how do you say? Phrase it delicately. And to be honest, people prefer to be entertained, rather than lectured."

"What's your truth?" Corwin asked.

"This is a great secret." Philippe's voice dropped to a whisper, although there was not so much as a sheep within sight. "Every land–not just Rome, not just Jerusalem—but every rock and pebble, is holy land to those who have eyes to see it. The Earth itself is not dross as we are taught from the pulpit. The Earth is a great resplendent goddess. She sleeps under a spell." Corwin's eyes grew as round as plates.

"Once there was a princess, who lived in the land of Plenty. Every day she danced, and where her foot touched, plants grew: Vines and grain, trees and gardens sprang up bringing forth abundant food. Every night she sang and the land rested and was replenished.

"The king of the neighboring kingdom was a grasping man, ever gathering, grudging even the planting seed, never letting a single field lay fallow, for fear of losing that much harvest. His land, after many years of his rule, became as barren as a stone. As his harvests grew leaner, he made more rules, more laws, more taxes that he laid on his subjects until they groaned with hunger.

"At last he came to despise his own land, viewing it as an empty husk, and he coveted the kingdom of the princess. He sent his messenger with a proposal of marriage but she, knowing his ways, refused. He amassed a great army and attacked by night, when all the land and the princess's subjects slept. They found the princess by her song and brought her to the king.

"But a strange thing happened. As soon as the warriors laid their hands upon her, she fell into a sleep so deep that none could wake her." Philippe stopped and took a bite of cheese.

"And then what happened?" Corwin asked.

"And so has she been ever since, while we poor mortals eke out a slender living under the rule of the king."

"But isn't there an end to the tale? A great hero? A clever farm boy, perhaps?"

"Not yet. Perhaps you will be the one to write the ending. But in order to do that, you must learn your craft. What is this story about?"

"A princess and a king."

"Not at all. Look deeper."

Corwin chewed a mouthful of bread as he thought. At last, he swallowed and spoke. "A kingdom of famine and a kingdom of plenty?"

"Look deeper still. Both kingdoms lie within your own heart and that of every other man or woman who has ever lived."

Corwin thought again. He watched a flock of birds soar across the horizon, weaving through the mist. "So, the princess and the king would be two ways of thinking about your life—that there is plenty to be shared or that there is none to spare."

"I am impressed with your reasoning. Now, what would be the outcomes of these two modes of thought?"

Corwin thought a moment, and then brightened. "It is as Our Lord taught, 'As you sow, so shall you reap.'"

"Yes. And the Earth, the whole of nature, will respond in kind to the image of her you hold in your heart. She cannot pour out her abundance to one who would throttle her. So how would you end the tale?"

"I don't know. A hero could kill the wicked king, or the king himself could have a change of heart." Corwin thought for a moment, munching cheese. "He could die of old age and the princess sleep for a hundred years until someone comes to wake her who can value her gifts properly."

"*Tres bien.* I will give you another way to look at this story, as well, and this is for your ears only. The princess is the goddess, love eternal, a*mor*, and the king, well, he is this society we have created, the kings, the priests, the bishops, the opposite of a*mor*: *Roma*, that would use her gifts for their own purposes, not let her sing her songs and dance her dance.

"And there is another reason for the constant creation of new stories: When one has been around long enough, the evil king will take it and twist its meaning to suit his ends. We who serve truth must always stay one step ahead of him. The stories must be told anew to each generation."

"But the truth of Holy Writ . . ." Corwin said.

"That most of all. In the land of my birth, I was blessed with the opportunity to study the Gospels with scholars who knew them in the language that Our Lord spoke them. It is a strange thing, translating from one tongue to another. The words are rarely a precise fit. There is room to—shall we say—divert the stream, a tiny bit here, an inch there, but as surely as water runs down a hill, the meaning of a text will become perverted. *Non, mon fils*, the Carpenter of Nazareth was the greatest storyteller of all time, and so his works have been the most abused. In stories lies the power to remake the world."

"Of course you would say that, your brother the great Chretien, and your father the troubadour Henri de Troyes. And your mother?"

Philippe stood and brushed the crumbs from his lap. "Once one has discovered one's truth, then it is time to put flesh upon those bones."

Corwin's brow wrinkled. "What?"

"*Excuses-moi*, I have made a metaphor, a word-picture. You must create the flesh, the muscles of your story, with the actions of your characters."

Corwin nodded, then frowned. "Where do you get that?"

"That," said Philippe, "is a great mystery. Sometimes you cobble it together from your own life. Sometimes you hear a story and it sparks a new tale within you, like the many stories of King Arthur's knights. If you do it well, your characters will come alive for you and all you need do is remember their adventures."

"Ah," Corwin said. "And have your stories come from your life, my master?"

Philippe turned and set off down the path. "It is time that we continue our journey, and tell me your lessons. Recite for me the names of the kings who opposed Arthur and the number of knights they commanded."

\* \* \*

Their path turned westward. "Master Philippe?" Corwin asked timidly. They had walked all day without so much as a huntsman's horn to interrupt the birdsong. "Aren't we going to London? This path is taking us too far west."

"But of course we are going to the west," his master replied, not slowing his pace. "I have no wish to go to London. We are going to Cornwall."

"Cornwall! We might as well go to the moon! Why would you want to go there? Why not London? Perhaps we could even perform for the royal court."

"No," Philippe snapped, with the finality of a hangman's trapdoor. "I do not wish to perform for Prince John and his royal cousins."

"But Cornwall, of all places. They don't even speak the King's English there. How can we tell tales?"

"I have learned the language of Bretagne, which is much like that of Cornwall and Wales. I can speak it as well as I speak your tongue, or that of the Normans, or the Langue d'Oc of my home or Latin or Greek for that matter."

"My master, you speak many tongues. Do you know the meaning of the word *ksh*?"

Phillipe gave him a puzzled look. "I have never heard such a word. Where did you hear it?"

"A man carried me off when my village was attacked. He told me I would be safe from the *ksh* in the forest."

Phillipe shook his head. "It could mean war, or strife. Cruelty, perhaps. It has an evil sound, like the lash of a whip . . ."

"And *quetan*," Corwin said. "He called me 'little *quetan*.' What could he have meant?"

Philippe gave the boy a puzzled look. "That is a thing I cannot help you with. What I can do for you is teach you the language of Cornwall, for which you will have much use. I have not my brother's gift for rhyme, but I have his gift to learn tongues easily. And by the time we get there, *mon ami*, you will speak it as well."

"Why Cornwall? A land of poor fisher folk, I am told."

"Fisher folk, indeed, but there is more. For years I have followed the trail of my story, from the south of France to the north, through the Low Countries, to the Black Forest, into Bretagne, and the trail has led me here. It will end, I know, in Cornwall."

"Your story? The story of Tristan? Of Perceval?"

"No," Philippe snapped. "Those were my brother's stories, I told you. This one is mine." He strode ahead of Corwin, whose good sense directed him to ask no more questions that day.

Corwin had other things to think about. How could he tell his tale, the one that lived in his heart? Who would his hero be? A knight? What did he know of knights, other than the men who destroyed his village? They might have been knights. Some of them had horses. No. His hero would be . . .

*Me. But not me as I am. A better me. Strong, quick-handed, tall. What will I call him?* He followed Phillipe's long strides down the hillside. *What was the name of that war god Philippe mentioned? Um . . . Murdoch. Now, how will my listeners meet him?*

35

# Chapter 7
# Ragged Andrew

"This way," Holy Andrew's Voice told him, so he took the uphill road, thinking not of the extra effort but that each step would bring him closer to the heavenly abode of God. He limped along the road, his lame foot catching on the ruts, his staff making sucking sounds as he pulled it from the mud of the low places. At the crest lay a cluster of thatched roofs, the tiny village of Roaz. He made for the village, dogs and geese raising a chorus to greet him. "Begin," the Voice told him, as he reached the first of the houses.

"Make straight the way of the Lord!" he shouted, his reedy voice startling the flock of gray geese that had waddled over to inspect him. Wings spread, a gander hissed. "Make straight the way of the Lord," he shouted again, taking a swipe at the bird with his staff, his patched and tattered cloak swirling about him like autumn leaves caught in a gale. "Make straight the way of the Lord!"

Two brothers, weaving thatch onto the roof of the next house, stopped to watch the stranger limp past. "Ragged Andrew, after all these years," said one. "Thought he'd be dead by now."

The other grinned and called down, "Stopped any wars lately?"

Andrew had his work to do and no time for idle chatter. He shook his staff at them. "Make straight the way of the Lord!"

"I hear there's a war going on right now, between Amytans and Eslenburg. Too hot for you in Amytans?" The men laughed and went back to thatching. Andrew limped on.

"Here," the Voice ordered, and Andrew stopped. It was hardly a promising audience: three dogs and six snickering boys, two of them with rocks in their hands. A black cat with a white chest looked mockingly down from the broad branch of the chestnut shading the well, and four young women, there to fetch water, were engaged in watching the smiths at work, or rather, Andrew surmised, one of the smiths.

The master smith was a great bear of a man, with round sloping shoulders and hair sprouting where the leather apron did not cover. The younger of the two was even taller, smooth and muscular. His dark hair, damp with sweat, hung raggedly to his shoulders. As Andrew watched, he saw that the younger man was the more productive: quicker-handed, no gesture wasted. *Grace* seemed an odd term to Andrew to apply to a smith, but grace it was, an effortless quality of movement that made the forging and bending of iron seem a simple task, almost fit for a child.

And what a clatter these two smiths made: the *ting-ta-ting* of the hammers, the wheeze of the bellows and roar of the flame, the searing *hoooosh* as the red iron was thrust into the trough, all as rhythmic as some addled clock.

"Speak," said the Voice, and Holy Andrew began.

"My brothers in Christ, I beseech you, hearken to me. For it was given to me by the Mother of God to come to you and exhort you to live as He intended, in peace with all creation, to give up that foul, hurtful thing called war." A stone whizzed past his nose and he glared at the crowd of urchins. There were now five, he noted, and wondered where the other one was hiding. "My brothers in Christ," he shouted. "It is in your power to fulfill the words of Our Lord, that the lion should lie down with the lamb."

The smiths stopped working. They turned, the elder shaking his head fondly at Andrew, the younger glaring. Andrew knew that look and drew back, in spite of himself. Sorely had he suffered to bring the Word of God to a hostile world. Without flinching he had borne the price of others' ignorance and sinful ways, but he did not look forward to a beating from that one's hardened arms. "Although I suffer the fate of the holy martyrs, I will not be silent!" he called out, a bit too shrilly. God must be testing him as He had tested Job. Certainly, there was no one here to step forward and take the vow Andrew was offering. No point in staying.

"Speak," the Voice commanded.

Andrew looked around in desperation. Of men, only the smiths. The boys, perhaps? His eye caught the missing boy, resting on the branch next to the cat, arm raised to throw. "You!" he shouted, pointing. The lad jumped, dropped the rock, and scratched the back of his neck. "You can change the course of history. You can bring the reign of God to this miserable earthly plane. You! Yes, you, my son, by standing upon the great principle God has given us, '*Thou shalt not kill.*' Take my vow. You will not be alone. Imagine! All the men of all the nations following you! Imagine! Each, as his conscience bids him, joining you in this simple vow, to go to war no more. Imagine! A world of peace and plenty, a world without widows or orphans, where every man can live his allotted span, free of the fear of destruction, in safety, in a world at peace. Swear, my son!"

"I will swear." The words, coming from so close behind Andrew, startled him. He leapt and spun. There stood the younger blacksmith, his hazel eyes still burning, tears running down his cheeks.

"You?"

"They came through my village, men fighting. My parents, my sisters, everyone, all dead. I will take your vow."

"Then kneel and repeat what I say. I, say your name—"

"I, Murdoch—"

"—swear that from this day I will not raise my hand against my fellow man, be he friend or foe, nor engage in war."

Murdoch repeated the oath.

"This I swear upon the Holy Cross, upon the angels and most holy saints, and upon all that I hold dear."

"I swear this on my mother's soul."

Andrew looked into Murdoch's eyes and knew that the angels and saints were not needed.

# Chapter 8

The next two days were long and empty, between them a night's berth in a moorland hut, deserted since lambing season in February. In the dim hours of dawn, between waking and dreaming, Corwin remembered.

He had laid on a bed of leaves on the forest floor. Tovan had put him down to sleep, and sat with his back to the boy. Corwin could hear his conversation with another. He remembered sitting up and looking around, but had seen no other person there.

*No, Tovan, we cannot keep him. He would not survive the Dreaming.*

*I will gather more food, Dunwadi. There will be enough.*

*Long years, Tovan, since there was enough. Our realm has shrunk since the coming of the* quetan. *Leave him to his own kind.*

Corwin rolled over to find Philippe already awake. "My master," he asked, "how can you repay a debt, when you can't find the person you owe it to?"

"What do you mean?"

"My life was saved by a stranger named Tovan. He left me in the road for Oswy and Acha to find. I know he watched over me. I heard him say farewell, but they did not hear him."

"An odd name. What did he look like?"

"Dark hair and eyes nearly black. He wore a cloak of fur and there were leaves in his hair."

"A hermit, perhaps?"

"Perhaps. But how would that explain him talking to someone who was not there?"

"People talk to themselves."

"But I heard her answer."

Philippe looked perplexed. "That is most strange. But as for how to repay him, perhaps you cannot. You can only pass his blessing along to others."

They ate the last of the bread and cheese from Acha for breakfast, then walked endless miles with only the streams they crossed for drink. The heath was behind them now, replaced by forest. The path they followed roiled over hills and around bends. Occasionally Corwin caught sight of a lake, glimmering through the trees below them.

Corwin's lessons continued. The journey worked his mind as hard as the stones of the path worked his feet. Not a step passed without either a lecture from Philippe, or Philippe's request that Corwin recite what he had been taught. On it went—poems, epics, chansons, phrases in the language of the Celts, still spoken in Brittany, Cornwall, and Wales.

There was little else to do. They traveled a dour region of forest. In vain they searched the view for rooflines, for the smoke that would signal a woodcutter's hut or the lakeside home of a fisherman. At last, after the sun had passed its zenith on the second day, the path grew wider by increments. Their hearts rose when they came to a boggy place that had been filled in with gravel. Surely a town could not be far. Cresting the last forested hill, the apprentice and his master saw a church spire. Hunger spurred them on. As they had expected, a village large enough to support a church also supported a tavern.

They entered the beer-scented room, peering into the darkness as their eyes adjusted from the bright daylight outside. After a moment, they made out the broad shape of the barkeep standing behind the counter.

"Good day," said Philippe, bowing to the landlord. "We are troubadours wishing to exchange our humble services as entertainers for a meal this evening, and perhaps a place to sleep."

"Sorry," the landlord replied, wiping his hands on the apron that rode high on his ample belly. "We've got one for tonight. You might try the Ram's Head over Tudbury way. You can reach it by sundown."

Philippe looked at Corwin, his eyebrows raised in surprise. "Who would have thought it, *mon fils*? In such a remote place." He turned to the landlord. "We will refresh ourselves with a new loaf and a flagon of your fine brew before we journey farther. Is your minstrel here now?"

The man nodded and pointed toward the back of his establishment with his thumb. Philippe and Corwin peered into the darkness and could just make out the form of a solitary man seated on a bench against the wall. They approached.

"Master Thomas?" said Philippe. The white-haired man looked up wearily. The pitcher before him was empty, and his cup nearly so.

He squinted from one to the other for a moment, and then a smile deepened the creases of his face. "Philippe? Can it be? Bless my soul! Philippe d'Albi! What brings you so far from Provençe?"

"The troubadour's art, *mon pere*. But why are you in such a lonely place? As I recall, you prefer the life at court."

"And still do, lad. My, it's been a long time since Louvines. How have you fared? And who is this young man?"

"Ah! I must apologize. This is Corwin, my apprentice. Corwin, this is Thomas of Bristol, the greatest teller of tales your nation has ever produced."

"Hah!" the elder replied. "Now there's a fine example of tale-telling."

"It is true, *mon pere*, and you know it. Corwin, this man was the only Englishman ever to teach at the great School of the Troubadours in Louvines. He is a true master of his craft. So, why have you come to this desolate spot?"

Thomas said nothing. The landlord brought the loaf, two mugs, and a foaming pitcher. Thomas watched him return to his post by the kegs, then turned to Philippe. "Can he be trusted?" Thomas whispered, glancing at Corwin. Philippe and Corwin nodded gravely. Thomas filled the three mugs. "I am here because of Robin Hood," he whispered.

"The Sherwood bandit?" gasped Corwin. "You have met him?"

"Met him?" Thomas said with a snort. "I made him out of whole cloth."

Corwin's jaw dropped. Thomas ignored him and spoke, still in a whisper, to Philippe. "There I was in Rouen, well respected for my craft, comfortably lodged, a confidant of Queen Eleanor herself, with a few coins in the mattress and the love of the most beautiful of her ladies-in-waiting." He glowered at Corwin. "Don't smirk at me, lad. Beauty is not the same as youth, you know. Lady Marian is old enough to be the grandmother of a whelp like you, and fairer by far than a dozen simpering maidens."

"And the queen?" asked Philippe. "How does she fare?"

"Ah, the loveliest lady in the land, saving only my lady Marian. The gracious patron saint of poets, her eyes still as blue as the sky over the Pyrenees. But you distract me. Longchamps sent for me, for audience in his private chambers.

"'My lord,' I said. 'You honor me.'

"'You are worthy of it, good minstrel' says he.

"'You wish to hear a tale?' says I, knowing full well it was not the case. I thought, perhaps, he had a message for me to bear. A minstrel may pass where a royal messenger would raise suspicion.

"'Another time, mayhap,' says he. 'Today I require your talents for a far higher calling.'

"Here we go, thinks I, hoping it won't involve too much travel.

"'I want you to save the kingdom.'

"'My lord?'

"'I know you as a man of discretion, and so I will speak frankly. The king has divided his realm among his sons. Geoffrey gets the French domains, Richard the English, plus Aquitaine from his mother.'

"'What does John get?'

"'Money. A great deal of it, and his father's permission to try to make himself King of Ireland.'

"'But why should this involve me?'

"'Our good king, Henry, has made a kingdom of us, where once we were a nest of quarreling barons. Surely you remember the Anarchy that preceded his reign?'

"Of course I did. No one who lived through those dreadful times can ever forget it." Thomas took a sip of his ale. "God slept. Many fair castles were built while children starved. Many fine crops were trodden under the hooves of the war horses as the barons squabbled amongst themselves. I remember well the joy with which we greeted Henry's assertion of royal authority.

"'So,' Longchamps says to me, 'Richard is to be king after Henry.'

"He need say no more. King Richard is a magnificent warrior, a bold and clever strategist, but a man less interested in the work of governance I can hardly imagine."

Again, Corwin's jaw dropped. "But . . . but," he sputtered. "He is *the king*! He is . . ."

Thomas gave him a withering look. "Have you ever met our king, Corwin?"

Corwin shook his head.

"All he cares for is war. His only yardstick is one's ability at sword and lance. Nothing else counts—not intelligence, not devotion to any duty that lies off the battlefield, not—well, poetry, he's his mother's son there, but nothing else." Thomas shook his head in disgust.

"'And that's not the half of it,' says Longchamps. 'Geoffrey can be expected to busy himself in France, trying to overthrow his cousin the French king, or fighting off Richard. It's John Lackland that concerns me.'

"I could see his point. A weasel of John's stature could hardly be left out of reckoning.

"'God's legs, I grow weary,' says Longchamps to me. 'John could no more conquer Ireland than best his brother Richard at sword. Glanville, de Mandeville, all of them pleaded with His Majesty to afflict Ireland with Richard and let John be lord of something, to let him strut in peacock's plumage and busy himself with palace fêtes, but no. Richard, he said, would learn compassion from the exercise of kingship, and the conduct of war would strengthen John's character.'"

Thomas shook his head. "Henry saw his sons with a father's fondness. Richard is far too restless to sit a throne. When he comes back from this little camping trip in the Holy Land, he'll be off fighting somewhere or other. Longchamps feared that John would try to purchase the barons' loyalty and make himself king. It would have been the Anarchy all over again.

"'I have my duty,' Longchamps said. 'I cannot let this happen.'

"'But my lord, how can I possibly be of any assistance?' I asked.

"'I need a hero, and I want you to create him.'

"'My lord? How can that help?'

"'We must prevent the barons from siding with John. The only way that I see to do that is to create a force, loyal to Richard, to countervail against the barons. That means the townsmen and the peasantry. If they refuse to support their masters, then their masters' hands will be tied.'

"'But my lord!' I said. 'How can peasants prevail against armored knights?'

"'There is one weapon that will serve: the long bow. It is the weapon of every yeoman in the land and it will pierce armor like a needle through cloth. I fear that, should the royal brothers decide to reenact the Anarchy, a genuine hero may arise who would encourage the people to overthrow our entire system of governance. We cannot have that! Resistance to John's schemes must be in the name of loyalty to Richard.

"'Here are my requirements: You must create a hero that the people will love. He must not be one of them, however. He must be a knight, clever and daring, and handsome as well. No one likes an ugly hero. All taxation must be blamed on John, and it must be made clear that he is after the throne. Your hero must be an expert at the bow and, above all, his loyalty to Richard must be absolute. Have you got all that?'

"I sat speechless. He watched me from the corner of his eye. 'The salvation of the kingdom,' he mused. 'Never has so great a task presented itself to a troubadour. You will be recompensed, of course, in as great a measure as your services deserve.' He sat there, the fox, watching me like a fat goose.

"'Of course,' he said, 'we cannot expect that one of your years and popularity at court to travel the length of England singing of this new hero. We will find younger men for that. You need only compose the work and teach it to them. Think of it, good Thomas. The capstone of your career. The name of such a minstrel would live forever in the lore of England. What say you?' He looked at me and raised his eyebrow.

"That wily fox! Had I known what it would cost me I would have told him to take his hero and jump into the Thames!" Thomas pounded his fist on the table, making the beer slosh. He shrugged. "Of course I said yes."

"But you are here, *mon pere*, and not in London. What happened?"

"Well, dear lad, can we have a hero who is known to be the creation of a spinner of stories? My recompense turned out to be exile—oh, they did not call it such—Longchamps settled an estate on me in Suffolk, two hundred acres, a stone manor house, servants, horses—"

"*Tres bon!*"

"Good? To spend the day discussing the plowing of fields with one's seneschal and the evenings with neighbors whose idea of a good story is a recounting of the slaughter they committed on their last hunt? Suffolk was —suffocating. I was there a week. I thought it a year."

"But why not return to court?"

"I tried, and had I succeeded it would have meant my death. My brave lady Marian sent her servant to me with word that John had learned of Longchamps's scheme. He has sworn to kill me with his own hand, if I so much as show my face at court."

He sat silent, gazing at his half-filled cup. "And my dear lady Marian, having to suffer through verses written in her honor by inferior poets." He sighed, but after a moment a smile began to crease his face. "But the story lives, Philippe, does it not? Corwin, Robin Hood is known to you. Where do you hail from?"

"Northumberland."

"Northumberland!! Even there!" Thomas chuckled. "And that conniving blackguard's name will go down in history as the greedy lout he is."

"Prince John?"

"Him? No. The sheriff of Nottingham. Owes me a gaming debt of twenty crown."

\* \* \*

"Tudbury can wait. You have much to learn tonight," whispered Philippe, as the room began to fill with customers. "Pay close attention, for you will have few opportunities to see such a master perform." The night was a fine one for Corwin, as he watched Thomas ply his trade. Listeners filled every seat in the flickering firelight. He watched awestruck as Thomas made each person there feel a part of his story, become a part of a great living being that he took by the nose and led where he willed, into castles royal, dragons' dens, through wild and desolate places, and into fierce battles. Corwin and Philippe sat toward the back of the crowd. As Thomas performed, Philippe whispered to Corwin, marking the tricks of technique that Thomas used to work his magic. When the throng toddled off to their beds, the landlord brought another pitcher to the minstrels. "Anytime," he boomed, his great ham-like hand clapping Thomas across his shoulders, sending the mug in Thomas's hand sloshing. "Anytime you're in these parts, I'd be proud to have you back."

"Well, thank you kindly," the aged minstrel replied. "I'll remember that." Corwin lifted his mug to hide his grin and wondered if Thomas meant the invitation or the shower of beer he had just endured.

"And your friends, they can share the bed with you."

Thomas reached below the table and came up empty-handed. "Ah," he sighed. "No tablecloth."

"We're not at court, *mon pere*," said Philippe, grinning.

"Must make do," replied Thomas brushing the drops of beer from his jerkin and chin with his handkerchief. "Must have sold a good bit of beer tonight," he chuckled, eyes twinkling. "Drunk his share, too, I'll warrant." He turned to Philippe, suddenly serious. "And how goes the Great Work?"

To Corwin's surprise, Philippe, the urbane and masterful troubadour, seemed suddenly younger, an abashed schoolboy called upon to recite.

"Ahem," he began. "I am almost ready to compose."

"*Almost* ready?"

"Yes." He cleared his throat again.

"Philippe, you have your characters, you know your plot. What's keeping you?"

"There is a missing piece," he said. "And I know I will find it in Cornwall."

"Cornwall! Of all the . . . have you known of any troubadour telling of Arthur's knights who has actually *been* to Cornwall?"

"Precisely, and that is why their stories are no more than stories."

Thomas looked at Corwin. The twinkle had returned to his eye. "Of course they're stories. Told by *story*tellers."

"They can be more. You know that. Look at Robin Hood. You will tell me that is just a story?"

"And do you know how much time I spent in Sherwood Forest? Not one bloody day!" He took a long pull at his beer. "They climbed the hill. A road passed through the forest. They found a lake. The castle stood atop a cliff. Everyone knows these images, can see them in their minds. You don't need to *visit* a forest to tell your audience that something happened in it."

"Of course," said Philippe, his long fingers toying with the handle of his tankard. "The scenery does not concern me. It is the deeper threads, the inner story. As well you know, the roots of Arthur lie deep within the land of the Celts. I want to trace the connections. There is more, I know it . . . more that connects with my own tradition, that of the Langue d'Oc, and further, with that of the land of my birth."

There was a passion in Philippe's speech that ignited deep within Corwin, although he could not for the life of him understand what his master was talking about.

"France?" Corwin asked.

"No, *mon fils*, I told you, I was born in Jerusalem."

"In the Holy Land?"

"*Oui*." Philippe turned back to Thomas. "It is all of a piece, you will see, when I am done. And it is none of it, not one word, of Rome."

Corwin sat puzzling this out, regretting the fog the ale had hung over his brain. *Not of Rome?* Roma, *the opposite of* amor, *as the troubadours taught, but the one Holy Church was of Rome, the city of Peter, the city of the Pope, the keeper of the keys to heaven. Not of Rome?* Corwin shook his head and took another sip of his ale.

*But what Thomas has done! He's written a tale that came to life and changed the world. Philippe is right. Can I make such a story? How?*

The discussion continued, becoming more heated. Philippe, in his excitement, had slipped into Provençal, and Thomas followed him effortlessly. Corwin, unable to keep up, drifted into his own thoughts. *Well, if Murdoch has taken a vow, he must be tested. There must be a war. But who will start it? Not everyone can do that. . . .*

# Chapter 9
# Breakfast at the Castle

A fire flickered on the hearth in Gwalhafed Castle, making the figures on the tapestries that lined the walls dance. Snowflakes swirled and pecked at the leaded panes of the solar.

"Sit up straight, Highness, and stop squirming. You don't want to soil your dress. Here, let me tuck that in." Matilda Nursemaid had her hands full that morning. Princess Alana, just three years old, squirmed as Matilda tucked a piece of linen under her chin. She wore her favorite dress, bright red. Her hair, equally red, hung in two neat plaits.

"Grandpapa said he would bring me a present from Velendruch. Do you know what it is?"

"I am quite sure I do not, Highness." Matilda's long face, surrounded by her flawlessly white wimple, refused to smile. She finished tucking Alana's napkin under her chin and began to cut a slice of sausage into bits for her.

The door swung open. "Good morning, Your Highness the Prince Uncle Rolf," Alana said through a mouthful of scone.

"Don't talk with your mouth full," Rolf growled. He threaded his long legs over the bench and sat. His black hair curled over his shoulders. His pale blue eyes, so like Alana's own, refused to look at her.

She swallowed carefully. Rolf's squire, Valan, son of Lord Vilnius, followed his master through the door. His jerkin was fine wool, pale blue. A new sword, with an ostentatiously jeweled hilt, hung at his side, bouncing against his thin legs. "Good morning, Valan," Alana said.

He glanced at Rolf, whose attention was given to buttering a scone. "Good morning, Your Highness," he replied, with as little feeling as possible, and attempted to sit, with the sword getting stuck between his legs and the bench. He blushed and untangled himself.

Alana waited until Rolf had taken the first bite of his scone. "Did your flies win the race, Your Highness the Prince Uncle Rolf?" she asked. "Papa says you should find some good use for your gifts."

47

"Such as grooming horses?" He glowered at her.

"Don't talk with your mouth full, Your Highness the Prince Uncle Rolf." He looked at her darkly. She gazed back with wide, innocent eyes. Matilda Nursemaid, of course, did not smile, but Valan concentrated on his plate and coughed into his hand. Sarah, just up from the kitchen with a loaded tray, turned quickly toward the sideboard to hide her smile from Rolf.

"Good morning, all," said King Galeschin as he swept into the room, his father-in-law and chief advisor, Lord Hounshel, at his side. One could see the resemblance between Galeschin and Rolf in their pale eyes, but beyond that, they were no more alike than Jove and Saturn.

"Brother, Alana, Valan, Matilda, Sarah. And what have you brought us from Cook, this fine morning?" He began to lift covers and poke at platters. "*What* a fine brown sausage. Pork?"

"No, sire, venison."

"From the stag you brought in the other day, Rolf?"

"However would I know what the kitchen did with it?"

"Hmm . . . I suppose not. No eggs?"

"I was just about to bring up the other tray, sire."

"Ah. Very good. Just for a moment there, I thought Cook was slipping."

Alana sat in her chair, squirming just a little, her eyes fixed on her grandfather. With elaborate unconcern Lord Hounshel split and buttered a scone, spread it with preserves, and began to eat. His snow-white hair fell to his shoulders. The snowy beard that spread across his chest was rusty at the tips, a memory of his family's flame-red hair that now lived on in his granddaughter.

"Grandpapa?"

He looked up in mock surprise. "Oh! There you are! I hadn't seen you, Alana."

"I was right here."

"So you are, my dear, so you are."

"Grandpapa?"

"Yes, my dear."

"Remember you told me you'd bring me a present when you came back from Velendruch?"

"Did I?"

"You did, Grandpapa."

"Hmm, well, now that you mention it, I suppose I did say something like that." He began to pat his jerkin in an absent-minded manner. "Let me think. I did bring you a little something . . . I'm sure I have it somewhere . . . ah!" He pulled out a small, flat parcel, wrapped in cloth, tied with a thin red leather cord. "For you, my little princess."

Matilda Nursemaid wiped the sticky crumbs from Alana's hands before allowing the child to touch it. "It's not a doll," Alana said, as she took it in her hands. She shook it. It made no sound. "I don't think it's a toy. She ran her fingers around the edge of the parcel. "I think it's a book! Grandpapa! A book for me?" She tore off the wrappings.

It was a book, a small one, suited for a child's hands, about four inches wide and six high. The cover was of tooled red leather, the edges of the pages, gold.

"Hounshel," whispered Galeschin. "This must have cost you a fortune."

"And worth it, for this moment alone," Hounshel replied, not taking his eyes off his granddaughter. Alana sat, stroking the cover, tracing her fingers over the embossed designs. "Aren't you going to open it?" She opened to the first page. It was nearly filled with an elaborate letter A. Adam peeked out from behind the letter, an apple in his hand. Ants crawled up the greenery twining round its base.

"Oh, Grandpapa," she said with a sigh. "It's so pretty." She climbed down from her chair and came to sit on his lap. "Read it to me."

"Well, this is a list of all the things on this page. Here we have Adam, ant, ash tree, aster . . ."

"What's that?"

"That's this flower right here, I think. Is that correct, Matilda?"

She peered at the page. "Yes, your lordship."

The next page held a great letter B, with two marvelous golden bees curled in its loops, a green beech tree behind it, and betony clinging to it. Alana did not stop to find the rest of the things in the picture, but was off to C, which held a ginger cat comfortably in its curve. And so it went for the next twenty-some pages. Saint George killing a dragon attended by goats and goblins on the G page, Jesus crucified on the J, while weeping Judas watched, the noose already round his neck, and a jester sat and laughed and Saint Jehoshaphat jumped for the joy of salvation. After the letters came simple rhymes to help one learn the number of days in the month, gauge the coming weather, and comport oneself as a proper lady.

"Where did you get this?" asked Galeschin, admiring the book over his daughter's shoulder.

"I commissioned it from the Benedictines at St. Blethis Abbey last year."

"Grandpapa," said Alana, "you really have good remembery, don't you?"

"Well, I suppose so," he replied. "In any event, I could never forget *you*."

"He wants her to learn to read?" muttered Rolf.

"And why not, brother?"

"What need has a girl child to learn anything besides sewing and herb simples?"

"The ability to read is useful to a ruler, brother."

"A ruler?" said Rolf, but Galeschin had turned his attention to the trout on his plate and refused to speak further. Rolf glared at him for a time, and finally returned to his breakfast.

"I would ask your advice, brother," said Galeschin, after he had sated himself with the trout, a bowl of porridge, several scones, four apple dumplings, an egg or two and half the sausage. "Hounshel tells me that King Ambrahad refuses to reaffirm our treaty. I admit I can see no reason for it. You have a head for these things. What do you think it means?"

Rolf smirked a little at Valan. "Well, *brother*," he said. "It could only mean that Ambrahad intends to send Velendruch to war against Amytans again, couldn't it? After all, if Velendruch were to attack any other realm, our neutrality would be useful to protect his back, would it not?"

"Yes, I see. I had suspected as much. But how shall we respond to this?"

"It would seem to me that we should stay out of this quarrel as much as possible. We must grant the army of Velendruch safe passage through our lands and so avoid any harm to ourselves."

"But would that not leave us open to retaliation by Amytans?"

"We could then insist that we were taken by surprise and had not the wherewithal to resist. After all, Velendruch is one of the greatest military powers in the world, and it is well known that we of Gwalhafed are not."

"I see. Well, brother, I thank you." Galeschin patted his lips with the edge of the tablecloth. "I'm off to the stables. Care to join me?"

"I think not," said Rolf. "Valan begins his training at sword today."

"Is that so? Well, young man, I wish you well." Galeschin rose and turned to leave, then paused. "Oh, Hounshel, did you notice any interesting manuscripts at the abbey? Might they have Herodotus?" "I did inquire. No Herodotus, but a very good Latin translation of Avicenna."

"The Moorish physician? Come along with me, Hounshel, I want to hear about this."

"Abbot Prydieu grew quite excited when I mentioned your copy of Homer's *Iliad*. He suggested that we exchange manuscripts for the purpose of copying them." Their voices faded as they retreated down the corridor.

"Highness," said Matilda. "Come along. We've a busy morning ahead of us."

"I want to look at my book."

"Later, perhaps."

"Will you read it to me?"

50

"I am sure that I do not know how, Highness. Come along. Make a courtesy to His Highness." Alana bobbed a curtsy and allowed herself to be led from the room.

When the door had shut, Rolf turned to Valan. "Ruler. Did you hear that, Valan? He plans to set that snippet, that . . . that *wench* on the throne. He thinks he can pass over me entirely. What a fool he is. Look how eagerly he seeks my advice, being too stupid to comprehend the least bit of strategy on his own."

* * *

Galeschin loved the scent of horses, the rhythmic swish of the brush, and the soft sheen of a horse's well-groomed flank, but what he liked best about the stable was that Rolf would never set foot in it. "Most extraordinary advice, don't you think, Hounshel? Especially coming from my brother, the would-be warlord. 'Let them pass through! Say we could not stop them!' What ever happened to 'Death or Glory?'"

"It is as odd as Count Vilnius's lack of opinions on Velendruch's behavior," Hounshel said.

"Indeed. The man has forceful opinions on everything from the Immaculate Conception to the malting of barley. I think Velendruch is aiming at us, and that Rolf is at the root of it."

"Velendruch's ally Emond of Eslenburg is besieged by King Ulrik's armies," Hounshel replied. "I fear King Ambrahad wishes to break the treaty to attack Amytans through the pass."

"Rolf would grant him permission in return for my throne." Galeschin flicked a wisp of straw from the horse's fetlock.

"But still, there are no preparations for war, at least none that I could see."

"Velendruch is large. There are plenty of fortresses that you have not visited. And we are small. It would not take much preparation for them to attack us. An attack on Amytans, however, would be a different matter. All Velendruch would swarm with soldiery."

"And you think your brother has a hand in it?" Hounshel picked up a piece of straw and toyed with it.

"First, he states with utter assurance that an attack on Amytans is the *only* possible option. An attack upon Gwalhafed is obviously a possibility. He wishes to mislead me." The horse stepped sideways, spooked by Galeschin's vehemence. The king stroked its flank to calm it.

"Second, his advice that we put our heads in the sand is totally out of keeping with his nature. The reason for his doing so can only be to render us defenseless. Velendruch moves in, and fails to move out. Gwalhafed Castle is besieged, Rolf gains a throne, and I, at best, a dungeon."

"What do you propose to do?"

51

"We have several options. The first is to imprison my brother on a charge of high treason. However, I do not yet have proof to make the charge stick. There are those nobles who prefer his view of governance to mine, and I do not wish to create cause for civil strife. Under the circumstances, the best course might be to give him enough rope to hang himself, while preparing the realm against attack." Galeschin resumed his brushing.

"It would be noticed."

"True. And then Velendruch would be forced to intensify its preparations, which would bring their intentions into the open."

"But they would then say that the attack was aimed elsewhere," argued Hounshel. "Might we not appeal to Amytans?"

"They would then send troops over the pass and through our lands to attack Velendruch. King Ulrik values his honor highly and Whisted, his war duke, seems to delight in throwing men into the teeth of his enemies. What difference does it make whether Velendruch or Amytans strikes first if we are to play anvil to their hammer?"

"Quite, and if Ambrahad knows he will face resistance, he will just send that much stronger a force against us."

"Exactly. We must keep our preparations hidden."

"But how?"

"Indeed." Galeschin brushed his horse's already gleaming flank. "Hounshel, I ask a boon."

"Anything, sire."

"Your estate of Hirday lies on the border with Velendruch. It is there that the first blow will fall. You and your people must bear the brunt of this. I ask that you begin arming yourselves immediately. Train warriors, lay in stores, prepare for siege. Those I can trust to act in secrecy—Burrk, Strenholm, Mallow, and Cirgan—I will instruct to send aid to you. The others will come into line, I fear, only when the threat is made manifest, and even then, I wonder if some will not side with Rolf." He ran his hand across his horse's flank. "Ah, Rolf, my little brother. What am I to do with him, Hounshel? He is a man of talents, and needs a broader scope for their exercise than our modest realm can afford."

"Which is why you sent him to Velendruch last year, and look at the result. He has only learned more cunning and ambition. He means to supplant you. The greatness of his gifts cannot compensate for the meanness of his spirit."

"True." Galeschin pounded his fist against the stanchion with a thump that made the horse shy again. "Why can he not use his abilities for the good of the kingdom, rather than constantly envying my position? As king, it is my duty to use all resources for Gwalhafed's good. Why can he not do that as well? We must find something, some task that will gratify his pride, yet do no harm."

"I suppose so, but in the meantime, I have a concern with your plan. Velendruch is so much larger. They could tell off enough men to keep us trapped in Hirday and still have enough to conquer the rest of Gwalhafed. If we concentrate our forces there, we would leave the rest of the realm defenseless."

Galeschin sighed. He put the brushes together and laid them on the stanchion. "Then let us sleep on it, Hounshel. We'll discuss it again tomorrow."

* * *

"That was disgraceful, Highness," said Matilda, taking Alana by the hand. "There is no excuse for your behavior at breakfast today." For thirty years and more, her life had been devoted to taking unformed—albeit well-born—girls and molding them into ladies. "We are going to the chapel, Highness, to beg God's forgiveness."

Alana's lip began to tremble.

"To speak to your royal uncle in that fashion is simply inexcusable. Your mother, God rest her soul, would never have done so. She was a lady!"

Alana remembered little of her mother, save that her hair was the same vivid red as her own. Matilda had tangled the rest of her memories into the statue of the Virgin in the chapel.

The heavy wooden door creaked as Matilda opened it and it closed behind them with an echoing thud. "Kneel, Highness, and beg Our Lady that you might mend your ways and not grow up to be a sharp-tongued shrew. Think of your mother, Alana, suffering the punishment of the damned for bringing such a little sinner into the world."

Alana burst into tears. The Virgin's face was so sad. She could not bear for her mother to be so sad on her account.

"That's good, Alana, to show remorse." Matilda let her sob a while longer. "But remorse is not enough. You must determine to mend your ways and treat your uncle with the respect due a prince. Remember, Alana, no one loves a harpy, but everyone loves a meek-tongued lady."

"His Highness the Prince Uncle Rolf doesn't love me," Alana sobbed. "And I don't care. He's mean. He's mean to Papa, he's mean to me, he's mean to the horses, and he's mean to the flies. I hate him!"

"Alana!" snapped Matilda. "How dare you think such a sinful thought. How it must pain your poor mother. A devil could be sticking his pitchfork in her right now, Alana, for having given birth to such a rude, hateful child as you are. For shame!"

53

It was all too much for the tiny girl. She screamed and threw herself on the floor, kicking, weeping, and howling her rage and grief.

Matilda watched the child with stiff composure, waiting for the right moment. At last, when the tempest had subsided into shuddering sobs, Matilda knelt on the stone floor and touched the little princess's shoulder. Alana climbed into her lap. "There, there, now, Highness. This behavior is unbecoming," Matilda said tenderly, wiping the girl's nose with a square of linen and patting the tears from her flushed cheeks. "A lady must always retain her dignity. Blow. There's a good girl. What silliness was that about His Highness's racing flies?"

"But he did. He and Valan made their flies run in circles."

"Silly Highness, how could they ever do that?"

"They each pulled one wing off and the flies ran around in circles."

Matilda stood, and pursed her lips in disapproval. "Come, my little Highness, it's time for embroidery."

# Chapter 10

Corwin and Philippe took their leave of Thomas the next morning. Philippe rummaged in his bag and pulled out a slender golden ring set with a sapphire. "Take this to Marie de Champagne," he told Thomas. "She will recognize it. And tell her that Philippe d'Albi sends his most humble regards."

"If you go to Alnwick, ask for Father Anselm," Corwin told him. "He blesses the fishing boats at Alnmouth each Shrove Tuesday. No doubt he can find you a way across the Channel."

"Yes," added Philippe, eyes twinkling. "And make sure he tells Oswy and Acha that Corwin is much improved, and no longer eats bugs." Thomas's eyes opened wide and his eyebrows rose. Philippe smiled and pointed at Corwin. "And he will tell you about the bugs."

\* \* \*

Again, they walked south by west, through parts more thickly inhabited. Taverns and inns aplenty to perform in lined their way and Philippe's purse grew heavy. On the evening of the third day, they climbed the crest of a hill and squinted into the sunset, shading their eyes. A broad river ran below them, and between them and it lay Lancaster. From the height above the city rose the half-finished spires of a cathedral and the square tower of a castle.

"Well, my young friend, what do you think?"

Corwin stood speechless at the sight.

"Tomorrow we will enjoy noble hospitality."

\* \* \*

They found lodging that night at a farmstead, and bedded in the hayloft. As Corwin lay in the sweet-scented hay, he thought about Murdoch. His story had put him in a box. *There would be a war, a hopeless war. How on earth could Gwalhafed survive?*

*And why must there always be war?*

# Chapter 11
# The Plan

The cock crowed and the sun had not yet answered when King Galeschin awoke, a freshly minted idea gleaming brightly in his mind. He rose, dressed, and went immediately to where Hounshel slept. He pushed back the bed curtains and sat on the bed. "Hist! Hounshel, wake up. I've got the answer."

"Hmm what? Oh. Galeschin? Sire!"

"Listen. I've figured it out. It's the *Iliad* that gave me the idea."

"The *Iliad*?"

"Yes. What did the Greeks and Trojans do when they were stalemated?"

"Why, they chose champions to fight in single combat and decide the issue."

"Precisely. The tradition continues to this day. And that is what we shall do."

"We shall? But who will be our champion?"

"Rolf."

*"Rolf?"*

"Hush, man, you'll wake the castle."

"Your brother?"

"Yes. He prides himself on his swordsmanship, and justly so. It would give him the sort of heroic role he craves. That should end Ambrahad's invasion, but even if it didn't, his pride would not let him lose the encounter, would it? And of course, if he wins, Velendruch loses."

"And do you think he will accept the task?"

"If properly approached."

* * *

At the conclusion of breakfast, which featured an enormous venison pasty, Galeschin spoke to his brother. "I'd like your advice."

Rolf glanced at Valan. "Yes?"

"I think it time for us to attend to the kingdom's defenses."

56

Rolf patted his lips on the edge of the tablecloth. "Really? Why? I can see no imminent danger."

"Still, it is my duty."

"Duty. Yes, of course."

Galeschin leaned forward. "It has occurred to me that we have not the resources to build an army to match either Amytans or Velendruch directly."

"A very perceptive thought, brother." Rolf propped his elbow on the table and rested his chin on his fist. "How may I assist you?"

"We need a champion. Your blood is as dear as my own to me, so I would not think of—"

"A champion?"

"Quite," Hounshel added. "A hero, you know, to fight in single combat . . ."

"I know what a champion is." Rolf frowned.

"Yes," continued Galeschin, "and with your knowledge of swordsmanship, I thought you might be able to tell me the best man for the job." Rolf scowled. Galeschin continued. "Of course, I have always held your talents in the highest regard, but, after all, you are my only brother. I could not place you in such a position of risk."

Rolf's scowl deepened. "I see," he said. "I see your game. You think yourself clever, brother, to pass me over in favor of some lesser man. To build him up in the eyes of the people and thereby diminish their regard for me."

"Oh, no, brother! I simply could not ask—"

"Could not ask! Dare not ask," Rolf snarled. "You know what would happen if I were champion. There would not be a man in the kingdom who would support you, you flabby little glutton. I can beat you at chess. I can best you at sword. I am smarter than you, taller than you, and I'm even better-looking. It's only an accident of birth that has made you king."

Galeschin chose to ignore the insults. "Rolf! Brother! I could never deny you a task your talents deserved. Will you be Gwalhafed's champion?"

Rolf leaned back in his chair and smiled. "Of course, dear brother. It would delight me to. . ." And then he faltered and his smile faded. "Yes. I see it now. You think yourself clever, Galeschin. To send me out to be killed."

"Rolf! I told you—"

"Too late, brother, your plans are as clear as water, and as weak. I must decline this dubious honor." He rose. "I bid you good day, gentlemen." With that, he swept from the room. Valan bowed and scurried after him.

Hounshel sighed. "So close."

"Perhaps it's for the best," said Galeschin.

* * *

Rolf sat in his chamber, his mood foul. Valan's mood was worse, having felt both the weight of his master's sword and the sting of his sharp tongue throughout the morning's lesson. Rolf fumed, and Valan knew the reason. Galeschin, nowhere near the fool Rolf imagined him to be, suspected. Rolf paced, glowering. "Gwalhafed," he said. "A land of woolly-pated shepherds. A low place in a rutted road running through a bog."

A knock sounded. Valan startled, and had his hand on the latch by the time Rolf snapped, "Well, open it, will you?"

A bowing page presented him a letter. "From your father, Lord Vilnius, sir, just in by messenger."

Valan took the letter from him, and barely had time to close the door before Rolf snatched it from his hand. "Give me that!" he said, and tore it open. There were two sheets. He handed one to Valan, and took the other to his chair by the fire. Valan knew what his would say: reams of advice on everything from military strategy to the proper way to manage one's cape while mounting a horse. He stood behind Rolf's chair to read the more interesting of the two over his master's shoulder.

*Ambrahad has agreed to your plan. I will get the maps*
*from you when I visit at Yule and the invasion*
*will begin at spring plowing.*
*That fool Hounshel will be taken unawares at Hirday.*
*Your humble servant,*
*Vilnius*

Valan bent his eyes to his own letter as Rolf straightened and glanced behind him.

"Good news from your father," he said. "He will be with us at Yule. Let's take the dogs and hunt, shall we?" He tossed the message into the fire and strode from the room.

58

# Chapter 12

In the morning, Philippe and Corwin tramped down the hill to the city gate. They strode through the crowd with Corwin gawking like a farm boy at his first fair.

Philippe planned to approach the court and it would not do to have his apprentice look like a peasant. He led Corwin directly to the market square, where merchants laid their wares for inspection by the bustling throng.

There were woolen merchants and lace merchants; jewelers with glittering shelves and large, sullen assistants. Corwin saw a whole section set off just for the sellers of food: fruits and vegetables, meat, grain. Makers of pies and pasties, of sweetmeats and stews, bustled past, all crying their wares at the tops of their lungs until Corwin, accustomed to the simplicity of Northumbrian life, began to wonder whether he had landed in heaven or in hell.

Philippe purchased a loaf and a slab of cheese and they ate as they wandered the square. At last, on their second circuit, he stopped before a wizened old tailor, seated under an awning, with his bolts of cloth displayed around him. "This," Philippe said, touching a bolt of dark brown wool. "How much for a new suit of clothes for this young man?"

Corwin went dizzy with delight. "Master Philippe! This is too much!"

Philippe held up his hand. "Enough. The appearance of the apprentice reflects on the master, *non*? You need new clothing."

The tailor bustled about Corwin like a bee round a rose. After taking any number of measurements with his tape he said, "Ten shillings."

Corwin's jaw dropped. If his master had that much money, he would surely not spend it on a suit of clothes for his apprentice.

"You can easily tell by my speech that I am not from these parts," Philippe replied. "But surely you do not take me for a rich man." He lifted his foot and showed the pitiable sole of his boot. "Or a fool."

The tailor grinned and rubbed the palms of his hands together, like a woodsman preparing to cut an oak. "I'm a good Christian man and full of

59

charity, and so I might be able to make him something for nine and sixpence."

A young woman came up to the booth, carrying a basket with bread, fruit, and spools of thread. She had brown hair pulled back into two braids and stood looking indulgently at the tailor. "Father, surely such a thin young man could not require very much cloth."

"Mmh, perhaps. I'll tell you . . . eight even, because I like a lad with an honest face."

The girl rolled her eyes and took the basket behind the curtain into the back of the booth.

"I regret that I could not possibly pay more than five," said Philippe.

"Five!" the little man exploded. "Five! You mean to beggar me." The young woman popped her head out from behind the curtain.

"Alas, my young friend, it seems we must seek elsewhere for your garments," Philippe sighed. Corwin, crestfallen, began to turn away.

"Father," the young woman whispered. "You're being greedy. You'll not get a single bit of work today if you insist on such ridiculous prices."

"Oh, Emma, I suppose you're right," he said, watching them leave his premises. "Wait, wait, I can't stand to see a young man so downcast. Five shillings it is."

"Can the work be finished by noon?"

"Noon?" the little man shouted. "Noon and only five shillings?"

"We are but simple tellers of tales," said Philippe. "We are expected to present ourselves at the castle at noon and can hardly do so with my apprentice's clothing in such shocking condition."

"Seven and sixpence!" the tailor bellowed.

"Father!" said the girl. She turned to Philippe. "If you could tell us a tale while we worked, it would speed our hands."

He bowed to her. "You are the very queen of trade. We would be delighted. I have nothing to do save take my boots to that shoemaker over there. Allow me to do that small errand and I will gladly tell you a tale or two."

The tailor's expression brightened and he agreed. As Philippe turned to go, Corwin tugged at his sleeve and whispered, "I didn't know that we were expected at the castle."

"And the tailor does not know that we are not. It would be a shame to miss the noontide meal."

"And I have never seen better bargaining. How quickly you got him to agree to your price!"

"My price? Hardly. I have never known a tradesman who did not start at twice the value of his goods. Still, I do not know if it would have been possible without his sensible daughter. Tell them your mouse tale."

By the time Philippe returned with his newly soled boots, the tailor had marked the cloth and was cutting the sleeves with an immense pair of shears. His daughter had threaded several needles and was already stitching a shoulder seam. "A mouse with a tail like a rabbit," the tailor chuckled, "and I like the way that moon-woman put it about the cats, 'A king without an enemy is like a knife without a whetstone, soon dull and useless.' That's God's truth. If they don't have wars coming at them, they starts them themselves, so they can have the duty of protecting us and us of paying them to do it. Well, master storyteller, if that's the sort of yarn what the boy can spin, let's see what the man can do."

* * *

As the Prime rung from the cathedral, Philippe finished his last tale and the tailor handed Corwin his new jerkin and breeks and led him to the rear of the shop to change his clothing. He emerged in a minute, doing his best to see himself from all angles. Philippe paid the man his due and stood smiling at his apprentice. "We'll make a courtier of you yet, young Corwin."

As the crowd dispersed, Philippe nudged Corwin and pointed to one of the departing listeners. "Him, *mon ami*. He interests me. Perhaps he will become part of a story, *n'est-ce pas?*" As they followed the man, Corwin watched him closely, to see what it might be that so drew his master's attention.

There was no doubt as to the man's business, and even had Corwin not been raised in the family of smiths, he would have had no difficulty in identifying the man as one. The powerful arms, the hunch of the shoulders, the ingrained soot of his skin all marked his trade. Yet there was an indefinable difference about the man that set him apart from Oswy or any other smith Corwin had ever encountered—a nimbleness of movement, an air of assurance. They followed him through the narrow, twisting streets of Lancaster, toward the castle, past its gate, and around the outside of its towering walls. At last he went through a wooden gate between two houses in a small lane. He left the gate open and they followed him. The clang of the smithy rang over the walls and filled the street, echoing from the red stone of the castle rampart. The interior of the yard surprised Corwin, however.

There was no muck, no straw, no overwhelming smell of horse. Three journeymen sent up a mighty racket from a low shed at the further end, their hammers pounding steel. Two boys heaved at the tremendous bellows, by far the largest Corwin had ever seen, and a third stepped quickly to bring the journeymen what they needed. The yard was swept and every tool, every item, in precise order. The walls of the shed were set with pairs of pegs and from each pair hung a gleaming sword or dagger.

The master, the man whom they had followed, stood watching them as they entered. "Good day, Master Troubadour," he said to Philippe. "How may I serve you?" Corwin, ignored by the swordsmith, stood a-goggle, staring at the display of shining steel as though it were a sky full of lightning bolts, each in danger of striking him. *Why does he do this?* Raised by smiths, he knew the answer: mouths to feed. *Would men go into battle if there were no swords?*

"For the moment, I ask only that my apprentice and I may sit and watch you and your men at their work while we take our noontime repast." He took their bread and cheese from his bag.

"Why not horseshoes?" Corwin blurted. Phillipe shot him a look.

The smith frowned. "Boring, and this pays better."

"I apologize for my apprentice's rudeness. He lost his family to war."

The smith nodded. "'Tis sad that such things of beauty should cause death."

*Is this also the* ksh? Corwin wondered.

The swordsmith shook his head, then smiled at them. "Not many would think to eat in such a clamor. Please come into the house. My wife will serve you herself."

"Please, I do not mean to impose myself," Philippe said. "As one who has no skill with his hands, I am fascinated by those who have. I truly wish to watch you at your work."

The smith seemed pleased with his response. "As you wish, then. My name is Ian. These young men are my wife's nephews Roald and Dirk and my son Stephen. The boys are Saul, my youngest, and my nephews Samuel and John."

"I am Philippe, and this young man is Corwin, from Northumberland."

"Northumberland?" Ian scowled. "You wouldn't know of a tub of a merchant named Sommer, would you?"

Corwin swallowed nervously.

"*Ah, oui*," Philippe answered. "I had the privilege of rescuing this young man from his clutches."

Ian eyed Corwin curiously, leaving Philippe no choice but to tell the story. When they reached the point where Corwin began crowing on Sommer's doorstep, Ian called to his workers to cease their toil and sent the youngest to fetch his wife and daughters from the house. The women came out bearing mugs and a pitcher of sweet cider, and soon pealing laughter replaced the ringing of hammer on steel. As Philippe told of his ascent through Sommer's bedchamber window, the swordsmith looked toward his gate and his smile disappeared into a look of cold formality. An elegantly dressed young man stood just inside the gate, surveying the yard with utmost disdain.

"Well?" he demanded of the swordsmith.

Ian rose and went to the row of gleaming weapons displayed on the shed wall. "Here it is, my lord Shea," he said, taking a sword with a magnificently decorated hilt from its place and carefully handing it to the young man.

The man took a step backward, admiring the sword as he fumbled with the clasp holding his crimson cloak, its fur trim unnecessary in the warm afternoon. He let the cloak fall and kicked it to one side, freeing his arm to swing the sword and test its heft and balance. "Yes," he said at last. "This will be adequate." He reached inside his velvet jerkin and absently tossed a purse of coin to the ground at the swordsmith's feet. He picked up his cloak with the point of his sword and turned to leave.

"I have not received payment, m'lord," said Ian in an even voice that filled the small courtyard.

"Don't be absurd, churl. It's lying there at your feet."

"Perhaps, but I have not received it."

"Well, then pick it up, lout." The young nobleman looked about him nervously. The three burly journeymen rose from their seats and quietly took position between him and the gate.

"You received the sword from my hand, and I will receive my payment from your hand. I am a master of my craft and will not suffer coins to be tossed at me like a common beggar." Ian pulled on a thick leather glove and stepped back a pace, next to the forge.

"I'll give you payment, you impudent varlet," the young man said and he leapt forward and swung the sword at Ian. The swordsmith's gloved hand had already closed on the end of a steel rod, whose tip glowed dully from the heat of the fire. He brought it up and warded off the other's blow and then, before the young noble could recover, swept it back at knee height, forcing him to jump. He pressed forward with amazing speed, holding the rod's dull red tip close to his opponent's face so that the young man stumbled backwards and came to land on his back next to the purse.

"Now you can hand it to me," Ian said calmly. Shea did so. Ian handed the purse to Roald. "Count it."

"Twenty-three," said Roald.

"Two short," Ian told his unfortunate customer. The young man began to protest, but Ian moved the rod an inch nearer.

Shea's nostrils twitched at the scent of the hot metal. He reached into his jerkin again, took two coins from another purse and placed them carefully into Roald's outstretched hand. Ian stepped back. "A good day to you, m'lord," he said as the other rose and collected his cloak from the ground.

"My father shall hear of this!" the young man threatened as he swept through the gate.

"For my sake, I care not. For your sake, I hope not," the smith replied calmly to the young man's retreating back. He returned to his guests. "It seems hard to believe that the name 'Shea' means 'a courteous man,'" He turned to Philippe. "So, what happened after you climbed through his window?"

# Chapter 13

They left the lane and crossed the broad square toward the bulk of the castle. Philippe gave their names to the guard at the castle gate, who sent a page running to the seneschal. After a time, the boy returned with word that they were to enter and find refreshment. They followed him, a thin, towheaded lad of eight years or so, dressed in the livery of the great house of Lancaster. On their way to the kitchens, for that was to be their first stop, they passed a group of guardsmen at their drill. The men stood along the wall, arms outstretched, cobblestones in their hands.

"What are they doing?" Corwin asked.

"That's to make their arms strong," the boy replied. "Ooh! Look!"

A dapper man strode into the courtyard. "Put them down," he ordered. "Your arms, shake out. Into formation." The men ran into their ranks. "Swords!" They pulled their weapons and stood ready. Corwin stopped, his heart in his throat. He had only one memory of swordsmen, buried deeply, but forceful enough to stun him to immobility.

"So," the sword master said as he demonstrated the figure he wished the others to copy with such speed that his sword blurred into nothingness. "Against a short cut, you defend like so. Have you got it?"

The guardsmen nodded and lumbered through the drill. It was clear that it would be some time before the best of them had even the faintest grasp of what he had done so effortlessly.

"Again!" the sword master shouted. The guards leapt forward, swords making silver arcs in the sunlight. "Again!" They leapt again and brought their swords flashing to the left. "No!" the master said. "Be using your backs. Don't wave your arms like puppets!"

The men stepped and swung in unison, swords gleaming in the bright sunlight, throwing Corwin into a memory of Tovan carrying him down forest paths. At times, his rescuer's pace had slowed, and his hand darted here and there among the greenery and brought food to Corwin's mouth— tangy leaves, sweet fruit, earthy mushrooms, cool mint leaves. Corwin rested, content, his head resting on Tovan's fur-clad shoulder, the leaves stuck in his dark hair scratching Corwin's cheek.

Then the drums began to sound, coming from below them. Tovan ran deeper into the forest, uphill, away from the sound. When they reached the top, Tovan stopped and put Corwin down behind a fallen log. They lay looking down the hill through the screen of leaves.

The drums roared louder. Trumpets brayed. Two ragged lines of men ran toward each other, bellowing war cries that turned into the clash of swords and screams of pain.

*Why do you* quetan *do this?*

Corwin had no answer.

Philippe and the page stood watching the sword master perform.

"That's our new sword master," the page said with some pride. "The best in all Christendom. Just arrived this morning. Begging your pardon, good sirs, but Cook will be cleaning up the kitchen. If you wish to eat, please come as quick as you may."

He led them down a twisting stair and into the clatter of saucepans and crockery.

"Eh there, Hubert, my little love, what have you brought me today?" said a red-faced woman, as broad as a gate, with arms as great as those of any yeoman. The boy smiled shyly and pulled a wilted dandelion from his sleeve.

"Oh, Ellen, will you look at this!" the woman crowed to the scullery maid, who stood behind a great tub, smiling and cooing at the boy's gift over a pile of soiled crockery nearly as tall as herself. Cook dusted a blade of grass from the boy's jerkin and handed him a roll, still warm, from a basket on the great table in the center of the room. "Here. Eat up, lad. You're to grow big and strong and be the finest knight in Christendom."

The boy glowed pink with pleasure, took the roll and began to nibble at it. He suddenly jumped, as if pricked with a pin, straightened up and said, in the most formal tone, "Oh. Her ladyship commands that these two troubadours be fed." His duty done, he went back to work on the roll.

"Troubadours, is it?" she said as she deftly filled two bowls with a savory stew and placed them on the long table in front of the two men. "These new fashions. When I was a girl we had storytellers, or sometimes a bard would wander out of Wales and tell us a tale of some horrid great battle, all slayings and smiting and horses cut in half and what not, or of some magical thing, the saints preserve us. Is it true what they say?" She looked at Philippe from the corner of her eye, "That troubadours tell stories of love?"

*"Mais oui, Madame."*

"You're French!" she squealed.

66

"Provençal," he replied.

"And you, lad, are you from France, too?"

"Northumberland," Corwin said.

"Oh." She turned to Philippe coyly. "Is it true what they say about—"

"No," he snapped. "It is an utter slander. It is true, however, that this is the most delicious scent I have encountered in all England. It is with great regret that I tell you that I have taken a vow. I may not eat flesh."

"Oh dear," she said, her brow wrinkling. "Well, here now, we've a fine Cheshire cheese, just cut, and some fruit . . . Janet! Have we any greens for sallet? Make a great bowl full. This poor man can't eat meat." She bustled as she talked and laid a feast at Philippe's place that would have fed a regiment. "Fish, surely you can eat fish," she said, placing a bowl of pickled herring before him. "Look now, you've made me forget to give you bread." She cut two slabs off an enormous loaf. "And drink. Beer or wine?"

"Red wine?" Philippe asked.

"From Bordeaux," she whispered.

"Madame," he said, standing and bowing, "you are a worker of miracles."

They ate for an hour straight while Philippe extracted information about the castle and its residents from the knowledgeable cook.

"We are new in these parts. Tell us of your master."

"Mistress, 'tis, Lady Avice of Lancaster and in her own right, too."

"She has not a husband?"

"Widowed. 'E died of a flux of the bowels, campaigning in Ireland with King Henry."

"How sad. Has she children to keep her company?"

"Only her son, William."

"A child, I assume, since he is not on the Great Crusade."

"Not a bit of it," she chuckled. "'E's as full grown as you can get, and then some. Lovely large lad he is, to be knighted come spring. Oh, but didn't he want to go. Fought her on it for months. I heard them arguing about it at dinner one night.

"'Mother,' says he, 'I must go on the Crusade. I will be accounted a coward if I do not.'"

"'And you will be accounted a corpse if you do,' she answered him, quick as that.

"'But I am the Lord Geoffrey's squire, and where he goes, I must. I have sworn an oath to follow him.'

"'Geoffrey fully understands the realities of the situation and has released you from your oath. I spoke with him this morning.'

"'Mother! How dare you!'"

67

"'My responsibility is to the welfare of this duchy, and so is yours. I'll not have my only heir butchered by the Saracens.'

"'Nonsense, Mother, with the force of my arm, all will flee before me.'

"'You'll still have to drink their heathen water,' says she. 'How do you think your father died?'

"'To die for one's king and Our Holy Savior is a noble deed, be it at the hand of the enemy or from the flux of the bowels,' says he.

"'To have my castle go into the hands of your cousin Mortimer would be a dastardly act, and one which I will not permit. When you're married and have fathered heirs, then's the time to think about noble deeds, not when you're the duchy's only bulwark against that ill-mannered brat and my upstart sister-in-law. I absolutely forbid you to go!'"

Cook cut another slab of bread and placed it in front of Corwin. "My, but wasn't he in a snit then! But she's a doting mother, and she says to him, 'William, my love, your time here will not be dull. I've hired the best sword master in the world. My mother's third cousin, Count Ulrik of Flanders, spoke highly of him. I've sent word for him to come, just for you.' That cheered him up. If there's anyone for the warlike arts, it's our William."

*Ksh,* thought Corwin. *How could anyone enjoy fighting?*

Philippe nodded. "And they are both in residence here, now?"

"Them and the maidens," she answered. "Six of them this season." Corwin looked at her, puzzled. "To be trained, of course, in proper deportment. There's none better at such things than our lady, be it a horse or a headstrong mam'selle. But I don't doubt that there's more than one lord angling for young William of Lancaster as a son-in-law." She noted their empty plates. "Another help, master troubadour?"

"*Non, merci,* and with great regrets. This has been exquisite."

"And you, lad? You look like you could take a little filling out."

Corwin smiled and bowed in imitation of his master. "I can only regret that I have not four stomachs, like a cow."

She whooped with laughter. "Anything you gentlemen need, you just send to me for it. Four stomachs like a cow. Well, I never."

They followed William toward their chamber, waddling like Christmas geese. "Ah," Corwin said, as he reclined on the straw pallet provided for them, "I could get used to life in a castle."

"If you wish to, refrain from mentioning cow stomachs in the presence of the ladies."

"Do you think I offended her?"

"*Mais non, mon fils.* For her it was a perfect comment, but for one of these maidens, I think not."

"Are highborn maidens so different from ordinary women?"

"Yes and no. Their training is different, *certainement*, but underneath, it is all the same. There is a certain pride, a certain longing, great love, fear, all those things that live in the heart of every woman. Perhaps the recipe is a little different, because of the circumstances of their birth, but the ingredients are the same."

"Is the love of a noble lady as great as the stories say it is?"

"The love of a noble lady is a thing wondrous fair, but the love of even a scullery maid is not to be scorned." Philippe reclined on the pallet and yawned, preparing to give himself wholly to the business of digestion. "Always remember that."

* * *

That night, at supper, the minstrels were shown to a table just below the great table on the dais where Lady Avice of Lancaster, her son, and the six maidens sat. The lady was quite tall, with a narrow face and a long nose. William sat beside her, a great, handsome, broad-shouldered youth, with wiry red hair as convoluted as a thundercloud. Philippe and Corwin shared their table with the sword master.

"Good evening," said Philippe, bowing slightly, as he and Corwin reached their table. "It is an honor to meet one of your skill. I am Philippe, a troubadour, and this is my student, Corwin."

The sword master smiled and clasped Philippe's hand. His hair was black and curled thickly. He had broad, prominent cheekbones and a hawk's-bill nose. His dark eyes were as narrow as the windows of a castle dungeon. "Hallo, friend," he said in the most incomprehensible accent Corwin had ever heard. "Mordred of Varnik am I." Corwin winced as the sword master shook his hand. Mordred lacked the bulk of William and the guardsmen who sat at the next table at their beef and beer, yet he possessed an effortless force.

"Where is that?" Philippe asked as he casually flexed and straightened his fingers. "In all my travels, I do not believe I have ever been there."

"A wondrous beautiful land," replied the sword master. "By empire of Byzantium it is lying."

"Mordred . . . an unusual name."

"My mother was daughter to Duke of Bretagne."

Philippe grinned. "You have a tale to tell. I can smell it."

Corwin watched the muscles slide smoothly beneath the weathered skin of Mordred's face as he smiled back at Philippe. "A short one."

"Will you tell it?"

He shrugged and speared a grape from the wooden bowl in the center of the table with his dagger and peeled it as he spoke. "My mother, as I have said, a noble lady, youngest daughter to Duke of the Bretagne. My father a duke, ruling under the authority of the emperor, himself. My elder brother succeed him, and I as you see me." He popped the grape into his mouth.

"But how can that be?" burst out Corwin.

"Simple, my young friend. The elder brother is receiving power temporal, and I. . . a taste for life in castle, a horse, a sword, of clothes two suit and a purse of gold coin." He speared another grape, his gesture as graceful as his swordplay. "Oh yes, and blessing of Bishop of Justinia Prima, as out the door they are pushing me."

"You have traveled far since then," said Philippe.

Mordred shrugged. "No more than need. The lord of the castle see me fight and offer me invitation to be teaching his sons, training his soldiers. After a time, the lady of the castle is offering me her invitation. After a time I am needing a new castle." He sighed. "Is my sad destiny. You understand?" He looked at Corwin out of the corner of his eye and grinned.

Corwin nodded, blushing. Philippe asked, "But this, ahem, aspect of your reputation does not keep noble lords from seeking your services?"

"No, because is not known well." His white teeth glinted as he smiled. "At least among noble lords. What man announce himself a cuckold? And the ordeal. I am having the right to challenge my accuser with my sword to prove false his accusation, do I not?" Corwin and Philippe nodded thoughtfully as they worked through Mordred's tortured grammar. The sword master leaned back against the rough stone pillar behind his seat. He put his hands behind his head and regarded them through the slits of his eyes. "Always they most happy to be referring me to my next place. I would, of course, appreciate that my story is not into your tales its way finding."

"Agreed," said Philippe, as Corwin nodded, eyeing the well-worn sword hilt that hung from the man's belt. "Upon one condition."

The sword master's eyebrows rose in surprise.

"That I may use your name, Mordred. I like it. It is a fitting name for a bold and deadly handed knight."

The sword master roared with laughter and clapped Philippe on the back. "I lak you, troubadour. Yes, by all means. I am awaiting the tale most eagerly."

"I must leave you now and prepare for my performance," Philippe said, as he patted his lips with the edge of the tablecloth. He rose and bowed to Mordred. Corwin began to rise. "*Non, non, mon fils*, I do not need your assistance. Stay here with our esteemed friend and enjoy a second helping of beef, or perhaps try a little of this sallet. I fear Cook has sent me far more than I can eat."

As Philippe left them, Corwin noted the stoop of his shoulders. For a time the sword master spoke of his travels: of the land of Rus, where

Kazakhs lived on their horses; of the broad valleys of the Danube and Rhone; but as Mordred expressed no interest in Corwin's life, the conversation ended and the apprentice storyteller let his gaze wander the room.

At the table on the dais, the universe revolved around William as the maidens competed for his attention. Seven hulking guardsmen sat at on a long bench at the table below the one Corwin and Mordred occupied, chewing their way through their meal with great dedication. Corwin noted their potbellies and the way one slouched, the tendency of another to hunch his shoulders forward and tilt his head back to compensate. He glanced at William, and was surprised to see him as bloated, oversized. He wondered what change could have come over his sight to have caused the men of the castle to deform in this way.

Then he looked at his dinner companion and realized what had happened. Mordred ignored him and sat, toying with the stem of his goblet, watching the dais as though it were a play enacted for his own entertainment. There was not an ounce of flesh to spare on the man, and he seemed to be at once entirely relaxed and wound as tightly as a spring. His form was of such perfection that beside him every man, even the muscular William, looked somehow inadequate: crooked, either too big or too small. Corwin watched him for a time, and then turned to look at the dais. As he did, Lady Avice looked up and toward them. He watched as she fell through the slits into the dungeon of the sword master's eyes.

There was a stir in the back of the room. Swift steps sounded, and a man strode up to the dais and bowed deeply. He wore a loose, flowing robe of dark red velvet, bound at his waist with a broad belt. Gold gleamed from the heavy chain hung around his neck and from the rings, with their rainbow of stones, that flashed from every finger.

"Madame," he said. "Mademoiselles. My lord." He bowed, then turned to the rest of his audience. "My friends." Corwin could not believe his eyes. This kingly man was his master, Philippe.

The troubadour began at once, in his rich, deep voice, to tell of a knight of surpassing skill and the lady who with one glance had accomplished what no warrior had ever done: vanquished him utterly. The tale continued: A villain arose, the kingdom fell, the maiden lost, and the knight, distraught, wandered mad in the forest.

Corwin withdrew from that forest and looked at those around him in the hall. He could see that the vision of all in the room turned inward. William and the guardsmen had all become the knight. Each of the maidens mourned her treatment at the hands of the evil wizard and wept for her lover's travails, which the wizard forced to her to watch in an enchanted mirror. Even the stern Lady Avice had become the maiden as she listened.

71

Philippe continued his tale. The other men's eyes saw an inner landscape of dark forests, dread beasts, and mountain ridges sharper than knives, Corwin could tell as he watched the expressions on their faces: here a shudder as the hero stood on the edge of a precipice, there a twitch of the hand as he drew his sword. Corwin looked at his dinner companion, the sword master. He, too, was the knight, his eyes seeing far into that inner distance as Philippe's voice wrapped them all in its spell, but as in all else with this man, there was a difference. His hand moved, as the others' did, his expression changed, but his focus never wavered. He saw not the trials, but Avice, the end point of his quest. Corwin wondered what thoughts went on in his head.

At last, the knight found the castle of the evil wizard. He bested the wizard, who wounded him with a poisoned dagger. He entered the maze of the castle, dying, but kept on, walking, staggering, crawling at the last until he found his love. She held him in her arms. Her tears washed the poison from his wound and healed him. Spring came to the land, and the bold knight and his beautiful lady walked hand in hand in sunshine amid the blossoms.

The maidens, and even the guardsmen, wept. A noble light shone in the eyes of all in the room, transfigured by the alchemy of the tale. Philippe fell silent, his work done.

\* \* \*

It had been a long and very exciting day. Corwin lay on the pallet, unable to sleep, with Philippe's thunderous snores in his ears. He thought of Murdoch. It was time for him to be tested.

Murdoch's Tale
# Chapter 14
# The Muster

Murdoch and Algar the Smith were the last to hear the drum, there in the forge, amid the heat and clatter of their own work. It was only when Murdoch turned to feed wood to the fire that he saw the villagers gathered in the marketplace. He nudged Algar, and the two smiths stopped their work to watch. A dozen soldiers marched into the square, led by the drummer and a soldier bearing the banner of Lord Hounshel. At the command of their sergeant, they came to a halt, standing at attention. The sergeant came forward and addressed the crowd, his voice loud enough to echo from the buildings surrounding the square.

"By order of His Majesty, our beloved King Galeschin, and His Grace, Lord Hounshel, all able-bodied men are to come with us to his castle at Hirday to perform the service due them by right."

The crowd muttered. Spring plowing was just weeks away and the loss of their menfolk at this critical time would devastate them. "Why now?" shouted one from the back of the crowd.

The sergeant lowered his voice. "Gather round," he said. Murdoch left the forge to hear better. "There is villainy afoot," the sergeant told them, "and danger from Velendruch. King Ambrahad intends to attack. This I have from the mouth of Lord Hounshel himself. It is the duty of every able-bodied man to fight for his king." Murdoch stood with his arms crossed at the back of the crowd. Algar limped up to join him. "What's this?" he asked his foster son.

"They want us to fight Velendruch."

"Well, I'll have Ara pack you some bread and cheese for your journey." All around them men left the square, heading for their homes to pack, save for the graybeards.

"I have taken a vow, Father."

"So you have, Murdoch, but this is the king's command."

"A vow is a vow."

"You there!"

Murdoch looked up. The sergeant was pointing at him. "Kiss your sweetheart good-bye. We leave tonight."

"No," he said.

"You will do as you are told, serf."

"Freeborn," said Murdoch sullenly. "And bound by a vow." He turned on his heel and went back to the forge.

"Take him," said the sergeant softly to his men. By the time Murdoch reached his anvil and had put on his thick leather gloves, they were upon him. He seized an iron rod from the coals and spun to face them. None dared take a step closer. The sergeant, knowing a losing battle when he saw one, called his men back. He rode off, with his men behind him.

\* \* \*

The sun sank from the sky and Algar went into the house, leaving Murdoch to lock up. He banked the fire and put his hammer in its place. He counted the ingots of pig iron, and decided they would need more. War was coming: horses to be shod, pikes to be forged, helmets, breastplates. Would his vow forbid him to make them? He had not thought to ask Andrew, and now the man was gone. He closed the door to the smithy and fastened the lock. He heard footsteps behind him and turned. A blow struck his head and he saw no more.

"I'll not let such a one as him stay behind." said the sergeant. "Put him in the cart."

\* \* \*

Murdoch woke to find his arms and ankles tied with coarse rope and his mouth stuffed with a foul-tasting rag. He rolled about the bottom of a lurching cart, knocking up against the boots of the soldiers who rode in it. He moaned and the one nearest him picked up a cudgel and raised it. "Why bother?" said another. "We're there. If you knock him out again, we'll have to carry him." The other shrugged and dropped it.

Murdoch rolled as far onto his back as his bound arms would allow. He could see a flash of blue sky, quickly swallowed up by the dark stones of the gate of some fortified place. The sky returned, and the cart swayed to a stop. Murdoch's captors stood. Two of them pulled out knives. One went to Murdoch's feet and began to cut his bonds. The other remained at Murdoch's side. "Behave," he said, "and I'll have no cause to use this. Mind your manners, smith. You're at the castle of Lord Hounshel." They hauled him to his feet and he stumbled from the cart. "Line up there with the others."

74

There were more than a hundred recruits in the courtyard, in clots and scraggling lines. He took his place next to Wat, son of the wainwright, and the rest from his village. Armed men, in the red livery of Hirday, walked through the mass of yokels, looking at them disdainfully and bellowing at them to stand straight and mend their lines. Murdoch glowered.

"Well, you had it easy," muttered Wat. "Riding in the cart while we had to walk all night."

"And a blow on the head every time I waked. A real pleasure."

"Stop that chatter. Stand up straight."

"Do you have any water, Wat?"

"*You!*" The guardsman stood an inch from Murdoch and shouted into his face. "What are you hiding behind your back?" Murdoch turned and showed his bound hands. The man pulled out his dagger and cut the cords. "Don't get any ideas, troublemaker. I'll be watching you." With a last hostile look, the man departed to harass another recruit.

When the guardsmen were satisfied that some sort of order had been established, they withdrew to the sides of the courtyard. Two other men, with finer clothing and the bearing of knights, came forward. "Those of you having skill with a bow, come forward," ordered the taller of the two. About half the men present stepped from the lines and were led off. After they left, the knights began to walk through the ranks. As they passed each man, they looked him over and offered their verdict. "Pike . . . sword . . . sword . . . pike." A guardsman followed them and gave each man a shove, pikemen to the left, swordsmen to the right. The pair stopped before Wat—"Pike," and then Murdoch—"Sword."

"I will not fight." But the two were already on to the next man. The guardsman put his hand on Murdoch's arm. Murdoch braced himself. "I will not fight!"

"Good. I haven't time for it now. Stand over there. You!" he shouted at the next man. "That side." Murdoch saw that the future swordsmen were being bullied into a line and that a great plank table stood at the head of it, with servants hauling bread and pots out to load it. He joined the line.

He was thirsty and filthy, coated with the dirt of his journey and the soot and sweat of his previous day's labor in the smithy. He tasted blood in the corner of his mouth. His head throbbed and the edges of his vision shimmered. He waited doggedly with the others as the line wended slowly toward the table.

The first woman serving, a stern peasant woman with great arms rough and red from endless work, gave broad wooden bowls. The second, very young, fair and fat, handed out chunks of bread. A third, mostly hidden behind the other two, served broth with a great ladle.

He watched the ladle scoop and pour, scoop and pour, entranced by its motion. It was not simply that he was hungry and it held food. There was a rhythm, a flow, that struck him as the first thing of beauty he had seen since he had been ripped from his home. It was his turn to be fed. He took his bowl from the unsmiling woman, and his bread from the next, who looked disdainfully at his grime.

The ladle dipped and rose and his eyes followed the hand, the arm in its sleeve of plain wool, dyed with blue woad, to the head, with hair like burnished copper peeking from beneath a coarse kerchief. And then she looked up at him, with great, brown eyes burning in her pale face, and then was gone, as the line of men shoved him past and she bent again to her work.

He found a place to sit at one of the crowded tables and turned to his meal. "Now, there's a fiery wench," said a coarse voice at the other end. "I'll be the man to quench that flame."

*No, you won't,* thought Murdoch, as he dunked his bread in his soup. He did not know who the unfortunate woman was, but he already knew that he did not like the man speaking about her.

"Well, you're the man to do it, Turnbolt!" A chorus of laughter followed. Murdoch looked down the table. Turnbolt sat at the far end.

The man was big and beefy, with dark hair and beard, both cut short, and the smug expression of one who thinks himself more handsome than his features warrant. "Ah," he said, "I love those red-headed wenches."

"Charming, ain't he, our Turnbolt," said a voice from across the table. Murdoch turned to look at the speaker. He was a small man, a head shorter than the brawny smith, but strongly built, with twinkling blue eyes and brown hair that hung to his shoulders in tightly twisted curls.

"So he's yours, then," Murdoch said.

"My village's very own bully," the other replied, sighing. "You spend your whole life waiting for someone to get their comeuppance, but no, we've been here a week and he's already sword master Tillin's pet pupil."

"Lucky you," said Murdoch, and turned his attention to his soup.

"My name's Grimbold. What's yours?"

"Murdoch." He could see the castle gate over Grimbold's shoulder, and he could see the pikemen guarding it. *No way out there.* "Well, if you ever need a tonic or physicking, just let me know. My mother's quite the herbwoman and sent me with a boxful of her potions."

Murdoch nodded and dipped his bread into his soup. The sergeant ordered the men at the next table to move, but Murdoch was too hungry to let good food go to waste. Servants hauled off the great kettle and dismantled the plank serving table. The serving women returned to the kitchen with the empty baskets. Turnbolt stood and made kissing sounds at the redheaded wench as she passed. She stared grimly ahead. Murdoch

76

glared at Turnbolt, who grinned smugly back. Murdoch considered punching him, but remembered his vow.

A dapper man came striding up to the table. He was not large, but broad of shoulder, and wore a fine sword at his side. "Tillin," whispered Grimbold.

"Come along then, Turnbolt," he said. "The rest of you men fall in." They stood, all save Murdoch, who sat munching the last of his bread.

"Stand up, man!" Grimbold hissed. Murdoch shook his head. The sooner they understood that he meant to keep his vow, the sooner he would be out of there.

"You there!"

Murdoch looked up to see Turnbolt pointing at him and the sword master's frown. "I said, 'Fall in!'"

"Sir," Murdoch said, "I have taken a vow. I may not fight nor wield a sword."

Turnbolt snickered.

"Really?" said the sword master. "Well, I have something special for you." He led Murdoch to the side of the courtyard, picked up two weighty cobblestones, and placed them in Murdoch's hands. "Hold these," he said. "No, not like that. Stretch your arms out to the sides. I'll tell you when you can put them down. And I'd best not see those arms drop." He turned on his heel and ordered the recruits into formation.

They drilled. Tillin barked orders and they followed, blunt practice swords cutting the air. An hour passed, then two, with Turnbolt smirking at him from the front row. Murdoch's shoulders ached, then burned. He shrugged them and stretched his neck, to no avail. He gritted his teeth against the throbbing pain. Turnbolt grinned. The recruits stopped their drill for water, but the sword master did not look his way. He put down the stones.

In an instant Tillin was on him, sword drawn. "I did not give you permission to put them down," he said quietly, his sword inches from Murdoch's throat. "You will hold those stones in your outstretched hands until I order you to do otherwise. Or are you ready to join us for drill?"

Murdoch picked up the stones. His shoulders screamed as he raised them.

# Chapter 15

"He won't come!?" Lady Avice's voice echoed down the stone corridor. Philippe and Corwin, just emerging from the room they shared, looked at each other, eyebrows raised. They heard an indistinct reply from the servant who had brought the message, followed by the lady's command to order the grooms to ready the horses. Philippe beckoned to his apprentice and they withdrew down the corkscrewing stairs to drink at the font of castle knowledge, Cook.

"He won't come? Hah," spat Cook. "When the bishop's away, the ferret will play, won't he, Master Troubadour?"

"*Madame?*" Philippe asked.

"Our brimstone-belching Father John. Father Petronius, her ladyship's confessor, is well on in years. The poor, dear man's as frail as last autumn's leaf. When he's not well enough to say Mass, her ladyship sends to the bishop for some priest to come to the castle and carry out his duties. But the bishop's gone to Canterbury, and Father John left in charge. He won't come. If that don't beat all."

"But why would he not come?"

"Well, it's hardly for me to say," she replied, rolling her eyes, "but I think if you'd ask him, he'd say that the power spiritual outshines the power temporal. Like the sun outshines the moon—yes, that's how he put it in his sermon last week."

\* \* \*

In an hour's time, the grooms stood at attention, holding the horses' bridles as the lady, her son, and the maidens mounted. Then the gates swung open and, led by a score of halberdiers in the livery of Lancaster, they left in procession for the church. First came William and Lady Avice, then the maidens, two by two in order of rank, followed by another twenty guardsmen and then the rest of the household. Despite the lady's proud carriage, it seemed as though no one was looking forward to attending Mass that fine morning.

At the church Lady Avice, William, and the maidens took the front row, but because the church was filled with the townspeople who normally heard Mass there, the rest of the folk from the castle had to find themselves seats wherever they could at the edges or in the back. Cook bustled in and took Corwin and his master under her ample wing. "Follow me," she whispered. Cook plowed through the throng like a great ship, and Philippe and Corwin slipped along in her wake. They found themselves seated in the first row of pews in the transept, beside the altar, their view of it blocked by the great pulpit, but their view of Lady Avice, William, and the maidens unsurpassed. Avice and her companions sat fanning themselves in the muggy air, sweetly scented with frankincense and myrrh.

"Wouldn't miss this for the world," Cook whispered to Corwin.

The choir began to sing and they all stood. An altar boy emerged from the sacristy, followed by Father John, a bulky man with his brow furrowed into a permanent scowl. His mouth smiled, though—smugly, Corwin thought—when he saw the lady and her retinue. The Mass began.

As the choir sang the Gloria, Corwin let his gaze wander from statue to stained-glass window to the heights of the ceiling. Then they all sat, and Father John climbed the steps of the tall pulpit, making the polished wood creak beneath his weight. The gospel that day was the tale of the loaves and fishes, and Corwin recalled the sermons of Father Anselm, and how he would use this gospel to encourage everyone in the village to share with those less fortunate, but when Father John looked up from his reading to begin his sermon, the fire in his eye wiped the smile from Corwin's face.

"SINNERS!" the priest roared, slamming his palm onto the polished wood of the pulpit, and the entire congregation jumped. Corwin looked around. Cook seemed to be enjoying herself. Avice looked at the priest with a defiant air.

"The blessed Apostle Paul says, 'Thus I teach to all the churches of the saints: Let women keep silence in the churches, for it is not permitted them to speak, but let them be submissive, as the Law also says.'"

The priest paused and glared at the maidens before continuing. "'But I would have you know that the head of every man is Christ and the head of the woman is the man, and the head of Christ is God. For man was not created for woman, but woman for man.'"

This last was aimed directly at a plump maiden in the first row, in the seat farthest from the duchess. The girl blushed as red as a beet. It seemed to Corwin that Father John was preaching his entire sermon to her ample bosom.

"Hear my words!" The priest's voice echoed against the stone walls. "This is the Word of God as revealed by the blessed Apostle Paul. 'Let women be submissive, for the man is the glory of Christ.'"

79

"'. . . and the woman the glory of the man,'" muttered Philippe, completing the verse under his breath.

"'. . . but every woman with her head uncovered disgraces her head, for it is the same as if she were shaven. This is why the woman ought to have a sign of authority over her head . . .'" He paused for effect. "'. . . because of the angels!'" He brought his fist down on the pulpit again. Everyone jumped.

"To think otherwise is a foul sin, the deadly sin of pride, deadliest of the seven deadly sins. Women, be submissive, as God commands!" He stopped and licked his thick lips, eyes still fixed on the maiden.

"'For as the body is one and has many members, and all the members of the body, many as there are, form one body, so also is it with Christ.'" Then he began again, his voice gentle. "'God has set the members in the body as he willed so that there be no disunion in the body, but that the members may have care for one another. . . . Now you are the Body of Christ, member for member . . . .'"

"I wonder which member he is," muttered Cook. "Od's little Bodikin?"

A laugh escaped from Corwin and Father John glared in his direction. Corwin coughed several times, as Philippe patted him on the back. There seemed to be an epidemic of respiratory ailments in the great cathedral.

The priest's glare raked the crowded cathedral. Suddenly he stared into space and blinked. "Amen," he said quickly, blushing, and then descended from the pulpit and hurried through the rest of the Mass.

The cathedral was beautiful, the Gregorian chant lovely, but Corwin had other things on his mind. His characters were leaping about in his head, and he had to watch what they were doing.

# Chapter 16
# Turnbolt

At last the day ended. One by one, the ranks were dismissed to place their practice swords in the racks and line up for supper. Murdoch stood, cobblestones in his outstretched hands, shoulders burning, wrists on fire. Tillin ignored him.

Menservants walked past, bearing planks to set up the trestles. Tillin turned toward where Murdoch stood. Turnbolt went to Tillin, and asked him a question. Tillin drew his sword and demonstrated a parry. He turned to leave. Murdoch watched intently as Tillin turned in his direction. Turnbolt, grinning at Murdoch, tapped Tillin's shoulder and asked him another question. Again, Tillin drew his sword and demonstrated. Murdoch considered pitching a cobblestone at Turnbolt's head, but remembered his vow. Tillin sheathed his sword again and turned. Turnbolt tapped his shoulder again. His friends chuckled as Tillin turned back.

"Master Tillin!" Grimbold's voice rang out from next to Murdoch. "Might you show me how to parry a short cut from a left-handed swordsman?"

Tillin turned. "Like this," he said, and demonstrated. "Now, enough. My dinner grows cold." His eye swept across Murdoch and he turned and walked to the armory door. He put his hand on the latch. He turned. "You may put them down, smith," he said.

Murdoch lowered his arms and gritted his teeth so he would not scream. He forced his spasmed fingers to release the stones, and his arms, freed of their burden, rose back to shoulder height. Turnbolt and his friends guffawed. In a heartbeat the courtyard filled with laughter.

"Planning to fly away, my fine chicken?" said Turnbolt, as he swaggered over. His friends gave a chorus of clucks. "How's your back?" And he slapped Murdoch on the shoulder.

Murdoch nearly swooned from the pain. He watched Turnbolt's grin through a fine red haze of anger. His hands balled into fists.

"Tut, tut, now. Remember that vow of yours," Turnbolt chided. The scullery maids came in bearing baskets of bread. Turnbolt watched the redheaded wench, his grin turning to a leer, and he followed her.

"Tincture of wolfsbane," Grimbold said, holding up a flask. "Good for sore muscles. Think you'll be able to feed yourself?"

* * *

Murdoch lay on his back on his pallet like one crucified, around him the hum and bustle of the recruits settling down for the night. He stared at the ceiling, exhausted, but in too much pain to sleep. Even in that crowded space, with the voices of a hundred men competing, he could hear Turnbolt.

". . . like a chicken. How perfect! That coward. Bwawk buk a buk. . ." The voice grew louder, and then Turnbolt's face appeared over Murdoch's, a gobbet of spit drooling from his lips.

In an instant Murdoch was on his feet, pain forgotten, drowned in his wrath. He rose so quickly, the gob missed his face and landed with a plop on the pallet. He grabbed the astonished Turnbolt by the front of his shirt, spun him around, and picked him up by the shirtfront and a leg and tossed him, like so much refuse, at the clot of recruits who had gathered to gawk, spilling them like ninepins.

"I'll get you for that, smith!" Turnbolt shouted, but he showed no sign of attacking. Instead, he nearly fell over himself as he and his cronies retreated to their pallets at the other the end of the hall.

"What about your vow?" asked Grimbold.

"Wasn't a war," Murdoch said, lying down again and resting his hands behind his head. "Didn't use a weapon. And did I raise my hand against him?"

"Well, it did go up a bit toward the end when you tossed him."

"Didn't hit him, though, did I?"

"No," Grimbold said. "I suppose you kept your vow, after all."

Murdoch stared at the ceiling for a bit, as Grimbold settled on the pallet next to him. "I've a question."

"What's that?"

"What was that you were saying to Tillin about a short cut? Both edges of the sword look the same size to me."

"Long is forehanded. You can reach farther. Short is back-handed. Your reach is shorter. Why do you ask?"

"No reason. Just curious."

82

# Chapter 17

The next morning Philippe and Corwin sat on a stone bench in the outer courtyard of the castle digesting their breakfast, a great satisfaction filling their souls. Philippe wore his usual attire and only one ring, the one given him by Lady Avice the previous evening. They had leave to stay in Lancaster as long as they wished, or as long as Philippe's trove of tales would last them, content to rest from the rigors of the road.

"My master," Corwin asked. "What would *amor* say to Father John?"

"In a moment, *mon fils*. It is not healthy to think too hard after such a large breakfast. I must compose my wits."

The sweet summer air was altogether too fine for anyone to stay indoors. The maidens came out like a multicolored flock, with servants carrying their embroidery and blankets for them to sit on in the shade. They roosted about thirty feet from the troubadours, cooing like doves in admiration of one another's handiwork. Last of all came Lady Avice, with servants carrying her embroidery stand, her thread basket, and her chair. The servants settled her a bit to one side of the maidens, the better to watch them, and then stood to one side, in a precisely straight row, waiting for whatever she might command next.

The minstrels stood and bowed. Lady Avice acknowledged them with a gracious nod, and with a wave of her hand allowed them to sit in her presence, although she did not invite them to join her. "A pretty sight, *non?*" said Philippe to Corwin. "But there is more here, I am sure, than meets the eye. Note how they all face toward the courtyard. I am certain that if they only meant to enjoy one another's company, they would sit facing each other, *n'est-ce pas?* Let us watch and see if we can learn the answer to this puzzle."

A few minutes later, a swift bay warhorse, lather flecking its flanks, galloped in through the gate, bearing the red-headed William. He leapt from the saddle and flung the reins to a groom perfectly positioned to catch them, then splashed water on his face from a basin held by a second servant. He pulled off his sweaty shirt and exchanged it for a fresh one held by yet another servant. There was a rustle among the maidens as he did so. He began his exercises.

Corwin glanced toward the maidens. There was precious little sewing going on, and all of it by Lady Avice's capable hands. She watched her charges as she stitched. "Decorum, ladies," she warned.

William grabbed hold of an iron bar set on posts to hang just above the height of his head. He was engaged in touching his chin to it repeatedly.

"Thirty," murmured a dreamy-eyed maiden with golden-brown ringlets and a pert, turned-up nose.

"What was that, Lady Maude?"

"Hm, what? Oh. Begging your pardon, Lady Avice. It was nothing."

"Lady Maude. Your father is Duke of Kent. No doubt you shall be at least a duchess by right of your eventual marriage. A lady of your station does not prattle about nothing if she wishes to keep the respect of her servants."

"Yes, my lady," Maude replied meekly.

"Forty-five," sighed another of the maidens, short, slender, and blond as flax, wearing a blue gown.

"Lady Marie!"

"I am truly sorry, Your Ladyship."

"Your father is only a baronet, young lady; however, the same goes for you. Nobility is a quality of one's person, not merely assigned by one's birth. I expect no less of you than of Maude."

William finished his chin-ups. A servant stepped forward and handed him a cloth to wipe his brow. A great stain of sweat spread across his back, making the shirt cling to his muscles. Another rustle passed through the crowd of maidens, like a breeze across a barley field. Lady Avice swept her sharp eye across them, and they bowed their heads to their work, like grain falling before the scythe. William stretched himself face down on the sward and began to do push-ups. The maidens sewed, with only surreptitious glances directed his way. Corwin heard a whispered, "Twenty-five." Lady Avice appeared not to have heard. A great, fidgeting cloud of silence hung over the courtyard. "Fifty." When the whispered count reached seventy-five, the maidenly breeze fluttered again. At ninety-two William slowed. Eventually he stopped. "One hundred and three," came the whispered count. "Imagine what it would be like to be underneath." The cloud burst, releasing a rain of giggles, Lady Avice serving as the thunder.

"Great heavens! Have you all become serving wenches! You've no more dignity than a gutter full of crows. On your knees, all of you, and say two paternosters immediately. Not you, Rose. Two rosaries for you, Lady Alyce, and consider yourself fortunate that I don't wash your mouth with soap."

"Why not Rose? That's not fair!"

"Because she had the decency to blush at such crudity and not twitter like a common sparrow. Her behavior has proven what I said earlier. Her father is a mere knight, but she has shown you all up." Corwin noted that Rose was the maiden who had been the object of Father John's attentions.

With only a few disgruntled mutterings, the maidens knelt to pray, their eyes still on William, whose damp shirt clung to his massive arms and chest. He stretched and shook them and then picked up two weighty stones and held them in his outstretched hands, as though he were the crucifix to which the maidens were praying. The maidens finished their prayers, all but Alyce, and turned again to their work.

"I think it is time for your lesson," Philippe whispered, smiling. "After all, we cannot let Father John go unanswered." He cleared his throat.

"Courtly love," he began, aiming his voice at the cluster of maidens with the accuracy of a Sherwood archer. Their heads spun toward him as swiftly as weathercocks in a gale, even that of Lady Avice.

"This I have learned at the court of Marie de Champagne, patroness of troubadours and the queen and arbiter of the Court of Love."

"Ah, Master Philippe?" One of the serving men stood bowing before them. "Lady Avice requests that you and your apprentice join her."

"*Certainement.*" They bowed to the ladies. A second servant emerged with a chair for Philippe, which he set next to Lady Avice. Corwin found himself a seat on the grass to one side.

"How goes it with my cousin Marie?" asked Lady Avice.

"Ah, *très bonne.*"

"And your father, who might he be?"

"Henri de Troyes."

"You are related to the great Chretien!"

"*Mais oui.*"

A puzzled look crossed Lady Avice's brow. "But my fifth cousin, Nicole, his mother, only had one son before she died . . ."

"Half-brother," Philippe admitted.

"Ah." She nodded knowingly. "And your lady mother?"

"You know, I misspoke. All is not completely well with your cousin Marie. This past winter she had a great loss," he replied. He shook his head sadly. "She had three dear little cats that she named *Un, Deux,* and *Trois,* and she delighted in their capering."

The sword master, Mordred, emerged from the armory. He and William crossed swords and began to spar.

"They would frolic on the ice on the moat of her castle. It was most amusing." Philippe sighed. "But alas, one day, as they scampered most comically, the ice broke, and *Un, Deux, Trois,* cats sank."

85

There was an instant of silence, broken by the clang of William's sword as Mordred skillfully disarmed him, and then the laughter of the duchess and the maidens as they got Philippe's bilingual pun. All but Rose, that is, the knight's daughter, who wailed, "Oh, the poor little kitties!" to the redoubled laughter of the others.

William scowled at the maidens and glared at Mordred, who turned to bow to Lady Avice. She however, was looking at Philippe.

"Quite droll, master troubadour," she said smiling, "but tell us of courtly love."

"Ah," he said, eyes twinkling. "Father John would not approve."

"Good," said Avice, with fire in her eye.

"Under the law of *Roma*, as we have so recently been told, the woman is under the power of the man, his to do with as he wishes, *n'est-ce pas?*"

They all nodded.

"He may marry his daughters to his advantage, put aside his wife to get another, take his pleasure where he will, is this not so?"

"But Holy Writ says that a man must cleave to his wife," said Rose.

"Of course, but do they? Our good Archbishop Geoffrey, is he not the natural son of King Henry? And after he was acknowledged as Henry's son, did Henry continue to be king? Of course! And what might become of the child of a lady, were she to have one by a man other than her husband? Would a man of such parentage become an archbishop? Hardly! Would she be sent off in disgrace? Well?"

Philippe's voice had grown louder to be heard over the combat between William and Mordred. William's sword fell clanging to the ground again, leaving a silence in which Philippe's "disgrace" echoed. The maidens and Lady Avice, eyes riveted on Philippe, all nodded. William blushed crimson and grimly picked up his sword.

"And yet what is a woman to do? How is it that she may live a happy life when all about her is circumscribed by duty? How may she retain the respect and honor of her husband when the entire law, the force of *Roma*, is set against her and teaches her that she is to be despised?

"Yet the Lord, when he walked among us, taught of love. And what are we to make of this riddle? The law, *Roma*, has come between us and love, *amor*, has it not?"

Again, they nodded.

"So you see," he concluded, "that marriage, which should be the pinnacle of Christian love, has become, not a joining of two people in the most perfect love, but little more than a business arrangement, a tool of political power. And the power—saving your grace, my lady, who rule capably here in this great city—the power belongs to the man. . . ."

"This is true, ladies," Lady Avice said. "Although the previous Lord of Lancaster was my father, when I married William's father he gained the rights to the castle and gave the commands. Were I to marry again, my husband would rule, not I."

"*Exactement*," Philippe continued. "And the remedy for this sad situation is courtly love." The ladies' attention was riveted on Philippe as the sparring continued between William and Mordred. William's face grew red with anger and exertion as the sword master gracefully parried and sidestepped his blows.

"Courtly love calls a man to a higher standard, and it is the woman herself who must set this standard. True nobility, as you said earlier, Madame, is a quality of character. To be wealthy or titled, this is an accident of birth. Are those qualities alone sufficient when choosing the one to whom you will give your heart?"

William charged at his teacher, swinging wildly. Mordred stepped lightly aside and tripped William, sending him sprawling. His sword flew in a glittering arc and landed, hilt first, in the watering trough.

"*Non!*" said Philippe. William glared at him.

"So, you see, the lady must first test the man, to see if his heart be gentle and true, to see if he is worthy of her. To this end, she must hold herself aloof, she must make it clear to him that it is he who must prove himself."

Mordred offered William his hand, but William arose and stomped off alone. Mordred turned, grinning broadly, toward the ladies and swept an elegant bow.

But no one was looking at him. He scowled and stormed off after William.

* * *

At lunch that day, Philippe sat at the left hand of Lady Avice, the two of them engrossed in their conversation to the exclusion of all else. The maidens all seemed to sit a little straighter, all save Rose, at the far end of the table, who merely stared at her trencher. Corwin shared a silent table with the sword master, who left, glowering, before the roast was even carved. William appeared late, and ate in silence. None of the maidens looked at him. Lady Avice dismissed the maidens at the end of the meal and requested that Philippe speak with her privately.

Corwin, full of Cook's excellent wares, wandered the castle grounds. He found his way into a privet maze, but could not find his way out. The air was so soft and the day so pleasant, he hardly cared. Marveling at the ease of a troubadour's life, he lay down in a patch of shade and fell asleep.

He dozed, and dreamed he stole milk from a cow, squirting the creamy goodness into his mouth, feeling the ache of hunger vanish. Somewhere in the back of his sleepy mind, he wondered how he could feel hunger, with his own belly so full. Somehow, in the twisted way of dreams, it reminded him of Tovan.

As the shadows lengthened toward midafternoon, he dreamt he heard a woman crying, and eventually his muddled senses told him this was no dream. He lay on the grass blinking.

"Oh!" He heard Rose's voice, on the other side of the privet hedge. "I'm sorry, Your Lordship." Her skirts rustled as she stood. She sniffed, then hiccupped.

"Why are you crying?" William asked.

"Oh, sir, 'tis nothing for one of your station to hear, but thank you for asking. It's just they . . . they . . ."

"Who?"

"The other maidens, Your Lordship. I am so ignorant, I should not be here. I'm only here because my father saved your father's horse in battle against the Irish and he granted my family this boon. This is all too far above my station. I am a simple fool, who should be home darning my brother's socks. I should not even be speaking to you. I can leave if you—"

"I suppose you would prefer it."

"Your Lordship?"

"No one cares a fig for me, since that sword master humiliated me this morning."

"He did? How awful! What did he do?"

"You were there." William sat heavily on the stone bench. "Sit, please."

"Humiliate you? But he didn't speak to you . . . I don't recall him saying anything—"

"Speaking to me? He knocked the sword from my hand! You all laughed! This morning, in the courtyard."

"He did?" There was silence as she puzzled it out. "No, my lord, they were laughing at a jest of Master Philippe's. I didn't get it." She sniffed again. "Then they laughed at me for that."

"The troubadour! He called me a disgrace!"

"Oh no, my lord! Master Philippe was discussing the law of *Roma* and that of courtly love; how the bastard son of a man could become a bishop, while a lady would be disgraced by bearing a child out of wedlock."

"Then why won't anyone talk to me? No one looks at me! What have I done?"

"Master Philippe says that the man must prove himself worthy of the woman. He is teaching us the ways of courtly love, teaching *them*, at least." She let out a long, shuddering sigh. "This is all too much for me to understand. All I want to do is marry a nice man and have lovely fat little babies." She burst into tears again.

"Here," William said. "Use this." Corwin heard her blow her nose. "That's what I want, too, Lady Rose. To find a nice woman to come home to between wars. None of this troubadour nonsense, nor Father John's beastly theology. I was angry on Sunday when I saw the way he looked at you, Rose. I wanted to grab his fat neck and wring it like a goose."

"Oh, Your Lordship!"

"William." he said. "Please call me William." He paused. "Will you share a trencher with me at dinner tonight?"

A servant cleared his throat. "Her Ladyship requests your presence, Mademoiselle."

"I will escort you," said William. He turned to the servant. "So, she's finished talking to the troubadour, eh, James? That's one man I'd hate to be," he whispered to Rose. "Our new sword master has sworn to kill him the next time he sets eyes on him."

# Chapter 18

"Master Philippe!" Corwin whispered. He found his master pacing the room they shared. Philippe held up his hand for silence. "But my master! The . . ."

"I am composing a *chanson* for the duchess. Do not interrupt me." Corwin stood, fidgeting from foot to foot as Philippe paced.

"What?" the minstrel shouted at last. "It is utterly impossible to work with you here. Out with it and be gone!"

"Mordred of Varnik has sworn to kill you!"

Philippe stopped his pacing. "For what cause?"

"His lordship did not say, but I believe it is because Lady Avice now speaks to you, and not to him."

"*Merde*," Philippe said. "And it is of the sword master that she speaks to me. How shall she ascertain that his heart is true? Were someone else in this predicament, I would find it *très amusant*. We must go to her at once and seek her protection."

They hurried down the long corridor and around the corner. Mordred paced before the lady's chamber door, his sword in his hand, mercifully with his back to them at that moment. Philippe grabbed Corwin by the scruff of the neck and yanked him back.

"We must find a page to send her a message," Philippe whispered. They tiptoed back the way they had come and found no one. "To the kitchen, then. Surely Hubert will be there." He reached for his bag and began to pack his belongings. "I must remember this for a story."

"We're leaving?"

"If we cannot find help before the sword master finds us, we will have little chance of returning for our things."

Corwin stuffed his clothing into his sack.

Minutes later, they crept down the stairs to the kitchen, which was filled with bustling servants. Cook stood over a broad copper pan, whisking herbs into a sauce. "What are you two doing here? I've no time for a chat."

"I was looking for Hubert."

"At his riding lesson with the rest of them, no doubt. The pages are not allowed in here while we're cooking, nor should you be. Mary! Bring me more thyme! Have you finished mincing the parsley?"

"There is no help for us here," whispered Philippe. "You see the danger of being tempted from your quest by an easy life. We are off to Cornwall, *mon fils.*"

They left the kitchen by the stairs to the courtyard and crept along the edge toward the gate. They had nearly reached it when Mordred's voice cried out, "I am seeing you now, coward! Like a man stand and fight!"

Philippe and Corwin broke into a run, with Mordred screaming a stream of oaths after them in his native tongue.

*Surely,* thought Corwin, *this must be the* ksh.

They ran through the gate and along the side of the wall, following the path toward the sword smith's. Soon his gate came into view. Philippe pounded on it. Behind them, they could hear Mordred's incomprehensible oaths growing louder.

"Who is it?" called a voice from inside the gate.

"Philippe and his apprentice! I beg of you, let us in!" The gate opened and the pair nearly fell through it. Philippe slammed it shut and dropped the latch. "He means to kill me!"

"Who?" asked the smith. "And why?"

"Mordred of Varnik, the castle sword master," said Corwin. "For jealousy."

"You're the one?"

"He was here?"

"Just after lunch. Bought a new sword in your honor. I'd no idea it was you he was after. Some chambermaid?"

Philippe put his finger to his lips. Outside the gate, they heard Mordred's running footsteps pass by.

"Lady Avice, upon whom I have no designs. It is all a misunderstanding, but he is a hasty man and there is no way to explain it to him. He has sworn to kill me as soon as he sees me."

The smith scratched his head. Suddenly there was a furious pounding at the gate. "Let me in, smith!" shouted Mordred.

"*Mon Dieu,*" whispered Philippe. Corwin crossed himself.

"This way," Ian whispered. He led them across the courtyard to where a cart stood. "In here. My sons will be taking it to the docks in the morning to get a load of pig iron."

"Let me in," roared Mordred. "I am needing your help!"

"For God's sake, don't make a sound," the smith said under his breath. "Coming!" he shouted toward the door. "What's all this, to take a man from his work?"

They spent the night in the cart, listening as Mordred ranted his way through dinner, and any number of beakers of ale, becoming more inebriated as the hours passed. Corwin and Philippe lay on the hard boards of the cart, not daring to move, scarcely daring to breathe.

After midnight, Philippe began to snore.

"What is that?" he heard Mordred mutter. "That damned snore I know. The Frenchman is sleeping here!"

Corwin held his breath.

". . . Ah . . . my nephew, Samuel. Snores, he does, like a bloody thunderstorm."

"It did not come from the house." Corwin heard the bench scrape on the cobbles as Mordred stood. He reached over to Philippe and pinched his nose shut. Philippe woke with a sputter. Corwin pressed his finger against Philippe's lips to silence him. He felt the troubadour stiffen in fear as Mordred's footsteps drew closer. Then he heard the sound he feared most: the whisper of a sword being drawn from its scabbard.

"Mordred! Friend!" Ian called. "We've half a pitcher of ale pining for us here."

"It didn't come from the house," muttered Mordred. "I mus' find him. I mus' kill him."

"It's too hot in the attic. My nephew sleeps in the shop in this weather. Come, friend. I can't have you damaging my bellows-boy."

Through a crack between the boards, Corwin saw Mordred, sword in hand, standing about twenty feet away. If he came any closer, he would be able to see over the side of the cart, to where Phillippe lay, wide-eyed. Corwin closed his eyes and prayed silently.

"Come, friend." Ian's voice sounded closer. Corwin looked through the crack. Ian stood beside Mordred, offering him a full tankard. "Here, drink this and tell me if you don't think my wife brews the best ale in England." Mordred took the cup from him. Ian put his arm around Mordred's shoulders. "Now tell me again the tale of your triumph at the tournament in Alsace."

Mordred took a deep pull at the ale and allowed himself to be led back to the table. "Johanna, her name it was, wife of . . ."

Mordred fell silent shortly before dawn, save for his echoing snores. Philippe and Corwin's brief sleep was broken when the smith's sons hitched the mare to the cart and took their seats.

". . . and make sure that it's good clean iron—none of that rusty stuff you brought back last time." The smith's voice dropped. "I've done my best to convince him that your running from him is the end of the matter. Go with God, friends."

92

# Chapter 19

The smith's nephews left them at a crossroads and turned toward the docks. Corwin and Philippe took the southward road. Each evening, they found an inn or tavern in which to barter their skills for bread and board. Life had returned to normal, it seemed.

The fourth evening found them in a small tavern where the road skirted the border of Wales. Corwin told one of his Mouse King tales. Philippe told a tale of love, and sang two songs. They sat at a long table in the back corner, where high-backed benches gave them some privacy, dining on bread and cheese and, to Philippe's delight, a good Bordeaux. In an hour, they would perform again.

"Life, *mon fils*, is good," said the troubadour, and took a sip of his wine.

Behind them rose the contented murmur of the crowded inn. The hinge squealed, another customer arriving. "Your pleasure, sir?" inquired the landlord.

"Wine," came the reply. The accent was barbarous, and unmistakable. Philippe laid his hand on Corwin's arm in warning. Corwin stopped breathing. "A friend of mine I am seeking," the voice continued. "French, a troubadour . . ."

"Might his name be Philippe?" offered the helpful landlord. Philippe slid beneath the broad table and tugged at Corwin's sleeve. Corwin followed. The landlord's voice grew closer. "Well, you're in luck, then. He's right here!"

Corwin sat frozen, looking at the legs of the innkeeper and the sword master. He could see that two swords hung from the man's belt, and he knew for what purpose the second had been purchased. *Ksh!* No doubt remained in Corwin's mind that Tovan's word applied to Mordred. Corwin froze, huddled there under the table with Philippe, hardly daring to breathe.

"Well, he was right here," said the puzzled landlord. "Probably stepped away to use the outhouse."

"Wait I will."

Corwin slid back as the sword master sat and swung his legs under the table. Time passed. The minutes stretched to hours. The landlord came, again and again, bringing wine, apologizing, then complaining, as the time passed and the troubadour did not return to perform as promised. Corwin pressed further and further back as Mordred slumped more in his seat with each glass of wine.

The room grew quiet as the customers left. The innkeeper approached the sword master's table. "We've room in a bed, if you want," he said. "You can have the troubadour's place. He's not honored his half of the bargain, and I'll be damned if I give him and his boy lodging."

"You warned him, didn't you?" the sword master said.

"Warned him? I took you right to him." The innkeeper sat across from Mordred. Corwin and Philippe pressed back against the wall. "What d'you mean, warned him? You said he was your friend. What do you want with him?"

"Revenge," Mordred was slurring now, much the worse for drink. "My life has he destroyed, my livelihood. Sword master was I to the court of the Lady of Lancaster, and she her eye had set on me. Then this . . . this . . ." He lapsed into his native tongue. The words were incomprehensible, but his tone made their meaning clear. He spat on the floor. "Suddenly, she will not look at me, but at him only. I did what in such a situation a man of honor must do. I swore to kill him." He drained his glass. "The coward ran. The matter, I thought, was at an end, and the way to her clear. But then . . ."Again he stopped to curse in his native tongue. "Then to her chamber she summon me and I go, I am thinking—but. . ." He gave a long, shuddering sigh.

"She threw you out, didn't she?" asked the landlord softly.

". . . She said I am not worthy. Me, son of a duke! Me, who has tournaments won against the finest blades!" He staggered to his feet. "Me, who has won the favors of noble ladies from here to the Black Sea! And she is giving me no reference!" He pulled the dagger from his belt and threw it. It whistled across the room and stuck, trembling, in the door. Mordred sagged onto the bench. He put his head on the table and said no more.

"You," whispered the innkeeper, "a drunken hothead, no matter who your father was."

Philippe reached around Corwin and tugged at the innkeeper's apron. The man looked down, and his jaw dropped. "Get him upstairs," whispered Philippe. Wide-eyed, the innkeeper nodded. He pulled the drunken sword master to his feet. "Come along then, to bed, Master Hothead." By the time he returned to lock the door, the troubadours were gone.

94

# Chapter 20

They ran, not looking back. At dawn they left the road, climbed across stiles, the short stairs that breached the hedgerows between the fields, and followed footpaths, winding their way south. The first night, warm and clear, they spent in a ditch. The next afternoon, gray clouds rolled thick overhead and they could smell rain. The trees showed the undersides of their leaves as the wind raced through their branches. "We must find shelter, master," said Corwin. The ripening grain whispered as they strode through it.

"We cannot risk being known," replied Philippe. "No one must know our trade, nor that I am not English."

They climbed a stile. A house, of sorts, stood at the bottom of the field.

"Leave this to me," said Corwin. "Act sick."

From the other side of the house, a woman's voice called the chickens, and the hens cackled as they scurried into the house. The door thumped shut as they rounded the corner of the hovel. Fat drops of rain began to spatter. Corwin knocked urgently at the door. "Please," he called. "We are travelers. Please give us shelter!"

The door remained shut. "Who are you?"

"My name is . . . Peter," he answered. "I am traveling with my uncle, the scholar . . . Petronius . . . from Oxford. Please! He has taken ill!" Philippe coughed and nodded at Corwin. The wind picked up and the skies opened. Corwin felt cold water soak through his hood and drip down his neck.

"Please?" He asked again. The door opened a crack. "We have a little money and can pay for our lodging."

An eye peered out, in a wrinkled face, with a faded kerchief on top. "Well, I suppose," the woman said. "But I'll warn you. My two grandsons are here and they have sticks, should you try anything on a poor old woman."

In response Philippe coughed again. "Our thanks, good missus," said Corwin. "He's frail, he is, and has lost his voice."

95

She opened the door. Her sons sat at the table, eating soup and bread. One was a grown man with a dull-witted look. The younger was Corwin's age, fair-haired and handsome.

"Move over, Paul," the woman said to the elder. "Make room by the fire for this poor man. I fear we've not much to share, just barley gruel with not so much as a bit of meat to go with it." Philippe smiled and nodded. "Finish up and give our guests your bowls, boys, so they can eat," said their mother.

Corwin looked at the room. It was small, not four strides in any direction, with a low loft at one end for sleeping. Chickens scratched the dirt floor. Two ragged cloaks and a shawl hung on pegs beside the door. "Please! Let them finish! We can wait."

He settled Philippe on the bench and held his cloak near the fire to dry. Philippe said nothing, and remembered to cough occasionally. The three finished their meager meal while Corwin and Philippe nibbled bread and sipped mugs of weak beer.

"So where are you from, Master Peter? And where are you going? And what do you study?" The woman's questions were endless and Corwin's imagination hard-pressed to provide answers. At last, satisfied that they were indeed going from Oxford to Carlisle to lecture upon the movement of the planets and their influence on earthly events, she wiped her son's bowls with a corner of her apron and filled them for her guests. When he had finished eating, Philippe reached into his purse and put four farthings on the table.

"Four!" the woman said, her eyes growing wide. "And with no meat in the pot. Here, Alfred, sing them a song to earn all this money. He's a lovely voice, my Alfred does. Sings in the choir on Sundays. Sing them the *Panis*."

Alfred stood, his blond hair like a halo. He sang the *Panis Angelicus*, as if he were one of the angels himself. His high, pure voice filled the room.

"That's beautiful," whispered Corwin. Philippe nodded, and coughed.

"Now sing him one you made up, my lamb." She winked at Corwin. "He's clever, my Alf is."

Alf grinned and sang:

*In days of old when knights were bold and ladies they were merry,*
*One lady fair beyond compare was queen of two great countries.*
*She went away on the bold Crusade a'camping in a tent.*
*How many men she vanquished there would fill a regiment.*
*Oh, Eleanor is a gay old lass, a lusty buxom lady.*
*She tossed old Louie on his arse to marry our King Harry.*

96

"Stop!" roared Philippe. "Stop, you filthy, ignorant swine, or I will tear out your lying tongue!"

He leapt to his feet and hurled the clay mug at the singer. It missed Alf's head by a whisker and shattered on the stones of the mantle. The room, so merry just a moment before, was filled with the growling mutters of Alf's brother. Thunder pealed directly overhead and flashes of lightning showed through the cracks in the shutters.

"Now Master Petronius, it was only a song. No harm meant," said the whey-faced Alf.

"You damn fool. You should know better than to sing a randy song about a queen of France to a Frenchman," hissed his mother.

"I didn't know he was French! They said he was from Oxford."

"You said he couldn't talk! Who are you?"

"Corwin, gather your things. We cannot remain beneath this roof," Philippe said. He strode to the door and held it open. Rain hissed and splashed onto the floor.

"Master Philippe? What are you doing? They have apologized. Master Philippe?" The troubadour had vanished into the drenching rain. Corwin turned to the woman and her grandsons. "I am sorry. I must go after him. I don't understand what could have come over him. He usually has the sweetest of dispositions. Master Philippe?" Paul grabbed a cudgel from its place beside the hearth and took a step toward Corwin. Calling after his teacher, Corwin ran out the door into the deluge.

Philippe refused to answer, but continued down the road with great, angry strides. Corwin splashed after him through the mire, calling his name all the way.

"My master," he puffed, when he finally caught him up. "This is madness! What have you done? By tomorrow everyone in ten miles will know we have been here! We must go back and apologize . . . explain to them—"

"Never!"

"We must find shelter. We'll freeze. We'll drown. We'll be struck by lightning!" As if to confirm Corwin's judgment, thunder rolled over them and lightning sizzled through the sky.

"It would be a pleasure by comparison." The troubadour sloshed through a puddle.

Corwin realized that he was going to have to do the thinking for both of them. The lightning flashed again, revealing a ramshackle hut not far from the path. Corwin seized Philippe's arm and dragged him toward it. "Quickly, my master. In here. We must shelter ourselves." Philippe, at last, allowed himself to be led. The stench, as they approached the shed, was vile. They could hear the bleating of sheep. "Are you sure you don't want to go back?" Corwin asked.

"*Oui*," Philippe answered, his chin firm and his look filled with pride.

Corwin sighed and pushed in the door. They found the driest corner with the aid of a flash of lightning and elbowed their wooly companions out of it. They settled themselves in their drenched clothing to wait out the storm. Furious at the loss of a dry bed and the promise of breakfast, Corwin turned to Philippe. "Have you lost your senses? Why should you care about a stupid song about the queen of England?"

"Before that she was queen of France, and before that the duchess of Aquitaine."

"So? Noble pride is one thing, but this has cost us serious discomfort. If word gets back to Mordred, it could cost you your life."

Philippe turned his face away. "A small price."

A long, flickering sheet of lightning illuminated the troubadour's noble profile. Corwin could not be sure, with all the moisture about, but it seemed to him that Philippe's face was wet, not from the rain, but from tears. "My master," Corwin said gently. "What is the lady Eleanor to you?"

The minstrel turned and looked at him. "She is my mother," he said.

### Philippe's Tale

"I was raised by a minor magistrate in the Kingdom of Jerusalem, and as a youth was brought by him to the south of France, to the troubadour's school at Louvines. On my sixteenth birthday, we had a visitor of note, Henri de Troyes, father of the great Chretien, minstrel to Marie de Champagne. After he performed, and listened to the students of the school perform in his honor, I was called to his chamber. I thought, perhaps, that my song had pleased him, and was proud to have been singled out. He began by complimenting my work, but as I stood blushing, he became suddenly overcome with sadness.

"'What is it?' I asked, thinking only that my poetry had had some flaw in rhyme or meter.

"'Sit, please,' he replied. He sighed, and the tears stood in his eyes. 'I am your father,' he said. 'Please forgive me, for our long separation has been required for your safety.'

"Henri had won renown as a poet and as a troubadour at an early age, a gift the Lord had given him, he said, along with his twisted foot, which caused him to limp most awkwardly and kept him from knightly adventures. He'd married, of course, but had lost his beloved wife shortly after his son, the great Chretien, was born. It was only natural that he would be presented at the court of the greatest of all patronesses of poets, the granddaughter of Duke William, the first troubadour: Eleanor, Duchess of Aquitaine and Queen of France.

"'Philippe, *mon fils*,' he said, 'it was as though the sun rose for the first time upon me when I beheld her. Although I had once or twice thought myself under love's spell, it was not until then, when I saw her at the side of Louis, her husband, that I understood the sweetness and the burning pang of love.

"'I sang for her that evening, a little ditty I had made to flatter her, of which I had been quite proud. It seemed a poor, trite thing as it fell from my lips. I felt like a cat bringing a dead bird to its mistress. Still, she nodded kindly and I thought, perhaps, that her eye lingered on me.

"'I was invited to remain at court, and I contrived as much as possible to be in her presence. I amused her, and thought that I, such an insignificant cripple, could not hope to do more. How could I? She was a high-born lady, the faithful wife of the king, surrounded by noble lords and brave champions, all of whom would die for but a smile or a kind word from her lips.

"'Louis, king though he may have been, was a suspicious, squint-eyed miser, fit only to play the part of *le jaloux*. He had no more understanding of courtly love than a fish understands fire.

"'When the Pope called for a Crusade, to come to the aid of the beleaguered Kingdom of Jerusalem, Louis was only too eager to curry favor, and reluctant to leave his honest lady wife alone in France.

"This was for her the last straw. For ten years she had been his wife, borne him a daughter, and felt the brunt of his anger for having borne him no son. But he was king! And his command had the force of law, and so she must endure the journey to the land of the Moors. Worse yet, her court might not come, save for a few ladies to wait upon her. I think it was for this reason that Louis was so eager to go on the Crusade, to separate his wife from all she held dear and to keep her under his jaundiced eye.

"She begged, she pleaded with him, she flew into a royal rage, and finally he agreed to allow one minstrel to accompany the expedition, on the excuse that someone must record the brave deeds of the crusaders in song. And that minstrel was myself. I am sure he approved of me only because of my deformity. And so, it seemed to me, as well, as we marched eastward, until that night.

"Late at night, unable to sleep, I rose and walked through the camp. The full moon, as red as a burning torch, hung just above the tops of the pavilions. It was a place so strange, one could hardly imagine it in a dream, so dry and sere, the never-ending wind whispering as it rushed through the ravines. Such an eerie land that somehow it seemed quite ordinary that a serving woman should come to me and beckon me to follow her. She led me to the presence of the queen.

"'Leave us now,' Eleanor said to the woman, 'but stand guard faithfully and your reward will be great.'

"'I have watched you, Henri,' she said. 'From the moment you entered my court. I have tested you endlessly, to see if your heart be gentle. I have seen that only one lady is enshrined in your heart, and I say to you that the fire that burns within your breast has kindled mine. Tonight, I will grant you mercy.'

"From that time, we were as one, sharing the delights of *amor* in the face of harsh *Roma*. By the time Jerusalem was won, I had felt you move in her womb beneath my hand. Now came the most dangerous part of the game, and the most sublime. She convinced Louis to stay in Jerusalem for the Easter season, but she kept herself at the court of her uncle Raymond of Antioch. There, you were born. After the birth, Philippe, she sent you away by that same faithful serving woman into hiding. Then, still in childbed, she confronted her husband.

"'I have borne a son,' she told him.

"He stood counting on his fingers, the dyspeptic fool, and answered,

"'It cannot be mine.'

"'You will accept him as your heir or be branded the greatest cuckold in Christendom.'

"'I will do neither. I will have you slain for adultery.'

"'Should you do that, Aquitaine will rise up in rebellion, and you know it. No doubt the Angevin will find it to his profit.'

"He flew into a rage at her words. He knew as well as any that the thread by which he ruled Aquitaine lay entirely in his wife's hands.

"'Witch!' he screamed. 'You are not fit to be the wife of a monarch, nor will your bastard sit the throne of France.'

"'And what do you propose to do?' she asked, crossing her arms, as cool as a sorbet.

"'I shall find the child's father and have him slowly roasted to give him a taste of Hell on his way there.'

"'That you shall never do. Surely you do not think I would open my mouth if he were within your reach. Nor shall you ever see the child.'

"'I shall . . . I shall send you back to your benighted Aquitaine, and may a plague be upon it.'

"'And so ends the line of Charlemagne.'

"'Hah! So you think. I shall have this charade of a marriage annulled. The Pope will do my bidding in this as I did his in the Holy Land.'

"'And brand yourself cuckold?' He stood before her, speechless.

"She continued, 'In token of the love I bore the king I married, let me advise the monk he has become. Appeal to the Pope on grounds of consanguinity. I'm sure he will find sufficient cause.'

100

"The Pope, however had his own ideas, and urged the two of them to repair their marriage. My lady conceived in Rome, on their way back from the Crusade, but it was another daughter, and so at last it was done, and the marriage annulled. Within two months she was the bride of Henri who became the king of England. My lady Eleanor sent me from her, to the court of her daughter Marie.

"She never sent for me, and so I have lived, in the most sublime and bitter happiness since, my heart being given wholly to her, the Earth about which I orbit, her subservient moon, having so much joy in my pain that I am sick with delight."

* * *

"So then, my master Philippe, by your lady mother you are Duke of Aquitaine and, were Louis not so proud, the king of France." Corwin, in confusion, went down on one knee in the mud.

"Yes," answered Philippe. "And I am telling you this tale in a sheepfold in the rain." And he began to laugh.

# Chapter 21

In the morning, they dragged themselves from the sheepfold and took their bearings. The main road lay to the east of them, the last place they wished to be, so they followed a footpath away from it, hoping to find another way south. They found a stream and washed in it, rinsing the straw and muck from their clothes.

When they reached a southward path and the warm day had dried their clothes, their spirits recovered. They bought bread, cheese, and cherries in the market square of a village, but did not stop to eat until they had walked for another hour.

They sat in the shade of a hedgerow, next to a stile that led to another westward path.

"If we continue south, we will eventually reach the sea," said Philippe. "From there, we can decide what to do—take ship or try the eastward road through Devon, *mon fils*."

Corwin nodded, spat out a cherry pit, and then lay on his back, almost asleep, watching the clouds make themselves into castles.

The birds twittered overhead.

He heard hoof-beats on the path and sat up. "There's a horse coming," he said.

Philippe gathered their food and stuffed it into his sack. "Quickly, over the stile."

They crouched behind the hedge and peered through the leaves. The horse, ridden at a brisk trot, grew closer. It was Mordred. Corwin closed his eyes and prayed. The hoofbeats approached and continued southward. Corwin exhaled.

"We must run," said Philippe, and took the westward path.

* * *

Tired and footsore, they climbed down the rugged Welsh hills toward a tiny village. They were miles west of their intended route, which followed the Severn to Gloucester, then along the coast through Devon and into Cornwall. Pursued by Mordred, they had wandered ever westward, following paths and byways, seeking a road to the south. All nature conspired to keep them on a westerly path, deeper into Wales. They stopped at the crest of a hill. The coast of Cornwall showed as no more than a dark line of cloud on the southern horizon in the slanting afternoon light. "*Mon Dieu*," said Philippe, mopping his brow with his sleeve. "We shall have to take ship to reach Cornwall."

"I've never been on a ship," said Corwin, pleased at the thought.

"Then you are a lucky man. It is far worse than the Bed Perilous. Every moment there is incessant movement, and it is impossible to retain one's nourishment." He sighed. "There is no point in putting off the inevitable. We must emulate the heroes whose tales we tell and gird ourselves for the ordeal. One must not think that a quest such as ours is to be easily obtained."

As Philippe spoke, Corwin's eager eyes took in their surroundings. The path before them dropped sharply, twisting as it descended the hills that bordered the sea. The shrubs leaned away from the incessant wind that growled through the sparse grasses. Far below, a single figure moved, tiny as a bug, climbing the path toward them.

They began their descent, carefully picking their way down the steep path. As the trail wound down the hill face, at times they could glimpse the other traveler approaching. As the stranger grew larger, he was revealed as a cloaked figure, clad in dark gray, who strode purposefully up the slope, head bent. They could not see his face. He carried a stout staff and as they walked they found they could think of little other than this sinister figure.

They came to a place where a tree lay across the path, its wind-shaped branches still struggling to put out a few leaves. "We will wait here," said Philippe, putting his hand on Corwin's arm.

In a few minutes, they could hear the hooded man's footsteps on the path below them. He came around a bend in the path and toward them slowly, his face still hidden by his hood. Only the sudden straightening of his back betrayed his surprise.

"Good day," said Philippe.

The man said nothing. He drew back slightly, but still did not speak. Philippe and Corwin exchanged looks. "*Bon jour?*" Philippe ventured, and then quickly added the same greeting in the language of Brittany and Cornwall.

At last the figure recovered his voice and spoke. "I have been sent to guide you to my teacher. Come."

Philippe glanced nervously at Corwin. "And what might be his name?"

"Her name," the stranger replied, though he did not give it. "Come with me."

As the last of the twilight faded, the hooded man led them to the bottom of the path, through the twisting streets of the seaside village of Llanywth, then along the water's edge where the waves lapped sullenly. Corwin wondered how the man could find his way, with only the setting crescent moon for light. Finally, he turned his back to the wind and strode through a tunnel of briar rose. A house rose before them, its thatched roof and whitewashed walls pale in the moonlight. Their guide knocked at the door in a peculiar rhythm, a hinge creaked, and a sliver of ruddy light slid through. After a whispered exchange, they were allowed to enter.

"Who are you, and why do you seek us?" To Corwin's surprise, a woman's commanding voice addressed them.

Corwin looked around the room. The only light came from a hearth at the far end. A long table filled the center of the room, with six people, men and women both, seated at benches at each side and a deep, carved wooden chair at its head, its back to the fire. Sacks of grain, bundles of herbs, skeins of undyed wool, and braids of onions hung from the rafters.

Philippe bowed deeply. "I am Philippe of Albi, a troubadour, and this is my apprentice, Corwin, from Northumberland." Absorbed as Corwin was in his inspection of the room, his bow came late. "I am engaged upon a quest to learn the wisdom of your noble tradition," Philippe said.

"He is a spy for the monks, Mistress Gwyneth," whispered the one who had opened the door for them.

"Nay," Philippe said sternly. "My tradition, that of the Pure, is as much at odds with Rome as is your own. We, too, must fear her spies in our land."

"Then you have your tradition. Why would you meddle in ours?" said the woman.

"There is much I do not know," replied Philippe. "Yet it seems to me in my travels that the old wisdom was everywhere the same at one time, and that in my land and in yours it has survived in its most pure form. I also see that in my sunny land of Provençe, the storm clouds of persecution gather and I see that here you brace for the storm. I would gather these teachings and record them, lest they be lost."

"Write them down?" sneered Gwyneth. "Books can be burned, as we well know here."

"True," Philippe said. "But my intention is to codify them in the form of stories. Thus concealed, they will live."

"Let me throw them out, I pray you, my mistress," said their guide. He had removed his hood, and his sharp-featured face looked sullen in the flickering light. "They are ignorant. They wish to use your learning for their own ends."

"No, Dylan," she replied. "Did not the raven cry as I stepped over the threshold this morning, saying 'Bacach! Bacach!' from the direction of the hills above the town? And did you not find them just as I scryed in the basin? No, nephew. Long have I waited their coming. Let them remain. I would speak with the elder." She turned to Philippe. "To what end would you put my learning? To make little tales for the entertainment of great lords?"

"My lady," said Philippe. "You know the stories as well—nay, better—than I. You have Pryderi, at two the size of a six-year-old child. You have Peredur, named in my language Perceval, driving home wild deer, thinking they were goats. Cuchulainn, no stranger to you, is killing men at the age of six, and Roland, a hero of my land, strikes a man with such force that he splits helm, head, body, and horse. These are the tales that we tell the great lords, and what do we get? A land ruled by brutality, where might makes right and the strongest may do as they please. And why not? What tales do we give them? What standards do we make for greatness? The ability to strike off a man's head and drive it home with a stick!

"These great lords, I know them. They are decent men, many of them, trying to live up to the standards we set for them—we, the bards, the tellers of tales, the keepers of tradition. They train to fight, to hunt, to rule, to dominate. They have, for the most part, no more imagination than . . ." He looked about him, then pointed. "Than yon braid of onions.

"In this moment, the warriors have gone elsewhere to carve out empire in the name of God, and so the land will be at peace for a time. But a new generation of knights is practicing at sword and their energies cannot be turned outward forever. No. Again there will be war. There will be widows, orphans, destruction. In the tales, war is glory. Only heroes fight. Only heroes die. In life it is otherwise.

"And this is our responsibility. We are the tellers of the tales that form their thinking. And their thought must be changed." The fire crackled.

"What do you want of me?" said Gwyneth, still speaking from the shadow of her high seat.

"I wish you to be my partner, to collaborate with me in the writing of my master work."

Corwin heard gasps from those gathered at the table and looked at his master closely, wondering if he fully understood the audacity of his request. Philippe looked like a man entranced by a happy dream. Cornwall, the goal of Philippe's long quest, still lay a day's voyage away. "This work shall be as a child to us, the happy joining of my tradition with yours."

The voice of the bardess trembled. "Tell me of this work. What does it concern?"

"A king who rules for right, for the good. A king who personifies all the qualities of a just and merciful monarch, to whose court the greatest knights are drawn as by a lodestone to fight, not for power, not for rich reward, but for gentleness, for purity, for truth."

"Tell me of this king," she said, leaning forward a little, so that Corwin could see her profile silhouetted against the fire, revealing a straight nose, round cheeks, and a small chin that showed great determination. Her hand moved, and he saw a band of intricate embroidery on the hem of the sleeve, a swirling, knotted design of bright green on the white cloth.

"He is the son of the High King and a noble lady of the lineage of the druids, whose passion burns so brightly that they cannot wait for the bonds of matrimony to sanction their union. They marry, but the king dies before the child is born, leaving the kingdom in chaos and the child's life in danger. He is hidden for his own safety and grows to manhood unaware of his heritage."

"But how, then, does he claim it?"

"By pulling an enchanted sword from a stone. You know of this king. I have traced his legend across the known world. Its roots lie nearby. His name is—"

"Arthur. And yes," Gwyneth said, standing and coming forth into the light. Her eyes were large, blue, and shining and her thickly curled hair showed silver mixed with black like Philippe's own. She was a tiny woman, as fragile as a bird, and stood barely up to Philippe's shoulder. She took his hand. "I will be your partner. This work will be as a child to us."

"What?" Dylan demanded. "How can you do this? They are strangers! Foreigners!"

She looked at the fuming young man calmly. "Who are you to question my judgment, nephew? Am I not the daughter of the druid?" Corwin watched in amazement, as Dylan's mouth opened and closed twice like a landed fish and the man fell silent. Corwin looked at Gwyneth. She stood there, calmly watching Dylan. "It is late," she said. "You may go to bed now. The rest of you, see to it that our guests are fed and have a place to sleep."

\* \* \*

As they lay on the straw pallet provided for them, Philippe gave a contented sigh. "One can trace the hand of God in everything. For years I thought my quest would end in Cornwall. But God sent Mordred to put us on the correct path. This quest has ended so much better than I ever dreamed it would." He turned on his side, and his snores quickly began to fill the chamber.

But as tired as he was, Corwin's characters would not let him sleep.

106

# Chapter 22
# Discovery

Had it not been for the love of a lowly chambermaid, the plot would not have come to light. When Daisy came in to straighten Rolf's chamber, she swept the hearth and pocketed the charred scrap of parchment she found there. Then she burned the rushes in the fire and spread new ones. Any other maid would have tossed the charred scrap of parchment in with the rushes, but Daisy had her eye on Lloyd, apprentice to Thomas the clerk by trade, and poet by preference. Parchment being a precious commodity, she would save any scrap with a blank face and present it to him at their nightly rendezvous outside the scullery door.

His poems were about her, he swore, although they all referred to women named Phoebe or Artemis. He explained that this was the custom among the poets of the arts of love, and who could doubt his word, with his eyes such a warm and liquid brown, like those of her father's heifer. She listened wide-eyed to his soaring phrases and ringing proclamations and then, in the moonlight, granted him a kiss and pressed the charred scrap into his hand.

It sat for some time in the box where he kept his deepest secrets, away from the prying eyes of his master, passed over again and again in favor of less damaged scraps. Then the first geese of spring flew overhead, provoking such a gush of poesy that Lloyd was forced to use it. It was after lunch, and secure in the knowledge that Thomas would nap for an hour, he took the box from its hiding place behind the dusty row of scrolls on the top shelf and wrote furiously.

With a sigh, at last, he put down his quill, collected his bits of parchment, and savored his creation. As he read each verse, he put that scrap down beside him on the bench. The poem completed, he leaned back with his hands clasped behind his head and idly gazed out the slit of window above his writing desk.

He jumped as the door scraped open, hastily grabbed the bits of paper, and flung them into the box.

107

"What's all this?" Thomas asked, his voice stern. He strode across the room on his spindly legs and darted his long arm down to snare a scrap from the floor. In spite of his panic, Lloyd could not help but think of a stork spearing frogs with its beak. "What have we here?" thundered Thomas. "Not more of those scandalous rhymings, I hope."

Lloyd babbled an explanation, but Thomas, reading the paper, did not hear it. His eyes opened wide in horror and he dashed from the room, leaving Lloyd to wonder if he should begin to pack or just leave immediately.

Thomas flapped down the corridor to the king's chambers, his sandals slapping the stones, only to find the room deserted. He next tried Hounshel's room, which was as empty as a robin's nest in February. In despair he raced down the spiral staircase, his monkish robes billowing up his pale, twig-like legs and then, in mid-stride, collected his wits and sprinted to the stables.

"Sire," he gasped, falling to his knees in the straw and thrusting the paper beneath Galeschin's nose.

"Thomas! Is the castle aflame?"

"Villainy, sire," the older man puffed. "Of the vilest sort. Read it." He wiped his sweating brow with his sleeve.

Galeschin read the paper. "This is dreadful. Hounshel, look at this. Have you ever seen anything more appalling?

> *Oh Phoebe, I am guided by your glow*
> *As when the peasant homeward wends from mow-*
> *ing, steps guided by that radiant disk, I risk—"*

Thomas stopped mopping his face. "Not that side!" he gasped, grabbing the paper and turning it over. "Look!"

Galeschin read.

> *your plan. I will get the maps*
> *hafed at Yule and the invasion*
> *pring plowing. That fool Hounshel*
> *nawares at Hirday*
> *vant,*
> *s*

"You were right, Hounshel. Thomas, where did Lloyd get this?"

"I do not know, sire."

"I can guess," muttered Hounshel.

"Well, let's find the lad and ask him, shall we?"

The library proved empty, but not so the narrow chamber that Lloyd shared with two of the pages. Even before they reached it, they could hear a furious bustle within. The king himself pushed the door open. Lloyd, busy stuffing smallclothes into a sack, jumped half a foot and spun to find his worst nightmare exceeded. He gaped, his jaw working soundlessly, and then fell to his knees, his hands over his head as though he expected a beating.

"Lloyd, look at me," Galeschin said gently. The lad looked timidly up. "Where did you get this?"

"From the muse, Highness. It wasn't me that wrote it. I mean, it just came to me out of the blue when the geese flew overhead—"

"Not the poetry, Lloyd. It scans poorly, the sentiment is over-sweet and the rhyme could use work, but it is hardly treasonable. I mean the parchment."

"Scans poorly?"

"Lloyd, this is important. Did you read the other side of this paper?"

"No, sire. I was trying to be innovative, to break through the stagnant forms, to create some—"

"Lloyd," said Galeschin sternly. "The parchment. Where did you get it?"

"And what's wrong with the rhyme?"

Galeschin sighed. "I promise you I will read the entire poem if you will tell me *where you got this piece of parchment.*"

"Sire? Oh, thank you, sire. Daisy gave it to me."

\* \* \*

"She's in for it now," whispered Annie.

"Serves her right for putting on airs about the clerk's boy," muttered Flossie as she applied her ear to the crack of the throne room door. It was hard to hear what the king was saying over Daisy's blubbering.

"He didn't touch me! I vow it! Just a kiss, a little kiss on my cheek! Not even on the lips!"

Galeschin handed her a handkerchief. He sighed again and glanced at Hounshel. "If a pretty young girl wants to have a sweetheart, I suppose the sun will continue to rise." He paused while she blew her nose. "And I am certainly glad that you have the sense to know where to draw the line with this young man. Not every woman shows such restraint in the face of poetry. However . . ." Her wide blue eyes looked at him above the wad of linen. "I do want to know where you got this piece of parchment." He held it out.

"It wasn't stealing!" she blurted and began to cry anew. "I only take what's been thrown out. Look. It's even partly burned. Nobody could have wanted it. Have mercy on a poor honest working girl, sire."

Galeschin gritted his teeth, but his voice remained as patient as ever. "Daisy, look at me. No one cares whether you burn the scraps or write poesy on the backs. But this parchment has something else written on it and I want to know where it came from."

109

He handed the scrap to her. She turned it over in her hands. So many scraps . . .

"Try to remember. Look at the shape. See how this edge has been burned. Please, Daisy, think carefully." She chewed her lip as she turned the scrap over and over in her hands. "I think. I think," she said at last. "I think I can't remember."

Her eyes told Galeschin that she spoke the plain truth. "Go," he said softly. "Tell your friends listening at the door that you are not in trouble. Say nothing else of this to anyone. And if you remember anything about the scrap, tell me at once." She bobbed a thousand grateful curtseys on her way out the door.

"Lloyd," he said. "Tell me about Daisy."

"She's . . . she's very sweet," he stammered.

"Very sweet. I see. She's quite fond of you, you know."

Lloyd said nothing.

"I suppose someday you'll wish to marry her." Galeschin watched Lloyd's Adam's apple fidget. "A wonderful state marriage. To have one's home, the ministrations of a dutiful wife, and then the children, one after another, at your knee, all looking up to their dear papa, the source of all their sustenance. And you, so fortunate, with two strings to your bow. If poetry doesn't feed your family, you can always copy off a manuscript or two. What could be a finer life, eh, Lloyd? Lloyd?"

The youth smiled wanly. "Oh yes, sire, if you say so, Your Majesty."

"Or then, there are the privations of the minstrel's life . . . constant travel, life at strange courts, the pressure of creation. . . ."

"Yes!" said Lloyd. "I mean, yes, of course, sire." He did his best to arrange his expression to show that such things were unpleasant to him, and failed.

"Thomas, take this young man back to his desk." High above, endless waves of wild geese sang their way northward. "Hounshel, we have little time," he said, when the pair had closed the door behind them. "The news of this discovery will be through the castle in an hour's time. We can wait no longer."

"I shall leave for Hirday at once, Galeschin," said Hounshel.

"No. *We* shall go to Hirday. Rolf will come with us, tied in a sack, if needs be."

# Chapter 23

The household woke each morning in the gray of dawn, spending time in meditation before breaking their fast on bread and gruel. Then Gwyneth would teach, sharing the wisdom and lore of the druids, of whom she was the last survivor. After lunch, the students worked at the chores needed to keep the household in order, while Gwyneth, regal in her great chair, received visitors, a line of townsfolk bringing sacks of grain, eggs, fruit, and fresh fish, leaving with herbs for sick children, potions for ailing elders, and sage advice for their personal difficulties. Chores completed, the students returned to their pallets and laid heavy stones on their stomachs, the discomfort designed to keep their bodies awake while their minds spun stories, each member of the household trying to outdo the others in creativity.

In the evening, after the dinner with its wit and cheer, each student took his turn, standing before the group, telling his latest tale, striving to make the others laugh, shudder, or cheer as their characters' actions might dictate. Gwyneth would render her verdict and suggest ways the tale might be improved. Philippe would critique the delivery, and then the students would add their own suggestions. Corwin delighted in his new life, at times so keenly that gratitude brought tears to his eyes.

Philippe spent his days with Gwyneth, as they worked to polish their tales of Arthur and his knights. When each story was perfected, they called upon Corwin to stretch his parchment and write. They took turns speaking, Gwyneth seated in her chair, Philippe by her side, their hands clasped, eyes shining as they gazed at each other in the candlelight. Corwin filled page after page with Gwyneth's tales of Merlin, Morgan LeFay, and the enchanted sword. Then they turned to Philippe's tales of the knightly adventures of the Round Table. As Yule approached, Philippe completed his final tale.

The Yule fire crackled in Gwyneth's hearth, the table cleared from that night's feast, and the students sat on the benches that lined the long table, eagerly awaiting the latest tale of Arthur and his knights. Gwyneth reigned from her chair at the head, Philippe at her side. Corwin sat at Philippe's right hand with his parchment stretched on a board, goose quill sharpened, pen at the ready. This, Philippe had told him, was to be the capstone, the triumph of the love of Lancelot and Guinevere over the stifling forms of Roma. Philippe and Gwyneth exchanged a smile, eyes alight, and he cleared his throat, ready to begin.

A knock sounded at the door, not the peculiar rhythm that signaled a household member, but a dull pounding: four strokes and a pause, then four more. Gwyneth and Philippe exchanged a worried look. With a nod of her head she sent Dylan to answer it.

He opened the door a crack. A brief conversation followed, too soft for Corwin, seated at the opposite end of the room, to hear. Dylan shut the door and went to his aunt. "Sir Sigmund, he calls himself, from Denmark. He says he loves nothing more than tales of Arthur and his knights. He showed me silver coins and says he wishes to be entertained."

"He is not a monk, come to threaten us with tiresome hellfire?" Gwyneth asked.

"No, he wears the clothes of a gentleman, and has a horse tied outside."

"Then let him enter."

Dylan went back and opened the door. Mordred of Varnik stepped across the threshold. Corwin's heart froze. "No!" he shouted and rose from his seat, spilling the inkwell across the table.

Mordred ran toward him, drawing his sword, so quick and unexpected that the other students, seated on the benches, could not react. Corwin held the board before him as a shield against that deadly blade, but Mordred slammed into him, tossing him aside like so much chaff in a whirlwind.

As Corwin fell, he saw Mordred thrust at Philippe, but Gwyneth was faster. She threw herself across her beloved and wrapped him in her arms. She screamed in pain as the sword ran through her and into Philippe. Then Dylan ran up with the threshing flail, screaming his rage, and struck Mordred on the head again and again until the sword master lay senseless on the floor. "Bind him!" Dylan shouted, and the others finally came unfrozen. Some ran to get rope, the others to the aid of their mistress.

Corwin stood and went to Philippe, stepping across the unconscious Mordred. Philippe's face was as pale as milk, and his breath came labored. *"Non, non, mon amour! Mon Guinevere!"* Tears ran from his eyes and splashed upon Gwyneth's face. She looked up at him. "I'm so sorry, so sorry," he whispered.

"My love," she said, and life left her. Philippe groaned in anguish. Corwin's vision blurred with tears.

The students gathered around them. They moved the table and dragged the trussed, unconscious Mordred to the corner. Dylan, weeping, held his aunt's body as Corwin pulled the sword from Gwyneth and Philippe and threw it, in disgust, into the fire. Dylan pulled Gwyneth's corpse from the arms of the weeping Philippe and laid her on the table. "Send for the sheriff," Dylan said.

"My master, you are wounded. Let me help you," Corwin said. Philippe did not answer, his eyes fixed on Gwyneth, but his breath came ragged. Corwin found a cloth to stanch the flow of blood and opened his master's bloodied jerkin. The sword had entered his ribs well to the left of his heart, and not penetrated all the way through. Corwin washed the wound, dressed it with honey, and bound it, wrapping a cloth strip tightly around Philippe's ribs, but as he looked into Philippe's eyes, he realized that some wounds cannot be bandaged. Philippe sat, staring at nothing, his face ashen, aged twenty years in an instant.

The others paid them no mind, but stood gazing at their late teacher as she lay, pale, her red blood oozing across the table, mingling with the black ink that Corwin had spilled in his vain effort to stop Mordred.

* * *

They laid Gwyneth to rest on Christmas Eve, and the whole town attended, even the priest. They dug her grave outside the churchyard, near the holy spring, and buried her. Then the crowd moved to the market square to see Mordred of Varnik hanged for his crime. He said nothing, as each witness gave his testimony, but stared at Philippe with unremitting hatred. When his sentence was pronounced, he laughed bitterly. They placed the noose upon his neck and asked him for his final words. Glaring at Philippe, he said, a satisfied smile on his face, "You have done this to me, and I have made you suffer for it."

Philippe stood as if he had not heard, looking into some interior distance.

* * *

All through the winter, Corwin tended Philippe, living still in Gwyneth's house, but no longer part of the household. Philippe said little, and for the most part sat staring out the window in the room he had shared with Gwyneth, gazing at the steeple of the church beside the holy well, where Gwyneth lay buried, and beyond that to the black branches of the snow-covered trees. Corwin fed him, tended to his wound, and did chores to see that the house was supplied with wood and water, but the others ignored him. He knew they held Philippe to blame, and Corwin was Philippe's. He did not wish to force the issue, as he and Philippe had nowhere else to go in the deep of winter. If he had to endure their shunning, he would pay that penance. It had all happened because of the question he had asked Philippe that day in Lancaster. *Again. Again, I am in a place I do not belong. Is this to be my life? Why could the men have not attacked my village? Why could Tovan have not kept me? Why did I ask that stupid question?*

After the New Year, the students began to leave, one after another, until only Corwin, Philippe, and Dylan remained.

* * *

One evening, as the world began to green, Dylan came in, slamming the door behind him. "Have you looked in the pantry lately?" he demanded.

Corwin nodded. "We are grateful to you, and I will see what my master can do to repay you."

"A gold merchant has arrived in Llanywth. If your master has entertained in as many castles as he claims, no doubt he will have gold trinkets to sell."

Corwin went to Philippe. "My master, the food is nearly gone. Dylan said a gold merchant has come to town. Will you sell one of your rings so that we may repay his hospitality and continue to eat?"

Philippe stared out the window, where the trees on the Welsh hills had begun to leaf, casting a pale green mist over the gray branches. "Mordred has destroyed Camelot. I cannot stay here."

"Yes, my master, he has." Corwin sat beside him on the bed. "But, like the heroes of our tales, we must go on."

"I'm too old for life on the road," Philippe replied.

"But what shall we do?"

"A friend of mine from Albi, a Cathar like myself, is now an abbot at a Carthusian monastery in Bretagne. He will give me shelter."

"And what am I to do?"

"I am certain they will take you in, if you wish." Philippe continued to stare blankly out the window. "Tell our host I will seek out the merchant in the morning, and that after I repay him, we will leave."

Corwin was not so sure he wanted the life of a monk. Father Anselm had taught him to read, and no doubt his skill as a scribe could earn him a place, but he was not old and tired of life, like Philippe. His life stretched before him, a great unknown, and he had yet to explore it. So many possibilities. Wealth? Well, probably not that, but love, certainly, and high adventure just waiting to be formed into tales. And another thought came to him, the one that had haunted him his entire life: *Can I find Tovan?*

# Chapter 24

Corwin whimpered in his sleep. His heart raced, his breath came in gasps. He ran through the moonlit forest, hounds baying behind him, his only thought the river ahead. Pain cut through him, slicing through his ribs from back to front. He felt the pain, then saw himself from a distance, writhing on the forest floor in agony, but it was not him. "Tovan!" he screamed and woke to find Philippe shaking him.

"Corwin!"

The boy gasped. The pain subsided. "A dream," he said, voice shaking. "A bad one." He looked at his chest, surprised to see no blade protruding from it, then lay back on the pallet, still struggling to breathe.

* * *

That day, he and Philippe packed their precious manuscript and set off with Dylan for the gold merchant. As they walked through the town, Corwin contemplated the strange path his life had taken, and wondered why God had found it necessary to spare his life that day. Why Tovan, his rescuer, had left him with Acha and Oswy. Why he had proven so useless at the forge. Why the lord of Alnwick failed to pay his debt to Oswy, so that he could become a lettered man and aid Philippe and Gwyneth in their creation. And how that had gone so horribly wrong. *Why did I ask that question, of all the things Philippe has to teach me? Gwyneth's death is my fault.* Corwin no longer dreamed of the horrible day that had ripped him from his childhood village. When he'd spoken of it to Gwyneth, she'd looked at him keenly and said he'd been touched by the faery folk, the People of Peace, but she had no knowledge of what the *ksh* might be. Gwyneth, whom he had tried to save, and failed. *Everything I touch turns to ashes.*

* * *

115

They reached the bustling market square. The dais stood there, where Mordred had met his end. At other times, it served as a pulpit where mendicant friars preached the Gospel. On this day, they witnessed upon it a most unusual sight. A fiery streak of red and brown flew across the dais, twisting and tumbling in midair as the crowd gasped. It stopped and became a person who stood and bowed, and the crowd burst into applause. Corwin, forgetting his master, wormed his way closer to the platform.

The performer wore a man's brown leggings and jerkin, which fit closely, emphasizing, rather than concealing, the slender woman's shape. Her copper-red hair fell in a thick braid to her waist. Her face, flushed with exertion, glowed with the fire of health and youthful strength. She turned sideward to her audience, bent backwards like a bow, and stood on her hands. She walked on them across the stage and then back, and regained her feet in the same manner she had left them. Corwin could not have found a woman less like himself, and so it was inevitable that he could not take his eyes off her. Dylan and Philippe strode ahead. Corwin hesitated. If he were not to follow Philippe and become a monk, he would need to perform, he realized. And there was no point in putting it off.

The woman bowed again and picked up her cap from the edge of the dais. Motioning for the throng to clear a space, she left the dais in a twisting somersault and landed, cap extended for their donations. The crowd roared with delight and chanted her name: "Lyneth! Lyneth, Lyneth, Lyneth!" As she moved through the crowd, laughing and joking good-naturedly, coppers jingling into her cap, Corwin clambered up the dais and began to pace its length, waiting for her to finish her collection and the company to settle down. He knew what tale he would tell—not a Mouse King tale, fit only for children, but the tale of a real hero.

He had learned a great deal these last months. He had seen his master take the stuff of his own life and weave it into legend, had he not? He had heard the tales of the great heroes, and even been a part of their making, had he not? He had seen how such talents, well used, had brought the admiration of ladies to his master, had he not?

He had. And his industry these past months had gone beyond the writing of the words of Philippe and Gwyneth. In the dark hours of the night, when dream and thought commingle, he had continued his own tale. And today he would share it.

At last the crowd quieted, wondering what amusement might come next. They turned their faces toward the dais, where he greeted each of them with his eyes. Corwin held out his hands for silence, and when everyone looked to him, he found Lyneth in the crowd and bowed.

"For you, fair lady," he said. She smiled and seated herself on the edge of the dais.

"I tell the tale of Murdoch this day, a hero unknown to you until now, although . . ." He held his finger up for emphasis. "He could be any one of you." He pointed at the crowd. He looked into their eyes as his finger swept across the marketplace. He had them.

"It began one autumn day, when a wandering beggar, a holy man, came to the village of Roaz. . . ."

# Chapter 25
# The Courage of One's Convictions

At Hirday, training continued. The recruits drilled and progressed to sparring. Murdoch stood, cobblestones in his outstretched hands. *He's not using his back*, he thought, watching the nearest recruit.

"You there—" shouted Tillin, as he thwacked the unfortunate recruit with the flat of his sword. "Put your back into it!"

When Murdoch was a child, at Algar's forge, he would lie in the loft, up high, away from the shooting sparks, and watch his foster father at work. As he grew bigger, he fed the fire and pumped the bellows, his eyes taking in Algar's every move. So it was, that when he grew old enough to take hammer in hand, he already knew what to do. He had learned by watching. And so it was, that as he stood, day after day, his arms and shoulders burning, will he or nill he, he learned the art of the sword.

He watched Turnbolt as well, to try to understand what made him the best of Tillin's pupils. The man was strong, no doubt about that, with an eye for his opponent's weakness and the will to exploit it. He fought to win, and had no scruples. Yet, since their encounter in the barracks, Turnbolt had delivered his taunts from a safe distance.

The wind turned that morning, and spring retreated. Winter attacked, with stinging sleet falling thick from the sky. The recruits complained, but Tillin kept them at it. Murdoch stood, feet frozen, ice beginning to glaze his hands, envying those who could warm themselves by moving. His arms and shoulders were numb for now, but soon, he knew, they would resume aching, then burning, and then cycle back to numbness again.

The menservants came out and set up the serving trestles in the lee of the great hall doorway. The men would fill their platters there and eat in the hall this night. Murdoch would be last in line. *I will stand in the freezing rain. Eat the crusts and the scrapings from the bottom of the kettle.* Tillin walked among the sparring pairs, correcting form, shouting orders. *To move. To be warm. To be fed.*

118

Tillin looked his way. "Are you ready to join us, smith?"

A figure brushed past him, swathed in a cloak, carrying a basket of bread, a damp strand of red hair straggling out from beneath her hood.

"My name is Joy. I admire a man with the courage of his convictions," she said as she passed.

Murdoch returned Tillin's glare. "No." A great warmth filled his heart, and the rocks felt as light as feathers.

# Chapter 26
# To Hirday

The sun stood high over the courtyard of Gwalhafed Castle. At the edge, near the armory, a troop of pikemen drilled. In the center, Valan had his sword lesson from Rolf.

"One! Two! Three! Good, Valan! Again!"

The lesson had gone on for two hours and Valan was ready for it to end. Rolf, however, had other plans. He could see Valan's fatigue in his slowing reflexes and the scowl on his face.

"Time to spar," Rolf announced with a smile. He drew his sword. "You first." He stood ready.

Valan stepped toward him, sword raised over his head, and swung downward. Rolf stepped back and brought his sword whistling down on top of Valan's. With a clatter, the sword fell from the young man's hands. Two servants came out and set up a trestle to one side of where Rolf and Valan sparred. "Again," Rolf said.

Valan tried a forehand cut. Again, Rolf stepped back, then stepped in and knocked the sword from Valan's hand. The pikemen stood to attention.

"Eyes right!" their sergeant ordered.

"Again," Rolf said.

Valan shook his stinging fingers. "I'd like a cup of water, if I might."

"Later," said Rolf. "Again."

Valan scowled. The servants returned and set benches to either side of the table. Valan swung blindly. Rolf sidestepped.

"Forward!" ordered the sergeant. The pikemen began to march around the edge of the courtyard.

Rolf allowed Valan a few more swings and then disarmed him. The servants returned, one bearing a tray with four goblets and a pitcher, the other a platter of cheese and apples. The pikemen continued their march.

"Again," said Rolf.

Valan attacked with a roar of rage. Rolf parried his blow, sidestepped, and struck upward. The sword flew from Valan's hands and fell clanging to the cobbles.

"Again," Rolf said.

"I think our young Valan's in need of a breather," said Galeschin. He and Hounshel sat on the bench facing the courtyard. "Come, sit, refresh yourselves."

"Attention!" shouted the sergeant.

"As you were," replied the king.

"Forward!" The pikemen resumed their maneuvers.

Valan sheathed his sword gratefully and came to the table. Rolf followed, scowling. "I really cannot have you interfering in the training of my squire, Galeschin."

"Have some cider," Galeschin replied.

Valan drank thirstily.

"I would have your advice, brother," Galeschin kept his hands below the table.

"Surely this could wait until after the lesson," Rolf snapped.

"Right face!" ordered the sergeant. His troops turned and continued their march.

"No, it cannot."

"Well, what is it then? Get on with it."

"I would like your opinion of this." Galeschin put the charred scrap of parchment on the table.

"Company, halt!" ordered the sergeant.

Valan put down his cup. Rolf stared at the parchment. Galeschin watched the cogs of Rolf's mind turn behind his eyes. "'Tis . . . 'tis nothing but a scrap of charred parchment."

"With the words *invasion*, *spring*, and *Hirday* on it. Do not try to play me for a fool, Rolf."

"You have no proof to connect me with it."

"I merely asked your opinion. It appears your opinion is that I should have cause to suspect you."

"I never said that!"

"Left face!" ordered the sergeant.

"We leave for Hirday tonight. You will accompany us."

"I've had quite enough of this treatment! I leave for my own estates." Rolf stood.

"Pikes down!" ordered the sergeant.

Rolf felt one touch the middle of his back.

"Disarm them and bind them," Galeschin said. "Keep them in the dungeon until I call for them."

"I want to go with Papa!"

Alana stamped her little foot. The look on Matilda's face told her that she had made a mistake. She did not want to be hauled to the chapel again. "I'm sorry, Lady Matilda," she said meekly. She had already thought of another plan.

That night she made herself stay awake, pinching herself and sticking her feet out from beneath the featherbed so they would stay cold. When Matilda's snores filled the chamber, Alana crept from the bed, got her cloak and shoes from the chest, and took her favorite possession, her book. She crept from the room, through the silent halls of the royal quarters, and down the stairs.

There were a lot of people up that night. Servants scurried, carrying armloads of clothes and scrolls, boxes, and chests. She could hear her father calling orders to the seneschal, and Hartendon repeating them to the servants. At each footfall, she shrank back into the shadows; the adults, busy with their work, passed her by. At last she reached the door, where servants and guards bustled in and out. Hiding in the shadow beneath the stair, she waited.

* * *

At Hirday, the sleet storm passed like an evil dream, and the next day spring returned. Life, and training, resumed. It was the feast of St. Wenus, patron saint of Hirday, and that evening the castle celebrated. After the evening meal, which featured collops of roasted ox instead of the usual soup with their bread, Lord Hounshel's musicians set up in the courtyard and played.

Murdoch leaned against the wall in the shadows. All around him the crowd danced and chattered. He watched the glad capering of the recruits and maidservants from the secrecy of the darkness.

Joy was there. She danced with one man and then another, her graceful movement all the more exquisite for being in its proper element, no longer restricted to the carrying of trays and the wielding of the soup ladle. But between the figures she would leave each partner and her gaze would roam the crowd, carefully avoiding Turnbolt. Then, as the music began again, another man would ask her to dance and she would oblige, but not without a last look around the courtyard.

Finally, one of the figure left her near the shadows. She thanked her partner, turned, and saw Murdoch. She came toward him smiling. "Why do you hide?"

He shrugged. The music began again. She reached out her hand. He had never felt so awkward in his life.

"Well, sir blacksmith, will you dance with me or no? Surely you have not taken a vow against that as well."

"I don't know how," he said, giving her a timid smile. "Our priest, Father Anselm, preached against it. He would allow no dancing in our village, for fear of bringing in devils."

"Oh, bosh," she said and took his hand. "I can think of nothing more divine than dancing. Here, I'll teach you." She led him away from the wall. "Here. Step left, right . . . no, forward with your right foot . . . that's it, now left again. Good. You learn fast. Now in time to the music."

And they danced. Angels provided the music, it seemed, because the musicians and all the others vanished from the courtyard as soon as Murdoch caught its rhythm. They swept round the cobbles, eyes seeing only each other, until the walls themselves melted and vanished and they danced free over the fields, through leafy forests, along the razor-sharp ridges of mountains, and across the billowing tops of the boundless sea.

* * *

King Galeschin stood in his chamber in Gwalhafed Castle, giving orders to his seneschal. ". . . And the scribe's boy, our young poet. We'll need his services."

"Already waiting in the third cart, sire."

"And my dear brother?"

"Firmly trussed in the second cart."

"Excellent."

"And his squire?"

"In the dungeon, with a cup of water and a crust of bread."

"Well done. We'll let him stew there. Thank you, Hartendon."

Alana heard her father's voice, and at first wondered why her bed felt so cold and hard. Then she remembered and pinched herself for falling asleep. He was leaving! Right now! He swept past her hiding place.

She waited until the last of the flock of courtiers had passed and then followed them into the dark courtyard, squeezing past the door just as it swung shut. The king's coach rattled through the palace gate. Staying in the shadows at the edge of the courtyard, she scurried down the line of carts. At the end she found one not yet loaded, with boxes and barrels piled behind it. She climbed the pile and stepped into the cart.

"Come on, Hugh!" growled a voice, "The king's already left. Let's get this done! Get in there; I'll hand the boxes up." Alana crept to the front of the cart and hid under the seat. One after another, boxes and barrels thumped into the cart and were shoved roughly to the front. One hit her hand and she cried out, then covered her mouth with her hands.

"What was that?"

"Probably a rat."

123

"I hate rats. Give me your knife, I'll kill it." Alana heard the scraping of boxes being pulled away. She shrank back under the seat and covered her face with her hands.

"Pox take you, Hugh. We've got to get this cart loaded. You can kill it when we get to Hirday."

Grumbling, Hugh shoved the boxes back and the thudding and scraping resumed. By the time the cart lurched into line with the others, Alana was asleep, clutching her book.

* * *

"Damn, it's cold. I think there's a blanket beneath the seat. Hand it up, Hugh."

Hugh reached under the seat, and gasped. "There's something down there!"

"Yes, Hugh, it's called a blanket, and maybe a basket of food, if we're lucky."

"No, John," said Hugh. "It's alive. I felt warm breath on my hand. I'm not putting my hand down there. I might get bit."

"Pox take you, Hugh. Here, take the reins." John bent down and looked under the bench. There was a shape in the dark, too big for a blanket. He touched it, and felt the contours of a knee beneath the cloak. He ran his hand along the leg, and found a tiny foot.

"We've a child on this cart! A little one!"

"Well, don't wake it up," said Hugh. "I hate crying."

* * *

Alana woke shivering, and her teeth chattered. She did not know where she was. She opened her eyes and saw boots in the dim light and heard the jingle of harness. That was it! She had escaped Matilda and was following her father and grandfather to Hirday in a cart. When she planned her escape, she had not thought how cold it would be or how hungry she would feel.

"You're awake, then, little mouse," said John. Alana stifled a gasp. "Oh, come up here on the bench with us. You'll be warmer." Alana crawled out and John helped her up to the seat between himself and Hugh. It was still dark, with only a faint lightening of the edge of the cloudy sky before them to hint at the coming dawn.

"So, what might a young snippet like yourself be doing in this cart?"

"I escaped," she said with pride. "I'm going to Hirday with Papa."

"Ah," he said, "And who might your papa be? One of the guards? You should be home with your mother. She'll be frantic."

They had reached the turning of the road below Hirday Castle. For the past few miles the road had run beside the deep, fast-flowing River Shales, which had gouged a cleft between the cliff topped by the castle to their right and a steep, pine-forested slope topped by a guard tower to their left. As they reached the end of the ravine and entered a broad meadow, the east wind picked up, sending the clouds scudding away from the growing dawn. A hundred yards beyond the cleft, a plank bridge crossed the stream. The road began to rise from there, winding up a gentle slope planted with hundreds of fruit trees and studded with beehives.

"My mother is in Heaven," she said, "and my papa is the king."

John turned his head to look at her. Hugh stared. At that moment, the sun peeked over the horizon, and its beams revealed the scarlet wool and golden trim of her fine cloak and the distinctive red of her hair. "'God's breath," said John.

"Are we in trouble?" asked Hugh.

\* \* \*

The first carts of the convoy had already reached Hirday Castle. Galeschin and Hounshel went straight to Hounshel's chamber and called for Lloyd, the apprentice scribe. The cart on which Alana was perched between Hugh and John was the last to enter.

The hubbub of the royal convoy disgorging baggage filled the courtyard. To one side, a line of recruits doubled back on itself, waiting for the morning meal. Servingmen carried a great cauldron of gruel by a stout pole threaded through the handles. Alana saw a copper-haired woman carrying a huge ladle stop, stare at the line of carts with Lord Hounshel's and the king's banners hanging from the first, and then dance a caper for sheer joy.

Hugh handed Alana down to John, who led her toward the doorway of the keep. There seemed to be a lot of bother going on at the second cart. Whatever baggage being unloaded there was not cooperating.

"Mmmmph! Arrgh!"

"Pick me up," ordered Alana. From John's arms, she could see her uncle bound and gagged, being hoisted by four men-at-arms. "Good morning, Your Highness the Prince Uncle Rolf," she said, and giggled. "You look silly."

He turned, surprised, and glared at her. Then another expression came over his face, and she did not like it at all. She hid her face against John's shoulder and said in a tiny voice, "I want my papa."

John carried her up the stairs and set her on her feet at the top. As they entered the chamber, they passed Lloyd bowing his way out, a delighted grin on his face and a bag of coin in his hand.

"Papa!" Alana cried, and she dropped John's hand and ran to her father.

"What are you doing here?" Galeschin glared at John. "What is the meaning of this?" Shocked by her father's reaction, Alana began to cry.

125

John knelt and bowed his head. "She hid in the cart, Majesty. We were nearly here before we knew it. We thought her a child of one of the guardsmen, until the sun rose and we could get a good look at her, and by then we were at the bridge."

Galeschin sighed, and picked up his daughter. "It was very wrong of you to come."

"I want to be with you, Papa."

"I know, child, and I with you, but we are in a war, or will be soon, and you must be kept safe."

"If I'm with you, I will be safe."

"If only that were true."

"I'm hungry."

Galeschin sighed again. "Have the seneschal assign her a chamber and a maid." He put the little girl down. "Now, go with John and have your breakfast." Alana skipped off, holding John's hand.

"She will have to be sent back tomorrow," said Hounshel. "Should we fail here, she must be sent to refuge in Amytans."

"I know," said Galeschin. "But let her be happy for now."

# Chapter 27
# Granton Abbey

As Lloyd slogged over the long, muddy road to Granton Abbey, he entertained himself with fantasies of the stir his arrival as personal emissary of the king of Gwalhafed would cause at the cloister.

As a royal emissary, he would be shown to an anteroom, he decided, as he waded along the muddy road, its ruts turned to twin streams by the melting snow. He would sit before a blazing fire, drying his cloak and boots while the monks served him a loaf and a wedge of cheese with a stoup of the abbey's famous red wine. *Yes,* he thought, as he turned from the track through the monastery gates and climbed the hill past endless rows of vines, his feet wet and numb. *And soup. They will bring me hot soup.* He picked up his pace.

"That way," said a tired-looking monk at the door when Lloyd had stated his business. "Up the stairs, end of the hall, then right."

Lloyd hardly needed the directions. The line began halfway up the stairs, and after an hour Lloyd reached the top to find that a line twice as long stretched from there to the corner. He distracted himself from his freezing toes and the wet spot on his back by counting his fellow petitioners and trying to guess at their business with the abbot. Most seemed ordinary enough, merchants there to trade for the fine abbey wine, petitioners for favors, one richly dressed man to whom messengers came now and again, bearing scrolls and whispers. Even he, Lloyd noted with dismay, stood in line in wet boots. At noon, two monks came down the hall with a basket of bread and a platter of cheese. As Lloyd munched on the last of his bread and cheese, he reached the corner. Far ahead, two burly monks stood flanking a door. At two, the kitchen monks returned with flagons of cider. At five, Lloyd reached the head of the line.

An elderly monk stuck his head out of the study door. "State your business, my son."

"I am here to see the abbot, and have been instructed to say nothing of my errand to anyone else," Lloyd replied. "I'm sorry," he added, when the monk scowled at him. "Please may I see His Holiness . . . I mean, His Honor . . . I mean, the abbot?"

The monk's wrinkled face suppressed a smile. "Can you do this quickly?"

"Oh, yes!"

"Then come in." He turned to one of the monks guarding the door. "This is the last for today." Lloyd followed him in, glowing with relief. The door shut, cutting off the moans and complaints from the hallway.

The abbot's round face smiled at the young minstrel. "What is your errand, my son?"

Besides the expected attributes of sanctity and knowledge of Holy Writ, Abbot Prydieu of St. Blethis was known for his deep knowledge of Greek and Roman literature, his connoisseurship of wine, and his wisdom. Shelves filled with books and scrolls lined the walls of the room. Several especially impressive volumes lay open on stands, the gold of their illuminated pages glowing in the last embers of the day.

Lloyd went down on one knee. "I bring a message for your ears only."

Abbot Prydieu nodded and the elderly clerk left by a side door. "My king, Galeschin of Gwalhafed, asks a boon."

"And how is dear Galeschin?" asked Prydieu. "Has he sent you for his *Iliad*? We've not yet finished copying it, I fear."

"No, sir . . . sire . . . um . . ."

"'Father' will suffice."

"No, Sir Abbot. He asks that, when Ambrahad of Velendruch and his army travel to Gwalhafed, you will accompany them to minister to their spiritual needs."

"Ambrahad goes to Gwalhafed?" He pondered this for a moment. "Oh, dear."

"Sir? I mean, Your Abbotship?"

The abbot looked at the perplexed young man. "Of course I shall. You may stay the night here and return to Galeschin with my reply tomorrow. Of course, this is to be repeated to no one but him or Lord Hounshel."

Lloyd stood shuffling and cleared his throat. "Sir, I mean, Your Holiness, um, Your Abbothood . . . "

Prydieu's eyebrows rose above his tired eyes. "Yes?"

"The king has instructed me to return only if your answer is no."

"Really?"

"Yes," said Lloyd with some pride. "I am to continue south and attend the great school for troubadours at Louvines, by his order."

"I see," said Prydieu, pursing his lips. "Is there a young lady involved?"

128

"I, er . . . well . . ."

"No matter," said the abbot. "But if you would entertain at court, you would be wise to learn your forms of address. You may stay the night and break your fast before you go. Go with God, young man."

When Lloyd had gone, the abbot sat deep in thought. "Ambrahad takes his army to Gwalhafed." He sighed. "May God protect us all."

# Chapter 28
# Swords

That morning, Tillin led Murdoch to a pile of weaponry in a corner of the courtyard. Murdoch stood, arms folded across his chest, and glowered.

"They tell me you're a smith by trade."

Murdoch nodded.

"Since you won't wield a sword, we've another task for you." Tillin pointed to the pile of swords. "Inspect them."

"I will not touch a sword."

"You'll do as you're told, you pig-headed serf."

"Freeborn," said Murdoch, scowling.

"Velendruch is poised to attack us, you oaf. Do you think they'll spare your life, or that of your family, because you won't pick up a sword, halfwit?"

"I don't care. I will not commit murder."

"Exactly. And that is why you will inspect these swords. Perhaps you think you can run away or spend the battle in the safety of some dungeon, but any man who goes into battle with a defective sword is a dead man. Do you wish that burden on your soul?"

Murdoch had run out of arguments. Reluctantly, he sat on the bench and picked up the first of the swords.

\* \* \*

The hours passed. The sun rose high and the piles of swords at Murdoch's feet grew. This one, fine. That one, a notched blade, to be ground down and resharpened. That one, cracked, to be reforged. The recruits drilled, the sergeants bellowed, and at the conclusion of that morning's drill, they were called to attention to trade their practice swords for real ones. Turnbolt, as the best pupil, got his sword first, amid the cheers of his friends and a telling silence from the others.

Across the courtyard, the servants began to set up the trestles and the women to bring out the food and trenchers for the noontime meal. Murdoch watched for Joy. She came from the kitchen, carrying a basket full of loaves, and darted back down into the scullery. *She dances*, he thought, *even with a basket of bread, she dances*, and he felt again the swaying delight of her in his arms. He laid the sword on the reject pile and reached for another of the few that remained. The day had warmed and the recruits dispersed to drink and douse themselves with water from the barrels. Some lined up near the trestles. Turnbolt and his friends loitered near the scullery door, waiting for the wenches.

Murdoch picked up another sword and examined the edges of the blade, then where the hilt joined. Finding no defect, he sighted along it and found that it was not straight, that it canted off at a slight angle. He turned it over and, about halfway up from the hilt, located the defect, a tiny crack, hardly discernible, but which would shear the blade in half at the first blow.

"Enough! You great lummox, get your hand off me!" Joy's voice rang out across the courtyard.

Murdoch stood, the sword forgotten in his hand. Turnbolt, his hair still dripping from its dousing, had hold of Joy's arm and was pulling her basket away from her.

"Just this one dance, my proud lady. Let me show you what it's like to dance with a man."

"I'd as soon dance with a pig as with you. Let go!"

"Let her go, Turnbolt." The words were not loud, but Turnbolt recognized the voice. He turned.

"Well, if it ain't her ladyship's pig." The crowd of recruits guffawed. "And what's this?" he said, looking at the sword in Murdoch's hand. He drew his own and smiled.

* * *

"Sire," said sword master Tillin, bowing to Galeschin. "How may I serve you?" The page who had summoned him bowed and left. Galeschin and Hounshel sat on a balcony overlooking the courtyard. The king waved Tillin to the empty chair beside his own and handed him a cup of wine.

"We have need of a swordsman of superlative skill," Galeschin said. "One who could serve as King's Champion."

"Champion, sire?"

"No doubt you are aware that Velendruch is both larger and richer than Gwalhafed, and you understand the impossibility of our raising an army large enough to defend ourselves, should they decide to attack." Lord Hounshel, seated beside the king, nodded his agreement. The sword master did likewise. "And so, it seems to us—to Lord Hounshel and myself, that is

131

—that in order to defend ourselves, we must draw on a tradition as old as warfare itself. We need a champion to fight in the name of the kingdom."

"I see, sire," the sword master replied guardedly. "Whom did you have in mind?"

"You are a master of the craft. I was hoping you would . . ."

"Sire," he said, eyes wide, "I could not be your champion." He drained his cup and then cleared his throat. Twice.

"Oh. I see. Could you suggest someone else?"

"Sir Brian Borrenough, champion of Velendruch, is the most dreaded swordsman in these parts. He is enormous, unstoppable, enduring—."

"Quite so," interrupted Hounshel. "We need a swordsman who can best him.""

"Sire, if I may be so bold, this idea is madness. Firstly, there is no one that good. Secondly, if there were, Velendruch would be able to outbid you for his services, just as easily as they can support a larger army. You ask the impossible. Even Turnbolt, the most talented pupil I have ever taught . . ." The ringing of swords interrupted his speech. "What the devil?" he said as he looked down into the courtyard.

* * *

Turnbolt leaped at Murdoch and brought his sword whistling down. The serving wenches scattered, squealing, and the recruits drew back, leaving space for the two to settle their differences.

Murdoch leaped backward and brought his sword up, taking the blow near the hilt, so that his sword would not break. Turnbolt's blow glanced off the edge of it. Murdoch whipped his sword in a circle and brought it crashing down. Turnbolt staggered backward, so the blow would land on his blade, not his wrists.

The recruits whooped. Of all the men in the castle, Murdoch was the last one they expected to test Turnbolt's mettle. Turnbolt roared, fury in his eyes. He swung, aiming for Murdoch's waist. Murdoch hopped nimbly backward and then, before Turnbolt could bring the sword back across, he darted in and brought his sword crashing down near the hilt of Turnbolt's.

It was not the blow of a swordsman. He had not learned it watching the drills. He had done it himself a thousand times, a thousand thousand, by the side of Algar. It was the blow of a blacksmith.

The force of it bent his blade. The shock of it stung Turnbolt's hand like a hornet and his sword clattered to the stones of the courtyard. Murdoch stood, his bent sword pointed at Turnbolt's belly.

He had broken his vow. But that was not the worst of it. He stood, waiting for a thunderbolt from the sky to strike him. The sun, instead, shone merrily. He could see Joy, her eyes glowing, running to embrace him.

Surely the stones of the courtyard would crack beneath him and demons drag him down to the flames. But there were only the cheers of the recruits echoing as they chanted his name. But that was not the worst of it.

It felt good. An enormous sense of well-being, a feeling of power, welled up in him.

Turnbolt looked at him, fear and amazement in his eyes. Murdoch gazed at his sword, bent at a wild angle. He raised it over his head, grasped the blade and brought it down, striking the flat of it on his knee. It broke. He threw the shards clanging to the ground and turned, walking away with the blood dripping from his left hand.

"God's arms," whispered the sword master. Hounshel and the king looked at each other and smiled.

\* \* \*

Murdoch sat on his pallet, morosely clutching a blood-soaked rag in his wounded hand.

"God's legs man! That was amazing! Where is that oil?" Grimbold rummaged through his box of potions. "I know Mum sent some with me—here—no, that's not it." The collection of little crocks rattled against one other as Grimbold pulled corks and sniffed the contents. He pulled one from the box triumphantly. "Here! Red oil for wounds and cuts. Let me see your hand." Murdoch offered his bleeding hand for inspection. Grimbold poured a small puddle of the oil into the palm and began to spread it with the cleanest corner of the rag. "What is it with you, smith? Any other man here would be crowing like a rooster. You'd think that great lout had beaten you, not the other way around."

"I broke my vow, Grimbold, sworn on the memory of my mother and all the holy saints. Don't you see what that makes me?"

"It makes you one hell of a swordsman, smith. You were wasted shoeing horses."

"It makes me one of them. No better than those devils that killed my family." He grabbed Grimbold's shirtfront and pulled him down to eye level. "My entire village died in a war they did not choose and had no stake in! And if we men continue fighting, more innocents will die, don't you see?"

"And, unfortunately, if we do not fight, Velendruch will slaughter us all on their way to Amytans for the real war," Lord Hounshel said, standing in the barracks doorway. "The king would have a word with you, smith."

\* \* \*

"Sit," said King Galeschin, indicating the chair to Murdoch. Murdoch remained standing.

"Damn it to Hell,'" muttered the sword master. "I believe you see the impossibility of your plan, sire."

"No, this is quite interesting," Galeschin replied. "I understand that you have no interest in swordsmanship."

Murdoch shook his head.

"That was quite an impressive performance just now," the king said. "Why did you fight?"

"To protect Joy."

"Ah. You love her?"

Murdoch nodded.

"You wish to marry her?"

Again, a nod.

"I see." The king considered a moment. "So, why is it that you do not wish to defend your kingdom?"

"I took Holy Andrew's vow."

"Ah, Ragged Andrew . . . so, he finally found a convert. Sword master Tillin tells me that until now you had suffered quite straitly to keep it. I like that. It shows great force of character."

Murdoch blinked in astonishment and almost smiled.

"An admirable goal, Andrew's, the ending of all war." The king leaned forward in his chair. "But in the meantime, what are we to do about these folk poised upon our border? They, too, have taken a vow: to slay all whom their king bids them slay. I have no more desire to see slaughter committed than you do, smith. You have a Christian name?"

"Murdoch."

"Named for the old god of war? You are a puzzle."

"They killed my family, my whole village. I was the only one left. When Algar and Ara found me, they named me Murdoch, since the war had given me to them."

Galeschin looked at Murdoch and held his gaze. "If you could prevent the sort of battle that destroyed your family, would you do it? Would you be willing to do what needs to be done?"

In the silence, Murdoch wavered.

The king waited, then spoke again. "You realize, of course, that I cannot allow just anyone to marry Joy."

Murdoch's look turned puzzled.

"Go to her now and ask her why the daughter of Sir Stancel Tavis should work in a scullery. Then bring her to me."

\* \* \*

Murdoch descended into the heat and clatter of the kitchen. Vast cauldrons belched and burbled on the cavernous hearth, and distorted flames reflected from the shining pots hanging from racks above the great, broad tables. Wenches and menservants scurried everywhere in the seeming chaos, moving the river of food needed to feed the army. At last he saw Joy, loading bread from the cooling rack into baskets to be hauled outside. He reached her side and touched her arm. She turned and smiled at him, tears glistening in her wide brown eyes. He led her from the din, silencing the protestations of Cook with the words, "The king commands it."

For a moment, the room hushed, but when the pair left, the hubbub began anew. He led her across the courtyard, past the gawking recruits, and they climbed the stone stairs to the walkway atop the battlements. There they stood with the sun on their faces, looking southwards across the green breadth of Gwalhafed. The warm wind smelled ever so faintly of the sea.

"Do you despise me, lady?" he said at last.

"Despise you? Why?" She looked at him, amazed.

"I have broken my vow."

She nodded. "Thank you."

"You don't despise me for breaking my word?"

"You did it for me. That is a high compliment."

Murdoch turned to look at her. "The king has bid me ask you how the daughter of Sir Stancel Tavis has come to work in the scullery."

She gazed toward the south, watching the flight of a lone bird. "My father was a cruel man and a drunkard. I did not weep when he died, though I well might have had I known what would come next. My brother Walter, a weasel-hearted worm, had need to pay the inheritance fee to Prince Rolf, his overlord, or forfeit our lands. Our family's most valuable possession was a golden medallion, a gift from old King Hume to my father's father. Rolf demanded it, but my father had picked out the jewels to fund his descent into drunkard's hell.

"We brought it to Rolf, at his castle at Parcell. He threw it in my brother's face. 'Damaged goods!' he shouted. 'Do you think to win my favor with damaged goods?'

"My craven brother actually smiled at him. 'Please, my lord,' he whined. 'Do not blame me for my father's sins. You know what sort of man he was. Take this and any other thing you desire, even my sword, or Dennys my horse.'

"Rolf scowled at first, but then cast his eye upon me and smiled. I felt the ice run up my spine. 'I'll take her, then,' he said. I cried out to my brother but he, that coward, said, 'Now, Joy, this is little enough to do for your family.' He turned on his heel and left me there, alone and friendless. Rolf's men dragged me off to his chamber.

"He came to me later. He had eaten well, I'll warrant, by the stink of garlic on him, and had drunk even more. I had eaten nothing since leaving my home that morning and was dizzy and faint. 'Do you think you'll starve me into submission, then?' I asked. 'I will never consent to be your wife.'

135

"'Don't give yourself airs,' he snarled at me. 'I will marry far better than the daughter of a common knight,' and he seized hold of me and began to tear at my clothes."

"Did he . . . ?" began Murdoch.

Joy smiled. "I thank God I am not one of those genteel ladies who sit all day at embroidery. I milked cows at home and carried the pails to the buttery. He got more than he bargained for, but no, he did not get *that*. It was then that he called his men and . . ." Just for a moment she faltered.

"And?"

"And they hauled me off again, this time to the dungeon." She gazed again off toward the sea.

Murdoch watched her face closely. "How did you come to work in the scullery here?"

"There was a woman, a good woman, who brought food to the prisoners and the guards. She pitied me, and on Michaelmas, put herbs in the guards' wine and freed me while they slept. Hirday is the nearest estate to Rolf's domain and so I ran here to plead my case, but Lord Hounshel was away, and so here I have stayed, telling my tale to neither man nor woman, lest the prince find me."

"And that was the whole of it?"

She did not speak, but stared off southward, jaw tight, and nodded. "We must go to the king," Murdoch said.

\* \* \*

Galeschin sighed when he had heard her tale. "So, Murdoch. Need I tell you that my brother is in league with Velendruch and at the root of this attack we now face? What say you? You have left your vow. Will I do as I bid?"

Murdoch did not speak. He glanced at Joy.

"He looks to you, my lady," said the king. "I sense you have more power in this matter than I. He is of common blood, and you the daughter of a knight. If his valor proves him worthy, I will knight him myself so that he may marry you as is his heart's desire. Are you willing, my lady?"

Joy burst into tears. "Oh, yes, sire. A thousand times yes!"

Murdoch gazed into her eyes. His soul wavered, on a knife's edge. He had made his vow, on his mother's blood. And he had broken it.

He could say no to a sergeant. He could say no to a sword master. He could say no to a king. But he could not say no to Joy.

"I will," he said.

Galeschin smiled. "Master Tillin, I cannot spare you from your duties here. Choose a man to escort Murdoch to Master Beecham. I understand that he lives in the forest near our border with Amytans. Have them stop at my castle and have my armorer Cedrik take his measure."

136

"Yes, Highness," Tillin replied with a crisp bow.

"Lady Joy, you will accompany them as far as Gwalhafed Castle, and will care for my daughter until she is returned to Lady Matilda's keeping."

"As you wish, Highness," she answered, with a deep curtsy.

"Smith, I hold you responsible for their safe arrival."

Murdoch nodded.

"Bow," whispered Joy. He did his best.

A knock sounded at the door. The servant opened it. Two guardsmen entered, wearing mud-splashed tabards and dirty boots, dragging a body between them. Joy looked at the body and stepped closer to Murdoch.

"Report," said the king.

The pair dropped their burden and knelt. "We found him skulking in the forest nearby," one said. "When we challenged him, he ran, and we gave chase. He put up a good fight, I'll give him that. We found this on him."

He handed Galeschin a dagger with the dragon signet of Velen-druch on it.

"If Velendruch has spies this close to Hirday," said Galeschin, "I cannot risk my daughter's leaving the castle. She will stay here. You, Lady Joy, will act as governess. Tillin, find your man. Murdoch, pack your gear." He turned to the servant. "Give orders to the kitchen to pack food for their journey, such as can be eaten in haste." He turned to Murdoch. "Ride hard, and may God go with you."

Murdoch felt Joy's hand reach for his.

Galeschin smiled. "You may kiss her, smith. It will be some time before you see her again."

# Chapter 29
# Beecham

"Why are we all the way out here?" asked Murdoch. They were on their second day of travel from Hirday, close to the border of Amytans.

"You're to study with the best," said Robert, the soldier who had been sent to guide him.

"The best? We're out in the middle of the woods!"

"That would be sword master Beecham. He retired after his wife was murdered."

"Murdered? Did he take revenge?"

"Quite thoroughly, but only on those who committed the crime. He could not touch the one who ordered it. Kicked it in, he did."

They had reached a crossroads. The road climbed straight ahead, toward Amytans. To their left, blocked by a massive fallen tree trunk, another path sloped downhill, toward the Swanswater ford. Robert turned to the right and they began to climb a steep path, hardly more than a deer trail.

"So, who ordered it?"

"No one knows."

Murdoch thought about that as he walked. He would have a wife soon, and thought that would mean a happy life. It occurred to him that nothing is simple. They crested the first hill.

"Beecham!" shouted Robert. His voice echoed in the forest silence. Only a crow responded. "I know he lives nearby." The track grew steeper and rockier. By the time they crested the next rise, they had broken a sweat. Robert cupped his hands to his mouth. "Beecham!" he called again. They heard no answer.

"Wait," said Murdoch. "I smell a bit of smoke." They stood silent, turning their heads and sniffing, trying to make out the direction from which it came.

# Chapter 30

Corwin's audience sat enthralled. The shadows lay long upon the cobblestones. Lyneth's gaze had not left his face for an hour. The merchants' stalls stood closed and silent.

The hooves of a single horse echoed along the stone walls like the beating of a drum. Corwin looked up as a white horse, richly caparisoned in blue, gold glinting from bridle and saddle, entered the square. The rider, no less elegant in a blue surcoat with ermine trim and pearls stitched on with gold thread, fixed Corwin with his gaze, and Corwin faltered in his telling. His audience, like sleepers waking, turned and began to bow and murmur. "The prince. The prince. Rhodri ap Anieran. Your Highness."

Rhodri ignored their greeting as his bold eye swept the throng. He was young, broad of shoulder, and fair of face, although one could already read the stamp of dissolution on him. His gaze fell upon Lyneth and stopped.

She shivered under his look. He rode his horse into the throng, which parted before him wordlessly. When he reached the dais, he smiled at Lyneth and reached out his hand. She mounted behind him, like one in a trance. He set spurs to the horse, and they were gone.

Corwin stood, stunned, and the crowd wandered off until only Phillipe stood watching him. "You did well, Corwin. You had them in the palm of your hand."

Corwin shrugged.

"I have sold my rings and paid Dylan. I have enough for two passages to Calais. Will you come with me to the monastery? The boat leaves on the tide at midnight." He began to walk toward the docks.

"My master, I do not want to part from you, but I have no desire to become a monk."

"You have learned much of the craft in a short time, but I still have much to teach you."

*Which you could have done this winter.* Corwin dismissed the thought as unworthy. *All this came from my stupid question, and he has never rebuked me for it.*

They reached a tavern. "Come, you must be thirsty." Philippe held up two fingers to the barmaid, a scowling woman of middle years. "Come, sit, and we will discuss this."

The woman brought two tankards and stood eyeing the pair as Philippe fumbled in his purse for a coin. There were few others in the dim chamber, just a bulky young man, her son by his looks, putting benches atop tables and two idlers of similar age lounging on a bench along the wall.

"You have truly been as a son to me," Philippe said. "And I would not part with you, but my heart is dead, and I can no longer tell my tales, do you understand?"

"You have not forgotten them. Your heart will heal, my master."

"No," Phillipe said. "This I can do no longer. All my life I cared for nothing but my craft, and it has killed my love, my Gwyneth, my *joie*." He wept.

The young man swept, and the idlers' conversation, at first a murmur, grew louder, until it impressed itself on Corwin's hearing.

"—English, I'd say. You can't hardly understand what the old one's saying, and if the young one can, then he must be one, too."

"I think it is time that we left, my master," whispered Corwin, as he stood. Strong hands grasped his shoulders and shoved him back down on to the bench. "Please, we bear you no ill will," said Corwin, "but we must leave so we may find our way to our lodgings before dark."

"Before dark! Before dark, aye! Do you not know," said the tallest of the three, seating himself next to Corwin, "that the faery folk haunt these hills?"

"Alan, be off to your mother," snapped the barmaid.

"Later, missus, I've souls to save here. The faery folk, do you understand? They will take any man they find and keep him for a tithe to pay the devil."

"Then we must leave now." Once again Corwin tried to rise, only to have Alan grasp hold of his arm and pull him to the seat again. "Isn't that right, Dru?"

The second idler, fatter than Alan or the barmaid's son, ambled across to Corwin, a drunken smile on his face. "It's God's truth, friend. But here's the only remedy." He pulled the cork from a small flask and thrust it under Corwin's nose. The acrid smell of whiskey made Corwin sneeze. The three roared with laughter. "Aye. They'll get you for sure, such a little dishrag as you. You're not man enough to fight off a faery. You're not even man enough to take a swallow of good honest whiskey!"

140

Philippe watched anxiously. "Gentlemen, please! He has done you no wrong."

"An Englishman who has done us no wrong!" jeered Dru, and the three guffawed. Dru pinned Corwin to the bench with his meaty hands. The barmaid's son stood with his back braced against the front door, grinning. Like cats with a mouse, they wanted only to amuse themselves. The barmaid threw her hands up in disgust and left the room by the back door, muttering.

Dru held Corwin's arms to his side. Alan pinched his nose and when Corwin gasped for breath, poured half the flask into it.

Corwin sputtered and coughed as it burned a swath from his lips to his belly like an invading army. Tears ran from his eyes as he choked. His tormentors guffawed and pounded his back. "There's the lad! Let's see you do it again!"

Dru released his arms and Corwin seized his tankard, to wash the taste from his mouth. He drank, and it was whisked from his hands and the flask thrust into them.

"Go on, drink up," Alan whispered into his ear, tilting the flask toward his mouth and pinching his nose shut again. Corwin swallowed and the fire razed his gullet. He sat, staring dully at the appalled Philippe.

"Is he ready, Gorlyn?" asked Dru.

"Let's see him walk," replied the barmaid's son. Dru heaved him to his feet, and Corwin staggered across the room.

"He's ready," said Alan, and the three bellowed with laughter.

Philippe stood. "You have had your amusement with him. We will go now."

Dru leapt at Philippe and shoved him. "Shut up, old man." He seized Corwin by his collar. "Out you go, dishrag. Go find the faeries." Gorlyn opened the door with mock courtesy and Corwin stumbled through it into the street. Gorlyn slammed the door behind him. "Now, old man, we've not had our fun with you—"

"Nor will you," said a quiet voice. The captain of the town watch stood in the doorway to the back room. The silhouettes of two pikemen showed behind him, in the light of the lantern in the barmaid's hand.

"He's English!" Gorlyn protested. Lloyd and Dru nodded. "What do you care what we do to him?"

"I'll keep the peace in this town," the captain said. He took a step toward them. "If you go home quietly, there should be no need to take you to jail."

Without a word, Lloyd and Dru slunk out the door.

"Follow them," he told his men, "and see that they do no more harm. Help him up." Gorlyn obeyed and helped Philippe to a seat on the bench.

Philippe stood. "I thank you, sir, but I must go. My friend has been turned out to the streets in a most drunken state by these louts. I must find him before he comes to harm."

"I will come with you," the captain replied. "And I'll have words with you in the morning, Gorlyn Atwood."

The streets were empty, but for mist and shadows. Although they hunted the whole night long, they found no trace of Corwin.

# Chapter 31

Corwin opened his eyes, and when his vision cleared, saw that he lay in a forest glade, a clump of mushrooms in front of his face, his head pillowed on a stone. He rolled over onto his back and lay there, staring at the branches interlaced above him, the green of their budding leaves like a mist in his blurry vision. At last he sat up, chafing his hands against his damp sleeves, willing heat into his numbed fingers. The toadstools, he saw, formed a ring around him.

*My master!* he thought. *I must find him.* He leapt to his feet, then sat back down, as a wave of nausea swept over him. *I need water.* He looked at the forest surrounding him, and listened for the sound of a stream.

From the corner of his eye, he saw movement. He turned his head, and the world swayed. He saw no one. A deer, perhaps, its coat the same hue as the tree trunks? It would lead him to water. He staggered to his feet and walked toward it. He did not get far. He stopped and leaned against an oak, turning his head slowly so as not to dizzy himself, scanning the forest for movement. He saw it again, from the corner of his eye, when his head was turned to the left, a flicker of movement directly in front of him, too big for a bird or a squirrel. He followed.

So it went, in fits and starts, until he staggered downhill and found the stream. He splashed handfuls of water onto his face, then cupped his hands and drank. The sun gleamed through the branches onto a flat shelf of stone beside the stream. Corwin climbed up and lay there, soaking in the heat from the sun.

Exhausted, head still throbbing, he was neither awake nor asleep, the thoughts running through his head. *My master! How will I find him?* He blinked, and looked at the unfamiliar forest. The chill wind whispered through the trees and distant birds twittered. *Where am I?* Despair overtook him, and tears welled in his eyes. *Why has it come to this? What would my life have been if Tovan had kept me?*

The world went silent, as if holding its breath.

The sun had swung round, moving the sunny spot. He rolled onto his side to follow it, and gazed across the stream. He could not believe what he saw. He sat up and rubbed his eyes, the world swaying about his addled senses.

The hoofprints of a deer led toward the stream, and on the other side, bare human footprints led away from it. He stared wide-eyed, and felt his heart pound in his chest. He blinked and saw a single movement on the other side of the stream. A red apple, wizened from winter, rolled down the slope toward the stream, and stopped next to one of the footprints.

*We share food with you.*

He looked up, startled, but saw no one. Then his heart leapt with joy. *Tovan? Tovan!* He looked into the forest, scanning for view of his old friend.

*See what is,* quetan, *not what you wish.* The thought paused. *Ksh.* This last felt regretful.

Corwin stopped, puzzled. *Ksh?* Had he harmed something? He looked again, scanning the forest without expectation. He saw her, standing not ten feet away, her shapeless shift the mottled gray-green of the tree trunks, her hair woven with lichen and moss, as much a part of the forest as the trees themselves.

She had the most beautiful face he had ever seen, although he did not understand how it could be beautiful. The coal-black eyes were of differing sizes, and set at different angles in her head. The nose was crooked and the smile slanted, yet taken together she possessed a radiant loveliness akin to some wild glade where ivy and briar intertwine. Moss grew in her hair. Whispers clung to her. He could almost hear them, almost make out what they said, but they eluded his grasp, like thistledown in the wind. Were the voices ghosts? He looked around but saw nothing but sunlit woodland.

She looked at him closely and he heard Tovan's name repeated, like an echo, but not with his ears. *Not the usual sort She chooses.*

Her mouth did not move, nor did he notice the lack as his eyes swam in and out of focus.

*You're awake now. Come.* There was more, a whispering stream of thoughts intertwining with the little he could pick up. She raised her head and looked around as warily as a doe.

"Who are you?" Corwin asked, and his whisper seemed to boom in that woodland stillness.

She held her finger to her lips. *No noise! Ranell.*

He held his head in his hands and moaned.

*Enough!* she ordered. *You drink stupid uisque stuff?*

He nodded as best he could without making the world sway too badly.

144

She shook her head. *Water helps. Drink, then come with me.* He obeyed, drinking his fill and then crossing the stream. He picked up the apple and ate it as he walked.

She began to lead him, then stopped and turned to him sternly. *Quiet! Want hunters? Watch.* She turned and walked silently, not a leaf rustling, her shoes leaving the tracks of a doe.

She slipped through thickets that clawed his skin and grabbed his garments. He followed clumsily. She flowed up crevices and boulder-strewn slopes as easily as water flows down, while he panted and struggled behind. He could hear her thoughts. She looked different. Her shoes . . . He stopped, cold sweat running down his neck and soaking the coarse wool of his jerkin. What was she? Why was he following her?

Seized by blind panic, he turned and ran. *Stupid* quetan, he heard her think. *Can't find your way. Don't know what to eat.* He could not escape the silent voice. He ran blindly, head pounding with the effort, lungs bursting, branch and bramble tearing at him until he fell, tripped by a tree root, and landed in a panting heap on the chill, leaf-strewn earth.

*Come, guest.* She stood beside him, not breathing hard. *The Lady does not choose every* quetan.

*The Lady? You?*

*No.* She pointed to herself. *Ranell.* Quetan *name for Lady is Faerie Queen.*

*You're a faery!?*

She drew herself up with dignity. Faer. *Our name.* Faer. *Not faeries.* She grimaced. *Quetan all wrong.*

He sat up and gaped at her.

*You* quetan *confuse us with butterflies.*

He blushed.

She began to walk away. *Well, come.* And again, the whispering thoughts trailed off, too swiftly for him to follow.

\* \* \*

He followed her for miles, climbing into land ever more rugged and desolate. As the sun grew low, gray clouds scudded in the chill wind. They came to a ruin of a great, many-branched oak, its trunk split near the ground. *In there.*

Corwin crawled into a tunnel of twisted roots and packed dirt with Ranell close behind. After a few yards, the tunnel widened into a small chamber, high enough to stand in and lit with a flickering torch. The withered old woman sitting in it looked up. Her skin was as creased as old tree bark and lichen entwined in her graying hair.

"Greetings to Your Majesty, Queen of the Faer," said Corwin, bowing as his master had taught him.

His mind filled with a torrent of laughter, that of the woman and of Ranell. *Thank you for the Lady,* chuckled the old woman, in the wordless speech of the faer, and she and Ranell redoubled their laughter. He felt no malice in it, just a stream of mirth as broad as the sea. *Funny quetan. All the way here, Mother, 'Greetings, Majesty.' Steps in holes, falls over roots, tears clothes,* Ranell told the old woman, shaking her head.

The old woman shook her head, smiling. *Ksh.*

Corwin froze. What had he done? He meant no ill to them. *What is . . .*

The old woman looked at him intently, and the thought of Tovan came to his mind.

*You knew my son.*

With a sudden jolt, he felt the pain from his recent dream pierce his side, and he gasped. Sorrow stabbed through him, so keen his heart ached.

*Yes,* quetan, *he was killed by your hunters, just two nights ago. He thought of you often.*

Corwin stood stunned, tears running down his cheeks. To have come so close to finding Tovan, only to lose him. "He saved my life. I—I never thanked him."

She looked at Corwin, and smiled sadly. *The ways of the Lady are a mystery to us all. In time, her wisdom will be revealed.* Then, just as suddenly, her sadness vanished. She smiled. *Manners! Mirna.* She touched her hand to her chest to indicate this was her name.

"Corwin," he replied, and bowed again.

She looked up toward the tunnel, and a man's head popped through, his hair wild and unkempt—long, matted, and crowned with a wreath of ivy. He slipped through the opening and stood. Corwin's heart froze. From the waist up, the man seemed human enough. He was as small and thin as Corwin, but wiry and tough, with the fierceness of a falcon in his eye. But from the waist downward, he was covered with soft, gray-brown fur, and where he stepped, he left cloven tracks. He eyed Corwin. Quetan. The thought held no mirth, only wariness. *I caught two, Grandmother.* He held up two rabbits.

*Brave, Aelvan! Tuunma and Boronil brought greens. Good soup tonight.* Mirna rose and took the rabbits from him and left the chamber through a second tunnel. Corwin could not keep his eyes off the satyr. Aelvan sat and pulled at his foot. After some tugging, the cloven-hoofed shoe came off. Corwin started and let out a shout of surprise. Aelvan and Rannell jumped at the sound and stared at Corwin. In a rush of relief, Corwin realized that Aelvan was dressed in leggings of rabbit fur, a token of his skill as a hunter, as was the cloak of rabbit fur draped across his shoulders in place of a shirt. Aelvan stared at Corwin. No thought came from him.

146

*Stop, Aelvan. You're scaring him. He's harmless.*

*Harmless? Harmless* quetan?

*The Lady wants him here.*

*I'll not argue, but I'll not trust.*

Three more men came through the entrance, each bearing a rabbit or squirrel. They were like Aelvan: small, tough, wary, and clad in skins, but older, their faces weathered and creased. Their hair was mossier, the lichen growing more thickly through it. Each regarded Corwin silently before passing through the second tunnel to deliver their catch. A moment later, Mirna returned. *Bartrym*? she asked.

Aelvan shook his head.

*Not with the others. I'll seek him for you.* Aelvan put his shoes back on and went up through the tunnel as swiftly as smoke. The old woman stood watching a moment after he had gone, her anxiety plain. Then she turned to Corwin.

*Sit. Food will be ready soon. Ranell, bring water.*

Ever the whispering stream of thought continued, swirling around the little that Corwin could understand. The questions in Corwin's mind fought one another and Mirna regarded him, a knowing smile on her face. *Slow, young one. All in time. 'Tis a long time since your kind was with us.*

*I never thought . . . I only dreamed. You can't understand. I thought faeries were . . . I mean, the* faer *. . . were children's tales, but I always wished they were real. I didn't know that Tovan . . .*

Mirna smiled. *The Lady chose you, no accident.*

*The Faerie Queen! Is she here?* He sprang to his feet and began to brush the dirt and leaves from his clothing. *Will I be presented to her? And the king, is he . . .*

*King? No king.*

*But if there is a queen, there must be a king. Who would rule the kingdom for her?*

*Queen? Kingdom?* Quetan *thoughts. We are the* faer, *the kindom of* faer. *All kin. No kings. No queens.* She looked up at a soft sound from the entrance. *Bartrym!*

Corwin felt her relief so keenly, he sagged against the wall. The man who stood next to Aelvan was straight-backed, his face thickly lined and his hair entirely covered by lichen, with patches of moss extending down the back of his shirt. In his hand he held a bundle of roots with their wilting leaves still attached. His face was marked with self-contempt.

*Old. Slow,* he apologized and walked past them, ignoring Corwin. Mirna watched him pass, and exchanged a worried look with Aelvan.

*Caught nothing, not come empty-handed. Gathering roots near Mother Holly.*

*Elder. He should no longer hunt*, replied Mirna.

*Elder. He should teach young ones*, answered Aelvan, and Corwin felt an unfathomable bitterness behind the thought.

Ranell returned bearing water in a bowl made from a hollowed section of log. *Food soon*, she told them. Corwin, then Aelvan, washed their faces and hands in the crude basin. Aelvan's eyes lingered on Ranell's face. She looked down and watched his reflection on the water. The three then followed Mirna through a gap in the tree roots.

This chamber was larger than the first, lit only by the red coals' glow around the bottom of the clay cauldron and the torch that Mirna had brought with her from the other room. Smoke found its way out through a hole far above them and the walls, lined with great tree roots, seemed to writhe like snakes in the flickering light. Mirna set the torch in a crevice in the wall, and Corwin noted that there were other torches lining the walls, unused. He felt the eyes of the others upon him.

There were twelve. Five men and seven women of the *faer* ringed the fire. Of these, only Ranell was clearly young. Corwin could not guess the ages of Aelvan and the other three hunters, all hale, but with weathered faces. Of the men, only Bartrym looked old. With the women, it was different. Mirna, whom Corwin had thought of as old when they met, seemed of middle age compared to the five women who tended the fire, their hands as gnarled as ancient branches. In the dim, unsteady light, Corwin could not be certain whether they were plant or person, save for the fact that they could move. He could not tell where their hair ended and the lichen entangled in it began, or their green robes from the moss that grew upon them.

*So. The* quetan, came the thought of the most decrepit of these.

*Yes, Dunwadi*, replied Ranell. *Like you said, lying dead drunk, head on a stone.*

The crones nodded, exchanging glances. Dunwadi turned her head and regarded Corwin, betraying no thought, her eyes glittering like black coals. *Welcome to the kindom of* faer, *young one.*

Corwin looked around him, his imaginings confronted with a hard reality. Where were the golden plates? The gossamer gowns of the faery . . . not faery . . . *faer* maidens. His mind raced, naked for them all to see. He looked around at them, at the mirth in all the faces but Aelvan's, who regarded him with the same stony contempt as earlier.

"I mean, thank you, my lady," he stammered at last.

She nodded. *Sit, young one. We eat. You will learn all in time. We give thanks*, she stated, turning to the others, *to the hunters: to Aelvan, Dworning, Rennor, Anil, for bringing us meat, to Tuumna and Boronil for gathering; to Bartrym, no empty hands, he. We give thanks, Lady, mother to all: horned, winged, swimmers, green shoots, mighty trees, and we, who walk her hills.* At this, Ranell handed her the first of thirteen small wooden bowls. Dunwadi grasped the wooden ladle with her trembling hand. With Ranell guiding the ladle as one would for a tiny child, she filled the bowl. This was passed around the circle until it reached Tuumna, the woman on Dunwadi's left. The remaining bowls followed the first bowl's slow progress. Corwin could hear the ladle scraping the cauldron's bottom as she filled the last. Two of the men then removed the cauldron from the fire. As the others watched reverently, they poured the last drops of the soup onto the ground, poured clean water into the cauldron, and stood it again atop the coals.

Corwin looked at his dinner, a mass of greens and chunks of root floating in broth. He ate his way through them by tipping the bowl to his mouth and sipping its contents slowly, like the others. At the bottom he found a few bones with tough scraps of meat attached. Hunger still gnawed at his guts. He looked at Ranell. *Is . . .*

*Rude to ask.* He felt something brush his arm. There was now another bit of meat in the bottom of his bowl. The crone to his left grinned at him toothlessly. *Thank Boronil,* Ranell told him. *She gifts you.*

Before he could even form the thought, he felt the crone's eyes on him, felt them to his heart. For one so old, as gnarled as granite, to have such aliveness, and such longing in her gaze. Embarrassed, he nodded his thanks, then looked away and gobbled the meat.

Ranell took his bowl and gathered those of the others. She and Mirna began to clean them with hot water from the cauldron on the fire. Two of the men and several crones brought out knives with cunning stone blades, to work at carving, or to trim hides into strips to braid slings. The others reached into baskets behind them and took out their handwork, simple looms that they held on their laps.

Leaving Ranell to finish, Mirna helped them set themselves up to work, looping the end of each woven cloth strip around the weavers' toes to maintain tension on the work, putting their thread and shuttles where they could reach them.

Aelvan, with a glare at Corwin, sprang to his feet to help Ranell empty the weighty cauldron and move it to its niche at the side of the chamber. Corwin, blistered by Aelvan's black gaze, thought it best to watch the crone nearest him at her work. Her fingers seemed to know what to do without any conscious thought on her part. As the *faer* settled into their evening tasks, Corwin felt the group's attention turn to him.

*Name?* He thought it was Dunwadi who addressed him, but the question seemed to come from several sources at once.

*I am Corwin.* The *faer* nodded and exchanged glances. There were no further questions, although the group continued to watch him closely. The only sound was the soft, hypnotic swish of the shuttles.

Corwin swallowed hard, under their eyes. *What do you want of me?*

*The Lady sends you.*

*How long will I be here?*

*As the Lady wills.*

*But my master . . . my work . . . he will worry.*

"*Master?*"

*My master, Philippe of Albi. He is teaching me the art of the troubadours,* Corwin replied with some pride.

*Troubadours?*

*Tellers of tales of courtly romance and knightly deeds.*

*Knights!* A wave of fear swept through them. *Iron men. Do not tell their tales here.* This last, an order, he felt from Aelvan.

*You tell* faer *stories?*

Corwin nodded. *Oh, yes. Many stories.*

Once again, the dark eyes met each other across the fire. *Perhaps that is why he is here.* Faer *stories? Tell us!*

*Oh, yes! I will tell you a story of my own making,* Corwin replied, and then stopped in confusion. . . . *If you will not be offended. You see, I am one of those who thought that faeries . . . I mean the* faer *. . . were small and had wings like butterflies.* Even Aelvan smiled at that.

*Forgiven. Be true from now,* Dunwadi replied. The murmured thought went around the fire. *The Lady sends him to learn and tell the* quetan *the truth about us.*

Corwin collected his thoughts and then began.


### The Mouse King and the Gold

*On that day, the Mouse King walked through the land to help the poor, dressed as a beggar, his fat purse hidden under his rags. As he walked along a stream, a hawk attacked, screaming as it dove from above. Quick as thought, the Mouse King drew his sword and slashed at the talons of the hawk. With a cry of surprise, the great bird left him in peace, and went off to find something easier to eat for breakfast. But the king, dismayed, realized that his purse had fallen into the deep, swift stream. He paced up and down its banks, wringing his hands and crying aloud.*

*Soon he heard faery laughter, and mocking voices crying,*

> "*Mouse King, Mouse King,*
> *Greedy thing! Greedy thing!*"

150

"I am not!" he shouted. "That money was for the poor!" But they only laughed louder. "Come out!" he shouted, taking his sword in his hand, "Come out, you cowards, and dare say that to my face!"

Instead, the voices left him, with a rustling of wind and tiny, tinkling laughs like the twittering of birds.

He spent some time by the stream, probing its bottom with twigs, but the clear stream was broad, a river by his reckoning, and its deep current too swift for a mouse, even a strong, brave one such as the Mouse King, to swim. At last, he sat on the bank of the stream, his head in his paws, and wondered what to do.

After a time, a rat came by, a fine, fat merchant, leading a pack mole laden with goods. The rat saw the Mouse King sitting beside the road in his patched cloak and stuck his nose in the air with a haughty sniff. "Lazy good-for-nothing," he said. "Get you out of the way of honest, hardworking citizens."

The next to pass was a high-born lady mouse and her children, with a retinue of guardsmen. "Oh, faugh," she said, when she saw the Mouse King in his beggar's garb. She turned to her children. "Let this be a lesson to you," she said. "Do you see what happens to people who do not eat their vegetables?"

The Mouse King decided to stay where he was, and see who else might come along and what they might say. The next down the road was a clerical frog, dressed in the rich vestments of a bishop. "Do you desire forgiveness, my son?" asked the bishop.

"No. I'd just like my money back. It fell in the river," replied the Mouse King.

"The judgment of God is not to be denied, sinner," thundered the bishop. "There will be no help for such a proud one as you until you beg God's forgiveness for your sins!"

"But—" said the Mouse King.

"Enough!" the bishop shouted, and he hopped down the road, grumbling about pearls and swine. The Mouse King sat down again, and listened to his stomach growl.

Then a tiny old woman came along the road, all bent over, carrying a basket, leaning on a stick. "Can I help you, Mother?" asked the Mouse King.

She sighed with tiredness and smiled at him. "Such a weary way I've come, such a weary way I must go, even to the ends of the world," she said.

"May I carry your basket for you?" She handed it to him. It was empty. He walked by her side along the river.

"Where are you from, good mother?" he asked.

"From forever and forever, down the long years' time."

He didn't know what to make of that, but it seemed strange to him to walk along with someone and not talk to her, so he tried again. "Where are you going?"

"To forever and forever, down the long years' time."

Addlebrained, he thought. What a pity. He shifted the basket to his other hand, as his arm had grown tired from carrying it.

After a few steps, he shifted it back. His arms ached and he found that, as slow as the woman's hobbling pace was, he could scarce keep up with her. Soon he began to sweat and had to grasp the basket with both hands. "May we stop and rest a moment?" he asked.

"Never a rest, never a rest, forever and forever, down the long years' time," she said, hobbling along so quickly that he had to trot to stay beside her.

The basket grew heavier with every step. "Please stop!" he cried, but she seemed not to hear. At last, after dragging the basket, breathless and aching, he thought, Well, if I stop she'll have to stop, or lose her basket. So he stopped, just like that, and sat down in the middle of the road, huffing and puffing.

She went on a step ahead and turned. As she came back toward him, her ragged cloak fell off and her beautiful faery wings began to unfold. The sunlight shimmered on her garments, and her limbs were lithe and her movement graceful.

"Empty the basket," she said. At first, he did nothing, because the basket, he could plainly see, was empty. "Empty the basket, Mouse King," she said again. He tipped it over and a shower of golden coins fell out, all that he had lost that day and more. The basket, once again, was light as a feather. She took it from him. "Let that be your lesson," she said to him. "Your life will be as heavy as your desires make it." And with that, she flew away.

There was a long silence when Corwin had finished. Only the hands of the weavers moved in the dim light. *So that is how you see us,* came their thought, at last.

*I am sorry,* replied Corwin. *I did not know that it was all such lies.*

*Lies? How can you think that?*

*That you have great wealth, that you keep an abundance of gold, when you live here in such dire poverty.*

*Wealthy still,* Dworning replied.

*Really?* Corwin asked.

Aelvan's thought was filled with anger. *See? Quetan. Gold. Ksh. Same as the others.*

*I'm sorry,* Corwin replied. *I did not mean—*

*You did.*

*No, really!*

*Enough!* Dunwadi's thought rose above the rest. *Wealth is not in things.*

*So then, the tales we tell of a Golden Age are lies.* Corwin frowned, crestfallen.

*Lies? No,* Bartrym answered. *There was a Golden Age, yes, young* quetan. All around him, Corwin felt the thought of the *faer* change. He could not understand the feeling that swept over him, of longing and sadness but with it a fierce joy, a wildness that made his heart race and his lungs draw deep.

*You cannot know land as I, nor I as my grandfather and his grandfather. Golden Age. Golden sun on the waters, gold ripe grain under a clear blue sky. The land is so bare now, no hands to tend it, to repair tears in the Lady's gossamer gown. Yes. Her green, living gossamer gown. Herds of* quetan *tear at her, plow her, gut her, rend her living garment. They slaughter the* faer, *all in order to change living essence for dead shining metal. They love dead things, not life. Understand, young one?*

Corwin sat bewildered. *But surely the plowman must plow, if we are to eat? Surely the cattle must graze?*

*Look, Anil,* thought Aelvan. *He is* quetan. *Full with fear. He can learn nothing.*

*Many years I have watched the* quetan, replied Dunwadi. *You all think you deserve more than your share, so you never have enough. That is the cause of your fear. We live. Long years. The Lady fills us from Her living self.* Quetan *are not satisfied to have today's food in their bellies. They take, never giving back to the Lady. There were many* faer *once, living with Her other children, never in want. No more. You have taken the land, cut the trees, dirtied the water, stolen the songs of the forest.* The shuttles swished rhythmically and Dunwadi's thought continued, wordless, as Corwin felt himself slip into a waking dream.

He watched Boronil's contorted fingers slip the shuttle endlessly between the warp, and the plain linen fabric, dyed a dull, uneven green, slowly grew. He seemed to come closer to it, as if touching it with his nose. The plain weaving took on a dimension and richness of detail that astonished him. Leaves sprouted from branches, vines encircled them and grew crazily: the whole luxuriant, of infinite variety.

And then he walked within it, a living tapestry as precious as the hangings in a king's court, with the added dimension of life. The leaves caressed his hands, and he breathed the scent of unknown flowers, felt the coolness of a breeze cross his brow.

And the sounds! The cries of birds, the hum and chirp of insects wove a tapestry of their own. His walk, the simple motion of his body, became a dance to the rhythm of this great chorus. He passed into this enchanted landscape, becoming part of the tapestry, knowing each plant, each leaf, seeing a fallen branch, freeing the living branch entangled with it, finding a patch of bare earth, the rain washing the brown soil, leaving shining pebbles behind. He grasped a handful of leaves and covered Her nakedness, leaving the broken branch atop the leaves to keep it in place.

He heard a rending. A knife cut through the fabric, its threads popping, the vines withering, leaving a raw edge that unraveled, taking with it all— leaf, trunk, and root, its singing silenced, leaving only a plain, small, ragged piece of linen cloth, crumpled and useless. Senses spinning, he slept.

# Chapter 32

*What a story this will make!* Corwin followed Bartrym as they hunted for rabbits in the clear light of the following morning.

*Too much noise, Corwin. We'll catch nothing today with you crashing through the brush.*

Corwin stopped, then took a cautious step, doing his best to make no sound in the fallen leaves of the forest. By this time Bartrym was five strides ahead. *Wait! I can't walk that fast and be quiet.*

*Here, watch me.* Bartrym turned and set off at a swift pace, walking with such care that Corwin could not hear a single leaf rustle or twig snap. He turned and explained as he walked back toward Corwin. *Put the side of your foot down first. That way you have more control. Walk with care. Listen for your own sounds. Look for the place with the best footing. Feel what you are stepping on. Pay attention.* They set off again, Corwin's attention centered on his feet.

*This is impossible. I'm not a faery, I mean* faer. *I—*

*Do you see them?* Bartrym asked. *There are three rabbits watching us. Can you see them without frightening them?* Corwin stood stock-still, his eyes roving as they tried to find what Bartrym had seen so effortlessly.

*Two are over here, by the fallen log.*

*Good. And the third?*

Corwin concentrated. At last, he saw it. *At the edge of the thicket.*

Bartrym nodded. He fitted a stone to his sling and then, with a flick of his wrist, sent it flying toward the nearest rabbit. It struck the rabbit's head and it fell. The other two scattered. Bartrym fetched the rabbit, held it in his outstretched hands, and thanked the Lady for the gift of food. They walked some distance before he stopped to gut the rabbit, leaving the entrails buried under a layer of leaves. He put the rabbit into his bag. *We'll need five more.*

*Why not one for each of us? They're not so big.*

*Our realm has shrunk since the coming of the* quetan. *Each year it grows smaller. We cannot take more than it can give us.* Bartrym set off again, with Corwin struggling to keep up.

\* \* \*

As Corwin became more comfortable with his new way of walking, his thoughts turned to Ranell. He saw her in his mind's eye, so beautiful, smiling at him, her shapeless shift hiding—

*Corwin! Must you blather on so?*

*What? I haven't said—*

*You've never stopped. I wonder where we're going? How many rabbits are around here? How did he make that sling? Must you share every thought that goes through your mind? And now Ranell. How can you* quetan *live like that, locked inside your heads? Blind to all around you, seeing only things that are not there and ceaselessly blathering about it?*

*But how do I know when I am sharing my thoughts?*

*By your use of the* vaira. *Only use it when you need it.*

*The what?*

*The* vaira. *You really must learn to pay attention.*

*Pay attention to what?*

Bartrym looked around. Corwin had the sense that he was gathering something, although his hands did not move. The thought of threads went through his mind, although he could see none. *Threads?*

*Silence,* Bartrym replied. *We must gather food.*

*But what is it? How can I be using it if I can't see it and don't know how it works?*

*It is everywhere, and we are all, every single thing, connected by it. You must learn how to use it.* Bartrym paused, thinking. *Like a child must learn to use its hands to grasp, its feet to walk.*

*But how—*

Bartrym smiled and shook his head. *Enough! Thoughts will not feed us. Come, we must go to the river to get more stones. Walk silently, and when we get there, I expect you to tell me all the animals we passed on our way.*

\* \* \*

The next day Corwin helped gather wood. Each of them wore a loop of cloth draped over one shoulder to hold the fallen branches they found. Aelvan and Ranell strode off, leaving Corwin to follow Anil through the trackless forest.

Corwin picked up a piece of fallen branch and put it into his sling. *Anil, could you teach me the* vaira?

Anil stopped and looked at him, puzzled. *Did you need to be taught to breathe?*

Corwin rolled his eyes. *I'm* quetan, *remember? It's not that easy for me. Is there a way for you to tell me or show me what you are doing when you use the* vaira?

*Can you tell me or show me what you are doing when you use your eyes?* Anil squatted and began to snap twigs off a fallen branch and put them into his sling.

Corwin thought about that for a moment. *No, but I could tell you what I see. I see that tree. I see the squirrel perched on the branch.* He craned his neck. *I see a hawk overhead.*

*Has the hawk connected to the squirrel?*

*Has he what? How could I tell that? What does it mean?*

At that moment the hawk circled and dove. The squirrel tried to run to the trunk of the tree, but too late. The hawk carried it off in his talons.

*That's what it means,* Anil told him.

*You could see that before it happened?*

*No, I could tell the* vaira *connected the hawk and the squirrel. I couldn't tell what the outcome would be.*

*What does the* vaira *look like?*

Anil broke the branch over his knee and put the pieces in his sling. *It's not so much how it looks as how it feels.*

*And what is that like?*

Anil stared off into the distance. *Like a current in the water feels to a fish? Or the wind to a bird? Like a plant's roots feel the soil? How can I even speak of these things? I am not a fish, or a bird, or a tree. Come, we must gather wood or there will be no dinner tonight.*

\* \* \*

The next day Corwin went with Boronil to gather. He walked with his head down.

*Why do you feel shame?* she asked.

*I have failed at the men's task and am sent out to do woman's work.*

She stopped and looked up at him, concern in her eyes. *Woman's work? What do you mean?*

*The men hunt. I failed.*

*No, Corwin. We have no separate work for men and for women. At least, we did not when we were a whole people, and not this tattered remnant. I have hunted, and I have gathered the leaves and roots as I do now. It is just that my hands are no longer quick and I can only catch what is slower than I am.* She loosened the soil with a stick and pried a cluster of roots from the ground. Carefully, she broke one of the tubers from the cluster and replanted it, patting the ground back over it like one would tuck a fretful child into bed. *There, little one. Sleep and grow. We give thanks for your gift.* She turned to Corwin and smiled, holding the roots aloft. *See, I can still outrun this.*

He smiled in spite of himself.

157

*Tomorrow you will hunt again.* He nodded, smiling. *Or try to.* His face fell. She smiled and stroked his cheek. *Learn all you can, young one. You will need it.*

He followed her that day, and watched carefully as she gleaned what the Lady provided. Many plants she left alone, but pointed out their properties to Corwin: some for healing of illness or the treatment of wounds, some to be harvested later in the season, places where she had taken plants before that must be left undisturbed while they recovered. She read every tree, every bush, every tender stalk as carefully as Father Anselm had read the parchment scraps that Corwin brought him. By the time the sun crested at noon, Corwin realized that this crone carried as much wisdom as a library within her, and that every minute he spent with her was a gift. As the shadows began to lengthen, they stopped at a stream and scrubbed the dirt from the roots. *Boronil, what is* ksh? he asked.

She busied herself with her cleaning. *You are* quetan. *How can you not know?*

*Tovan used that word when the men destroyed my village, killed my family. And Ranell used it when we met, because I did not see her at first. How can it be, that murder and war can be the same as just not seeing something?*

She looked up from her work. *How can they not be the same?* Then she shut down her thought, leaving Corwin to puzzle it out for himself.

Corwin carried the full sack down the tunnel through the tree roots. At the entrance to the chambers, Aelvan took the sack from him with a curt nod of approval and gave it to Ranell, keeping himself between her and Corwin. The crones and elders smiled at Corwin, thanking him for the work he had done to feed them.

Corwin's heart drank in their praise. He smiled shyly. *It was Boronil. I just carried the bag.*

*Did you learn from her?*

He nodded. *Many things. I hope I can remember them all. So many plants, so many places to remember which ones can be harvested and which ones must rest. I don't know how she remembers it all.*

*Remember?* Boronil answered. *I remember many things, but I do not need to remember these things. The* vaira *shows me.*

*Bartrym told me of the* vaira, *but he said it had to do with directing one's thoughts. Anil says it's about connecting things, like a hawk and its prey. What is it?*

They looked at him, dumbfounded. *How can he not know the* vaira?

*Ksh,* Dunwadi explained.

There was that word again. Corwin felt it like a slap across his face. *Tovan used that word when the men burned my village, destroyed my family. How can that be the same as not knowing which plant to harvest?*

Aelvan shook his head. *Stupid* quetan.

Mirna glanced sidelong at Aelvan, rebuking him before responding. *The* vaira *is life.* Ksh *is what we call the* quetan's *blindness to the* vaira. *Do you understand?*

Corwin sat, puzzling it out. *So* ksh *doesn't mean killing?*

*We kill to eat,* Bartrym reminded him.

*True. But how is that not* ksh?

*The* vaira *changes constantly. If we take a hare or a hawk takes the hare, or if the hare dies from age or from accident, the* vaira *is affected in the same way. But if we were to take more than we need—*

*Like you* quetan, Aelvan burst out, anger filling his thought. *Not branches gathered for fire, but a tree cut down. Not a tree cut, but the whole forest. And your minds so filled with imaginings, you do not see the* vaira, *the way you tear it, burn it, weaken it. Do you not see this,* quetan?

Corwin sat silent, eyes downcast, avoiding Aelvan's glare, willing himself to understand. *I can tell the difference between a forest and a field.*

Exasperated, Aelvan stormed out.

*Was it always so between the* faer *and the* quetan?

*Once we lived as neighbors. Even then they had the* ksh. *We thought them clever at first, and learned from them: how to weave, and make our knives and slings for the hunt, our pots for cooking.*

Bartrym leaned forward. *We learned skills from them that we turned to the protection of the* vaira, *but there are so few of us now. It is all we can do just to provide ourselves with food.*

*But they never learned from us,* Dunwadi answered.

Ranell's brow furrowed. *Perhaps they cannot. Perhaps it is like teaching a blind person to see a sparrow's flight.*

*It may be so,* Dunwadi answered, *but I think it was once a choice on their part. They chose to notice the things they wished to create, that we could not see, and chose to ignore what we can see, what they would destroy in order to create. At first, the things they changed were small, a leaf here, a twig there, but as the long years passed, and they lost all awareness of the* vaira, *the changes they wrought became bigger and bigger: not a twig, but a tree; not a tree, but the whole forest fell to them. We left them then, fleeing to the safety of the forest, ever retreating until this is all we have left.*

# Chapter 33

Bartrym and Dworning's thoughts wove themselves into Corwin's dreams.

*I think he's ready.*

*Are you sure? We can't afford to have anyone falter on this faring.*

*Yes, and besides, we will need six to carry the filled sacks and one to carry Dunwadi. We must take him.*

He opened his eyes to find them watching him in the dim light of the underground chamber. The fire had died, but faint streaks of morning sunlight made the two elder *faer* into strange silhouettes, with their shapeless cloaks and wreaths of leaves tangled in their unkempt hair. Although he had become much stronger, and learned to think of them as *faer* rather than faeries in the time he had spent with them, Corwin still always outslept them. He wondered: Do they sleep at all?

Dworning handed him a wooden bowl. *Up, lad. Eat quickly. We've miles to fare this day.*

Corwin obeyed, eating the portion of boiled moss and berries the others had left for him. *Where are we going?*

*Barley,* Dworning replied, his dark eyes quick and expressive in his lined face. *Anil and Aelvan watched them reap yesterday. There is a whole field that the* quetan *cannot harvest. We will eat well this season.* Corwin followed Dworning to the outer chamber, where the rest of the faring waited. All the men were there, with the crone Dunwadi and Ranell. *Keep an eye on him,* Dworning told Ranell. *Don't let him fall behind.* The maiden nodded and bent to put on her shoes, which left the tracks of a deer.

Corwin did the same. Like the others, they wore cloaks of mottled, faded gray-green. Beneath hers Ranell wore a shift of the same nondescript color. Corwin, like the other men, wore leggings of rabbit skin, fur side out. Dunwadi hobbled over to Corwin, a bowl of green slime in her hand, and smeared some on his hands and bare torso. He smelled the bitter scent of

160

rue in it, to mask his scent from any dog's nose. She put the bowl down and lifted her hands. *May the Lady watch over us, her children.*

They climbed through the passage to the outer world, settled Dunwadi on Rennor's back, and walked toward the rising sun, making no more sound than a herd of deer, and leaving no more than the tracks of deer behind them. They moved swiftly, scattering through the wild so that Corwin, had not Ranell stayed by his side, would have been hard-pressed to know which way to go.

*There. Nion's stone. Yes, I see it, and there, where they found Ennet, when the dogs had savaged him. Yes, he led them from Netumna and saved her. Yes, but she lost the baby—lost the baby. The hazel is burdened this year. She will drop her fruit by new moon. Oh, look! My birthing was over there. Yes, I see it. And there, that stump, was the tree Arnil hid in when they took Brakka. We are bearing too far south. Quickly, toward the cave where we stayed the season of the Head High Snows.*

He could hear the thought of the others even without seeing them now, but still had not learned the knack of locating them by it. Still, he noted with satisfaction, he now could keep pace. *Don't feel so pleased,* Ranell told him. *We're going downhill. It's the coming home laden that will test you.*

Before they had walked an hour, they reached the boundary of their realm. They splashed across a waist-deep river and the land lost its ravines and boulders. Its wild tangle of green growth muted to gently rolling, forested hills with sparse brush. *Huntsmen frequent these woods. If we hear a hunting party, we must hide ourselves until they pass. Do not make a sound.*

Corwin followed her, glancing nervously about him, but they heard nothing and passed unhindered. They walked for the better part of the day, during which the land grew steadily flatter and plowed fingers of land stretched amid the forested tracts. There, they came upon Bartrym and Dunwadi. *It is not far now. You must take a turn,* the white-haired elder told him. *We've saved the easiest part for you.*

Corwin understood the slight, but made no reply. He squatted and Ranell helped Dunwadi to mount pig-a-back on him. He stood, and she seemed to weigh no more than a child.

*Grandmother,* he asked, *why do you come with us? Why not stay home with the crones?*

*I come because I must,* she replied. *There would be no point in this journey without me.*

Corwin struggled with the question in his mind, trying to word it in a polite fashion. The effort was, of course, useless and he felt the bubbling mirth of the faer rise up in her before she replied.

*Only I can call them,* was all the answer he got.

They came to a stream, its banks overgrown with moss. He carried her across, and set her down for a moment. As light as she had seemed at first, he felt glad of the rest. He cupped water in his hands to drink.

*No,* Ranell ordered. *This water comes from the lands where your people live. Do not drink it.*

*But why not?*

*Your people put the spirit of illness in water that flows through their dwelling places. We do not drink it.*

*How ridiculous,* thought Corwin.

Dunwadi looked at him sternly. For just an instant, his vision was filled with her memories, of babes lying dead and bloated, of twisted corpses, frozen in their final agonies, and then there was naught but he and the two women beside a chattering forest stream, with a bird twittering far away.

She felt heavier when he lifted her again to continue the journey.

They came upon the others as the sun reached its height, Corwin dismayed to find they had settled themselves in the midst of a thicket of briar at the crest of a hill. Ranell slithered in quickly and even Dunwadi, bent nearly double with age, entered the thicket easily, avoiding the thorns with a wood-wise skill that seemed magical. Corwin sighed and followed with painful slowness, the sharp thorns grasping at his cloak and stinging his skin.

Mercifully, no one commented. Their attention lay elsewhere. Below them stretched the barley field, the far end cut to stubble, but most of the stalks in the near end lying on the ground, flattened by some squall. *A grove stood there, in the far-off days. Tall oaks with holly set between. They burned it when I was a child,* Rennor told them, *and have no doubt forgotten it ever grew, but the Lady does not forget. See how she provides for us! Anil, Aelvan, you have led us well.* Approval rippled through the thought of the group, while Corwin looked on, appalled at the idea of harvesting the field grain by grain. He felt acutely aware of their mirth, and of Ranell's defense of him: *He's only* quetan.

*Well,* he thought angrily, *how are we to get the grain into the sacks? This is a hopeless task.*

*Don't worry, young Corwin,* Dunwadi replied. *I will see to it.*

*You?!* He envisioned the crone crawling across the field, placing one grain after another in the sacks with her gnarled fingers. Their mirth redoubled and he scowled. *Enough,* ordered Dunwadi, at last. *We must eat, and rest. Tomorrow will be difficult.* She patted Corwin's knee. *Be patient, young Corwin. You will learn all in time.*

Corwin stayed by Dunwadi, who wrapped herself in her cloak and became as still as a stone. The others melted into the forest and returned, after some time, with apples, berries, and mushrooms. They ate and waited. The field

162

below them lay deserted, although they could hear the song of harvesters and the swish of scythes through the hedgerow at its lower end. The *faer* sat motionless, wrapped in their green cloaks, and Corwin rolled himself into a ball and slept in their midst.

They saw only one person, a peasant furtively poaching rabbits. The man spent some time peering into the thicket, but could see only briar rose arching over great mossy stones that had not been there the day before. He soon left, muttering and making signs against the evil eye. Corwin woke at twilight, as the group began to stir.

Dworning carried Dunwadi to the center of the field. Anil arranged the sacks around her, their mouths facing outward. The two *faer* returned to the thicket. Corwin squinted. Dunwadi appeared to be no more than a boulder that had magically appeared in the middle of the field. As the full moon rose, and his eyes accustomed themselves to its light, he could see only one hint of movement: Where her hand emerged from her shapeless robe, her fingers drummed monotonously on the earth. At last he grew bored with his vigil and slept again.

\* \* \*

He dreamed he looked down at Tovan, a much younger Tovan. *When I am grown, I will find my brother for you, Mother.*

Corwin felt Mirna's sadness. *It has been long since I have felt him.*

*Perhaps he has forgotten us.*

Corwin felt his hand tenderly stroke Tovan's cheek. *No mother could ask for a finer son than you, Tovan. You are the Lady's gift to me.*

\* \* \*

Corwin woke, alone, with the bright moon full in his eye. He sat and stretched his stiff limbs and pulled his cloak tighter against the chill. He crawled out from under the sheltering thicket and went down to the edge of the field. Dunwadi still kept her vigil, her hand tirelessly thrumming the earth. Wondering what could possibly be happening, Corwin stepped onto the field. Instantly, Ranell was there, clasping his arm and drawing him back.

Ksh*! No!*

*But why not? What is she doing?*

Ranell touched the ground. After a moment, she brought her hand up. *Look closely.*

She held her hand inches from his face. He saw black spots milling about on it, exploring the fingers, congregating on the palm. Each was an ant, burdened with a grain of barley. *They do us this service. It would be wrong to treat them so heedlessly.* She lowered her hand and the ants trailed back to the ground. *Go back to the thicket, will you?*

\* \* \*

His head felt clogged with too much sleep when Ranell nudged him awake in the gray chill before dawn. *Come.* She thrust a sack of grain into his hands. A confused ant clung to it. He brushed the ant off and shouldered the sack. *Here.* Ranell handed him an apple. *You must eat as we go.* Her thought held a focused urgency. She set off at a trot. He struggled to keep pace. They came upon Rennor at the stream, transferring Dunwadi to Aelvan's back. Rennor picked up Aelvan's sack and vanished into the wood. *Stay close to me,* Ranell told Corwin. *The* quetan *hunt here.*
*Perhaps they will not hunt today.*

*Perhaps.* She gave no further reply. Corwin looked around nervously and plunged after her. The woods were open here—too open—great oaks and beeches widely spaced, the shade of their high canopy leaving little sustenance for undergrowth. He noticed Ranell stayed within sight of Aelvan and Dunwadi. *We must protect them,* she explained. *Aelvan is laden heaviest and cannot move as fast. We will need to divert any pursuit.*

As the sky turned from gray to golden, and the first beams of the sun glittered on the dew, the hounds began to bay. Instantly, Corwin felt the thought of his companions. *The Lady preserve us! To the river!* Ranell sprang away from him and he found it all he could do to keep up with Aelvan and Dunwadi. The baying grew louder, and he could hear the thudding of hoofs and the winding of the hunters' horns. His lungs bursting, legs aching, a stitch paining his side, Corwin at last heard the plashing of the river ahead. *Faster!* ordered Aelvan. *You do not want them to catch you.* They crested the hill and ran down to the river bank. *Take off your shoes.* Aelvan stepped into the water, kicked off his own, picked them up, and crossed the stream, Dunwadi still clinging to his back. *NOW, you stupid* quetan*!*

Corwin did as he was bid, and splashed into the river. The current threatened to tear his feet from the slippery stones and forced him downriver with each step. He waded through chill water up to his waist, holding the sack on his shoulder and his shoes above it. The cries of the hounds grew stronger by the minute. He reached the opposite bank and began to climb its steep, rock-strewn shore. Aelvan emerged from the brush and grabbed Corwin's burden. He tossed it into the bushes and then turned, clasped Corwin's forearm and pulled him up the bank. They crouched in the bushes beside Dunwadi as the hounds reached the opposite bank and milled about in a confused mass, sniffing for a scent.

In a moment, six mounted hunters joined the dogs. "What sport!" cried one, letting loose a blast on his horn.

Corwin watched them, motionless, as though they were a breed of animal he had never seen before. They were huge. It was not just the fact that they sat upon great stamping horses, but that Corwin, grown accustomed to the companionship of the *faer*, had forgotten their thinness and small stature. These humans seemed grotesque, too tall, layers of fat beneath their belts and under their sweating skins, their bright clothing and shining spears garish in the cool green of the woodland.

"They have crossed the river," said a second. Cautiously, they urged their horses into the stream. The first hunter had nearly reached the opposite shore when he let out a shout as though he had been stabbed. The tracks, in the muddy space beyond the rocky stream bed, were not those of deer's hooves, but of feet. Aelvan, Dunwadi, and Corwin crouched in the brush, ten yards away, not daring to breathe, as the hounds milled about the horses, whining at their masters' sudden dismay.

"Mother of God," said one, a burly man mounted on an elegant bay. He crossed himself.

"This is faery magic," said the horn blower, his eyes darting about nervously. A rumble of dismay passed through the group. Aelvan and Dunwadi began to breathe again.

"Back," said yet another of the hunters, an older man whose iron roan matched his grizzled hair and beard. His word carried weight, as the others immediately turned their horses and recrossed the stream, all save one.

"Squire Giles!" ordered the graybeard, but the young man sat entranced, his chestnut mount still knee-deep in the stream. "Squire Giles, come. We will seek other game."

"Nay, Uncle," said the young man. "I will follow this trail where it leads. I have mind to ask a boon of these folk."

Aelvan inhaled sharply. Ksh. *The Lady preserve us. There's always one.*

"Nephew, your father has given you into my keeping. I cannot permit this."

"Nor can you hinder me," shouted the young man, setting spur to his horse. It leapt up the bank like living flame and disappeared into the forest, three of the hounds at its heels. The uncle and his companions sat thoughtful astride their horses. At last the graybeard spoke. "I am not of a mind to spend the day chasing that hot-head through the forest. A pox take him. If he comes not home tonight, we will send the huntsmen to find him in the morn." With that, the party left by the way it had come.

*We must join the others at the oak grove,* Aelvan told them. *By now they have laid a long, confused trail for this* quetan. *If we go the most direct way, we may reach them before he does.*

He put on his shoes and picked up Dunwadi again. Corwin, again shod, picked up his sack. They crossed the trail and climbed straight up the hill before them. From its crest, they could see the tall crown of the circle of oaks directly before them and hear the racket of the knight and his dogs off in the distance. They plunged down the hill at a dead run, leapt the narrow stream at its foot and struggled up the low hill crowned by the oaks.

165

The trees of the grove were of huge girth, planted in a circle by the Ancestors' hands. They had grown to such a great size that there was scarcely room to step between them, save at one end, where a space had been left for entry, and another, almost directly opposite, where one of the giants had fallen outward, leaving a rotten stump and a log whose hollow was large enough to hold a man sitting upright.

As they reached the fallen tree, Corwin could see the others race into the grove from the opposite side. Ranell ran to the log and thrust her sack and shoes into it. The men tossed their burdens out of the circle and turned, slings ready, each loaded with a stone.

The hounds burst into the clearing. Instantly, the men let fly their stones, each striking its target, a dog's head, with a loud crack. The dogs fell as though they had been turned to stone themselves. The faer melted back through the trees. Corwin crouched behind the log with Aelvan and Dunwadi, gaze fixed on the clearing. Ranell fidgeted beside him. *Be still,* he thought angrily. *The hunter is not far behind.*

*I know,* she replied, and with that she stepped into the clearing, just as the squire rode into it from the opposite end.

She was naked.

Corwin leapt after her, to save her from this amazing piece of folly. Aelvan grabbed his arm and pulled him back, sending him sprawling on the soft forest floor. *Watch and learn!* he commanded. Corwin peered around the splintered end of the tree. Ranell stood, her back to him, her skin so smooth. Aelvan nudged Corwin's ribs with his elbow and gave him one of his black glares. Corwin turned his gaze to where Squire Giles sat astride his horse, gaping at the dogs and at Ranell.

*Why do you pursue my people?* Ranell's thought thundered in the silence.

Giles sat astonished for a time, and then replied, his voice harsh in Corwin's ears. "I wish a boon."

*Name it,* came the wrathful reply.

He swallowed hard. "I wish to gain the love of the beautiful Marie, daughter of my lord the duke."

*You must travel far, until you can gain the branch of the living tree that bears blossom, leaf, and fruit together. Only then may you gain your heart's desire.*

He looked dismayed at the impossibility of such a task.

*Further, you must leave this place and harass my people no longer, or forfeit your life.*

His Adam's apple danced again and he looked about nervously.

She clenched her fists and glared at him. *NOW, or suffer the fate of your dogs!* The horse spun round and he was gone in a flurry of hoofbeats.

166

Corwin crouched behind the fallen tree, his mouth agape. The mirth of the faer rose around him. Ranell came back and calmly began to dress herself.
*He could have killed you!*
*He could have killed us all.*
*You were naked. He might have raped you. What possessed you to do such a foolish thing?*
Ranell slipped her shapeless shift over her head. *Would he have believed I was a "faery" if he saw me in this?*
Corwin stood slack-jawed, buffeted by the gales of the *faer*'s mirth. He imagined himself pushing invisible threads away, lest they all feel what the sight of Ranell's naked body had inspired in him. He took a deep breath and glanced at the others hoping it had worked. *That was amazing*, he conceded.
*It is an old strategy.*
*He could hear your thought.*
*Given enough of a shock, most* quetan *can. You are unusual only in that you can hear us without it.*
*You granted him a boon! The tales are true!*
*Not a one.*
*But—*
*I told him that if he left here and never returned, and found something that does not exist, he might get what he wants. I promised him nothing.*
*You had your weapons. You could have killed him.*
*Yes*, replied Aelvan, *and had his uncle's huntsmen tramping all over our domain seeking vengeance. Better to scare him off.*
*But you've sent him on a fool's errand. He may spend years—the rest of his life—he may die seeking something that does not exist.*
*We may all die, young Corwin*, replied Dunwadi. *In fact, I am sure of it. And the things you* quetan *seek, it seems to me, are mostly fools' errands, in any case. Mayhap he will learn from his quest, mayhap he will die. It is no concern of ours. What concerns us is that there is one less* quetan *persecuting us.* She cocked her head and breathed deeply. *Come, the air smells of rain. Let us bring the barley home before it starts.*

* * *

After dinner, Corwin left the others to their evening tasks, and wandered alone in the darkness. He climbed the ancient oak that hid the *faer*'s cavern and rested in the crook of a massive branch. It took all his strength of will not to think of Ranell, not to see her naked before him. Instead, he drew his mind to Aelvan, the way he kept himself between Ranell and Corwin, blocking, always blocking his way to her. He tried to understand the situation as a *faer* might, not simply as a *quetan*, intent upon only his own desires. *I understand his feelings. He has known her for long years, and she is meant to be his. He is* faer, *and I am not. He has the skills to hunt and gather in the forest to feed her and their children. He can see the* vaira, *while I am cursed with the* ksh *and unworthy of her.* He hung his head, and remembered the stories Philippe had taught him, how the knight would serve his lady without thought of reward. *So must it be between Ranell and me.*

* * *

The next morning, Corwin awoke in the dim light of the cavern. Ranell handed him a bowl of barley gruel. *We must gather wood, Corwin.*

He took the bowl from her, careful to keep his eyes downcast. *Where are the others?*

*The men have all gone to hunt, and the crones to gather. Food grows scarce, and many hands are needed. That leaves us to feed the fire and bring water.*

Corwin nodded as he ate.

*Have I angered you?*

Corwin's heart leapt, as he tried to conceal his feelings. *No! Why would you think that?* He looked at the bowl in his hands.

*You hide. You will not look at me.*

*When I look at you . . .* He stopped, unsure of how to express himself. *My feelings are too big. I am afraid they will offend you . . . and the others. I am afraid I would do nothing but look at you.* He dared to look at her feet, clad in their shoes, then looked away, afraid of the way his eyes wanted to rise up her legs. *You are Aelvan's. I have no business interfering with that.*

*What? I am Aelvan's? What am I, a rabbit skin? A pair of shoes?*

Corwin stopped in confusion. *You know what I mean.*

*No. I do not.*

*Then why does he always stand between us? Why does he look at me with anger if I so much as look at you?*

*Because you are* quetan, *and the* quetan *have done us such harm. He fears you, Corwin.*

*Fears me?* The thought had never occurred to him. Certainly no quetan had ever feared him. *But he's bigger than me.* Corwin felt her annoyance through her thought.

Ksh. *He fears* ksh.

*But I've learned.*

*You only know what you have learned, Corwin, not what you haven't learned.*

The thought stopped Corwin in his tracks. *Perhaps there are things that the* quetan *know that the* faer *do not. Bartrym admits that you learned from us at one time,* he argued.

*Yes, but we stopped when we saw where your path leads.*

She followed him through the twisting passage to the surface and they began their task. *How can I be worthy of her? I must learn to use the* vaira. *But how? I can't see it, or hear it, or however they are aware of it.* He puzzled over this as he gathered fallen branches, trying at the same time to remember Bartrym's lessons, moving silently and noticing everything around him. He found he could not do it all. Either the thoughts had to go or the silence and the noticing. His thoughts got him nowhere, so he abandoned them. At last, his sling was full and he turned back toward their shelter.

Ranell stood before him, hand outstretched. *If the* vaira *were something you could see, it would look much like this.* In her hand, she held a snail shell. She traced its spiral with her finger. *It goes like this.*

*So, the* vaira *is something that moves.* At last, Corwin felt he had a toehold in understanding the *vaira. Does it move like the wind? Or like a bird on the wind?*

*No.* He felt regret in her thought. *It doesn't move like we move. It just is.* She stood, brow knitted in concentration. *It connects all, and feels like this.* She placed the shell in his hand. *Come, we must gather more wood, and we have yet to fetch the water.* Corwin tucked the snail shell into the waistband of his leggings and followed her.

# Chapter 34

The wind turned chill, these many days. The leaves faded and withered, flying thick through the air, leaving naked branches that scratched the sky. At last the days grew longer, but snow still covered the land. Aelvan and Anil had been gone for two days, upon what errand Corwin did not know, and none would tell him. The last of the barley, the Lady's precious gift to them, had gone into the breakfast pot. Corwin rubbed the sleep from his eyes and saw the lone bowl of it, left there for him. He reached for it and began to eat, panic knotting his gut. Was this to be his last meal? Had the *faer* abandoned him? Again? *Dunwadi!*

He felt Dunwadi's thought. *It is time.*

*Time for what?* Corwin asked.

*Come with us and learn.*

He ate the last of the gruel, cleaned his bowl, and climbed out from beneath the roots of the oak. He stood alone, with no sound but the sighing of the wind in the great trees that towered over him and no companion save the chill that cut through him, laughing at his meager cloak. Snowflakes fell, swirling through the black branches of the trees. He looked, scanning the forest, careful to keep his mind open, not filled with expectation, and saw no one. His fear resurfaced. *Where are you?*

*Come with us and learn.*

He reached within, breathing deeply, calming his fear. The snow swirled around him, covering any tracks the others might have left; the chill wind tingled the edge of his nostrils.

Then he felt it, something he could not define, pulling his attention ahead and slightly to his right. He walked, simply drawn. He recognized Nion's stone, named for the one who had died there, where he and Boronil had foraged. The roots nearby slept now, their dead vegetation hidden beneath the snow. No food here until spring, he thought, his panic rising again. *Where are they? What if I cannot find them?* He pulled his cloak tighter around him and climbed a steep, rocky hillside. A deer trail ran just below the top of the ridge, sheltered somewhat from the wind, and he followed it.

Where another trail crossed it, he saw tracks in the snow. The boar and his sows had taken the same path, not long before. He stopped. Danger lay that way, but he could feel the pull directing him along the path. His toes, wet now with chill snow soaking through his shoes, began to ache from the cold and he wrapped his cloak tighter, rubbing his hands on his upper arms for warmth. Cautiously, he followed the path.

And then it split. The pig tracks led downward toward water and the deer trail continued along the ridge. He stopped, waiting, looking ahead for some sign or intuition that might lead him. He did not want to meet the boar, with its short temper and long, razor-sharp tusks, but the path along the ridge did not call to him. He took the downward path.

Ahead, he could see the pigs, drinking from the ice-rimmed stream at the foot of the hillside. He willed himself to move silently, as Bartrym had taught him, placing each foot with care. The boar raised his head and sniffed the air. Corwin froze, averting his eyes so the boar would not think him a predator.

And then he saw it. A pit filled with ash lay nearby, cold now, and filling with snow. Even without that, he knew, with a certainty that astonished him, that he had found the others. The boar grunted and went back to drinking. Corwin made his way down the hillside, a step and a pause, then another, ever keeping his awareness fixed upon the boar.

A copse of fir stood close against the hillside, near the firepit. He crept along the uphill side of the pit and peered into the copse. Dimly, he could see a fracture in the rock face large enough to admit him and he slid between the stiff branches, not quickly as the others would, but at least without harm. This much he had learned. He then followed the twisting course of the crevice by touch until he saw a faint red glow that led him to the round chamber where the others waited.

It was comfortable in there, with glowing rocks piled in the center, and the walls warm to the touch. This, then, was Aelvan and Anil's errand. *I thank you, brothers, for making this warm place.*

*You have learned well, young Corwin,* Dunwadi greeted him. He looked quickly to Ranell, who smiled at him. He did not look at the others: at the crones who nodded and smiled at the look that had passed between him and Ranell; at the men, Aelvan especially. He quickly sat next to Trilma, away from Aelvan's black glare.

He heard a whisper of sound from the cave entrance and Bartrym joined them. He looked at Corwin and smiled. *No,* quetan, *you were never alone.*

Corwin looked down to hide the spasm of emotion that crossed his face. Relief and gratitude filled his heart. *I give thanks.*

*How did you find us?* Ranell asked.

*It felt like I was pulled. I had to think about you, and then I felt something guiding me.*

A rustle of thought went through the *faer,* like a breeze through tall grasses. *So, the* quetan *can feel the* vaira*!*

*But it didn't feel like you said it would, Ranell, not all curly like a snail shell.*

*Perhaps the* quetan *feel it differently.*

*And how will they use it?* asked Aelvan. *Will they break it, like everything else they touch?*

Corwin had no answer. They sat in silence, until Dunwadi asked, *Where shall we go?* Corwin now knew better than to ask what this strange request meant. They were in a cave, in a great ruddy hole in the ground, with only one entrance which Anil and Rennor had blocked with sacks full of dry leaves. There was barely enough room for the twelve of them. He thought of Tuunma. She had always frightened him: too wizened, too knowing, like a witch out of some tale with her withered skin, glittering black eyes, and thoughts he could not fathom, but she was dead now, gone foraging too close to the river and shot through with an arrow.

As much as he had feared her, he grieved her loss and his part in it, for being the one more mouth that had sent her farther and farther afield to forage for the group and brought her into the range of the hunters that pressed closer upon the domain of the faer with each season.

*Wait. I have a gift.* He recognized the thought as Boronil's. Sweet Boronil, a young girl's heart still beating within her crone's body. She had fed him, many times, a bite of food from her own dish. Even after he knew enough to realize what this cost her, she insisted, feeding him with such love that he could not refuse her, but bent himself to master the sling and the hunting lore and take his place with those who gathered food for them all. Boronil, as generous as the Lady herself. He wondered what she had been like as a girl.

She fumbled with the lacing of her shift and reached into the neck to pull out a flat pouch, hung from her ropy neck with a leather thong. Carefully, she slipped it over her head and untied its fastenings. She unfolded the packet and held it up in the glow of the stones for all to see. There, protected from sweat and grime, ancient, faded almost to nothing, lay a scrap of cloth. On it, two rabbits whirled in a dance, as rabbits will

172

when the madness of spring is upon them, against a background of what once had been green grass. Corwin stared in amazement. Although faded, they seemed alive, just frozen in the moment, about to leap off the cloth and dance for them all. *Where did you get this?* Corwin asked.

*My mother wove this for me when I was a child. It was part of a dress.* Corwin felt a shimmering dizziness take hold of him as he entered the memories of the *faer*. They swirled round him: faces; scraps of cloth; an endless stream of smiling mothers; great breasts dripping milk bent to his lips; clothing, bright patterns in the reds and ochers of the earth itself.

*I give this to you now, Ranell. I am old. You must keep it for us now.*

His mind still whirling in a fog of faces and bright patterns, he saw Ranell solemnly take the cloth, bind it in its wrapper, and slip it over her head and beneath her dress. He dropped his head into his hands, overcome, and let the rushing thought take him where it would.

The rabbits danced, their colors bright and new, then disappeared in a swirl of red and brown, then reappeared, then gone again as the little girl spun, her jet-black braids standing out straight from her head, the bright fabric of her dress swirling out to show her chubby legs. *Oooh, Boronil! So pretty!*

*My mother made it for me! See how much she loves me!*

*Oooh, Boronil, stand still. I want to pet the bunnies.*

*Oooh, Boronil!* The other children crowded round, smiling, touching, eyes alight.

*Here, Boronil. Let me see your beautiful dress.* A woman came toward the children, carrying a basket filled with ripe grapes. She set it down and got down on one knee, to be at Boronil's height. Corwin gasped. The woman was tall, full-bosomed, and carried herself with a regal dignity, her clothing vividly patterned, making her dark beauty shine in the dappled sunshine of the forest. *The Lady!* thought Corwin.

*Hush!* warned the others.

The woman stopped and stiffened, then relaxed. *The Unseen Ones are here, Boronil. I think they have come to look at your pretty dress. Can you feel them?* The children quieted, listening. One by one they nodded.

*Who are they?* asked Boronil.

*Others,* the woman replied. *The Ancestors, perhaps, or those of us not yet born. I don't know.*

*Why do they feel so sad?*

*I don't know, Bartrym . . .*

*Bartrym?! You?*

*My grandfather. Hush.*

*Your grandfather? But . . .*

*Hush, Corwin.*

*. . . mayhap they miss us, mayhap they miss the feel of the wind, the gold of the sun. Let's see this new dress of yours, child.* Boronil held out the skirts with her hands and spun again. *And what is this on the front? Look at these two! Oh, Boronil, your mother does the finest weaving of us all.*

None of them saw him come, but there he stood, arms folded, watching them all, smiling. Again, Corwin felt his breath catch and he remembered his talks with his master, the troubadour Philippe, and understood, at last, how men in ancient times came to believe that gods walked the earth. *Nion.* He had come upon them without warning, despite the brilliance of his garb, his movement as silent and graceful as a great stag. The children saw and called to him. The woman turned and, finding his eyes upon her, blushed. He sat beside her and stroked her cheek.

*The Unseen Ones are here.*

*Are they?* He reached down and plucked a mushroom and held it to her lips.

*And how have you fared?*

*Another group of them has come. They passed by the grove beyond the river with their great stinking beasts. They seem as stupid as the first. We left food for them, but they trampled it.* Again, he reached down. He plucked a leaf, admired it, and then ate it.

She shivered. *They frighten me. They come from nowhere and will not meet with us.*

*They are uncouth, Brakka, but they are beneath fearing. I do not know where they have come from, but it seems such a shabby folk must be moving because they could not prosper where they were. They are blind, Brakka, afflicted with the* ksh. *They will not last long here.*

*But still, Nion . . .* He put his arm around her and pulled her close. With his free hand he touched her face, his fingers gently tracing the curve of her cheek. *Nion, the children.*

*The Unseen Ones, the children . . . I think you do not love me anymore.* Nion turned to look at the children, appealing to them with his eyes. Grinning and giggling with the inward mirth of the *faer*, they turned and left.

*I want to stay.*

*You can't, Corwin. No one here has that memory. There is more to this, but not with them.* The children ran along a path, past patches of grain and laden vines twining in branches high overhead. The vision split apart and shimmered, signaling to Corwin that this memory came from several of his companions. He caught glimpses of the men and women of the *faer* as they bent to the tasks of harvesting the Lady's bounty, all in the golden sunshine that scattered itself on the brown forest floor.

Then suddenly it was as though he had hit a great stone wall, a nightmare of terror and grief, wailing chaos surging through them all. Nion passed through them like the wind. Brakka gathered up the frightened young ones and guided them to the murky darkness of a cave, where they waited until dusk brought the others. Slowly, they gathered. Women, then men, and last of all Nion, his bright clothing torn, bleeding from a gash on his forehead.

*Talnor was gathering cress near the stream, and a party of them took him and bound him. Handruth is dead, and Mantur, and Dworning the Elder. Mirna, I am sorry. We went to them, to bring back Talnor, but they attacked as soon as we showed ourselves. I saw him, once, fastened about the neck like they do their animals.*

Mirna fell to the ground, caught by Brakka, and sat, rocking, her arm covering her head, as if it could ward off the loss of her son and his father.

*One hit me with a club and the world grew blacker than night. I fell down the steeps to the stream. They let me lie, thinking me dead. When I could see again, they were gone. I will follow them with whoever will come with me. I will not rest, my sister, until I have brought him back to you.*

Corwin was buffeted by a storm of grief and anger, his heart filled with the anguish of the *faer*. Deeper still, a profound uncertainty, for they were a people who killed only in order to eat, and now found themselves hunted with less reason and less regard than the forest beasts. They plunged deeper still into dark places haunted with nameless fears, deeper, deeper yet, until, from the depths, a glimmer of light emerged, growing clear and radiant as each one reached it, joined with it, and clung to it for comfort.

The Lady came to them. *When the child who was stolen returns a man, then shall you take your place as the elders and teachers of the* quetan.

Corwin saw Dunwadi come forward, white-haired but straight-backed, and place her hands on Mirna's head. The grieving woman stopped rocking, her body relaxed, and she seemed to sleep. Brakka and another woman spread cloths for her to lie upon and two of the men placed her on them. Something about this surprised Corwin, until he realized that he had never before seen one of the faer sleep.

*I will stay with her until the Lady returns her to us. Nion, come, let me see your wound.*

*Dunwadi, what shall we do?* Nion asked, anguished.

*Our Dunwadi?*

*Yes. Hush.*

*We must send watchers to observe these people and learn what we can. Then we must council among ourselves.*

175

Corwin felt his heart ache to bursting, like the lungs of a drowning man, drowning in sorrow. All around him, the fist drove home, both Seen and Unseen keened their silent grief.

*Dunwadi, this is too sad.* It was Bartrym. *Take us back further. Take us to the Far Days, before the coming of the* quetan. The vision glimmered and gained a single focus. All the *faer* rode on the back of a single thought, back, back, to the shining bliss of the Far Days.

# Chapter 35

The smell woke him. Putrid and foul, it filled his nostrils and dragged him bodily from the sun-dappled forest; from a deep, sweet dream of feasting; from the silver gleam of the moon on the dancers in the grove. He shivered. The stones before him had lost their glow, and the wall at his back sucked the heat from his bones.

His eyes opened into a rustling darkness, filled with stench and jostling as hands reached to unblock the mouth of the winter cave. The thin, sharp breeze blew sweet, giving Corwin the strength to crawl toward the faint light that trickled through the cave mouth.

*Not yet, Corwin. We must help the elders.* He remembered Bartrym had been next to him and found him by feel. The elder clasped his hand in greeting. *Come, let us get Trilma out.* Corwin reached back to her and found the crone's claw-like hand. It gripped his and he and Bartrym between them pulled her to her feet and supported her as she tottered toward the cave mouth. They wound through the narrow passage, Bartrym leading, Corwin behind, hands beneath her elbows holding her weight, until they emerged in the gloom of the firs.

Just ahead, Rennor and Dworning were settling Dunwadi on the soft, damp needles of the forest floor. Behind them came Ranell, leading Duthuna and Mirna. Last of all came Anil and Aelvan, supporting Arna and Cuthnil.

Corwin helped settle Trilma and sank down beside her, gratefully gulping the fresh air, his head swimming from stench, hunger, and the effort of moving after so long. The wind, though chill, bore the scent of earth and the sound of birdsong. It was some time before he raised his head to look at his companions. *Where is Boronil?* He started to rise. *I'll get her.*

*No,* Aelvan answered. *Couldn't you smell her?*

Corwin stared at him, blinking in confusion, the great, crushing weight of guilt bearing down upon him. *Boronil, who gave me her food. Oh, God! What have I done?* He curled into a ball, the loss of her mingling with the losses, so many of them, that he had only begun to perceive. He felt his world shift, disintegrate, but this time it was not from the thought of the others. The *faer* sat silent, watching him, holding their thought in stillness. This was his own private hell.

He rocked, the motion comforting somehow, soothing the rawness that devoured him. He wanted to cry, to scream, to lash out, but could not. His burden was too great, immobilizing him. And then, as soft as a butterfly, he felt a hand on his shoulder, then another, and another as the *faer* drew close about him. *Corwin, child, she has chosen to stay with the Lady. Do you not know that?*

*I killed her. I took food from her.*

*It was her gift, Corwin, not your taking.*

*I didn't know. I am a stupid* quetan. *You should kill me so that there will be more for you to share.*

*Corwin . . . Corwin . . .* He saw Boronil again, with shimmering, shifting vision: young, in the flush of her womanhood, on her hands and knees, digging. She turned, picked up a tiny bundle of bright cloth, and unfolded it. It held a baby, tiny and stillborn. She stroked the tiny face with her finger, covered it with the cloth, and placed it in the hole. She sat, looking at it, her dark eyes frozen, and reached out to touch it, patting it, arranging the cloth, and at last smoothing the earth back over it, and carefully replacing the leaves.

He saw Boronil, still young, on her hands and knees, digging. She turned, picked up a bundle of plain cloth, a bit larger than the last, and placed it in the hole. She sat, looking at it, her dark eyes frozen, and reached out to touch it, stroking it, arranging the cloth, and at last smoothing the earth back over it, and carefully replacing the leaves.

He saw Boronil, older and older, digging, again and again. . . . She had borne many children, and she had lost them all.

*Corwin, never say that. You were the Lady's gift to her. It is fitting that you mourn her as your mother,* Dunwadi told him.

*I can't remember my mother.*

*The Lady chooses her gifts well.*

*There is a hole where my heart should be.*

*It will always be so. Fill it with the sweetness of her memory.*

*It is not enough.*

*It is never enough, and yet it is.* He felt Dunwadi place her thin hands on his head. Corwin stopped rocking. His world, so lately shattered, began to draw together, the ground solid again beneath him, the hands touching him warm, magnetic.

He saw Boronil in his mind's eye, a withered, stooped figure, grinning at him as she dug roots from the ground with a blunt stick. She pointed to a plant, a small, soft herb—cress, he thought it was—stroked its leaves, and

178

held her hand up to him to smell. She plucked a leaf and fed it to him, before plucking more to put into the bag he held for her and he saw her smile slyly when the taste of it burned his mouth and he dropped the bag and ran off to the stream.

*He is good, Corwin. He makes you strong, that one.* He felt the love flow from her, filling his heart, connecting him to her, to the cress, to the stream, to the cold clear water and the muck beneath his feet, to the hands that rested lightly upon him still. Corwin raised his head and looked into the fathomless depths of Dunwadi's eyes. He felt it there, too. He could see it radiating from her in all directions, to the earth, to the firs, to each of their companions, and again from each of them the same, a tapestry of light that wove him in its web, that held them all, warm and safe, proof against harm: the *vaira*, the shining embrace of the Lady.

*Come, Corwin, we must gather food, and eat.*

# Chapter 36

They spent the next winter in a different cave. It would be years before they could return to the cavern where Boronil lay decomposing. Corwin had gone with the men to prepare next winter's cave. They took the bones of Sherra, who had died two years before Corwin joined them, and buried them beneath the Mother Holly.

They lost another that year. And the next. And the next. And then there were a few years of respite. Or were there? The years, as Corwin entered the mind of the *faer*, lost distinction. His life with the *faer* commingled with their memories, and after a time he could no longer tell which were his own. Only the shimmering tapestry of the life of the *faer* remained.

He thought of Tovan at times, sometimes of watching the battle with him; at others, he recalled the memories that he once thought were dreams. These mingled with the memories of the others: of Ranell, playing with her brother Tovan when they were children; of Tovan, a silent, wide-eyed newborn, suckling at Mirna's breast. The power of that tiny mouth surprised him. He rubbed his nipple, surprised to find it small and flat.

The present, ever bright and new, grew deeper and more detailed. He saw and heard what had once passed beneath his notice. The cries of birds, the subtle shifts of the wind on his skin, the scents it brought him held more information than any library. He smelled Man, on occasion, hunting in the forest, and stayed away, finding the scent of what had once been his own kind a stench.

Bartrym, who had taught him to hunt, gone. Mirna—kindness herself— mother of Ranell and Tovan, left in the cave where Boronil had died, her bones removed to the Mother Holly in their time. The crones, the elders, in ones and twos, dead, their memories with them, only the echoes of them living in his brain.

Dunwadi endured. Eldest and frailest of all, she lived. Each year there were fewer to carry her to where the ants might gather grain for them. Each year, there were fewer to feed.

They sat in the cavern under the great oak, their summer shelter. *They are dying*, thought Corwin, and immediately regretted it.

*We know*, came Dunwadi's reply.

*Let me take you back with me. Dylan respects the old ways. Perhaps he would shelter us and feed us.*

*Corwin, your kind would not allow it.*

*But Dylan—*

*And what of it, Corwin? We would be prisoners in his house. You know that those in the village would harm us if they saw us.*

Aelvan stood and left the chamber. *It is the way of your kind to strike out at what they do not understand.* Corwin felt the anger behind Aelvan's thought.

*Why does he hate me?* asked Corwin.

*Not hatred.* Dunwadi looked at her gnarled hands, clasped on her lap. *Great sadness. He shares our memories of what our life once was, but he will never know that life for himself.*

Corwin nodded.

*But there is hope*, Dunwadi continued. *The Lady protects us. She is nearly ready.*

*The Lady?* he asked. *Ready for what?*

But he got no reply.

\* \* \*

He and Aelvan went perilously close to the dwellings of men that year, scouting for the field that the Lady would give them. After three days searching, they separated. The year grew late, and a field must be found before the rains of autumn spoiled the grain. Apart, they could search more quickly, cover more ground. *Do nothing stupid*, quetan, was Aelvan's parting thought, before he disappeared into the brush.

\* \* \*

It was late in the day and hunger gnawed at Corwin's belly. He was closer to a village than he would have liked, and the forest plants he had learned would sustain him were few. He smelled the stench of a farmstead above the ravine he followed. Cautiously, he crept up the bank. Swiftly, from handhold to handhold—a crevice, a clump of grass, the trunk of a slender sapling—he rose silently.

The house was small, and not far from the ravine's edge. A fenced meadow lay to his left, in the slanting sunlight a cow ambled toward the gate. *Milk!* Ducks and chickens scratched among the flowers behind the house and in the garden, where turnips and cabbages stood in luxuriant rows. *Eggs!* Nearest him stood a bed of peas, their vines climbing a tangle of twigs stuck in the dirt. Corwin crept closer, out of the ravine, and picked a handful. Then he saw it. The field next to the cow pen was planted to wheat, half of it flattened by a squall. The Lady's gift. *Aelvan! I have found it!*

A woman's voice sounded from the cottage. "Elyn! Feed the baby while I cook. Henry, fetch eggs. Mind the broody hen."

Corwin slid over the edge of the ravine. The kitchen clatter grew louder, momentarily, as the heavy door swung open, then shut. A boy, perhaps four years of age, came out with a willow basket and began to peer under the foxgloves and lupines that surrounded the cottage.

Corwin shrank back, crouching in the ravine, his head, with its wild hair, camouflaged by the ivy that twined through it. *Eggs!* He'd had none since spring, when the wild birds had laid theirs. An egg would be good. He munched his peas, not bothering to shell them, and watched. The cow reached the gate and mooed thunderously. Corwin jumped.

"Thomas! The cow." Again, the door swung back, and a hulking, half-grown boy came out with a wooden bucket and stool. He went to the gate and the cow stood, chewing placidly, while the boy went about his business. Corwin heard the sizzle of the milk hitting the bucket and his stomach growled.

Henry was coming closer, peering under cabbage leaves. The chickens and ducks gabbled at him good-naturedly and lazily strutted out of his way. Thomas milked the cow dry and then stood.

*Lady, could you give me some of that nice warm milk?* Corwin asked.

Suddenly, one of the cabbages exploded, or so it seemed to Corwin, but it was only Henry finding the broody hen. The child dropped the basket and ran. Too late. The chicken, enraged by motherly feelings, went for him, flapping and striking at him with her beak. The little boy screamed.

Thomas dropped the bucket and ran across the yard, shouting and waving his arms. Milk splashed on the ground, but the pail did not overturn. The hen scooted back to her nest among the cabbages. Thomas scooped up the wailing Henry, blood gushing from a slash in his calf, and carried him into the house.

The pail of milk stood unguarded. Corwin scurried around the edge of the yard, picked up the pail, and crouched behind the fence. He drank his fill and thanked the Lady, feeling not a little guilty about Henry, still shrieking in the house. The bucket was still three-quarters full. He crept up cautiously, and put it back. He slipped over the edge of the ravine and crouched, watching. Chaos still reigned inside the house; the baby crying now, as well. The basket of eggs lay on its side, not more than twenty feet away, tempting Corwin. Silently, mindful of that devilish hen, he crept over to it. There were five eggs. He took one.

"Mummy! There's a faery in the garden!"

"Not *now*, Elyn, we've no time for your nonsense. Go to the attic and gather cobwebs. Your brother's bleeding!"

Corwin looked up. The girl stood framed in the half-opened doorway, frozen, staring at him.

*Mind your manners.* He was not sure whose thought that might be, but he obeyed. Slowly, he stood and bowed, and then ran to the edge of the ravine and dropped over. He landed halfway down the steep slope, missed his step, and slid down the rocky slope. His foot caught, and he tumbled forward, his mind focused on preserving the precious egg. Pain seared through his ankle.

*Ksh!* Aelvan stood at the bottom of the ravine. Corwin's foot was wedged in a crevice, and twisted at an odd angle. He had saved the egg, though, cupped in his hand.

*Want an egg?* Corwin asked.

Scowling, Aelvan climbed up from the stream bed and stood next to Corwin. *Stupid* quetan. *You will be the death of us all.* But he took the egg, expertly broke it, and sucked out the contents.

Corwin painfully pulled his foot from the crevice. The ankle had swollen and a bruise had already begun to form. He tested it, cautiously putting weight on it, and winced.

Aelvan's fury seethed through Corwin's thoughts. *How will we bring enough grain? Ranell and I cannot carry it all and Dunwadi as well.*

*Leave me here to mend while you get them. It will be four days at least until you return.*

*Not here. Too close.* Aelvan put his arm around Corwin's waist and helped him climb down.

*She is almost ready.*

*What? Who, the Lady? Ready for what?*

In response, Aelvan only glared at him and shut his thoughts down entirely.

\* \* \*

Corwin spent the next four days alone, in the ravine, with a pile of nuts and roots that Aelvan had foraged for him before leaving. They had found a place where the waters had cut an alcove, not enough to be called a cave, but enough of an overhang to keep prying eyes away. Corwin kept his ankle submerged in the stream, even though it smelled of cow and chicken. The coolness soothed his ankle and brought down the swelling. Twice a day, he limped upstream, to where a smaller, clean spring bubbled into the larger one. There, he drank. Although his ankle was still bruised and painful to the touch, he could walk without limping by the time Aelvan returned with the others.

The sun drew low. He found their thought.

*If we don't wait, we will have to return on the full of the moon.*

*No, they will use the full for their harvesting, working long after the sun has set. We can hardly be out there gleaning while they are swinging scythes.* Corwin, in his mind's eye, saw the flash of gleaming blades and felt the others shudder.

*Should we wait until after?*

*No. Do you not see the clouds? There will be rain in three days' time and we must have the grain gathered and sheltered by then. There is no choice.*

*Where are you?* Corwin asked.

*Not far.* This thought was Ranell's.

*At the farm where you took the egg.* That was Aelvan's. *Meet us at the field.*

Corwin climbed the bank above him and cut along the hedgerow at the top of the cow's pasture. The field, with its flattened stalks, lay before him. He crouched in the shadows, waiting. As the shadows lengthened toward sunset, they came to him. Aelvan carried Dunwadi; Ranell, the sacks.

Aelvan crouched about ten feet from Corwin. Ranell put down the sacks and helped Dunwadi sit on them. She stayed close to Dunwadi, smoothing the elder's hair, offering her water from a flask. Aelvan settled himself between Corwin and the women and glared.

*What now?* thought Corwin.

*She is almost ready.* Dunwadi thought.

He peered over Aelvan's shoulder. Dunwadi was smiling, Ranell her back to them, pulled food from a sack.

*All these years and I will never be one of them. My best efforts only slow them, cause them pain. I don't understand anything. Lady, why am I here?* Feeling lost, Corwin sat watching the wind ruffle the ripened wheat.

*The Lady is wise,* Dunwadi answered. *Her acts are never purposeless. You will see.*

* * *

The ants filled both sacks for them, and Corwin didn't step on any. That was something. As the eastern sky lightened, Aelvan carried Dunwadi. He insisted that Ranell walk in front of him, carrying one of the sacks. Corwin followed Aelvan, carrying the other sack. At the place where Corwin had stayed, they rested.

*It is better to fare at night. Fewer* quetan. *Fewer hunters.*

Corwin nodded. Ranell unpacked the sack that hung from her belt, bringing out bowls and smaller sacks that held food.

Corwin had an idea. He held out his hand to Ranell. *Bowls.* He took two. *Back soon.*

184

He climbed the slope. His ankle twinged faintly. He reached the top. The cow had begun her slow progress to the gate. He ran, crouching, toward her.

"Shhhh," he whispered as he reached her and put his hand on her flank. She did not seem to mind, or notice, and continued down the hill toward the gate. She reached the gate and stopped. He put the bowls beneath her and began milking, hoping that she would feel no need to call the boy from the house.

His ruse worked. The cow stood placidly as Corwin worked to relieve the pressure in her udder. He squirted milk until the first bowl was full, then aimed the teats toward the second. The cow moved her hoof. Startled, he put the first bowl behind him and continued on the second. He filled it, and still there was no movement from the house. He put the second bowl beside the first and squirted milk into his mouth, feeling the creamy bliss of it on his tongue, down his throat, filling the gaping ache in his belly.

A rooster crowed. He heard the creak of the farmhouse door. Regretfully, he let go of the teat, grabbed the bowls, and scurried off in a half-crouch, careful not to spill a drop. Before he had gone ten paces, the cow, puzzled by her still-full udder, mooed.

"Thomas! The cow!" Life went on in the world of the *quetan*.

Carefully, Corwin descended into the ravine. He handed the bowls to Ranell and Dunwadi, and could not help grinning at Aelvan's angry stare. Ranell poured the milk into the two empty bowls, distributing it evenly. Corwin took his bowl and poured half of its contents into the others. *I already had some.*

Ranell and Dunwadi gave thanks and smiled at him. Aelvan drank his milk in silence.

# Chapter 37

The first night's journey proved uneventful, but the next night the moon rose full. Corwin crept from beneath the bramble thicket where they had rested during the day. He turned and clasped Dunwadi's hand. Slowly, with Ranell's assistance, she emerged and stood beside him, leaning on his arm for support.

She turned her head and looked up at him. *This may be my last faring, you know.* She told them that every year, but still, he worried. He felt her hand, as fragile as a bird's claw. She was old, he knew, even by the standards of the *faer*. He knew from their farings in Dreaming that even Ranell, who seemed just past her girlhood, had a life that spanned many lives of men. Still, Dunwadi's frailty frightened Corwin. He could not bear her loss.

*Don't say that,* he answered.

*I didn't say anything. You know I can't talk.* She smiled at her joke. He returned the smile. His heart throbbed. He had never known such pure love.

Ranell crawled out and turned back for the sack of grain Aelvan handed her. Last of all came Aelvan. He heaved his sack, the heaviest, onto Corwin's waiting hands. Ranell helped Dunwadi onto Aelvan's back, and they took off downhill at a trot.

They crossed a series of low, rolling hills with little underbrush, the easiest going, and therefore the most dangerous. The trees towered overhead, their trunks spaced as evenly as the pillars of a cathedral. No natural wood, this, but the hunting park of a great noble.

This had its good and bad features. On the one hand, it protected the *faer*. Any peasant venturing into it to poach rabbits would find his life quickly forfeit. This left the rougher land encircled by it, the territory of the *faer*, free from prying eyes.

The price of this protection, however, was paid each autumn, when they had to fare through it to reap the Lady's bounty. Some years, they paid only in pounding hearts and a sense of dread as they crossed it. Other years, they paid in blood. *Interesting,* thought Corwin, *that* quetan *should think it is the* faer *who exact a tariff on them. You know that they believe that the Faerie Queen steals a human every Samhain to give to the Devil.*

*You people get everything backwards,* Aelvan replied.

They made good speed, reaching the tree where Attunna had been taken in long years past, now a rotten log. There, they stopped for Corwin and Aelvan to switch burdens. Corwin flexed his ankle. The soreness was coming back. He longed to find a cool stream and soak it. They set off into the moonlight.

Then the horns sounded.

*A night hunt! Run!*

There was no hope for it. It was the night of the Harvest Moon, and the hunters were taking advantage of it.

In the distance, Corwin heard the barking and baying. *May the Lady preserve us!* His ankle throbbed with each step and he rued bitterly his carelessness and recalled Aelvan's words: Ksh*! You will be the death of us all.*

*Help me, Dunwadi.*

The hounds were louder now, and he could hear the thud of horse's hooves, too many to count, in the distance. He felt Dunwadi's thought turn inward.

A great stag flashed across his path before them. The does that followed him surrounded them. Corwin ran, for a moment in the middle of the herd, and then they, too, followed the stag.

*What hunter will follow a lone boar when a herd of deer offer themselves?*

He ran, limping now, with Ranell and Aelvan far ahead. It was still a mile to the river. Ankle throbbing, he ran on.

Behind him, not as far behind as he would have liked, he heard a confusion of dogs, men, and horses. Then the hunt moved on, after the deer.

But not all of it. He heard the baying of three hounds that did not fade with the rest.

*Dunwadi? I cannot outrun them.*

*Do your best,* she replied, and he felt her go within again. Moments later, a boar fled across their path. *Thank you, my brother.*

Again, a moment's respite as the dogs milled and the riders argued. Then came the words Corwin dreaded.

"You take that one; we'll go after the other. What a feast we will have!"

*Run, Corwin! Aelvan, help us!*

The river was near. Corwin could hear the splash of the water. The hunters grew closer, the hounds louder. Aelvan ran back toward them. The hooves thudded. The dogs were nearly upon them. There was no time to shift Dunwadi from his back to Aelvan's.

*Run, fool, to the river!* With that thought, Aelvan ran past them, straight into the dogs.

There was no sound, as Corwin ran into the brush at the riverbank, save for the snarling of the dogs as they attacked. There was no sound, as Corwin stepped into the blessed coolness of the stream, save the whickering of the horses and the cursing of the hunters as they pulled up short where the dogs were savaging Aelvan. No sound from Aelvan reached Corwin's ears as he climbed the further bank and Ranell rushed past him to retrieve Aelvan's sack from where he had dropped it.

But the pain tore through Corwin. He felt teeth tearing his flesh.

*Lady, defend me!* came Aelvan's anguished thought.

"Back, Cael, back, Angus!" came the voice of the hunter. The dogs fell silent. "You stinking serf! Whose chattel are you?" A pause. "Speak! It is death for you to be here. Will you tell me and die quickly, or defy me and be left to the dogs?"

The pain throbbed through Corwin's limbs and his belly. He placed Dunwadi on the farther bank of the river. Defying the pain, he turned back.

*No, Corwin.* This came from Dunwadi.

*I must. I cannot leave him in their hands.* He passed Ranell, struggling back toward him, burdened with Aelvan's sack.

*No! Corwin! They will take you! Do not make his sacrifice for naught.*

*Aelvan! I am coming!*

*Idiot! Run! Take them to safety!*

"Cael! Angus! Get him!" A wave of pain hit Corwin, tearing through him, doubling him over, as the dogs tore into Aelvan.

*She is nearly ready. The Lady has chosen you, not me. You must live, so the* faer *will live.*

*Aelvan!*

*Protect them as I have.* And with that, Aelvan's thought ceased. Ranell grasped Corwin's arm and led him back to Dunwadi.

Clouds gathered across the moon's face. The dogs snarled, then grew silent. Dunwadi gave her judgment. *Ranell, take the lighter sack home, then come back for us. The grain must be sheltered before the rain begins.*

Corwin sat curled in a ball, rocking, his thought too anguished to form. He felt Dunwadi's hand, then Ranell's upon his back.

*I did this. I am responsible for his death.*

*No, Corwin. It is the will of the Lady.*

*NO! I will be the death of you all. He foresaw it.*

He felt Dunwadi's thought intertwine with his and lift him from his pain into the blessed bliss of the Lady.

# Chapter 38

That winter, they ate with salt tears to season their gruel. Only three remained: Dunwadi, Ranell, and Corwin. Again, the grain did not last long enough. The Dreaming was deep that year, as Dunwadi took them far within her memories, sharing ones that she had not in previous Dreamings. Pointed green leaves. Red underneath. Tiny prickly hairs. Square stems. Stops bleeding. Ants. Oak bark. Roots. Soaked three days and pounded into a poultice. Ants. Grain. A spiraling of stars. Ants. Grain. Ants. It was as though she felt the need to squeeze every drop of her knowledge into Corwin and Ranell.

Corwin felt the warmth of the sun on his face. He left the twisting maze of Dreaming and opened his eyes. He sat up and turned, light-headed after his long immobility. Ranell sat on the other side of Dunwadi. *Dunwadi?*

She did not answer. Ranell looked at him, wide-eyed. *Dunwadi?* Corwin put his cheek up to her face. He felt the faintest of breaths. *Dunwadi?* They each took one of her hands and chafed it, willing life back into her.

Dunwadi's eyelids fluttered. She looked at Ranell. *Fare well, little one.* Her eyes shifted to Corwin. *She is ready.* Then she smiled, and was gone.

Corwin looked at Ranell, and she at him, tears welling from her deep brown eyes and trailing down her cheeks. Suddenly, he understood. The knowledge welled from the core of his being. *Ranell, who had been like a sister to him; Ranell, the youngest of the* faer*; Ranell, the only woman of the* faer *young enough to conceive. She is ready.*

She looked deep into his eyes. *Yes, Corwin.* Then she leapt to her feet and ran from the cave.

His mind sat stunned. His body had no misgivings. He jumped to his feet and followed. She flew ahead of him through the forest. He ran, heart pounding, breath coming deep and slow. His mind seemed to be off to one side, watching as his pumping legs, his lungs, the branches swaying over his head and the first budding leaves of spring all danced.

189

Ranell ran. Their bodies, although twenty strides apart, shared the same rhythm with the leaves dancing overhead. A doe, startled, ran from them, her fawn at her heels. Overhead, a hawk wheeled and dived—all a part of who and what they were, who and what they were about.

Corwin could feel the air that had touched Ranell caressing him. Fifteen strides now between them. He, Corwin, would carry on the lineage of the *faer*. Twelve strides.

She reached a river and splashed across, the water up to her thighs, slowing her. Ten strides now. He hit the water as she reached the other bank and willed himself to move in tandem with her, to keep his legs moving in the same rhythm as hers, despite the resistance of the water.

He left the river, eight strides behind her, now six, as his longer strides closed the gap. Somewhere in the distance, his mind protested that he could not do this, that he had to be weak, dizzy from the Dreaming and the long fast. His body refused to listen. Now two strides, now one. He clasped her waist. She turned toward him. He kissed her. They were falling, falling, and were one.

# Chapter 39

A frost hung in the air that day, and heavy snow clouds crept down from the north. Corwin strode through the forest. His hair unkempt, bleached nearly white at the ends, crowned by holly. He wore the garb of the *faer*: a simple homespun shirt, leggings of rabbit skin, a cloak of faded green and shoes that left the track of a boar. Ranell, at his side, matched his stride with the tracks of a deer, her belly great with his child. Corwin no longer knew how long he had been among the people of the Lady. He had come to share their endurance, their oneness with creation. His eyes shone with the same fierce joy.

*Are you weary?* he asked. They had spent the better part of the day gathering such food as the autumn woods provided. The heavy sack on his back was filled with hazelnuts and hers was laden with roots. Corwin had snared rabbits and squirrels to make furs for her comfort and buntings for their child. These were already arranged in the Lady's cave.

*Of course not. I'm not the baby, remember?*

Corwin smiled, but underneath his joy, worry gnawed at him. Would there be enough food to last the winter? True, with only the two of them to share the forest's bounty, there would be more to go around than in previous years, but Ranell would be nursing. He remembered still how Acha had nibbled constantly when she nursed her bairns. They could not enter the Dreaming with an infant to be fed. Wouldn't it be better to find Dylan's house now, before the child was born? He looked at Ranell, knowing that she had read his thoughts.

*No, Corwin. I'll not live in a box.*

*Is it really so different from living in a hole in the ground?*

She looked away and strode angrily though the forest. He had to speed his pace to keep up. *How could I live, surrounded by the* ksh?

191

Underneath the anger he felt her fear, the well-earned fear of going among his kind, the kind that had so thoughtlessly murdered her kin, at times with a cudgel or a sword, at times by the theft of the land and its bounty, at times by the spread of sickness.

*You are young, and beautiful. It counts for a lot among my kind. I am sure Dylan would welcome you.*

*No, Corwin.*

He tried another tack. *If the child is to teach the* quetan, *how can he do so without living among them?*

*How will she know our ways if she grows up living among them? What would she have to teach? No, Corwin, I cannot live among your kind.*

*I know. I love you.* He surrendered to her. That thought—*I love you*—sang through his being and underscored his every thought. She was carrying his child. It had been centuries since any woman had conceived among the faer. The Lady's reason for choosing him was, at last, revealed. He would keep the lineage of the *faer* alive. *But for how long?* The thought slipped out.

*Corwin! Leave off!*

*I must think this through. I'm* quetan, *remember? This is how we deal with problems.*

*The Lady, Corwin; the Lady will take care of us.*

*The Lady sent me, Ranell. Consider that.*

*No, Corwin! What life would I live there? The Lady will provide for us. She always has.*

*The Lady has watched you all die, Ranell.* He regretted it the moment he thought it.

*Not all!* Ranell dropped her sack and ran from him. He picked it up, but burdened with both, he could not keep up with her. *Ranell!* He felt her rage and grief. *Come back.*

*No!*

*I don't want to leave you alone.*

*Enough. I need to be alone right now. I'll stop at the stream and drink. You go on ahead and build a fire.*

*It's their hunting season. I don't want to leave you alone.*

*I'll go to the stream near the oak glade. I can hide in the hollow log if I need to. Anyway, they make so much noise crashing through with their dogs and horses, we'd have heard them by now if there were any about.* Corwin sniffed the air. The chill north wind carried no scent of a hunting party.

He turned and trotted obediently up the hill, leaving the tracks of a boar.

\* \* \*

192

"I don't like it," said the huntsman. "A deer and a boar together. It smells of faery magic. We are within their lands. This will not end well."

"Faeries," snapped the mighty lord. "Arglebargle. I'll not spend the day out here freezing my arse off to come back empty-handed. The overlord brings his court to my castle tomorrow. You don't think I can feed them all chicken? What would they think of me?"

"My lord, the game is not so plentiful in these parts as in your father's day."

"And I'll not have it said that so renowned a hunter as my father can have a son who comes home empty-handed. Ride on." There were just the two of them, and only five dogs, kept strictly to heel. They rode northward at a walk, closely regarding the tracks.

"Look, my lord," said the huntsman when they reached the parting of the tracks. "The doe goes down toward the stream, but the boar keeps on. Shall we follow her?"

The lord thought a moment. Killing a boar would bring more renown, but with only two hunters and five dogs, there was no guarantee that the boar would lose the engagement. "After the doe," he said. "Let loose the hounds."

\* \* \*

Corwin reached the Lady's cave and placed the sacks full of food in the back. It was small, only four paces across, but the entrance bent toward the south, protecting it from the wind. He'd worked hard hunting, and gathered leaves for a soft bed. Ranell had worked with him to tan the skins and sew them together into warm blankets—a big one for them and smaller ones for their child. He started a fire in the shallow hearth, so that the space would be warm when Ranell arrived. All was ready, all prepared for the birth of their child, but satisfaction and fear warred in his heart. The child would come to them, but then what?

Then he heard the baying, and his heart froze. He ran out of the cave and up over the crest of the hill, directly toward the glade, his heart pounding. As he raced across the broad valley, past the Mother Holly—he could hear the thud of hoof beats in the distance. After he crested the second ridge, he saw the pursuit beneath him, through the sparse, leafless undergrowth. Ranell had reached the glade and was struggling to hide in the hollow log. The hounds, baying and growling, leapt at her. One caught hold of her foot. The hunters had not yet caught up with them. Corwin stooped, grabbed a heavy fallen branch, and ran onward. Then he was among them.

He raised the branch over his head and brought it straight down on the dog that had hold of Ranell. It yelped in pain and fell to one side, whimpering, its back legs motionless. The others wheeled to meet his attack. He swung again and swept the rightmost dog into its neighbor as the branch broke with a crack. He stabbed at a third dog with the remains of the branch as the other two leaped for him. He went down under their impact and felt their teeth in his left arm as they landed in a squabbling heap. He felt for the stone knife in his belt, grasped it, and slashed wildly at the dogs.

One yelped and loosed its grip, but the remaining three gnawed at him. He plunged his knife into the eye of one, and slashed at the other two in a crimson fury. They loosened their grip on him as he heard the sound of hoofbeats. He ran from the glade and concealed himself behind one of the huge oaks that lined the edge of the glade like rough gray columns.

"God's breath!" whispered the mighty lord, as he viewed the whimpering remnants of his cry of hounds. The huntsman dismounted and knelt to read the tracks.

"It was the boar." He crossed himself. "There is evil magic at work here. In all my years hunting, I have never heard of a boar come to rescue a doe." He dispatched the paralyzed dog with his knife and tossed its body into the brush. He mounted quickly and the pair spurred their horses, looking about nervously, leaving the whining dogs to limp home as best they might.

Corwin crept from his hiding place, his arms and shoulder burning where the hounds had savaged him. He ran to the log and slithered though the crevice to Ranell's side. As he embraced her, he felt her belly harden like a huge round stone against his.

*Ranell?*

*It's coming. It's going to be born soon.*

*Can you walk?* As he asked, he pushed himself out from under the log to better look at her foot. The dogs had torn off her shoe and left her foot a bloody pulp.

*I'll carry you.* He squirmed back out from the log and reached in to help her. *How far did you have to run?*

*All the way from the stream.*

*I love you.*

He carried her in his arms as the twilight deepened around them and snow began to fall. Corwin pressed on, hoping to reach the cave before the child would be born.

*Lady, help us,* he thought.

Soon, his arms began to stiffen and the fire of the wounds went out, replaced by a dull throb. The snow soaked his shoes and clung to them like a coating of lead. Ranell clung to his neck fiercely, the hardening of her belly becoming longer and more frequent. He began to stagger.

*Stop,* she said. *Put me down. We'll not make it at this rate.*

*No,* he replied. *You can't give birth here.*

*Corwin,* she began sternly, and then her thought suddenly stopped. Corwin was seized with terror as her thought disappeared.

"Ranell!" he said out loud. Her eyes were closed, her smooth brow furrowed, and she clung to his hand with such strength, he thought she might break it. After a moment the contraction passed.

*It's coming now. May the Lady protect me.*

Corwin looked around him at the snow-covered forest, hidden behind a screen of pale, falling flakes. In the growing darkness, he could barely make out the form of the Mother Holly, heavy with berries. He carried Ranell to it and they crawled under its rough protection, the sharp points of the fallen leaves piercing their hands, the bones of Ranell's ancestors hard beneath them. He took off his cloak and spread it on the ground for her. She lay on her side, curled in a shivering ball.

*You must help me off—*she began, only to be interrupted by another pang—*with my leggings,* she finished after the contraction had passed. *Quickly, Corwin.* He fumbled beneath her and there was a gush of hot liquid across his hands. She moaned softly. He smelled blood. *Dunwadi told me that when a baby comes out there will be a cord still attaching it to me.* She stopped again, breathing hard.

Corwin sat shivering, his hand on her belly. There was another liquid gush and the smell of hot blood. *This is a good place, Corwin. It's so warm here. It's a good place for a baby. Let me rest a minute, Mother, I'm so tired.* Her thought drifted off and left him.

"Ranell? Ranell!" He grasped her limp hand, and she squeezed his faintly in response. He could see nothing in the darkness under the holly, and the wetness had grown cold on his hands. He did not know what to do. "Ranell!" he shouted, close beside her ear. "Ranell, wake up! Ranell! The baby! Ranell?" He whimpered, squeezing her hand again. This time there was no answering clasp. She was cold. Her belly vast and soft. He clasped her to him, felt the child within kick twice, and then all was still.

\* \* \*

When the mighty lord took his guests hunting the next day, the forest was filled with the tracks of the boar. They never caught sight of it, nor is it recorded whether they found the bloodstained corpse of a pregnant woman beneath a holly tree.

195

# Chapter 40

Ksh*! I must run. She is in danger. Will there be enough food to last the winter? This makes three baskets of hazelnuts, and the beeches have not yet dropped their—Corwin, leave off. The Lady will provide. You are right, my love. The hounds run toward us, baying. The sound of hoofbeats grows nearer. We run from the stream to the grove and Ranell crawls into the hollow of the fallen tree. I crouch in the opening, knife in hand. The dogs attack and I slash at them, drawing blood, sending them away in dismay. Ksh! Blood. Ksh! Her blood is on my hands. No. The hunters ride up and I curl into a ball, concealing her, lowering my head so that only the moss and the ivy twined in my hair will show. The hunters sit on their mounts, aghast. "How can this be?" asks the mighty lord. "The boar has driven off my hounds, but no tracks leave this place." The huntsman's voice quivers with fear. "This place is accursed with faery magic. Let us leave, I pray you," and they depart. I turn to Ranell, and she smiles. Ksh! I must run. She is in danger. Ranell hides, curled in the hollow of the fallen tree. I run into the grove as the hounds enter. Bad dog! I shout. Heel! And the dogs obey, cringing before me. The hoofbeats approach and I stand motionless, my back against a tree. The hunters ride into the grove. They cannot see me, my head bent forward so that only the moss and the ivy twined in my hair and the gray of my leggings and cloak show against the gray of the tree trunk. They look in puzzlement at their dogs, who sit quiet, tongues lolling. I reach into the* vaira *and my thought thunders through the silence. How dare you enter the realm of the* faer*! Wide-eyed, they look about. I raise my eyes and glare at them. To them, it is as though a piece of the forest has taken shape as a person. Leave! I command. They turn their horses and flee. I must run. She is in danger. We enter the Lady's Cave, our burdens of hazelnuts and roots heavy. The cave is filled with the Lady's abundance, with only enough room left for us to lie down. I kindle a fire while she chops roots and greens for our dinner. She puts her hand on her belly. Corwin! The baby! Ranell. Oh, God. Ranell. The baby. Ksh! I must run. She is in danger. Her blood is on my hands. Ksh! I must run. Ksh!*

Corwin awoke sobbing, a mother's sweet, gentle hand caressing the tangles of his hair. He felt the smoothness of her dress, and the softness of her thighs beneath it as she cradled his head on her lap. He heard, not with his ears, her soft crooning, which wove itself into a lament.

> *Mouse King, Mouse King,*
> *I am bereft,*
> *My bairns are dying.*

His heart's woe flowed through the portals of his eyes as she sang to him. He remembered his time as a child with Tovan and the battle he had witnessed. The lines of men became the tides, ebbing and flowing red. He ground his teeth, anger filling him. *Fools! Let them destroy themselves.* With each pulse, the tide grew, his rage growing with it. The tides flowed across the land, across the seas, and finally engulfed the world. *Die! All of you! It is only what you deserve.* More images came. Men in strange dress, with coats of red, of blue, of gray, and then later of a dull mottled green, not unlike the color of the *faer* clothing. And the fighting—at first, things he could understand: knives, swords, and arrows, but later the sound of thunder and men exploding into bloody bits. *Yes! All of you! Die! You who would destroy, may it be done to you.* Finally, there was only a gray silence, with figures moving through it like charred ghosts.

He lay in bleak despair, and then felt the hand of the Lady stroke his brow. *Is that truly your will?* she asked.

Corwin felt the rage drain from his heart, leaving bitter dregs. Y*our people are all dead, and I a part of it.*

*No, child. It was not your doing.*

*But my people killed them. If this vision is true, they deserve to die.*

*Do they? All are my children, little* quetan. *The* faer, *the* quetan, *the four-legged, those of the waters and the air, those who move and those who do not, those seen and unseen.*

*But the* ksh—

*It is your blindness, and your gift.*

*A gift?*

*The* quetan *are blind to so much. They see only form, not the life that flows within it.* Her fingers smoothed the tangles of his hair. *But they also see what is not, yet can be, and they act upon that vision. Focused on that vision, they become ever more blind to all else. That is where the destruction lies.*

Corwin's vision shimmered and shifted, back to the tapestry he had witnessed the day he first met the *faer*. At first, he saw it from a distance — green, unchanging as a mountain. Then his vision grew closer and details emerged: the wind moving the trees; deer wandering forest paths, eating leaves; wolves on the hunt, rending deer flesh. He saw it a thousand times, a thousand thousand, on land, in the seas, in the air. The wolf dying, the vulture consuming; the vulture dying, the earth consuming, transforming dead flesh into fertile soil for the plants to drive their roots through, eating, eating, and being eaten in turn.

Revulsion swept through him.

*This is the* ksh, *the fear you* quetan *feel.*

He did his best to fight the fear, but the horror of Death crawled upon his skin.

*This is not Death, Corwin. This is Life.*

*But how can this be, when all is eaten and decays?*

*The* quetan *see only the husk of life, the outer shell. They see only form, Corwin. They cling to it, fear its loss, try to preserve it at all cost, but they cannot. No being has such power. Form changes. Life endures. Join us.*

As Corwin watched, the tapestry began to shimmer. And then he felt it, thread-like roots, shining, penetrating his being, weaving him into itself: the *vaira*. Twining through his body, threading through the earth. He sank into it, finding warmth, sweetness filling his heart. He let his thought travel along it. Tendrils of light stretched from his fingertips, spiraling outward in glowing, knotted patterns, burying themselves in the soil, growing, entwining, seeking the depths of the earth. He felt his awareness rise, and spread, felt the wind move him, the sun bless him, the sweet rain fall and caress him as he released each drop to the ground beneath. He lay overwhelmed by the wholeness of it all, secure in its embrace, no longer alone, a child of the Lady, no longer the orphan, the one who does not belong.

*You were never alone.*

The shimmering web of light grew, filling his senses in a way he could not describe: not seeing, not hearing, nor smell, taste, or touch, but all of these and more; it held him in a secure embrace. He let his thought run along the threads, feeling the life of the forest, the shift where the wild realm of the *faer* ended and the tended lands of the *quetan* began.

The *vaira* grew thin there, losing the deep memories of the trees, its harmony stunted. At first this puzzled Corwin, but then it came to him: His awareness of the *vaira* had reached a field of wheat, and had become a single line, losing the rich complexity of the forest. He stretched his awareness further and found the village.

Like an angry swarm of bees, it hit him. All the thoughts of the inhabitants, his fellow *quetan* buzzing and swirling through his mind. *Why her, and not me? I'm sure the miller has shorted me and stolen some of my flour. Will the crop be good? It hasn't rained in a week. There's a buxom lass. I swear I'll kill him if he ever does that again. I've naught to feed the children. What am I to do?* A thousand thoughts, from a thousand minds, all weaving together, scouring the *vaira* like a handful of sand scrubbing a pot, drowning it out, obliterating it, as rough upon his ears as fingernails on slate, on his skin like needles of sleet striking it, like the burning of hot coals.

Corwin wept aloud, understanding in full, at last, the patience and forbearance of the *faer*, who had sheltered him, allowed him to share their food, and shelter, while bearing the burden of the onslaught of his thoughts. Guilt flooded him as he realized how it had driven Ranell to her death. He pulled his awareness back, fleeing to the solace of the forest.

He came back to himself, resting in the lap of the Lady, her warm hand stroking his brow. The *vaira* faded, retreating beyond his ken.

For a time, he lay stunned by what he had experienced, but his memories crept back, and tears again flooded from his eyes. *Ranell.* He felt her smooth skin pressed against him, her lips upon his. He saw her face, a thousand memories of her. How happy they had been, waiting for their child's birth, the child that would carry on the lineage of the *faer*. *My child, never to be born.* He groaned. *I miss them so.*

*They are with you always.* Again, the swirling light returned, the images shifting as quickly as the sun-dappled woodland floor on a windy day. He saw them all, and more: Ranell suckling their son; Dunwadi, Bartrym, Aelvan, Boronil, and the memories of their forefathers and mothers stretching back through the generations, everything he had learned in the cold, hungry time of the Dreaming.

*But the* faer *are no more. Your prophesy, it was false.*

*No, child. Not in the least.* Her hand smoothed his brow.

*But the child who was stolen never returned.*

*Were you not stolen by Tovan that day? Did you not return to us?*

The thought stunned him. *This was your will?*

*Even the wisest cannot see the way their truth will come to be, little* quetan. *My children are no more, but they live in you. Have you forgotten the lessons of your master?*

Corwin lay silent, feeling her hand stroke his hair. *My master?* The world of men had grown so distant. Philippe's face came back to him, and his words: *Corwin,* mon fils, *it is the task of the storyteller to make the world right.*

He looked back upon the strange and twisting path his life had taken. Rescued, then abandoned by Tovan. Found by Oswy, and then sent to work off his debt, which led to his learning to read, which prepared Corwin for his apprenticeship to Philippe, which brought him to Wales, and to the *faer*, each turn of the path marked by disaster and loss. This, then, was the reason. The *faer* and their ways would survive. The truth of their kindom, of their riches would remain, long after the castles of the mighty lords had crumbled into ruin and the mighty lords had become themselves a tale told for the amusement of children. *So strange are the ways of fate.* He felt the soft hand of the Lady stroke his brow, and wept.

*There is no fate, only the echoes of past deeds, rippling through time.*

Eventually, his tears spent themselves, and as he drifted into sleep, his head pillowed on the lap of the Lady, her crooning once again formed itself into words.

*Seven hundred years, fourscore and three,*
*Until your work see light of day.*

It hit him like a bolt of lightning. *Seven hundred years!?*

*Shhhhhh*—she hushed him. *It is but a night's dreaming to me. Your kind live in the blink of an eye. You are not here long enough to see the consequences of your making. May it then be that they will see.* Her voice faded, and as close as he might listen, he could not discern her words from the sighing wind.

* * *

Corwin awoke, shivering in his sodden clothing, his throbbing head pillowed on a stone. Bracing himself with his hands, he rolled to a crawling position, where he remained for some while. When the discomfort of the cold outweighed his tiredness, he opened his eyes to see the pair of stone feet that had served as his pillow. He rose to his knees and became, to any observer, a common pilgrim kneeling before the roadside statue of the Virgin.

After a time, in which he strove to clear his head of the nightmare from which he had recently awoken and swore that he would never again touch whiskey, he stood and turned his face toward Llanywth. He shivered and walked slowly: cold, hungry, barefoot.

The grass showed green in the rising sun and new leaves peeked from their buds on the branches. The faint bleating of sheep came from a far hillside, and he could see the new lambs, straggling white dots, following their mother's cloudlike forms.

*What a dream I have had.* He looked at the sun, rising over the hills. *My master! Has he taken ship without me?*

# Chapter 41

Fretting and mumbling to himself, he walked faster toward the town. He came to a village that he did not remember, a collection of half a dozen cottages and a cowshed. He crept around the verges of it, and was delighted to find three eggs where hens had laid them and took them, wondering at the lack of guilt with which he did so. He broke them and sucked out their contents and continued on his way.

The town lay at the foot of the hill, with the sea glinting beyond. He saw a new wall. How had they built it so quickly? As early as the hour might be, already carts moved through its gate toward the markets and carts departed, filled with barrels of fish. There were so many! This must be a feast, or some special market fair.

Corwin hastened through the throng, his urgency so great that he did not notice the way people pulled back from him, crossing themselves, staring aghast at his strange attire, wild hair, and the straggling leaves of holly tangled in it. The town seemed strange, bigger, with turnings and buildings unfamiliar to him, but he finally found the market square and crossed it hastily, bearing toward the western end and the street that he knew would take him to the harbor and past it to Gwyneth's seaside cottage.

"Let go of me, you great lummox!" The cracked voice of an old woman echoed down the alley toward Corwin. As he rounded the corner, he saw her at bay, her walking stick raised like a cudgel at the three young men who hemmed her in. They hovered around the aged beggar woman, staying just clear of the staff's reach.

"Now begone w'ye!" she shrieked. "I've nothing for the likes of you."

"Well, give us a kiss, then," said one. "A kiss from the lips of dear Rhodri's beloved."

The staff whistled down an inch from his nose and he stumbled back into his friends.

"Never!" she raged. "I wouldn't stoop so low. I am Lyneth, the beloved of Rhodri ap Anieran and I'll thrash any man who tries to make light of me!" The three young men drew closer to her.

201

"No!" Corwin shouted. How could this ragged hag be his beautiful, young Lyneth? The three looked his way and then began to draw back, repelled by the wildness of his appearance. Crossing themselves, they turned and ran.

Corwin stood, too stunned to move, as the crone hobbled toward him, leaning on her stick. Her back was bent, and her gray hair, straggling from beneath her kerchief, showed pale red at the ends. Her face, lined deeply, still held the outlines of Lyneth's as he remembered it. She smelled of whiskey.

"Thank you, young man," she said, squinting at him. "Not from these parts, I see. One might think you were one of the faery folk," she whispered, crossing herself. "You've need of a comb. And a good meal, I'll warrant. Have you broken your fast?"

Corwin shook his head, the eggs having made no dent in his hunger.

"Well, come then. One good turn deserves another, say I." She hobbled off. Corwin followed.

"Those wretched louts," she muttered, as they wound through the narrow alleys of the town. "Daring to touch me! I was Rhodri's beloved, you know. He singled me out, from all the women in the square, and carried me off on that great white horse of his.

"Such a masterful man," she went on, and Corwin realized that this was a continuing monologue with her; it would go on whether he stayed with her or not. "He took me off that day to an inn. 'The best of everything,' he says to the innkeep as we sweep in the door.

"'Yes, my lord,' says the little weasel-faced sot, and he brought it to us —jugs of wine, wheels of cheese, fresh-baked bread, and roasted pheasant —all just for us in the best bed in the house. Such a man was my Rhodri! None could gainsay him. He loved me. I know it. He'd have married me but for that weaselly, pimple-faced sot of an innkeep.

"Next morning, he's up at dawn and drinks another jug of wine. There never was a man who could hold his liquor like my Rhodri! And down the stairs we go, with the horse all saddled and ready at the door, when up comes that greedy bastard and says, 'Four shillings, my lord.'

"Well, Rhodri looks at him and the man is like to crawl up his own arse. 'Please you, my lord,' he whimpers, 'but I've a family to feed and tradesmen to pay.'

"'I'm the prince,' says Rhodri. 'You don't think I carry money on me, do you?'

"'Please you, my lord,' says the sniveling snot, but Rhodri will have none of it.

"'Bah, keep the wench for your pay,' he says and leaps on his horse and rides away like thunder.

202

"Well, you can believe he never had no satisfaction out of me! I thrashed him good and his servingman, too, and ran straight to the castle." She stopped, eyes glittering with satisfaction, and pulled a flask from her bodice. "Want a drink?" she asked. Corwin shook his head. She took an experienced swallow, refastened the stopper, and continued her tale.

"The idiot gatekeepers wouldn't let me in, not even a month later when I came back and told them I was carrying Rhodri's bairn. Laughed at me, they did, and told me to go round the back of the castle by the midden heap. The scullery maids were kind to me, though, and saved out scraps from the prince's own table. I never had to root through the heap like some of those other women. So, *my* Rhodri ate as good as the prince himself and was born a fine strong boy."

She took another sip. "In his sixteenth year, off he went to the castle to offer his service. They took him on, and he did well. By the time he'd been there five year, he'd become like to his father's right hand and all said there was none like him for strength and endurance, nor—and they would say this in whispers—was there another who looked more like Rhodri in his youth.

"The time passed, and Rhodri at last decided to take a bride. He'd always loved me. That's why he never married all those years, but this was different. This was politics. He was to marry Susanna, a daughter of Llewellyn, the great overlord himself. He chose *my* Rhodri to be among those who would escort her." She stopped and took another drink.

"How could she help herself, the poor little thing? She was barely fourteen, and Rhodri, he was near forty, and too much of a man for her. And then, when she saw my handsome young Rhodri, well, how could she help herself? They ran off together and came back home to me. And they were so happy! She sang the whole time, near a week it was, before the soldiers thought to look here.

"They came, ten of them, with some great ugly drunkard shouting commands from atop a white horse and seized my Rhodri and took him in chains to the castle. Susanna, they left behind. Her father would have naught to do with her either, for dishonoring him. Such a sweet girl. She died after the baby was born. I named him Rhodri, for my love's sake. . . . What's this?"

They had reached a wooden shed built on to the end of a warehouse. Corwin could hear the crash and clatter of falling objects within its thin walls. "If it's those boys, I'll—" Lyneth said, grasping her stick. She pushed the door open. "Rhodri!" she shouted. "What in God's name are you doing?"

"Where have you hidden it, Grandma? Where's my father's sword?" Rhodri turned to face them. Corwin gasped, for there, poised on the cusp of manhood, stood Rhodri, a young Rhodri, with a light in his eyes that his grandfather's had never known. Corwin staggered and braced himself against the doorjamb.

"Good lord, son, you can't go to the castle! Your father—"

"My father was a hero and his father a prince. I am the grandson of Llewellyn himself on my mother's side!"

"Rhodri, you're a bastard. They won't accept you."

"Galahad was a bastard, the son of Lancelot, and he was accepted at Arthur's court. He became a great knight, the one who found the Holy Grail."

"Don't be a fool!"

"Grandmother, I will do great deeds. I will fight for the right, as Arthur's knights did. You'll see. Don't stand in my way. I'll make them accept me."

"Rhodri!"

"I want the sword. I'll tear this place apart if you won't give it to me!"

Corwin could take no more. He staggered back into the street and sat, while the argument raged. He tried to calculate how long he had been gone, but could not count properly. He tried again and again, but the toll always came to well above thirty years. Thirty years! He rose and ran toward Gwyneth's house, in terror of what he might find there.

# Chapter 42

The cottage looked abandoned. The once-neat yard grew thick with weeds, chickens sauntering among them, pecking the dust. The door was closed, but a drift of smoke came from the chimney, so Corwin pounded on the door.

"Who's there?" called an old man's voice. "What do you want?"

"A stranger to these parts," said Corwin cautiously. "I seek word of the troubadour Philippe." Corwin heard footsteps inside, growing closer.

"Go away. There's no such person here."

"But he was. I know . . . I was told that he lived here. What has become of him?"

"Your voice is familiar."

"You're Dylan, aren't you?"

Silence from behind the door. Then: "And who might you be?"

"Corwin, who was apprentice to Philippe."

"Corwin? Corwin, who disappeared? *That* Corwin?"

"The same."

The door opened a crack. Dylan peered through. "'Tis the same Corwin, and not aged a day. You've need of a comb, though. Where were you?"

"Among the *faer*."

"You mean faeries?"

"*Faer*. Their name."

Dylan looked at him, eyeing him up and down, and finally nodded. "There is nothing left for me here. Can you take me to them?"

"Oh, Dylan," Corwin said, and the tears ran down his face. It was some time before he could form the words. "They're all dead."

Dylan nodded, the disappointment clear on his face. "So much we have lost. Come in. Break your fast. We have much to tell each other."

Corwin spoke while Dylan pottered about the hearth, cooking eggs and porridge, asking questions. Corwin started at the beginning, with his waking in the circle of toadstools and ended at the feet of the Virgin.

He talked while they ate, and while Dylan fed chickens and ground grain in a stone quern. He talked while Dylan kneaded bread and through lunch and the long afternoon, while he and Dylan sat beside a stream with fishing lines in their hands. He talked through dinner, as if all the words he might have formed in all the long time of his silence among the *faer* had come at last unstoppered and gushed forth. All this time, Dylan listened and nodded. At last, Corwin stopped. He took a deep breath. "Thank you for listening. And for feeding me."

"What a tale that will make," said Dylan.

* * *

A week later, Corwin stood in the market square, the crowd attentive. Dylan had lent him a comb, and in return for help with wood splitting and planting, had given him clothing. Further, Dylan had gathered the crowd and told them a tale. Now it was Corwin's turn.

"I wandered off on Samhain eve. I admit I'd had a bit to drink." The crowd chuckled. "When I woke in the forest, in the gray dawn, she was there, Ranell, of the *faer* folk, the People of Peace."

Two of the women in the crowd, sisters by their looks, glanced at each other, crossed themselves, and moved off in the direction of the cheese vendor. It was one thing to tell the tale of some person in the far past consorting with faeries, but to claim to have done so oneself was another thing entirely.

"She spoke no word to me, nor did any of the *faer* in the long years I spent with them, yet I heard her thought as she said to me, 'Follow.'"

"Tell us about her gossamer gown," said a child near the front. "Was it pink? What color were her wings?" Her mother hushed her.

"No wings," said Corwin, "and dressed in clothes of homespun flax."

"Bah," said the child. "This isn't a *real* faery story."

"*Faer*, not faeries," said Corwin, annoyed. At the back of the crowd, he could see Dylan shaking his head. The crowd grumbled. Some left. "This is not a faery tale!" Corwin shouted. "It is true, every word of it!" More grumbling. Most of the people crossed themselves. All left.

"They don't want the truth," said Dylan. "They want a story."

# Chapter 43
# Master Beecham

Again, Corwin stood in the market square, telling the tale of Murdoch he had begun so long ago. As before, he held the crowd enthralled, but this time, no fine lordling came along to interrupt him.

* * *

Murdoch and Robert, searching for Beecham the sword master, followed the scent of wood smoke until they came to a hut as rude as any peasant's. It stood in a small clearing, not far from where a spring tumbled out of a rock face. There was a thatched lean-to behind it, sheltering furs stretched on frames to cure, and at the far side of the clearing the wreckage of a great tree, fallen in some storm.

"Master Beecham?" called Robert, and knocked upon the door.

Murdoch heard movement inside. The door pushed outward. "Robert," said a deep voice. "What brings you here?"

"Urgent business for the king."

"I've given it up." The door began to close. "He knows that. Tell him to find someone else."

"He did. You're to train him."

The door stopped, and then opened a bit. Murdoch caught a glimpse of grizzled beard.

"Well, he's big enough. Looks more like a blacksmith than a knight."

"I am a smith," said Murdoch.

"Has Gwalhafed fallen so low?"

"He's to fight Velendruch's champion."

"Sir Brian Borrenough?"

Robert nodded.

"Ah . . . no wonder. Good luck, young man," he said and closed the door.

Robert scratched his head, then brightened. "Well, I've done my bit. See you later, smith."

"What?"

"Those were my orders. Deliver you to Master Beecham, then come back. Bring provisions once a week. Talking him into it is not my job. Must be yours. Good day." And Robert left, practically running back to the horses.

Murdoch knocked on the door. "Will you talk?"

"Why waste your time? You'd best leave with your friend."

Murdoch remembered the logic that induced him to inspect the swords. "I'll have to fight this Borrenough fellow whether I'm trained or not. You wouldn't want that on your conscience."

"Go see Tillin, or Jameson, or Crivins. There's a dozen sword masters in Gwalhafed."

"They're all busy training recruits. Velendruch is planning to attack."

"Ridiculous! Why would they want to upset the treaty?"

"Rolf's involved."

"Oh. That whelp. I hope Galeschin's thrown him in some dungeon."

"That he has."

"Good. So that ends the war."

"No, Ambrahad's still coming. The king thinks we're just a stop on the way to Amytans."

"Not again." Beecham's deep voice trailed off into a long string of profanity and he opened the door a crack. His graying hair was cropped short and his beard grew long. He stood half a head shorter than Murdoch, with broad shoulders and a scar across his cheek, half hidden by the beard. "Are you old enough to remember the times before the treaty?"

Murdoch nodded. "I lost my family. That much I remember."

"Amytans's troops or Velendruch's?"

"I couldn't say."

Beecham nodded. "I feel for you, smith, but I told you. I've given it up."

The door slammed shut. Murdoch heard him bar it. Murdoch pounded until his fist grew sore, but Beecham refused to answer.

\* \* \*

Beecham refused to talk and Murdoch refused to leave. When the sun set, he looked about for a place to sleep. He pulled down a great bearskin stretched on a wooden frame and used it for a pallet. He spread his cloak over himself and lay on his back, pondering his situation as the moon rose.

Could this be God's answer? That he was not to fight? But no, he had given his word to the king. So, did that mean he would be sent in untrained against an opponent whom even experienced swordsmen feared? Was that to be his punishment for breaking the vow? Perhaps he should give up and go home. But what of Joy? He fell into a fitful doze.

Murdoch heard the murmur of voices. The moon had climbed the ladder of the stars and stood near the top, peering down onto the world.

"It will make a difference," said the unknown voice, a woman's, scarce more than a whisper.

"I am surprised to hear you say this, Dunwadi," replied Beecham.

"I understand," she answered. "I am myself surprised, but the Lady's voice is not to be denied. The time of the prophesy has not yet come. The child who was stolen has not returned, but he will, and this man will be a part of the prophecy's unfolding."

Murdoch kept to the shadows as he crept around the side of the hut. Beecham sat on a log in the moonlight facing toward him. Dunwadi stood facing Beecham. She was small, and wore a shapeless shift. White hair, brilliant in the moonlight, hung down her back.

"The Lady wishes bloodshed? This is a new turn of events."

"No, not bloodshed, but its avoidance. This attack must be stopped, and your guest has been chosen to stop it. You may join us," she said to Murdoch without turning her head in his direction, startling both men.

Murdoch came out of the shadow and walked over to them.

"So," she said to Beecham. "You will train him in your art."

"Yes, Dunwadi."

She looked at Murdoch, her dark eyes piercing his soul. "And you will win."

"I will do my best."

"There is more at stake here than you know. The fate of us all rests in your hands."

Murdoch swallowed. The fate of Gwalhafed was burden enough.

She smiled suddenly, reached up, and patted his arm. "You need never fear a bee." She walked off chuckling. Murdoch was never certain afterward whether she had simply walked into the darkness or vanished.

"Bees?" asked Beecham.

"I've never been stung. An old man in my village kept a hive. I would go there whenever I could." He smiled. "It was the honeycomb he gave me that kept me coming back, but I learned much from him. But how did she know that? Who is she?" asked Murdoch.

"You wouldn't believe me, smith."

"You haven't lied to me yet, so far as I know. So, who is she, your grandmother?"

"She's *faer*."

"A forest faery? They are real?"

"*Faer*. They don't like to be called 'faeries.'"

"But what is she to you?"

Beecham thought for a moment. "Well, if there is such a thing as a faery godmother, she may be it. See that fallen tree over there?"

Murdoch looked, and nodded. Even in the dim moonlight, he could make out the silhouette of the massive, splintered stump.

"I was standing beside it when it fell, three winters ago. I got far enough away that it didn't kill me outright, but I was trapped, my leg pinned beneath it. It was close to noon, but before dark three of them came: a healer-woman named Mirna and two young men. By the time the men dug me out from under the tree, she had a fire burning and hot soup for me. They stayed a week and left me with the larder stocked, a pile of firewood next to the hearth, and another week's worth piled right outside the door. I asked them how they knew I was in trouble. Mirna smiled at me. Beautiful woman, that Mirna, and the best healer I've ever encountered. She said, 'Dunwadi told us to go to you.'"

"That tiny old woman was wandering around in the dead of winter and saw the tree fall on you?"

Beecham shook his head. "The legends say that the trees carry messages to them, whispering from branch to branch. That one might be true as well. Get some sleep. We begin your training in the morning."

# Chapter 44
# The Abbot and the King

When King Ambrahad and his army reached the gates of Granton Abbey, he found the abbot waiting for him, astride his horse.

"Good day, my son," Prydieu's arm swept in a benediction.

Ambrahad reined in his horse, and the column shuddered to a halt behind him. "Good day, my good abbot," he said.

"I ask a boon," said the abbot.

Ambrahad's eyebrows rose in surprise. "But of course."

"Last night, as I knelt in prayer, a vision came to me, a vision of Mary, the Holy Mother of God. She vouchsafed to me that I am to accompany you and your army, and my monks are to minister to their spiritual needs."

Ambrahad stroked his dark beard. If Abbot Prydieu were with him, it would send a message to Galeschin as to just whose side the Church was on. He craned his neck and noted the casks of wine in the cart. The wine alone would be worth letting Prydieu tag along. And best of all, if Ambrahad let the monks come, God would owe him a favor.

"I would be honored," he said.

* * *

The shadows grew long, and Abbot Prydieu walked through hordes of bustling soldiers; between rows of tents; past horses tethered to picket lines, grazing or munching oats in bags hung beneath their noses. One of his monks followed him, burdened with a crate filled with bottles.

The king's pavilion stood on the highest part of the encampment, on the newly planted field of some unfortunate farmer. The tent was dyed crimson, and black pennons with the red dragon of Velendruch stood on either side of the entrance. Three chairs were set in front of the pavilion, a table with goblets and a carafe set between them. The king sat in the most ornate chair. The curtain to the king's pavilion swept back, and Sir Brian Borrenough stepped out, ducking under the entrance. He straightened and stretched,

211

standing a foot taller than the opening. He bowed to the king, then the abbot, and took his seat at Ambrahad's right hand.

Prydieu sat and stared, breathing a silent prayer for whoever in Gwalhafed might oppose Borrenough.

Ambrahad smiled and offered a cup to the abbot. "Wine, Father?"

Prydieu nodded and took the cup, his diplomatic manners shattered by what he saw.

"Impressive, isn't he?"

Prydieu could only nod.

* * *

The servants cleared the fish course and served the meat. Abbot Prydieu watched as Ambrahad swirled the ruby wine in his goblet, sniffed the bouquet, and sipped. "Well, what do you think of it?"

"Quite tasty, and you say it will age well?"

"Indeed, Highness. I believe the tannins will accentuate the inherent nutty undertones. What do you think, Sir Brian?"

"Um," said Sir Brian. He drained his cup. "Good wine. More."

"I was concerned at first, that the fruity bouquet might overwhelm the dry aftertaste, but so far, it seems to be mellowing nicely as it ages. I believe, in twenty years or so, this will be a legendary vintage."

"Well, I find it quite tasty," said Ambrahad, having run out of adjectives. "Might I have another stoup?"

"But of course." The abbot gestured to the nearest servant, who poured for the king and Sir Brian, who had already drained his second cup. "I've three more bottles of this, and some marvelous port to go with the cheese course, from our abbey near Lisbon."

The abbot sipped his wine. The meat was served, thick slices of roast beef on trenchers. *Not yet,* thought Prydieu. *That knight could drink an entire regiment under the table. If Ambrahad is not sufficiently mellowed by the time the port is gone, I'll have to break out the brandy.*

Another sallet course followed, then cheese, then fruit, each with its own wine, then blanched almonds in a small dish, which the king and the abbot picked at as they discussed the breeding of warhorses and sipped Prydieu's brandy. A separate dish of nuts was brought for Sir Brian, who scooped up the contents in one swipe of his massive hand. The brandy bottle emptied. The king had not yet begun to slur his words. The abbot despaired of finding an opportunity to talk him out of his plans.

"Abbot," said the king, "we are engaged in a mission vital to the well-being of Velendruch. I have become aware that Galeschin has allied with Amytans in violation of our treaty. You are a man of wisdom. Have you noticed any signs in the heavens of late?"

*One must make a start somewhere,* thought Prydieu.

"I have always marveled at the way God expresses himself in signs and portents."

"But have you seen any lately?" asked Ambrahad.

"Two nights ago, it was cloudy, yet as I knelt to pray after Nocturns, the clouds were sundered and a falling star flew past the window of my cell. It could portend dire events."

"Which way did it fly?" asked Ambrahad. "From the east or the west?"

Prydieu considered, then decided that Ambrahad would most likely interpret a meteor from the east as favorable.

"From the west," he said.

Ambrahad frowned and took a gulp of brandy. "Still," said the king, "one must do what one must do. For the sake of the kingdom, of course."

"Of course. I thank God that I was born a second son, and that my brother, not I, must bear the burden of rule. War is a terrible thing."

"I like it," said Sir Brian.

"Of course," said the abbot quickly, "and it is to men such as yourself that we owe our safety. Still, I simply cannot imagine what Galeschin is thinking, forging an alliance with Amytans in violation of the treaty."

"Quite," said Ambrahad. "And so he must be taught a lesson."

"'Vengeance is mine, saith the Lord,'" said the abbot.

"Exactly."

*Not what that means.* Prydieu fought the urge to lecture Ambrahad and kept his voice gentle. "Still, what could have possessed Galeschin to throw away his advantage by allying with Amytans? I could see Rolf trying such a ploy. After all, the treaty guarantees him nothing."

Sir Brian choked on his brandy and said, "But—"

Ambrahad eyes threw daggers at him. Sir Brian closed his mouth and held out his cup for another refill.

Abbot Prydieu studied his brandy and appeared not to notice Borrenough's outburst. "It is entirely possible that Rolf is misleading you, and his talk of an alliance with Amytans is a stratagem to incite you to attack his brother for his own benefit. I would proceed carefully, Majesty."

Ambrahad glanced at Sir Brian and then at his hands before meeting the abbot's gaze. "Of course," he said.

"Fortunately, I have heard he is captive, and you will be able to question him."

Ambrahad spoke more quickly than usual. "Excellent idea, abbot. I shall certainly do that." He stood and stretched. "Goodness, it's late. Goodnight." He turned on his heel and swept past the curtain and into his sleeping quarters.

"Well, Sir Brian, I do not envy the men who might oppose you."

The giant knight smiled. "Thank you. I always—"

"To bed, Sir Brian!" ordered the king, popping out of his chamber like a rabbit from its hole. "Good*night*, abbot. Guards! See that Abbot Prydieu is escorted to his tent."

Prydieu smiled and made the sign of the cross before him. "Thank you for dinner, and God's blessing upon you. Majesty, Sir Brian, I bid you good evening." The abbot turned and left the pavilion, ignoring the two men who walked beside him, their hands on their sword hilts.

* * *

"Brother Albert," he asked, when he had returned to his tent and his escort departed, "what news of Eslenburg?" The city was the westernmost of Velendruch's allies, small in size, but rich, controlling the strait of Unlent, a finger in the eye of Amytans's imperial ambitions.

Albert, who had soldiered before repenting, had spent the evening swapping tales with the officers. "Word arrived last week to Ambrahad that the city had fallen to Amytans. The archduke's army besieged them for months. Then Amytans attacked by sea, sailing into the harbor under cover of night. They hurled flaming pitch at the ships tied to the docks. Duke Emond had no choice but to attack with his remaining ships.

"In the gray before dawn, Amytans's fleet withdrew, and Emond gave pursuit. Once out of the harbor, the rest of Amytans's fleet attacked Emond's ships from the other end of the strait. While all were distracted, a party of four bold men scaled the walls with grappling hooks. Three died, but the fourth, they say, still lives. He lost all his limbs, save one, but not before he opened the gate. Archduke Whisted had marched reinforcements up in the dead of night and threw them at the gate at dawn. The sea battle lasted two days, but the city was taken before noon of the first."

Prydieu sighed. An army of that size had not been raised in a week. No, Ambrahad had intended to violate the truce months ago, and now was using the loss of Eslenburg as a pretext. He crossed himself and said, "Let us pray."

# Chapter 45
# Cedrik

The sun rose high, sending needles of light through the newly leafed trees. They had been at it since dawn. Beecham brought his sword crashing down. Murdoch blocked it with his shield and forced him to take a step back.

"No. That won't work."

"Why not?"

"I can't match Borrenough's strength, and neither can you. He's as big as an ox and as strong as two. If you try that with him, he'll break your arm. Blocking with your shield or with your sword at right angles to your opponent will only work if you're the stronger. Then you can push to get him off balance, but that's not the case here. Try blocking like this." He held his sword at an angle, point downward. "This is called the Fool's Guard. Few understand its uses. Rather than meet force with force, use your sword to deflect his, then follow up by attacking where his sword is not. You'll find it useful against his *Drei Hewes*. Again."

"Dry ewes? He's got sheep?"

Beecham rolled his eyes. "It's German, you blasted peasant. *Drei*, three. *Hewes*, strokes—you know, like hewing a tree. The first will take off your sword arm the second your shield arm, and the rest will split what's left of you down the middle."

"Ah," said Murdoch. "Too bad it's not sheep."

Beecham shook his head and raised his sword. "Again."

Murdoch's sword sliced toward him. Beecham blocked, and wound his sword past Murdoch's to strike him. Murdoch was quicker. His blade flashed and Beecham was forced to step back.

"Good!" he said, and twisted his blade, deflecting Murdoch's thrust harmlessly over his shoulder. Murdoch shifted his weight and stepped to his left, and the point of his sword, levered against Beecham's, clipped the sword master's head.

"Ow!" Beecham roared. "Well done!" His sword slipped past Murdoch's and sliced toward Murdoch's shoulder. Quick as thought, Murdoch parried with the Fool's Guard, and deflected Beecham's blow.

"Good," said Beecham. "You learn fast, smith." He wiped the sweat from his brow. "Again."

The clang of their swords drowned the sound of horses' hooves. When next they stopped to breathe, they heard applause. Robert sat astride a horse, clapping. A second steed stood patiently beside his. "Is he ready, then?"

"As any man could be," replied Beecham. "And I'll have need of your horse."

"My horse?"

"I'll be coming with him."

\* \* \*

"But when do I see Joy?" asked Murdoch, when they left the eastward road toward Hirday and took the road leading to Gwalhafed Castle.

"Business before pleasure, smith," replied Beecham. "We've your mail to fit. Cedrik, the king's armorer, is the best. He'd be highly insulted if you passed him by after all his hard work."

"How long will it take?"

"Depends on how much fitting is needed. A day or two—"

"Well, come on, then." Murdoch spurred his horse to a gallop.

\* \* \*

Cedrik was not tall, although he might have been, had his back not curved like a shepherd's crook. His arms were massive, and he carried the bundle of ringmail as though it were a featherdown pillow. "Here," he said. "Let's start with this one." He dropped it onto the sturdy work bench with a crashing thud. "I've left the sides open so I could fit it to you."

Murdoch stood, wearing a *cuir bouilli*—a coat of boiled wool—with a padded cap on his head. He bent to let Beecham and Cedrik pull the mail coat over him, then stood. The coat came to his knees, and the sleeves stopped inches short of his wrists.

"All right, now, stand straight, arms out." Cedrik went over him like a tailor, twitching the ringmail so it would lie properly and taking measurements with his thumb. "Bend your arm. Good. Now raise your arms over your head. Six rows more around the arm. Arms out again." He took a bit of wire and twisted it to hold the side seam closed. "Now bend forward. Bring your arms down like you would on the third of the *Drei Hewes*. Eight more in the chest. Beecham's been working you hard, I see."

"Can we go now? I want to see Joy."

"His first set of mail," Cedrik said. "You'd think he'd be excited."

Beecham shrugged.

"We're not half done, smith. Give me your professional opinion of this." He beckoned to Murdoch.

Cedrik strode to a storeroom, his limping gait oddly graceful. He threw open the door. There, on a stand was an aventail of fish-scale plate sewed to leather. It glittered in the dim light of the workshop.

Murdoch reached out to touch it. The scales were identical, polished to gleaming perfection, and lay in overlapping rows that began an inch above where the helm would cover and extended over the shoulders and upper chest. "This is fine work. I've never seen anything half so well made in my life," Murdoch said.

"Let's try it on, then, and the helm." Cedrik took a plain bread loaf helm with a nose guard from a shelf.

At last they were done: the aventail, helm, and padding packed and the mail coat in the hands of Cedrik and his assistants, who would work all night to finish it.

"Can we go now?" asked Murdoch.

"Without your armor? Have you a death wish? Ambrahad is on his way. You may need to go straight into battle. Here, smith, eat. Rest. Tell me about her."

# Chapter 46
# The Truth Revealed

"Well, where is she?" Murdoch said as they dismounted in the courtyard at Hirday.

"Patience, smith," said Beecham. "You'll see her when the king wills it."

Murdoch glowered at him.

"She's a lady, smith, not some farm girl with mud on her clogs. Look at yourself! We've got to clean you up."

The gates of Hirday rumbled shut behind them. Guardsmen stopped, necks craned. Everyone was looking at them.

"Murdoch!" shouted Grimbold, from atop the parapet.

Murdock waved.

"Follow me," said a familiar voice. Murdoch turned. Tillin stood, smiling. "Your lady awaits," he said. "Let's get you cleaned up."

"She liked me well enough as I was when she last saw me," he grumbled.

"She'll like you better clean, trust me. You might even grow to like it yourself." They led Murdoch through a warren of passageways behind the armory to a chamber where a barber waited beside a tub of steaming water.

Murdoch stripped and eased himself into the scalding heat. Knots he'd grown accustomed to untied themselves in his arms, his shoulders, the calves of his legs. *I could* come to like this, he thought. Afterward, he sat wrapped in a sheet while the barber went at him with razor, comb, and shears. Then the sword masters returned bearing guardsmen's livery: black leggings and boots, a linen shirt, and a dark green surcoat with the ram's horn badge of Gwalhafed stitched on the front.

"No one would know you for a blacksmith now," said Beecham, and Tillin nodded.

* * *

"Time for bed, my little red bird," said Joy as she finished Alana's braid.

"Tell me a story," said Alana.

"A short one," said Joy.

"A long one," said Alana. Joy had been different today. Laughing, happier than Alana had ever seen her, but distracted somehow, not really paying attention. All she had talked about was Murdoch.

"Tomorrow, certainly," said Joy, "but tonight your father has commanded that I attend a ceremony."

"A short one, then," Alana agreed, "but two stories tomorrow."

"We'll see," said Joy, laughing. "How about this one? Once upon a time, they lived happily ever after."

"That's not a *real* story, silly Joy."

"Perhaps not. Let's see. One day the Mouse King woke up and the sun shone brightly. The birds were singing, and everyone was happy. So they had a feast all day and sang songs all night in the moonlight. The end."

"That's not a *real* story."

"Why not?"

"Nothing exciting happened."

"Feasts are exciting. Don't you get excited at Yule?"

"Yes," said Alana, winding the end of her braid between her fingers. "But in a real story there's more than just *good* exciting things. There has to be a scary part."

"Well, sometimes, even in storyland, nothing happens. Life just goes on. The Mouse King can't be having adventures all the time. He'd get tired out."

Alana yawned. "I want a real story."

Joy looked at the lengthening shadows thrown by the light from the narrow window. Her love had returned, and was waiting to see her. She must get ready for the ceremony. "Two stories tomorrow," she said, "or better yet, we'll each make up a story and tell it." She smoothed the coverlet and kissed Alana's forehead. "Now, think hard upon the story you will tell me, my little red bird."

Joy let herself out of the chamber, dizzy with delight, and pulled the key to the garderobe from her bodice. Lord Hounshel had given it to her, with instructions to choose whichever kirtle suited her fancy. She hurried down the hall opposite Alana's chamber door and turned right at the next joining.

The castle had filled in the past few days, as Galeschin's allies arrived. Knights and their squires strode the hallways, making it difficult to get anywhere quickly, what with the need to exchange curtsies for bows every few feet. Tall Lord Mallow and Lord Cirgan, shorter by a head, whose fur-trimmed collars marked their rank, came out of a doorway a few feet ahead of Joy, intent upon their conversation. She fell into step close behind. The others stepped aside for the two nobles and she swept along in their wake.

"Well, what else could the king do?" said Mallow. "Could you best Borrenough? I know that I could not."

"Still, a blacksmith?"

"Tillin speaks highly of his talents. They all do, and he's had Beecham's undivided attention for a month."

"Borrenough's been at it his whole life. What are a blacksmith's chances?"

Mallow sighed. "If the smith wins, the whole thing will be averted. At the least, he will buy us time. Galeschin has messengers on fresh horses stationed every ten miles from here to the Amytans border. If he fails, we must then resist with all our strength until help can come from Amytans."

"*If* he fails? You know as well as I that no one's ever bested Sir Brian."

"Yes. Galeschin's no fool. He knows it's better to sacrifice a pawn than a knight."

They had reached the garderobe. Mallow and Cirgan walked on, but Joy stood, stunned. Numbly, she unlocked the door and hung the padlock on the hook inside.

# Chapter 47
# Oath Taking

The sword masters led Murdoch through winding back passages, coming out at last to the main stair. The high-arched door stood closed before them, two men in glittering mail and green tabards standing guard.

Beecham picked a piece of lint off Murdoch's shoulder. Tillin eyed his tabard and twitched it straight. He nodded to the guards, who swung the doors back.

A roomful of faces turned toward them: allies who had come to the castle's defense, Hounshel's troops, and the entire castle household, right down to the clot of scullery maids huddling in the back. The murmuring voices stopped. Necks craned.

Tillin and Beecham stood on either side of Murdoch. "Left foot first," whispered Beecham. They started walking. The crowd parted. At the far end of the room, on a low dais, the king stood before them. Beside him stood Joy.

No woad-dyed dress or apron, no servant's kerchief on her head. She wore the dress of a lady, a crisp white underdress peeking from beneath a kirtle that had belonged to Janet, Hounshel's daughter, who had been Galeschin's queen. Deep green it was, the color of Gwalhafed, with gold embroidery on the bodice and the hems of the trailing sleeves. Her hair, put up in complex braids, glowed like polished copper in the candlelight. Her face was as pale as death.

*She's not smiling*, thought the smith.

\* \* \*

Joy watched as Murdoch strode toward the dais between the two sword masters, taller than either, broader of shoulder, as handsome as any knight. Her heart pounded for love of him, and tears welled in her eyes. *What have I done?*

\* \* \*

They reached the dais. "Stand on the first step and take a knee," whispered Tillin. They knelt in unison with him.

"Murdoch Smith," said Galeschin. "Have you prepared yourself to be our champion?"

"Yes, sire," he whispered.

"Speak up," whispered Beecham. "Everyone in the room must hear this."

"Yes, sire!"

"Murdoch Smith, do you swear to defend Gwalhafed to the utmost, to the death, if needs be?"

He looked at Joy. Tears streamed down her face, but she held his gaze. What could he do, here in front of the entire household? He had already given his word to the king. He could not take it back now. "Yes, sire!" Murdoch shouted.

"Receive your sword, Murdoch Smith." Galeschin held the sword out to him, its three feet of polished steel gleaming.

Murdoch took it. As Beecham had promised, it felt as light as a feather. *What am I doing? My vow . . . it is broken.*

"Rise, Murdoch," said the king. Murdoch stared at the sword in his hands, transfixed.

Tillin nudged him. "Stand up," he whispered. Murdoch stood.

"Lady Joy," said the king, and she stepped forward. She held a belt in her hand, leather, black as night, with three silver disks on it, and a scabbard attached, covered in Gwalhafed's green with gold embroidery she had worked herself.

\* \* \*

Her hands trembled at the touch of him. She wanted to press herself against him, to be one with him, so that even should he die, she would be with him. *For me. He would do this thing for me.* The king stood, watching. A thousand eyes looked on. She finished fastening the clasp. Reluctantly, her hands returned to her sides.

\* \* \*

Murdoch stood, fascinated by the play of light on the intricate locks of her hair as she bent to her task. He had never seen anything so beautiful. He longed to throw himself at her—no, that would not do in this room packed with people. No, to kneel at her feet, to speak poetry, fine words that would befit her beauty, to let the feelings that soared through his heart pour forth, but they surged and crashed against his thick peasant's tongue and could find no way out.

"Turn around," whispered Tillin. In unison, they turned.

"Behold Murdoch, our champion!" cried the king. The crowd roared his name. Behind him, Joy burst into tears.

* * *

"She was crying!" Murdoch strode the length of Tillin's room above the armory.

"Women do that." Tillin, seated on the bench, pulled his feet out of Murdoch's way. He reached for the loaf on the tray and cut a slice.

"She's changed her mind. She doesn't want me."

"Women cry for all kind of reasons: happy, sad, not getting their way, getting their way, too, for that matter," said Beecham.

"But she didn't smile when I walked in."

"She probably didn't recognize you without your customary layer of dirt," offered Tillin.

"But what can I do? If she wants someone else, I couldn't force her to marry me. How could I? She'd not be happy and—"

"If you want to worry," said Beecham, putting down his tankard, "try worrying about Sir Brian. Unless you can get past him, all this talk of whether or not you'll marry anybody is so much hot air. Sit. Eat. Have some of this ale. After dinner, walk off your nerves. Then get a good night's sleep."

Murdoch sat. He tore the leg off a roast chicken and began to gnaw it.

"Murdoch," said Beecham, his voice, for once, gentle. "Have you not thought that she might be frightened? And would she fear for you if she did not care for you?"

* * *

Joy could not sleep. She lay in the bed beside the sleeping princess and tears ran silently down her cheeks, soaking the pillow. *What have I done? I have condemned this man to his death. And why? Because he loves me.* She burst into tears again. She could not sleep. She slipped from beneath the covers and through the bedcurtains. By the light of the candle left burning in its sconce, she found her shoes and gown. Queen Janet's kirtle lay folded on the chest where she had left it. She would take it back to the garderobe. It would be something to do to stop the thoughts running through her head.

She slipped from the room and down the hallway opposite the door. A guardsman dozed, leaning back against the wall, head lolling on his shoulder. The lanterns at the hallway intersections burned low. She reached the further hall and turned right. At the garderobe door she stopped and pulled the key from her bodice. The click of the lock echoed from the stone walls of the deserted hall. She pushed the door open. The hinge creaked. By feel, she put the lock on its hook.

*I should have thought to bring a taper.* The small room was dark, with only a faint smudge of moonlight where the narrow window pierced the wall. She felt for the dress stand and slipped the kirtle over it. Footsteps sounded in the hall. The guard, no doubt, had awakened and was making

223

his rounds. She tweaked the shoulders of the kirtle and felt along the seams, hoping that it hung straight, and turned to the door.

It was filled by a form too big to be a guardsman.

"Murdoch?" she said.

* * *

He knew her voice. "Yes, my lady," he said, and went down on one knee.

She burst into tears.

It was not what he had hoped for. *Maybe I should have knelt on the other knee. Have I given insult? She is a lady, daughter of a knight. She knows these forms, and I do not. How could I presume . . . ?*

"Forgive me," she said.

*This is it. She will tell me now. I have been a deluded fool, looking far above my station.*

"Were it not for me, you would be safe in the armory repairing swords."

He did not know what to make of this. "My lady?" he said.

"Oh, Murdoch," she sobbed. She ran to him and embraced him. Her tears fell hot on his scalp. "I'm so afraid I will lose you."

"Oh," he said, and his fears left him.

# Chapter 48
# War Approaches

Galeschin awoke to drums in the distance, long before the vanguard of Ambrahad's army appeared on the road that snaked from Velendruch to Gwalhafed. He had much to do that day, he knew, and would be busy with his kingdom's defense for what might prove to be the rest of his very short life. But there was something he had to do first.

In the gray time before dawn, he went to the chamber where his daughter slept. He rapped on the door, and heard a stirring within. Lady Joy opened it, holding her gown closed over her night dress, her eyes red from crying. He understood the reason, but there was nothing that could be done about it, and nothing he could say to sooth her pain.

"I would like a moment with my daughter," he said, and Joy curtsied and left the room. He pulled the curtain back and sat on the edge of the bed. Alana slept, her pale skin touched with faint freckles, her hair, the braid come loose in her sleep, as vivid as fire. *So like her mother*. He touched her warm hand, where it lay on the coverlet, and she stirred.

"Papa?"

"Yes, my little love."

"Tonight, Lady Joy will tell me a story and I will tell her a story. Would you like to hear mine?"

"It must be short."

She rolled her eyes. "Grownups always want short stories. But it is, Papa. Once upon a time, bad people came, and *monsters*, but Papa and Murdoch made them all run away. Then we had a feast and sang songs at the moon. That's a real story. With a scary part."

"That is a wonderful story, Alana."

"Papa?" Alana sat up. Galeschin knew she wanted something.

"Yes, my little love," he said.

"When we go back to Gwalhafed Castle . . ."

"Yes?"

She squirmed and took a deep breath. "When we go back home, can Lady Joy be my governess?"

"Well . . ." he said. He had seen little of his daughter of late, his days being filled with his kingdom's defense, yet she seemed happy, happier than she'd been since her mother's death the previous year.

"Please, Papa?" Her blue eyes brimmed with tears at the thought that he might say no. She sat up very straight, with her toes held precisely together.

"I suppose so," he said, and wondered if any of them would live to return to Gwalhafed Castle.

* * *

"I don't like it," said Lord Strenholm. "It's wrong. Against all the forms."

"Yes, quite," said Hounshel, "but the alternative would be to make our land a battlefield between Amytans and Velendruch again. You are old enough to remember those days."

Strenholm sighed. His massive shoulders heaved under his surcoat. "I know."

"We cannot let that happen, Uncle," said Mallow.

"If you won't, I will," said Cirgan. His curly head nodded emphatically.

"You're too short," said Mallow. "It's got to be Uncle and myself."

* * *

"Polish all the pots?" said Cook.

"By command of the king himself," said Joy. "Mirror-bright. Come, it will keep us busy, and that will lessen our fear."

* * *

"More wood," said the sergeant. "We'll need a hundred fires all through these woods. We'll have to be ready to light them when we get the signal. You there, musician. Have you got that fanfare?" The man nodded and went back to polishing his trumpet.

A soldier ran up to report. "The lines are strung, and the 'laundry' hung."

"Good," the sergeant replied. "Tell the men to mill about smartly."

* * *

Rolf sat in the darkness of the dungeon, aware of the bustle around him and the drums growing ever louder. His time had come. Ambrahad of Velendruch had arrived.

"Sotley!" he called through the gloom. The man ran up, bowing. "What is happening, friend?"

"A great army has come from Velendruch, Highness. They are preparing to attack the castle, I fear."

"From Velendruch? My God. We cannot withstand them. If only I were free to talk to Ambrahad. I know him and could reason with him. I know you for a good man, Sotley. Let me free. Do this, Sotley, for the good of Gwalhafed."

"I dare not," said Sotley. "I've got my orders and they don't come from you."

"Then we are doomed," said Rolf. "We cannot withstand the might of Velendruch. Help me, Sotley, and I will speak well of you and save you from the worst of it."

Sotley swallowed nervously.

"They will cut your arms from your body and leave you to die," said Rolf. "It is their standard punishment for resistance. As you lay dying, they will bring your family before you, one by one, and do the same to them. You will watch each other die . . . women, children, elders, all. . . ."

"That's not true!" said Sotley, but Rolf could hear the doubt in his voice.

"Alas, it is, and worse. Before they kill the women, they . . . no, it is too horrible. I cannot speak of it. I pray you, Sotley, set me free to help prevent this disaster."

Sotley took a step toward the cell, then stopped. "No, I have my duty. I —"

"I beg of you, Sotley. I have lived among them, and my brother has not." He watched Sotley's hand move toward the key on his belt as he edged closer to the cell. "I beg of you."

"No, Highness. I—" Sotley's decision came too late. Rolf's hand reached through the bars, grabbed him by the front of his jerkin, and yanked him, face-first, into the iron bars, again and again.

\* \* \*

"I want my book, Lady Joy," said Alana. "I left it in my room."

"As you wish," said Joy. They climbed the corkscrew stairs from the kitchen to the back hall. This was so much better than Matilda Nursemaid, whose dignity would never permit access to servants' passages. When they returned home, Joy would be her governess. They would learn all the back ways of Gwalhafed Castle and laugh and play games. She would only go to the chapel for Mass.

\* \* \*

Rolf dragged Sotley's body over to the pallet. He arranged it there, face-down, with the blanket over the head, and stood back to gauge the effect. *The very image of despair*, he thought. He locked the cell door and slid Sotley's keys into his jerkin. *Now for a weapon. . . .*

\* \* \*

The hallway was deserted. All the men who had filled it the night before had gone to the castle's defense. The women, those not polishing pots, sat in the great hall, rolling linen strips for bandages. Joy hurried down the hallway, Alana skipping at her side.

"Let's find your book quickly, my little highness, and then go to the parapet." *Soon, the army will be at our doorstep. Soon, Murdoch will step forth.*

Alana ran to her bed and reached under the pillow. She grasped the book and smiled.

"Well done!" said Joy. "Let us go."

Hand in hand, they stepped from the doorway and turned toward the stair. At that moment, knife in hand, Rolf came up the stair.

\* \* \*

Galeschin straightened his cloak. He mounted his horse and took the white flag of truce in his hand. The gate wards swung the gate open and he rode out alone. Before him, among the trees of Hirday's orchard, stood rank upon rank of the army of Velendruch, Ambrahad's dragon banner at the fore. The apple trees had bloomed early. Bees hummed among them, flying to and from the keps. Westward, from the forested slope across the river, the smoke of a hundred campfires rose and the banners of Gwalhafed, Amytans, and Hirday fluttered from the guard tower that topped it. At the edge of the wood stood Mallow and Strenholm, wearing the yellow and blue tabards of Amytans.

Galeschin stopped a hundred yards short of Velendruch's ranks. "I would parley with King Ambrahad," he called.

\* \* \*

"May I accompany you?" asked Abbot Prydieu.

Ambrahad considered. *Let Galeschin know whose side the Church is on.* "Of course, my good abbot," he replied.

"Why do you violate our treaty?" began Galeschin, when they reached him.

"In defense of my kingdom," said Ambrahad, "seeing as you are in league with Amytans." He pointed at the knights guarding the westward road.

"They are here because of this," said Galeschin, and he held out the charred scrap of parchment.

Ambrahad snorted. Abbot Prydieu took the scrap from Galeschin's hand. "It is damaged, but bears the words *invasion*, *taken unawares*, and *Hirday.*"

Ambrahad's brow furrowed. *That fool Rolf. Can he not be trusted even to destroy a secret message?* "A base forgery," he said. "You are not fit to rule."

"Shall we put it to the test, then?" replied Galeschin. "A battle between our champions."

Ambrahad laughed. "You know your puny army stands no chance. Are you fool enough to think you have a knight who can best Sir Brian Borrenough?"

"I think God will decide the right," Galeschin replied. "As you see, we are not defenseless." He turned in his saddle and gestured toward the ramparts, which glittered with ranks of helmeted heads atop them.

"If I may say, sire," whispered Prydieu to Ambrahad, "you would win either way, and a prudent man would choose the means less costly to himself."

Ambrahad smiled. "Single combat, then. Our champion against yours. Our men will stake out the lists on this spot. See that your man is here within the hour." He turned his horse and cantered back to his lines.

\* \* \*

"What's happening?" asked Cook. "I can't see a blessed thing with this saucepan on my head."

"The parley is over," answered the guardsman in front of her, peering between the crenellations. "The king's coming back. He's smiling. Ambrahad's agreed to a duel."

"Thanks be to God," said Cook. "Where's Lady Joy?"

\* \* \*

Joy froze, then seized Alana and ran down the corridor opposite Alana's chamber door. The further corridor lay ahead, branching right and left, a stairway at each end.

"You must give me your book," Joy whispered earnestly as she ran. She pulled Alana into the right-hand turning. "I promise you will get it back." She snatched the red leather-bound volume from Alana's reluctant grasp and tossed it to the floor of the left-hand turning.

Alana wailed in dismay. "My book!"

"Silence!" Joy hissed, with an intensity that terrified the child. Clamping her hand across Alana's mouth, she ran. She could hear Rolf's footsteps pounding up the corridor, growing closer. She could not reach the stairs before he reached the joining. The garderobe! She had not locked it the night before. She reached the garderobe door and ducked into it. She shut the door and grabbed the padlock, but there was no hasp on the inside of the door. There was no way to lock it.

She heard Rolf's footfalls grow louder, then pause as he stopped to pick up the book. She heard the pounding as he opened doors, searched rooms, and then slammed doors shut along the farther end of the corridor.

"Under here, quickly!" whispered Joy. She held up the skirt of Queen Janet's dress on its stand. "You must not make a sound. Do not move until I come back for you!" The sound of doors slamming came closer.

"Lady Joy!"

"Hush! This is the scary part of the story. You must be brave and do as you are told for it to end with happily ever after."

Another door sounded, flung back against its hinges. Joy picked up a red cloak and made a child-sized bundle of it. She opened the door a crack, glanced down the hall and slipped through, carefully locking it behind her.

Joy ran toward the stairs, holding the bundle in her arms.

Rolf came out of a chamber and saw her. She could hear his feet pounding closer. She ran faster. Almost there. Two more steps. She heard his breath behind her as she reached the stair. His hand grabbed the back of her skirt. "Fly, my little red bird!" she shouted, and threw the cloak back, into Rolf's face.

He yanked her backwards. She resisted. He pulled harder, and she pushed backward into him, landing her elbow in his ribs. He grunted. She screamed for help as loudly as she could and then his fist struck her head and sparks flew across her vision. She kicked, hoping to find a knee, but struck his shin. He pulled the cloak off his face. "You!" he snarled. Her fingernails raked his face. His fist crashed into her head again, and then she saw nothing.

# Chapter 49
# The Battle of the Bee Field

Ambrahad of Velendruch chose the location for the duel, in a clover meadow on the flat between two hillside orchards. The armies had pulled back from their positions, and two of his men and two of Galeschin's busied themselves ruling off the area for the trial: pacing off the square, driving in the corner posts, and stringing ropes between them.

Murdoch, with Beecham beside him, left the castle and walked toward the list. The sun shone with crystalline brightness, and the trees had never seemed so beautiful, with their new leaves and fragrant blossoms. Birds twittered, and beneath it all he heard the hum of the bees from the keps among the orchard trees. Silently, the troops of Gwalhafed parted for him. Galeschin waited at the front of his troops.

"There is much at stake for us all today," he said.

Across the field, about a hundred feet back from the combat ground, sat a black tent topped with the red dragon banner of Velendruch, the tent of the King's Champion. A knight came from it, the like of whom Murdoch had never seen. There were few men the blacksmith had to look up to, and this was one of them. Further, Murdoch could tell at a glance that this man outweighed him by a third.

"That's my opponent?" he whispered nervously to Beecham.

Beecham squinted into the bright sunshine, shading his eyes with his hand. "No," he said regretfully. "That's his little brother. There—" He pointed to a second knight emerging from the tent.

Sir Brian Borrenough was built like a great axe blade, set point down. His body was one long taper, from the ox-like shoulders to the narrow hips, slender legs and oddly small feet. And it was all encased in gleaming mail that glittered in the sunlight, as brightly as the four-foot-long blade he swung in great, swooping arcs.

"You can take him," said Beecham to his speechless pupil. "See how slowly he moves."

231

Borrenough walked slowly enough, Murdoch noted, but swung his sword so forcefully that the very air rattled.

"Go ahead," Beecham whispered. "Warm up your arm. Swing your sword. Don't let him intimidate you."

Murdoch drew his sword hesitantly. He stepped away from Beecham and cut a great circle in the air. The sword slipped from his nervous fingers, sailed through the air and landed, hilt down, about twenty feet away. There was a gasp from the Gwalhafed side of the field and a burst of laughter from Velendruch's. Murdoch could hear the word *blacksmith*, and then the laughter surged again.

"Good. Good, Murdoch," said Beecham. "Get him overconfident."

Murdoch stared at him, amazed that he was in earnest.

"Here," said Beecham. "I'll pick up the sword." He brought it to Murdoch.

"You can't let him touch you, Murdoch, but you can outmaneuver him. Remember, he won't be able to see much with that bucket on his head. He'll be swinging blind most of the time. You can take him, Murdoch. Stay clear, dart in just after the blade has passed, and, for God's sake, don't stop moving."

Sir Brian Borrenough removed his great bucket helm and walked to the square. Velendruch's marshals untied the ropes from one corner so he could enter. Murdoch stood beside Beecham, his helmet in one hand, his chainmail suddenly as heavy as an entire castle.

Murdoch looked at his own sword, three feet of shining steel that had seemed so deadly when he first received it. He took a deep breath.

"Let's get this over with," he growled. He put on his helmet and strode down the hill. Beecham untied the rope marking the combat ground, and tied it silently behind him. Murdoch strode forward.

Beecham crossed himself, and whispered, "God forgive me. I have just sent a man to his death."

Murdoch stopped ten feet short of where Sir Brian stood near the center of the list. The bees hummed in the clover. Sir Brian swatted one away.

A clatter of hooves on the castle drawbridge broke the sunlit silence. Rolf spurred past the mass of Gwalhafed's troops and across the gap to Velendruch's lines. He reined in his horse and turned. Before him in the saddle, wrists bound, mouth gagged, sat Joy. Murdoch leapt toward them, and Rolf, without a word, turned his horse and spurred toward Ambrahad. There, he turned, held his dagger to her throat, and shouted, "Surrender, or she dies!"

Murdoch stood stunned. He turned to Galeschin, who raised his hand for silence.

Galeschin rode forward, with Hounshel at his side, the cloth in his hand taking the place of a white flag. "Ambrahad, I would parley with you, your champion, and my brother."

The ropes were untied and the four rode to the middle of the combat ground. Abbot Prydieu, although uninvited, rode in as well, and directed his horse between Sir Brian and Rolf.

"It is quite like you to hide behind a woman's kirtle, Rolf," said Galeschin.

"Her life is in your hands," Rolf replied, with a smug smile.

\* \* \*

*This is my beloved they are discussing like some bargain at a horse fair.* Murdoch scowled and paced the edge of the enclosure, turned and strode back again, a bit closer, hoping to hear the negotiations. He sheathed his sword, an idea growing in his mind.

\* \* \*

"Surely, my son, this would not reflect well upon the renown of so great a land as Velendruch, that you would win this by holding a defenseless woman hostage," said Prydieu. He looked at Joy, the great bruise on her cheek, the fire in her eye, and the raw scratches on Rolf's face, and had some doubt as to how meekly she might have submitted.

"Still," said Ambrahad, "as you yourself have said, 'a prudent man would choose the means less costly to himself.'"

*A prudent man would endeavor to win in a way that would not show him to be an opportunistic brute*, thought Prydieu, but he knew better than to say so out loud. "One's reputation is not without value," he said. "I fear this may damage it."

"Let her go, Rolf," said Galeschin. "She is nothing to you."

"She is my chattel, and mine by *droit de seigneur*."

"She is freeborn, and the daughter of a knight," Galeschin replied, his brow darkening.

"She is *mine!* Ulp!"

A great shout came from the ranks of Velendruch, too late. A gauntleted hand came up from behind Rolf and grasped the wrist of the hand holding the knife. Murdoch pulled the blade from Joy's throat and quick as thought pulled Rolf down and his face into the range of his right fist. Joy fell with him, curling as she fell. She felt Murdoch's arm sweep over her head, heard the ring of Rolf's knife as it glanced off Murdoch's mail, and felt Rolf shudder as the fist drove home. The abbot's horse skittered sideways into Sir Brian, knocking him over with a clatter.

"Don't you *ever* touch her again!" roared Murdoch, to Rolf's unconscious ears. He helped Joy to her feet.

"This is a violation of truce!" shouted Ambrahad.

"And his holding a dagger to the girl's throat was not?" asked Galeschin.

"I believe we are back to the original terms of combat," said Prydieu.

"About time," said Borrenough. "Somebody help me up."

Murdoch escorted Joy back to Gwalhafed's lines, where he cut her bonds and removed the gag. She smiled and raised her lips to his.

"Ahem," said the king. He pointed to where Sir Brian stood, hands resting upon his sword. "The road to Joy lies through him."

Again, Murdoch put on his helmet and strode into the enclosure. The giant knight raised his sword. "Surrender," he snarled.

"Ballocks," the smith replied.

"Then die," his opponent roared and attacked. He strode forward and the massive sword whistled down, but Murdoch ducked under his arm and struck him a ringing blow on Sir Brian's helm with the flat of his blade from behind. The ranks of Velendruch growled, and those of Gwalhafed cheered. Sir Brian turned, and Murdoch slipped behind him.

"Coward!" shouted someone from Velendruch's ranks. Murdoch responded with another blow to the helm. Sir Brian, roaring with anger, turned the opposite way. Murdoch faced him this time, ducked under the knight's swing, darted in, as Beecham had told him, and thrust his sword into Sir Brian's armpit. The knight bellowed like a bull and backhanded Murdoch across the helm with his shield.

Murdoch reeled dizzily backward, and dodged the next blow Sir Brian aimed at him by luck more than anything else. He felt the breeze from that blow against his cheek and heard the ring of the blade as it grazed his aventail. He pulled his wobbling senses together by force of will and swung at Sir Brian's sword arm. Sir Brian stepped back and caught the blow on his shield, batting it away like a fly. Murdoch leaped backward to dodge Sir Brian's next blow.

The sun climbed. The hours passed. There seemed no end to the giant knight's endurance. Murdoch settled into a workmanlike rhythm, husbanding his strength as he would at his anvil. He took no hits, other than that backhand, but the many he inflicted on his opponent seemed to have no effect. A dribble of blood ran down Sir Brian's side from the wound in his armpit, and now, occasionally, after a blow to the helm, Sir Brian would shake his head as if to clear it. That was all.

\* \* \*

Rolf lay on the ground, feigning unconsciousness. How could the combat have gone on for so long? Borrenough must be slipping. Through slitted eyes he glanced at the men standing guard over him. Their eyes were locked on the combat. He looked about him, gauging the distance to the

234

nearest horse. One could never be too careful. Satisfied, he leaned on his elbow and watched the fight.

* * *

Borrenough's sword whistled down. Murdoch dodged it, closed, and thrust his sword upward again, deeper this time. Sir Brian roared, Gwalhafed's troops cheered, and those of Velendruch gasped. Few had drawn blood against Sir Brian and lived, and none twice. Again, the knight's shield slammed into Murdoch, sending him sprawling and his helmet flying.

He flew through the air and landed on his back, his ears ringing and neck burning from the force of the blow. The earth was soft, and his shoulder sank into it.

Velendruch's troops roared. Gwalhafed's moaned, but beneath the racket, close to his ear, Murdoch heard the ground around him hiss like a steaming kettle. He had no time to consider what this strange sound meant. Sir Brian was advancing with his sword raised.

Murdoch rolled to his feet. Sir Brian came on, faster now, gaining momentum like a stone rolling down a hill. The great sword swooped down. Murdoch deflected it and wound around it to jab under Borrenough's left arm. The sword bit, drawing blood for the third time, and Murdoch retreated to pick up his helm. He bent and grabbed it on the run and placed it back on his head. He spun around just in time to deflect another of Sir Brian's strokes and was astounded to see, in the brief instant before Borrenough's next blow, a bee with a bent wing clinging to the back of his gauntlet.

And such a bee! Longer than the first joint of his thumb. He had no time to consider this marvel. Again, he parried. Again, he retreated. He heard Beecham shouting, urging him to attack, but he had another plan. He retreated in a circle, step by step, back to the place where he had fallen.

The hissing in the ground grew to an angry growl. Sir Brian took another step and made another swing, an *oberhau*, the first of the deadly *Drei Hewes*. Murdoch dodged to his left. His sword rang as he deflected the blow with the Fool's Guard. He fell back. Borrenough stepped forward and swung again. The second stroke, designed to sever arm from trunk, sliced air as Murdoch retreated again.

Murdoch felt the ground sink beneath him and stepped back. Borrenough stepped forward, sword raised high over his head for the third stroke, and the ground gave beneath the weight of the giant knight and his heavy mail. His left foot sank in up to the knee, and a thousand golden-banded warriors leaped to defend their home. The hissing grew to a thunderous buzzing. Sir Brian had stepped into a nest of bees, his foot held fast in the earth.

The bees surged out of the soil, most trapped under his surcoat, the rest pinging against his mail. He flailed his arms. A hundred insects attacked each crevice. Sir Brian opened his mouth and screamed in pain. They flew through the slits in his helm and filled his mouth with their stings. His sword fell from his hand. He struggled to free his foot. The ground supporting his other foot sagged, then crumbled, releasing more bees as their hive was destroyed. He flailed at the bees, raging, bellowing.

Murdoch stood to one side, gaping at the sight, as the bees swirled around him, ignoring him as they attacked on his opponent. The words of Dunwadi came back to him. *You need never fear a bee.*

\* \* \*

*At last, God has given me something to work with*, thought Abbot Prydieu, seated on his horse beside King Ambrahad, and he vowed a novena for Sir Brian's healing. Ambrahad raised his hand to order the attack. "Hold, sire," said the abbot to Ambrahad, in the voice he reserved for preaching disciplinary sermons to the monks dozing in the back pews of the great chapel at St. Blethis Abbey. "See how the bees, symbols of the wisdom of God, attack only your champion. This is an omen, the clearest I have ever seen. Leave off this war, I pray you, or face the wrath of God."

Ambrahad glowered and ground his teeth. He looked at the ranks of Galeschin's troops between himself and the castle. He glanced at the castle battlements, where hundreds of helmets gleamed. He turned his head toward the bridge, where two tall knights in the livery of Amytans sat silently on their horses. Behind them sat a mounted messenger, his horse turned westward, looking back over his shoulder. Three banners flew above the pine wood, filled with a hundred campfires, each representing a troop of twenty men, and saw ranks of yellow tabards massed among the trees.

One of the knights raised his hand and the fanfare "Archers string your bows" rang out. A soldier ran out of the wood bearing a torch and stood in front of the knights. The bridge across the swift-flowing stream had been soaked in oil, no doubt. His troops would be trapped, unable to advance toward Amytans. The archers, safe on their hillside, would turn Ambrahad's entire force into pincushions.

He looked at his troops, who looked not to him, but stood muttering among themselves, watching the bees flying past them from blossom to hive and back. He looked at his invincible champion, flailing his arms like a giant metal infant throwing a tantrum as he uselessly swatted at the bees. He lowered his hand. "Bring Prince Rolf to me," he ordered.

A guardsman ran off, but returned moments later. "He is gone, Majesty, upon a stolen horse."

\* \* \*

Horrified, Murdoch watched Sir Brian writhe, then sheathed his sword and ran into the cloud of bees. "Fall backwards, Sir Brian, so I can pull you out!" he shouted.

Among Borrenough's screams was a sound that might have been "Never!"

"I can't lift the weight of you and your armor. Fall back and I will drag you out." The bees surrounded them, thick as a winter's blizzard. Sir Brian they stung, but they bounced off or crawled harmlessly on Murdoch.

Sir Brian screams continued, but he stood firm.

"Enough, then," said Murdoch. He went behind the giant knight and carefully threaded his fingers under the knight's shoulders. He could feel the bees squirming and the tickling of their wings between his fingers. With all his strength, he pulled. Sir Brian crashed backward like a cartful of scrap iron. Hundreds of bees, now released from beneath his surcoat, burst into the air.

Hounshel's beekeepers ran up with their smudge pots, more interested in capturing the bees than rescuing the screaming knight. Velendruch's troops kept their distance while the beekeepers brought the bees under control. Murdoch dragged Sir Brian, whimpering now, to the edge of the list. Now that he was free of the bees, Borrenough's squire and a crowd of healers ran up.

Galeschin dismounted. "Bring Achilles to me!" he ordered. A horse was brought, massive, black, with one white fetlock. "Murdoch, come here."

Murdoch turned from watching them tend the great knight. Borrenough's squire was trying to remove his helm. It appeared to be stuck. Lines of bees stitched the mail to his *cuir bouilli* with their stingers.

Amid the cheers of his countrymen, Murdoch walked to the king. "Remove your helm and kneel, Murdoch." Murdoch obeyed. The king drew his sword and tapped him three times on his shoulders: right, left, right. "Rise, Sir Murdoch of the Bee Field. Take this horse as my gift. My lady?" he said, beckoning to Joy. "Behold your champion."

She came forward, smiling. Murdoch handed his helm to Beecham and reached out his hand to her. She took it, and raised her face to his. He bent to kiss her.

Suddenly her face froze. "The princess!" she gasped.

* * *

It was boring there, in the darkness of the garderobe. Faintly, Alana could hear the cheers and shouts of the crowd. Something was happening, far away. It seemed like forever. She thought about crawling out from beneath the dress stand, then remembered the look on her uncle's face and decided against it. She napped at times, and thought about her story.

At last she heard quick footsteps and voices in the hallway. The lock creaked, the door swung back, and the dress and its stand were swept away. "Papa!" she cried. Joy and Murdoch stood behind him, hand in hand.

"Your story came true," her father said.

"Can we have the feast now?" she asked. "I'm hungry."

"A wedding feast," said Galeschin. "As soon as Cook can make it."

"And stay up late and sing songs at the moon?"

"Of course." He picked up his daughter and carried her out of the room. "You may kiss Joy now, smith," he said.

And Murdoch did.

# Chapter 50

The sun rode low above the rooftops. The crowd laughed and cheered as Corwin took his bow.

Dylan walked among them, collecting coppers in his cap. "You did well," he said, "for an English."

"Well," sighed Corwin. "It's a start."

## We are the agents of the Goddess on Earth,

and we participate in Her reemergence by recognizing and honoring the sacred in the ordinary details of life, by serving our planet and each other with humility, gratitude and awe. We give birth to the new story of connection and wholeness through these small, infinitely powerful acts of reverence.

—*Emily Trinkaus*

*Corwin's Chronicle* continues:

# Alana's Tale

Princess Alana, now eighteen, is betrothed to the son of Lord Mallow, and Gwalhafed prospers under the peaceful rule of her father, King Galeschin. But Prince Rolf sends his brother a heartfelt note, repenting of his misdeeds, and requesting to return from exile.

Rolf's arrival brings a string of disasters. At last, she and her champion, Murdoch, find themselves alone, on a desolate journey that will lead them to the realm of the *faer*. There, the ancient prophecy, "When the child who was stolen returns a man, we will become the elders and teachers of the *quetan*," begins to unfold.

# About the Author

Teri Gray grew up in the Jersey 'burbs, twenty miles from Times Square, in a town too small to have a traffic light, wandering the forest, fantasizing about people living in holes in the ground, long after the other kids her age had outgrown that sort of childish nonsense.

She came to writing like most everything else in her life. High school newspaper editor-in-chief followed by a degree in art ed, followed by a stint as editor of a small publication in Honolulu, in addition to a wide assortment of jobs ranging from restaurant hostess to bartender to field interviewer to postmistress relief to banking to her personal favorite, communications director of the Newark Food Co-op.

Along the way, wedged between work, raising three children, and the occasional bout of illness, she wrote. Eventually, she found out about the existence of critique groups and started actually learning how to write. She's not an example of the breakthrough novelist. If anything, she's an example of the motto, Persistence Pays. The child who was a toddler when she started writing *Corwin's Chronicle* is now pushing thirty.

She is a facilitator with the Alternatives to Violence Project, (www.avpusa.org) has worked with the AVP program at James T. Vaughn Correctional Center, and blogs about Corwin-related matters at *www.tfgray.com* and about gardening at *www. suburbutopia.com*

www.ingramcontent.com/pod-product-compliance
Lightning Source LLC
Chambersburg PA
CBHW070600130626
46556CB00001B/230